JUDITH PELLA
HEAVEN'S ROAD

BETHANY HOUSE PUBLISHERS
MINNEAPOLIS, MINNESOTA 55438

Heaven's Road
Copyright © 2000
Judith Pella

Cover illustration by William Graf
Cover design by Dan Thornberg

Unless otherwise identified, Scripture quotations are from the King James
Version of the Bible.

Published by Bethany House Publishers
A Ministry of Bethany Fellowship International
11400 Hampshire Avenue South
Minneapolis, Minnesota 55438
www.bethanyhouse.com

Printed in the United States of America by
Bethany Press International, Minneapolis, Minnesota 55438

Library of Congress Cataloging-in-Publication Data

Pella, Judith.
    Heaven's road / by Judith Pella.
        p.   cm.
Sequel to: Texas angel.
    ISBN 0–7642–2279–1
    1. Fathers and sons—Fiction. 2. Texas Rangers—Fiction. 3. Texas—
Fiction. I. Title.
PS3566.E415 H43   2000
813'.54—dc21   00–009844

JUDITH PELLA is the author of several historical fiction series, both on her own and in collaboration with Michael Phillips and Tracie Peterson. The extraordinary seven-book series THE RUSSIANS, the first three written with Phillips, showcases her creativity and skill as a historian as well as a fiction writer. A Bachelor of Arts degree in social studies, along with a career in nursing and teaching, lends depth to her storytelling abilities, providing readers with memorable novels in a variety of genres. She and her family make their home in northern California.

Visit Judith's Web site at: http://members.aol.com/Pellabooks

PART ONE

———✳———

Early Summer 1842

One

DEAFENING GUNSHOTS PIERCED *the chill air. Cries of shock, pain, and even defiance mingled with the shattering blasts. And above it all a voice shouted,* "Run, Micah! Run!"

The boy hesitated. "No, Uncle Haden."

"I said run! Your pa'll kill me if anything happens to you."

The boy looked at his beloved uncle, then beyond him to the wall of slaughtering Mexican soldiers. Micah could not have moved even if he had wanted to, frozen as he was with sudden panic. Men were falling everywhere. They were unarmed and helpless against their Mexican executioners, but many were fighting desperately against the massacre with their bare hands and with the butts of rifles seized from their attackers. Still, they fell mercilessly.

"Run!" *Uncle Haden's voice wrenched Micah from his panic.*

Two Mexican soldiers approached the boy and his uncle, ready to fire. Micah wanted to die with his comrades, but the voice kept screaming.

"Run ... run ... run!"

Haden then thrust his own body like a shield between Micah and the approaching soldiers. Only then did Micah know he must obey this man who was giving his life to save his nephew. That life could not be given in vain.

He turned and ran. A lead ball whizzed past his head. Another grazed his shoulder with searing pain, but he kept running. A thick stand of trees lay ahead, then the river. Upon reaching the cover of the trees, he paused to gasp in a breath but made the mistake of looking back at the field of slaughter. The two Mexicans were standing over Uncle Haden's body, firing into the fallen form as if he had not been killed by the first shot. Then the soldiers took off toward the woods.

After Micah!

He wanted to fight them. He wanted to kill them. But Micah had no weapon. Rage supplanted all fear and horror. All he could think of was getting revenge. And he knew now why he had obeyed his uncle. He would run now, but he would one day fight again. The Mexican murderers would pay dearly for what they had done at Goliad.

Micah turned and ran again. How he hated to run, but he now was buoyed by roiling thoughts of vengeance. He reached the steep riverbank, but as he was about to plunge over the side, another ball struck his leg. He made a desperate lunge over the edge, where he figured he would probably be dashed to bits by rocks and debris or frozen by the icy spring runoff. But miraculously he hit the water cleanly even as more shots rang above him. Gasping a deep breath, he went under. He held his breath until he thought his head would explode, and only then did he slowly rise to the surface of the water to carefully venture a look.

The soldiers had given up their chase, no doubt believing he had drowned. He swam to the opposite bank, crawled from the water, and forced his numb body to move.

"Run! Run! Run!" The words kept echoing over and over in his head. "Run . . . kill! Kill! Kill!"

1842

Micah felt a sharp pain in his side. He flailed with his arms and let out a shuddering groan.

"Hey, Micah!"

A voice penetrated the sleep-numbed fog.

"Get up 'fore you wake every Injun and greaser around."

Micah opened his eyes, panting as if he truly had been running. Sweat drenched him. He looked around. His friend Jed Wilkes was standing over him, looking perturbed. They were outdoors, and Micah was lying in his bedroll on the hard earth. Though still dark, the damp chill indicated it was the early hours of the morning.

"Can't a man sleep in peace?" Micah growled harshly to cover the shaky insides left in the wake of his fitful sleep.

"Sounded like you was havin' that nightmare again." A look of worry creased Jed's broad, simple face. "Ya looked awful scared, Micah. Ya ain't never scared 'cept when you have them dreams."

"And I ain't scared then either!"

Micah ran his hands over his face. That cursed nightmare! Six years had passed since the Goliad massacre where his Uncle Haden, along with four hundred other Texans, were brutally murdered. Yet Micah still could not get those sickening images out of his mind. He had been a boy of fourteen at the time; very impressionable, he supposed. Still, he was a man now—almost twenty-one. What must his partners think seeing him flailing around in his sleep, probably crying out like some yella' kid?

"Did I wake anyone else?" He looked around. Only Harvey was up. Joe was just starting to stir.

"It's time to get up anyway," said Jed, who then turned his attention to packing up his bedroll.

Then Micah remembered. They were supposed to be up several hours before dawn so they could start working. Smirking to himself, he thought of the euphemistic reference to work. Well, it *was* work. It kept him fed—that is, it usually it kept him fed. Sometimes the pickings were slim, and he'd get a bit slim as well. Only two weeks ago they had been unsuccessful in usurping a small herd of Longhorns. The owners had chased Micah and his partners into Mexico, where they had been living like animals since, trying to stay alive until something else came along. Running across the herd of mustangs two days ago had been better than finding water in the desert. Mustangs went for a lot more money than cattle. If they were successful this time, they should get a nice little wad of cash. The herd of about two hundred fine mustangs was grazing not far from them. All they had to do was round up a few of them.

"Rounding them up" was also rather euphemistic. The better word was "rustle." Yes, Micah Sinclair, son of a preacher man, was nothing but a horse thief. He only hoped his father knew about it and it was a nagging thorn in the man's side.

Harvey Tate, the erstwhile leader of the little band of rustlers, called everyone together. Micah stowed the last of his gear on the back of his roan mount and ambled up to the group.

"I could sure use some coffee," he grumbled.

"Sure, Micah, go ahead. Build a fire and warn everyone within ten miles that we're laying in wait here," sneered Harvey.

"Maybe I'll do just that and put an end to this stupid scheme." Micah stood toe to toe and eye to eye with Harvey. Micah could shoot straighter and was probably smarter than his boss. The only thing Harvey had on any of the other men here was age—he was almost ten years older than Micah. Thus Micah figured he'd let the man lead until he himself could garner the kind of respect afforded by sheer age.

Micah's pale hair, despite the streaks of red, and his fair skin made him look like a babe. He hated it, especially in that these traits had come directly from his father. He tried hard to cover them with a smokescreen of swagger and grit. He had probably killed as many men, if not more, than all his outlaw friends combined—that is, if one included the Battle of San Jacinto. But he sure didn't look like no war hero. He didn't look like an outlaw either.

"You got a better plan for getting those horses?" Harvey was saying.

"I don't like stealing from Anglos, that's all. And I got a funny feeling about that herd."

"Ain't no time to be choosy. We ain't had a good haul in a month." Harvey spit a stream of tobacco juice into the dirt. "Besides, they're Mexican. You saw how they were dressed."

"Yeah," put in Joe Stover. "I been a whole month without whiskey or women. I'll steal from my own mother if'n I have to."

"You ain't never been without whiskey," Micah retorted. "And I'll bet you ain't got no mother either!"

Jed laughed, snorting loudly. "He got ya there, Joe. You an orphan like me, Joe? Ha, ha!"

"Why you half-witted—" Joe began, turning viciously on Jed.

Micah stepped between them with fist raised and would have planted it in Joe's face, but Harvey grabbed Micah's fist from behind.

"No arguing, ya hear?" Harvey glared at his men, and Micah had to admire a man who could look fearsome like that—not that he himself was afraid. Nevertheless, he did back down. They had more important matters to attend to. Even Joe, an *hombre* every bit as tough as Harvey, relented.

"Listen, Micah, I don't want to steal from Texans either," Harvey said. "Shoot, we could hang for that. But they're Mexicans. I'm sure of it. And we're in Mexico, so it stands to reason."

"Nah, Harvey," put in Jed. "We crossed the Rio Grande yesterday, so we're bound to be back in Texas now."

"Not according to the Mexicans," said Joe, who fancied himself not only a lady's man but also a scholar because he'd read one book in his life. "There's never been agreement on that fact. The Mexicans put the boundary at the Nueces—"

"Shut up, ya bunch of yammerin' fools!" burst Harvey. "It's gonna be daylight soon, and we ain't gonna get nothing if we keep standing here exercising our jaws. I say them horses are Mexican, and that's that!" He swung around sharply toward Micah. "You with us, or what?"

Micah shrugged. "I guess so." He had no qualms at all about stealing from Mexicans. Truth be told, he wasn't squeamish about stealing from Texans, but because the penalties were a far sight stiffer, he tended to avoid it. Texans stealing from Mexicans were simply considered resourceful. But those stealing from Texans were labeled bandits and received no quarter.

The four outlaws mounted up and headed out. They rode for about three miles, slowing a safe distance away from the herd and covering the last several hundred yards as soundlessly as Indians. Their plan was simple enough. Under cover of darkness they would cut out about fifty horses and drive them to a box canyon Harvey knew of where they would lay low for a couple of days while they changed the brands on the animals. Then they would take the small herd to Laredo and sell the mustangs to a friend of Harvey's.

The four rustlers paused on a ridge overlooking the grassy meadow where the herd had been bedded down for the night. There was only one guard on lookout. Micah had noted when they first spotted them two days ago that they were running with a skeleton crew. His best guess was that there were no more than five or six drovers, including one driving the wagon. And he was certain one of them was a female, though he was baffled why there would be a woman present in this wild country. In any case, the drovers were for the most part outfitted like *vaqueros*, wearing wide-brimmed sombreros and mounted on Spanish saddles. But what worried Micah was that a couple of the men definitely looked like gringos. Still, it wasn't unusual for Mexicans to wear a combination of duds. The presence of the gal worried him, too, but if all went well, there should be no danger to anyone. And even if there was, Micah had no problem killing Mexicans. He would never finish exacting the debt owed him after Goliad.

A small part of Micah knew he was trying to justify his own questionable actions. Honesty had been drummed into him much too hard as a kid. He didn't *like* being a thief. He had just fallen into it. After San Jacinto he had been pretty aimless. A fourteen-year-old with no one but himself to rely on. His uncle was dead, and he sure couldn't return home. A life of crime had been far more preferable than facing his father.

Tom Fife, the man who had guided his family part of the way to Texas years before, had offered to take him under his wing. But Micah had been rather cocky after the heady experience of fighting a battle as well as any grown man. He had proven his prowess in battle and thought he could take care of himself. Fife had meant well, but Micah rather liked the new taste of independence he was feeling.

He had drifted around after that, hungry most of the time but too proud to let anyone know. He fell in with various gangs or worked by himself, doing whatever he had to do to survive, but never doing more than merely keeping himself alive. He joined up with Harvey last year, and it was then that he began his formal schooling in the art of preying on others for financial gain. Harvey had done everything dishonest that was possible in the States and had fled to Texas—just one step ahead of the authorities. He was a worthy teacher. They stole mostly from Mexicans. Micah liked to call it raiding, and in truth, he never had stopped fighting the war. At any rate, he figured it didn't count if you stole from Mexicans. When he was forced to steal from whites, he managed to justify it by telling himself that he was a war hero and deserved what he could get. He didn't doubt, though, that if caught, the Texans would hang him, war hero or not. And in that sense, his lot was cast. There was no way out for him now except by bullet or by noose.

Micah glanced up at the sky. The moon was up, bright and full. "Comanche Moon," he muttered.

"What's a Comanche Moon, Micah?" Jed asked.

"Nothing," Harvey broke in. Then turning sharply toward Micah, he added, "Shut up, kid. We don't need to hear none of that."

With a shrug Micah said no more. They all knew that, unlike other tribes, the Comanche had no fear about attacking at night, especially on nights like this when the moon illuminated their prey. The rustlers knew it also illuminated *their* prey and them as well. They'd had a long discussion about the danger of rustling under a full moon, but by then everyone was thinking more of full stomachs. Game had been scarce for a week, and even Micah, notably the most cautious of the gang, was easily convinced that such an opportunity would not come along again soon.

"Micah"—Jed's voice broke into his thoughts—"how much money you think we're gonna make today?"

Micah glanced over at his friend, a freckle-faced boy of nineteen. Jed was tall and rangy, a bit awkward on his feet but good with a gun. Problem was, his mental facilities were slower than his gun hand. His mind had probably been addled after seeing his family killed in a Comanche raid nearly ten years ago. Maybe he bumped his head during the raid, or maybe he just didn't see any point in facing life as an adult. Regardless, he was a good man and a loyal friend. He and Micah had met not long after San Jacinto. Jed, orphaned, had run away from a cruel foster father who thought regular beatings and hard work were all the kid needed. Micah saw that Jed would not make it on his own, so he let the kid tag after him. They wandered around together and sometimes starved together. Micah taught Jed how to use a gun and taught him how to steal as well.

"Enough money, I reckon," Micah casually replied. The money never did appeal to him. Besides the matter of survival, he figured he did what he did in large part just for the thrill. It beat the daylights out of farming and ranching. No way did he ever want to settle down to that kind of life.

"Harvey says we'll stay in Laredo after this and raise some Cain," Jed said.

"Sounds good."

"Time to move out," Harvey ordered.

Harvey led the way, and Micah followed with the others ranging behind. They picked their way with great stealth down the ridge. Micah made sure his rifle and pistol were loaded. They weren't expecting trouble, but they'd better be ready for it.

Two

AT THE BOTTOM of the ridge, Micah cut away from his companions. His job would be to eliminate the guard. In two days of covertly observing the herd, Micah had discovered something of the drover's habits. Each watch was about four hours long, and by Harvey's pocket watch, it would be a little more than an hour before the new guard came on duty. They planned their move near the end of the watch, when the guard was growing weary. The guard made about three or four circles of the herd in an hour, then usually headed up to the camp for a quick cup of coffee. The camp was not far from the horses, so striking while the guard was getting his coffee would not work because the man still had a good view of them.

There was no way around it. The rustlers had to get rid of the guard, and it had to be done quietly. This job fell to Micah, who made use of the guard's coffee break by slipping among the herd and taking one horse while the man was away. He noted that the horses were unusually restive, but the little bay filly he roped came fairly easily. He led the animal away toward a tall clump of mesquite. The guard would pass this clump on his rounds and see the stray and come to fetch it. At least Micah hoped it would work that way.

The wait seemed interminable. The man must have had two cups of coffee. Finally he started his ride around the herd, and when about halfway, he noted the stray.

"Don't know why the herd's so jumpy tonight," the man muttered to himself. He was wearing a sombrero and had a Mexican serape around his shoulders, but he didn't sound Mexican.

Shrugging away his disquiet, Micah pulled his bandanna over his nose and mouth, then drew his pistol. When the guard was well within range, Micah stepped from the cover of the mesquite.

"That's far enough, *señor*," he warned.

"What the—?"

"Easy, now, and no sound from you, or I'll be forced to shoot. Get those hands up where I can see 'em." The man obeyed, and Micah lifted the fellow's pistol from his belt. "Now dismount."

Up close, Micah saw the man was definitely a gringo. This made his task a bit harder, because he knew he'd pay dearly if he killed the man. A Mexican . . . well, that would be different.

"Lie down," Micah ordered. "Face in the grass." When the man had complied, Micah quickly took the rope he'd used on the bay and tied the drover's hands behind him. With a powerful blow, he clipped the man on the head with his pistol butt. That ought to put him out of commission for a long spell, but just to be safe, Micah also gagged the man.

Returning to his partners, the four began cutting out horses. They wouldn't be greedy. They could get away with fifty head without causing too much of a stir. This was a nice-looking herd, and even fifty ought to bring each rustler a fair bankroll.

Half an hour later the job was nearly done. Harvey and Joe were already well away with at least two dozen animals. Jed was a couple of hundred feet behind leading away ten horses, and Micah was about to lead away a dozen more. That's when it all broke loose.

Micah first heard a shout. He thought it might be the guard having regained consciousness and broken free of his gag. But it was coming from the wrong direction. Then a split second after the shout, there came a shot. Now Micah knew the sounds were coming from the camp.

More shots blasted, followed by loud bloodcurdling whoops that could only be Comanche. He heard a scream. The woman traveling with the drovers? Suddenly his thoughts were distracted when the horses began milling skittishly around him. His own roan sidestepped and whinnied. Micah tried to steer his mount away from the press of the herd in case they should stampede. An instant later another shot split the air, and the mustangs took off.

Micah tried to hold back his mount, but in doing so he jerked too hard on the reins. A stupid thing to do. He knew better. The roan was a good animal but young and nervous. All the sudden commotion was just too much for him. With a wild neigh, he took off with the other horses. Micah reined him hard, and the frightened beast reared. Micah knew he should have been able to control him and would have, given another moment. But just then the horse collapsed right out from under him.

Micah jumped from the falling beast to avoid being crushed under the weight of it. He bounced over grass and rocks until his head crashed against one sharp rock, stunning him. He lay still for several heartbeats, black and white spots undulating before his eyes. He knew he was about to pass out but willed himself to stay alert. He tried to stand, but everything was spinning too much for that. Instead, he crawled toward his horse, the ground seeming to rise up beneath him as he moved. His insides quaked. Hands trembling, he reached for his rifle and powder horn. He might not be able to walk, but he sure wasn't going to just lie there defenseless. Much to his dismay, he saw an arrow through the roan's throat. The animal was dead. A good horse, and his only means of escape.

His hands had barely touched the rifle when he heard another scream. It was closer this time, and it was definitely female. Using the fallen roan for support, he pulled himself up to a sitting position. When the spinning slowed, he saw a Comanche race away from the camp carrying a captive. The woman! And they were riding in his direction.

With hardly another thought, Micah raised his rifle and took aim at the moving target. The galloping Comanche was a good hundred yards away. It was a one-in-a-hundred shot, but he'd made harder ones, only this time his vision was still blurry. His finger moved on the trigger, then he stopped. The woman was flailing against the Indian, fighting for all her worth to free herself. A heroic effort, but it hampered his purposes greatly.

"Hold still," Micah murmured, as if she could hear.

Suddenly the woman sagged. Micah was almost certain the Indian had struck her. No matter, he had a clearer shot now. He squeezed the trigger. An instant later horse, rider, and captive toppled to the ground. Then all was still.

Had Micah killed them all? Forcing himself to his feet, he laid aside his rifle and made his way to the scene with his pistol drawn. He felt steadier now. The ground only quaked a little under his feet, and his vision, though still fuzzy, no longer had those sickening spots dancing before his eyes. Within a few feet of the fallen threesome, Micah saw movement. The passengers had been thrown free of the horse, and it was the woman who was now moving. As she sat up, Micah prodded the Comanche with his toe and found him to be very dead. The horse was alive, but its leg was badly twisted.

"You shot him?" the woman said.

"Yeah."

"Who are you?"

That was a good question. Micah reached up to scratch his head in thought and realized his hat was missing. He scratched his head anyway.

"Well, I was just riding by," Micah said lamely.

"I saw . . . no one. W-where were you?" She looked mighty pale, even in the moonlight, and her voice quavered as she spoke.

"The stampede spooked my horse." Micah jerked his head toward the dead roan. "I was just coming to from being thrown when I saw you and that Comanche."

The woman stood rather shakily. Micah gave her a steadying hand. Then she looked at the fallen Comanche and gave a shudder. There was a hole in his left temple. She swayed a bit on her feet, and Micah feared she might go down again, but she hitched back her shoulders, seeming to defy gravity itself.

Her eyes wide and her lips trembling, she said, "Y-you made that shot from way over there? I-I'm g-glad you didn't miss."

"Oh, I seldom miss. I was a bit worried though 'cause my eyesight was still blurry from knocking my head against a rock."

"B-blurry. . . ?" That was all she said before her eyes rolled back in her head and she started to topple over.

Micah lurched forward and caught her in time. For a moment he stood there helplessly holding her slender form, now slacklimbed as a rag doll. He glanced around as if hoping for rescue himself. There was still fighting in the camp, but the drovers seemed to be holding off the Comanches. He brought his attention back to his burden and saw by the light of the moon that she was a pretty woman. Well, *woman* was hardly the right description, because she was probably younger than he. Still, she was comely, and the feel of her in his arms was almost as dizzying as his fall from the roan. It had been weeks since he had even seen a woman, and as for holding one this close ... well, it had been far too long.

She moaned softly, and her eyes flickered open, then closed again.

"Miss...?" Micah murmured rather helplessly, but he could not bring her around.

Getting back his wits, which had been slightly stunned by her sudden nearness, Micah laid the girl down on the grass. Tucking his pistol back into his belt, he waved his hand several times over the girl's face. The moonlight glimmered off her creamy skin and illuminated a mass of curly dark hair tangled around her face. Her closed eyes were thickly fringed with dark lashes. She was beautiful. But still very unconscious.

Micah noted that the shooting up at the camp had stopped now. Looking in that direction, he saw the Comanches were riding away and knew he had to do something. It was a sure bet the drovers weren't going to buy his tale that he had just been riding by.

"Miss," he said determinedly, "wake up." He gave her shoulders a shake and considered leaving her. She wasn't dead or anything. But he couldn't leave her lying there like that. He didn't know, but maybe a woman could die of shock. In any case, with the roan dead and the Comanche's horse injured, Micah had no hope of getting far.

Finally the girl let out a little moan and lifted her head. "Wh-what happened?"

"Guess you fainted."

"I've never fainted before." She stated this so matter-of-factly that Micah actually began to wonder if he had been mistaken.

"That's what it looked like to me." Micah glanced toward the camp. The men were heading toward them.

"I thank you again, sir." She smiled and the gesture was sweet, warming her large dark eyes so that he nearly forgot his imminent danger.

He smiled back, stupidly, foolishly, like a gawk-faced schoolboy.

"Miss Maccallum!" called one of the drovers. "You okay?"

"Yes, Pete. This gentleman rescued me."

"I feared you was a goner when that Injun grabbed you." Pete turned to Micah. "Thank you for what you done."

"Weren't nothing" was all Micah could think to say.

"Sure was fortunate you happened along when you did," said another drover.

"Yeah, guess so," Micah replied vaguely.

There were now three drovers standing over Micah and the girl, both still seated on the ground. Micah saw that two of the men were indeed Mexican. One had his hand over a bloody shoulder. They were all armed. Still, he thought there might be a chance of bluffing his way out of this dicey predicament—that is, until two newcomers approached.

"Hey, look what I found!" said one.

"I got jumped," said the other.

"What're you talking about, Tandy?" the drover named Pete asked.

Tandy, whom Micah clearly recognized as the guard he had knocked out, brought a hand to his head and, as he rubbed, said with a grimace, "I say, I got knocked out and tied up."

"By Comanche?"

"No, you dim-witted fool! By a rustler. Leastways—"

Tandy's eyes suddenly took note of Micah. It had been dark back at that mesquite bush, even with the full moon, and Micah had been wearing his bandanna, but it would not take long before all the pieces fell into place right on top of Micah.

"Who're you?" the guard demanded.

Before Micah could respond, Pete spoke. "Said he was riding by when he saw the Comanche attack."

"I'd bet my boots that's one—"

But Micah did not wait to hear more. Quickly jerking his pistol from his belt, he grabbed the girl and pressed the barrel of the gun to her head. It was her gasp that drew the attention of the men.

"Drop your weapons now," Micah ordered, "or I'll have to shoot the girl."

"You ain't gonna shoot no girl," said Pete, who still appeared a bit stunned at the rapid sequence of events.

Micah cocked the hammer of his pistol. "Well, if it's her or me, I'm not gonna debate it much."

A tense moment followed. The other drovers looked to Pete, who did indeed seem to be debating in his mind just how desperate this baby-faced outlaw was. Reaching the only logical conclusion, Pete tossed his rifle into the dirt and signaled the others to do the same. That done, Micah gestured for the girl to stand. He rose with her, still holding her with one arm while with the other he held the gun on her. Only then did he really note how steady the girl was. She wasn't whimpering or crying or even shaking. His own knees were still a little mushy, but he attributed that to his fall from the horse. His head throbbed, but his vision had cleared.

Micah didn't like to leave the weapons within such easy reach of the men, but he could only handle so many details at once. He had to hope none would be fool enough to shoot at him while he held the girl. Nudging her along, Micah went up to where the saddle horses were hobbled in the remuda. Thankfully these had been unaffected by either the stampede or the Indian attack. On the way past the camp, he saw three bodies sprawled on the ground—two Comanches, one white man.

Nodding toward a nice sturdy-looking chestnut horse in the remuda, he said to the girl, "Saddle that horse up for me. Remember, I got my gun on you, and as you seen before, I don't miss."

She licked her lips, the first sign he noted of any stress.

"That's one of our best animals."

"If I'm gonna hang for stealing a horse, it may as well be a good one," he answered casually. "Go on now," he added, "and hurry up."

After she did as he asked, he said, "Now mount up."

"What!"

"The minute I ride away, your drovers are gonna start shooting. You're just gonna give me some insurance—only for a short distance. I ain't fool enough to take you far."

With a resigned shrug, she mounted. She had no difficulty at all with the large animal; in fact, she swung up into the saddle with elegant grace and sat as if she had been born to it. Micah stood for a minute staring in admiration. Then he remembered he was holding a gun on her, that she was his hostage. He mounted behind her, took the reins, and spurred the chestnut away. Again he had to remind himself that this was a desperate getaway. Yet feeling her close, her silken masses of fragrant hair blowing in his face, wrecked havoc with his sense of reality.

After a final warning to the drovers not to follow and assuring them he'd let the girl go soon, he rode about half a mile away before he stopped and let her dismount. The drovers had not followed. They were practical men and no doubt figured Micah was practical, too. He wasn't about to kill a girl if he didn't have to. And Micah figured they wouldn't waste time to go after one rustler when there was hope of still getting back their herd.

"Sorry I had to inconvenience you," he said as soon as the girl's feet touched the ground.

"I'm sorry your day was wasted, and you only got away with one horse." She smiled wryly.

"Maybe I'll do better next time." He decided to make no mention of the two or three dozen mustangs he hoped his partners had successfully made off with. The drovers might just think they had been lost in the stampede.

"Then until next time . . ."

Their eyes met and held for a long moment. It was the strangest moment Micah could ever recall experiencing. Her look made him forget who and what he was. It made him feel almost clean, like he might even deserve to have a girl like her look at him in that way.

Three

THE MACCALLUM RANCH was a large spread even in a land where everything was larger than life. Located a two-hours' ride south of San Antonio, it had been founded more than a hundred years ago by Joaquin Vasquez. The land had passed through his male Mexican scions until his grandson had only one child, a daughter. Rosalind Vasquez married an Anglo from Kentucky named Reid Maccallum, a Scotsman with red hair, towering brawny bulk, and a smile that could charm the scales off a rattle-snake.

Reid was a fine man, and his future father-in-law had no qualms about passing his ranch to his daughter to be run by the gringo. Tejas was changing, being overrun by gringos who even changed the name of the Mexican province to Texas. A gringo would better understand these changes and the irascible Americans who had brought them. Besides, Rosalind loved the Scotsman, and the Scotsman loved her. So what was a father to do, especially a father with no sons?

Lucinda Maria Bonny Maccallum, child of this union, thought about her Scottish father and Mexican mother as she rode up to the house where she had been born nineteen years earlier. She was glad to be home. How she had missed her papa, and how she wished her mother could be there to greet her as well. Mama had died two years ago of consumption, taking with her a little of the sweet life that had always infused the Maccallum place.

Lucinda, or Lucie, as most everyone called her, left her horse in the stable for one of the hands to tend. Usually she did this task herself, but she was anxious, for more reasons than one, to see her father. She wanted to get to him before their foreman did with the report of their adventures—or rather, misadventures—on the trail from Mexico.

She hurried around to the back of the house, slipping inside through the kitchen door. She always used this door but it was a mistake this time because she was immediately waylaid by Juana, their housekeeper, who would, however deservedly, require more than a cursory greeting.

"Oh, Señorita Lucie! You are home!" The woman quickly set down the basket she was carrying and threw thick, sturdy arms around the girl. Juana had been with the family for years and was practically a member. There was little, if any, servant-mistress formality between them.

Lucie kissed the woman on her plump cheek. "*Hola*, Juana."

"Look at you! I think you have grown an inch in the month you have been gone. But you have lost weight."

Lucie chuckled. To the housekeeper, anyone who weighed in at less than Juana's solid one hundred seventy pounds was a skeleton. "I am sure you will take care of that."

"Come, I have some nice sweet rolls warm by the stove." Juana tugged at Lucie's hand, urging her toward the table.

"I'm anxious to see Papa."

Juana's eyes, bright as lumps of onyx, clouded. "He is anxious to see you as well, *mi pequeña*."

"How is he, Juana?"

"Some days are better than others. But now that you are home, I think there will be mostly better days, eh?"

It was hard to believe that the large brawny Scot was not a well man. Reid Maccallum had the biggest, most loving heart in the world—at least in Lucie's world. But it was that very heart that appeared to be failing him now. It did not seem right that so soon after her mother's death, Lucie should have to face the possibility of losing another parent. She tried hard not to think that it was a very great possibility.

"Maybe I should not have gone to Mexico," she said with a sigh.

"Now you think that?" Juana said with a slight edge to her voice. She had been against the trip from the beginning. "Ah, Lucie . . ." The woman's tone softened. "Think nothing of me. Your papa no doubt would be the first to insist you live your life to its fullest. He would not want you to sacrifice it nursing him."

"It would be no sacrifice."

Juana raised a hand and gently patted Lucie's cheek. "Señor Maccallum has raised a precious child."

"It is only that he gives me so much. It would be a small thing for me to give to him in return. As it is, all I can do for him is to pray."

"That is a great deal, *pequeño!*"

"Of course it is—" Lucie stopped, momentarily distracted by the sound of footsteps in the dog run that divided the house in half, next to which the kitchen was located.

"Mr. Maccallum" came Pete Barnes' voice.

"I'm in the study," responded Lucie's father. "Come on back."

Well, it looked as if Pete had made it to her father first, after all. She hoped the foreman would be sensible enough to give a watered-down version of the troubles on the drive. Perhaps he would leave out Lucie's own close call during the Comanche attack altogether.

"I know one thing you can do for your papa," Juana said, drawing Lucie's attention back to the kitchen.

"What's that?" Lucie asked eagerly.

"Find yourself a husband so that he knows you will be taken care of."

Lucie could not hold back a responding groan. If dear Juana had one fault, it was this burning need to push Lucie into marriage.

"Oh, Juana . . ." Lucie glanced toward the door leading to the dog run as if contemplating escape.

"A girl your age should be married or at least betrothed."

"It doesn't seem to concern Papa," Lucie answered, perhaps a bit defensively. She wondered, though, if this weighed upon him now that he was ill. "Juana, I want to do what is right. But . . ." When she tried to put into words what she felt, it all seemed so silly. Juana, practical woman that she was, would not understand how Lucie wanted to find a special man to marry, one who she would love. She wanted what her parents had had. A bond of hearts and minds and souls. Perhaps it was expecting too much, especially in view of the fact that no man had yet come along who even came close to what she was looking for. Juana would say she was too choosy, that if she found a good, honest, decent man, she would come to love him in time, and that was enough to expect.

Lucie sighed.

Juana patted the girl's shoulder. "Come, *pequeña,* sit, and I will fix tea to have with those rolls. You must be hungry after riding all day, and it is a while until supper."

"Thank you, Juana, but I really want to see my father." She forced a smile to her lips. The woman meant well. Then Lucie left the kitchen.

A nice breeze was blowing through the dog run, which was, after all, the purpose of the open-air area. It became a necessity during blistering hot Texas summers, such as the one that was now descending upon them. Lucie followed the corridor toward the back of the house where her father's study was located. She wondered, as she often did, what the old house built by her great-great-grandfather had been like. She had only a vague memory of it, but Juana had told her it had been of a hacienda style such as could be found in Mexico, with arched porticos and tile floors. But a devastating hurricane had destroyed it when Lucie had been but five, and her father had rebuilt it in the style of the American settlers, two rooms divided by the dog run. However, in the case of the Maccallum home, there were several more than two rooms. They had been quite prosperous in those days.

When she reached the study, she heard the voices of her father and Pete. She hesitated before knocking. Maybe she should wait until Pete was done. But no, she missed her father and did not want to wait another minute. She raised her slim fist and tapped on the door.

"Who is it?" her father said.

"It's me, Papa."

"Lucie, sweetheart! Come on in."

She opened the door and entered. Pete Barnes was seated before the large mahogany desk that had once belonged to Joaquin Vasquez. Behind the desk sat Reid Maccallum, his great hulk filling his chair, which was at the moment tipped back, precariously leaning against the wall. His laced fingers were propped behind his head, and he looked rather imposing, especially with his untamed red hair sticking up everywhere. But the grin on his face warmed Lucie's heart down to its core.

Reid righted his chair and quickly jumped up, striding out from behind his desk and into his daughter's outstretched arms. He wrapped his own thick logs around her in a breathtaking bear hug, lifting her several inches from the floor in the process.

"Papa!" she giggled. "Put me down. I'm not a little girl, you know!"

"And what else are you, then?"

"You'll always be his little girl, Miss Lucie," Pete said.

"Oh well, then why fight it?" Lucie kissed her father's cheek. "It is so good to see you."

Reid put her down, then held her at arm's length. "You've grown and put a bit of meat on your bones."

"Not according to Juana."

"Ha! She won't be satisfied until you are as fat as she, with three double chins besides."

They both laughed until Reid paused, taking a sudden gasp for breath.

"Papa, what is it? Are you all right?" Lucie had seen this before in recent months since his heart trouble had begun.

"Oh yeah, fine," he said with a deprecating wave of his hand. "Sometimes my breath just gets a little behind, that's all. Now sit in that other chair. I'll just be another minute here with Pete."

"We can finish later, boss." Pete rose. "Lucie deserves a chance with you before me."

"Thanks, Pete. Come on back after supper."

Lucie took Pete's vacated chair. It was larger and more comfortable. "Papa, I am never going away for that long again," she said after Pete left. "I feel like it's been forever."

"You were the one who insisted on going," Reid said.

"Yes, I suppose I did have to twist that arm of yours, but you know Uncle Ramon preferred to turn the horses over to a member of the family. He didn't know Pete or any of the men. Besides, I really did want to visit with my aunts and uncles and cousins. Goodness, there are a horde of them, too! At least a dozen more than when we last went there before the war."

"Well, they are your family, and it is good to keep up the ties." His step seemed a bit heavier as he returned to his own chair. His color was a little pale, too. "Perhaps keeping up such ties will help hasten true peace between our two countries. Still, with all the unrest it was foolhardy of me to let you have your way."

"Papa, it didn't burden you with any undue worry, did it?"

"Of course it did!" he said with a gentle smile. "I worry about you whenever you are out of my sight. Guess I'm worse than a mother hen."

"I didn't think before I left that it might make you ill." She eyed him closely. Sometimes he seemed so well that it was hard to remember his illness.

"You are back safe and sound, and that's what matters. I would have worried a long sight more if I'd known about the Comanches. And rustlers to boot!"

"So Pete told you?"

"'Course he did, child! How else was he gonna explain the death of one of our vaqueros, not to mention the loss of seventy-five fine mustangs? And when I think how close you came—"

"Papa . . ." Lucie leaned forward and, reaching across the desk, took her father's hands in hers. "Please don't strain yourself over it. Praise our God, it all came out fine. Did Pete tell you how one of the outlaws saved my life?"

"Saved your life? What—"

"Oops!" Lucie lowered her eyes and leaned back in her chair. It seemed Pete had been more discreet than she gave him credit for. "Nothing, Papa," she added. "I forgot to tell you about the beautiful dresses I bought in Mexico City—"

"I think you better tell me about this outlaw." Reid narrowed his eyes in as stern a gaze as he was ever likely to focus on his daughter. "Out with it, Lucinda Maria Bonny Maccallum."

Lucie swallowed. When her father used her full name, he usually meant business. "Oh, it was really nothing to speak of. One of the Comanches grabbed me from our camp during the battle. He was riding off with me when a rustler shot him. I don't know how he got there—the rustler, that is. I suppose he was in the process of stealing some of our horses when the attack started. He must have been caught in the stampede. We later found his horse with an arrow in the poor beast's throat. But, Papa, you should have seen the incredible shot that man made! He hit a moving target at over a hundred yards and struck the Indian in the temple. I have never seen such shooting. And he said his vision had been blurry at the time from his fall."

As she paused to take in a breath, she noted her father was staring, or rather gaping, at her incredulously. She smiled weakly. She had probably again said more than she should have. But she was just too accustomed to telling her father everything.

When Reid finally spoke, his voice was barely a tight gasp. "Why, the fool!"

"He saved my life, Papa." She didn't know why she was defending the man. Yes, he had saved her, but he was also a thief, and he had used her as a hostage to escape. All that must negate his heroism. But somehow it didn't.

"He could have killed *you* with that shot. It was a fool, stupid thing to do."

"I guess it was." But she wasn't convinced. "Anyway, I had a feeling he knew what he was doing. But no matter—he could have stayed hidden, let the Indian carry me off, then slip away himself, unnoticed. But he even came over to make sure I was all right after the Indian's horse fell. And he caught me when I fainted and stayed with me until I came to, even though he could have been caught any time. Eventually he was."

"What's this?" Reid leaned forward raptly. The color had returned to his face. "Did my boys get that rustler?"

"Well..." Her father wasn't going to be happy at all when he heard the rest of the story. But why should it matter if her father was happy about some rotten rustler?

"Come on, Lucie, all of it," prompted Reid.

"The men came over before he could get away. Then one of them identified him as a rustler because he had knocked him out—"

"Who knocked whom out?"

"The rustler . . . um . . . knocked out our guard. Well, at least he didn't kill him, now, did he?"

"You seem a bit defensive of this man."

"He saved my life."

"He also stole our horses—"

"We don't know that. They could have been lost in the stampede."

Reid ran a hand through his wild hair. "Do you realize it is not likely your rustler was working alone? Pete said he found several tracks up on a ridge overlooking your camp. Figures there was four of them. Pete decided to round up what he could of the mustangs rather than pursue the outlaws. But other tracks indicated they almost certainly got away with a good number of our horses. Moreover, Lucie, before you start glorifying those men, it was pretty heartless of them to ride off when they could have helped defend my men against the Comanches."

"They didn't all ride off."

"You said yourself that fella's horse had been shot out from under him. He had no choice."

"But he did, Papa."

"Let's not argue over the matter, child. Of course you are grateful to the man. I suppose I am a bit, too. But don't ever forget he is still a criminal. Pete is gonna ride into San Antonio tomorrow and speak to the ranger captain and see if there can be some sort of search for those men. It is likely they thought they were stealing from Mexicans. They will see what a costly mistake that was."

Lucie didn't like it when steel glinted in her father's hazel eyes. She knew that though he was as loving and gentle as a father could be, he was also a strong, tough man. He had to be to survive in this rough frontier.

"Yes, Papa," she murmured contritely.

"Oh, Lucie, I don't want you to think I am angry with you." He rose from his chair, walked around the desk, and kneeled down before her. He took her chin between two fingers and lifted it. "Come now, let me see a smile." He prodded her with his own grin.

"Papa, will those men hang if they are caught?" She just couldn't smile.

"You know the law."

"Even the one. . . ?"

Reid nodded gravely to her half-spoken question.

"He was just a boy."

"A boy, you say?" When she nodded, he added, "A handsome boy?"

"Papa!" But her blazing cheeks belied her protests.

"Handsome or not, young or not, he is still a thief. If nothing else, he stole Pete's best saddle horse. He surely knew what he was doing."

"I suppose so . . . but Papa, if he is caught, could you mention what he did for me?"

"I'll think about it, my love, but only if you give me a smile."

Lucie did smile then because he asked, and it was hard to refuse her father. But also because she knew he was a fair man and would see that justice was done in the case of the young outlaw if he were found. She still secretly hoped the handsome heroic criminal was never caught.

Four

LUCIE HAD WANTED to go to San Antonio with Pete but simply could not justify leaving her father so soon again. Besides, what did she hope to gain by giving her side of the story to the authorities? Not that they would give much heed to a woman anyway, especially a young one.

But why did she feel so compelled to defend that rustler? Over and over she tried to convince herself that he was bad, a thief, maybe even a killer. But she wasn't convinced. Instead, Lucie kept remembering the gentle way he had held her when she nearly fainted. She had been conscious enough to feel his arms around her, and she even recalled a brief glimpse of his utterly distressed expression at her plight. She had caught a flicker of something else deep in his eyes. A wounded look, perhaps? And the kindly words he had spoken. He had been truly concerned for her. What she tried not to think about was his fine-looking visage. Eyes as blue as a Texas sky, hair like a red-gold sunset descending over that sky, and dimples forming in his ruddy cheeks when he smiled. And that smile! It had only flashed momentarily, but it had not been the smile of a hardened outlaw. Maybe that's why Lucie felt so compelled to come to his defense. It seemed to her when he had knelt over her, his concerned expression softening to that smile, that he was simply a nice boy. A boy her father would probably like. And now she was almost sure it was so. He had just taken a wrong turn in life and needed to be nudged back to the right path by a caring friend.

Her?

Well, she doubted she would ever find out. More than likely she would never see him again, and that was just as well. She didn't want to see him again, not if it meant he had been caught. Besides, her father would never let her be friends with an outlaw, even an ex-outlaw.

Lucie did, however, remember one thing she could do for the young man who had saved her life, one way she could repay him even if she never saw him again. She knew someone else who cared about him.

"Dear Lord, I think it is all right to pray for outlaws, isn't it? Now that I think of it, even you prayed for the outlaw who hung on a cross next to you. Well, I pray that my outlaw never gets to that place. I suppose it is wrong to pray that he never gets caught, but I do pray that if he is, you will somehow take care of him, protect him, maybe even help him to find you. I guess it is safe to assume that since he is an outlaw, he must not know you very well. I saw good in him though, just in the few minutes of our encounter. He saved me, Lord, so I pray you will save my outlaw."

My outlaw, Lucie mused. What a silly notion. But he certainly was God's outlaw if not hers. And thus, she left the young man— she did not even know his name—in God's hands.

———

"Lucie, we have company," her father called from the front of the house.

Lucie had been in her room taking a rest after the midday meal. Her room was the coolest in the house on these hot summer days. She rose from her bed and patted out the wrinkles in the beige-sprigged calico of her day gown. It was not her best dress for receiving guests, but if they had come unexpectedly, they surely would understand. She glanced in the mirror of her dressing table. There was not time to give her hair the attention it needed. The unruly curls never obeyed her combs and pins, but at least the long braid at her back, carefully plaited that morning by Juana, looked presentable. She repositioned the combs, doing her best to tame the dark auburn tresses. Papa often said her riotous mane best represented the mixing of her wild Scottish blood with her beautiful Mexican heritage. She thought it was usually more wild than beautiful.

As she entered the parlor, she saw the Carltons from the neighboring ranch had come to visit—Axel, his wife, Violet, and their son, Grant.

"Good afternoon," Lucie said with a smile at her guests.

The men stood and bowed slightly, offering polite greetings. Axel kissed her hand. He was from Virginia and fancied himself a true gentleman. Grant just grinned at her. He was twenty-one and fancied *himself* Lucie's prime suitor. Lucie didn't fancy either of them. She thought both Carlton men were too full of themselves. But she had to admit that Grant did appear to be prime husband material. In a land where the men were supposed to outnumber the women by ten to one, she had found precious few decent prospects—not that she was looking.

"We were so happy to hear you had come home," Violet said. "Come, sit by me and tell me all about your trip." She patted a place beside her on the couch.

Lucie liked Violet well enough, though she could be a bit simpering at times. That Virginian breeding, Lucie supposed. But she had been a good friend of Lucie's mother and had always been kind to Lucie. Before taking a seat, Lucie offered refreshments, but her father said Juana was already seeing to them. So Lucie sat next to Violet, who immediately put her arm around Lucie's shoulders in a motherly fashion.

"Your father tells us you were in Mexico City," Violet said.

"It was my first time—my first time in any large city, actually," Lucie replied. "I have never seen such splendid buildings. The Church of Santo Domingo, which I believe is the largest church in the Americas, was breathtaking."

"We don't hold with Papist trappings," Axel said dourly. "Not anymore since Texas is free of all that."

"Oh . . ." Lucie swallowed. She was not Catholic either—a sore point with her Mexican relatives to be sure—but beauty was beauty, and the cathedrals *were* awe-inspiring. She tried to politely counter Axel Carlton's rudeness. "Well, of course, there was much more in the city. Violet, you would have loved Alameda Park and the splendid courtship ritual that takes place every Saturday afternoon. The young girls, decked out in all their best finery, circle the fountain while the young men circle in the other direction, all hoping to meet a future mate. My *tia* Maria took me there."

"And did you join the ritual?" Violet asked breathlessly.

"Oh no. I would not want to marry a man who lived so far from home." Lucie regretted her words the minute Violet's gaze skittered toward her son. To cover her discomfiture, she quickly added, "And the shops! Papa gave me money to buy some new things, but I had the hardest time deciding. After we have refreshments, Violet, you may come to my room and see what I bought."

"That would be delightful!" Violet exclaimed.

"One day Texas will be just as prosperous as Mexico," Axel said.

"If we can ever get out of debt," Reid said.

"And curb all the lawlessness," Grant added.

"You are right there, son," Axel said. "Reid, our cattle were raided again. Those cursed Mexicans stole a hundred head—" He stopped suddenly as his wife daintily cleared her throat with a warning glance at Lucie. "Ah-hem. Well, of course, Lucie, my dear, I don't mean you. I hardly think of you as Mexican at all."

"But I am, Mr. Carlton," Lucie said softly and without apology, keeping ire from her tone as well.

"Only half," put in Grant. "And you seem as American as anyone here."

Lucie pasted a gracious smile on her face. "But I am *Texan*, Grant, both halves of me. Not American, if the truth were told."

"Of course. We're all Texan," Grant replied, "but not for long if a good portion of our citizens have their way."

"Unfortunately, we have little to give the States right now to entice them into offering statehood to us," Reid said.

Lucie knew that her father was one who would prefer for Texas to remain independent.

"And that brings me back to my lost cattle," Axel groused. "I do not mean to offend anyone present, but those Mexican banditos are wrecking havoc on local ranches. Something must be done."

"I have reason to believe there are gangs of gringo rustlers operating as well," Reid said. He paused as Juana entered the parlor with a tray of lemonade and coffee and an assortment of sweets.

"Thank you, Juana," Lucie said as the housekeeper set the tray before her.

Lucie poured coffee for Axel and her father and glasses of cool lemonade for Grant, Violet, and herself. Then she offered cookies and such to all. Juana had stood back to allow Lucie the place of hostess; however, the housekeeper did wait a moment to observe before exiting. Lucie smiled to herself. Juana was making sure Lucie had not forgotten her manners during her absence.

"So what is this about white outlaws?" Axel asked between sips of his coffee. "I know we have them, but as long as they keep clear of whites, I don't see the problem."

"I believe it is a problem no matter who they steal from," Reid answered dryly. "But they stole a good portion of the mustangs I had just purchased in Mexico. I figure they have certainly crossed the line."

"I am still more concerned about the Mexican banditos."

"Are you certain it was they and not the gringos who stole your cattle?"

"One of my men saw him. He was certain it was that black-guard Joaquin Viegas. I'm gonna personally attend his hanging when they catch him." Axel snatched up a cookie and popped it into his mouth as if this sealed the gruesome matter.

Lucie glanced at her father. His jaw was taut with repressed anger or pain, she couldn't tell exactly which. He lifted his gaze to briefly meet hers, then looked away. In that brief moment, Lucie knew it was mostly pain assailing her father, and not from his illness, but rather from a deep emotional wound. She wanted to go to him and hold him tight. She was feeling some of his pain as well. But they both sat still and politely entertained their guests, who were becoming more objectionable as the visit wore on.

"Mr. Carlton, please, this is mixed company," Violet scolded.

Dear Violet. She was an absolute saint to put up with a man like Axel Carlton, Lucie thought.

"Sorry again," the man said tightly, obviously not one bit regretful of his words but only of the fact that he might have overstepped etiquette a little.

The visit droned on, interminably it seemed to Lucie. Her only relief was when she and Violet retreated to her room, where she showed off her new gowns and trinkets from Mexico. Violet clapped gaily like a little girl, her pale ringlets bobbing around her head as Lucie paraded out each item. It was almost like having a girlfriend. Lucie hardly believed the woman was a matron of forty.

They returned to the men, and soon after the Carltons departed. As everyone was exiting the parlor, Grant Carlton contrived to detain Lucie alone in the room while the others made their way outside.

"Lucie, I must tell you I'm delighted to see you again," he said as he turned just the right way to block her exit from the parlor.

"I am glad to be home," she replied shortly. He stood within inches of her, and there was no way to escape without being rude.

"You look absolutely fetching in that gown."

She nearly replied, "This old thing?" in the coquettish manner such things were said, then remembered it *was* an old dress and looked horrid. Grant was just plying her with false flattery. And she didn't much like it.

"Grant, if I weren't around," she said mockingly, "I declare you'd make eyes at Juana."

He momentarily appeared affronted, then suddenly smiled. "There isn't that much of a dearth of women around here. There are, in fact, several young gals in San Antonio who might catch a man's eye. But you, Lucie, are the most beautiful—" He held up a hand to forestall her attempt to protest. "It is true, ask anyone. And it doesn't bother me much that you are half Mexican."

"Not much, eh?" she said sharply, then whirled away from his nearness, not caring a whit if she was rude. "If my father heard you say such things, he'd challenge you to a duel." That, of course, was not true, since Reid deplored such senseless violence as dueling, but she didn't know how else to vent her ire. She'd had just about enough backhanded slurs from the Carlton clan in one day.

"Please forgive me." Grant followed her around until he was near again, then put his hands on her shoulders. "When I am around you, I get positively senseless. You make my head spin, Lucie. I don't—"

She glanced at his hands reprovingly. "Please, Grant, you are indeed forgetting yourself."

He dropped his hands, a flash of shock in his dark eyes indicating his realization that he had indeed gone beyond his carefully honed Virginia chivalry.

"Lucie, there is to be a ball in San Antonio next week. Will you do me the honor of accompanying me there?"

"That is really too much, even for you." She attempted to affect her father's stern gaze. Failing at that, she let a slight smile slip on to her lips. "I believe my father will escort me to the ball, but I shall certainly give you a dance or two."

He smiled. "Two! More than I could have hoped for. Thank you, Lucie. I will look forward to it!"

She watched him go, bemused by the entire scene. For all of Grant's past attempts at wooing her, this was the most forward he had ever been. Perhaps he had spent her absence fearing she would find a husband in Mexico, and now that she had returned still unattached, he decided he must take more affirmative action. It was almost enough to turn her head.

Almost.

Grant was a nice-looking man. Tall, broad-shouldered, with a trim waist, fine features on his clean-shaven face, neat brown hair. Even his teeth were straight and fairly white. But she simply felt nothing for him, except when he was boorish, as he had been this afternoon. Then she felt sheer distaste. But he wasn't always a bigoted boor. He could be charming, and he did say the sweetest things. She knew better than to be enticed by flattery, but at times he did sound so very sincere. What girl didn't like to hear she was beautiful?

Maybe Juana was right. Her choices were limited. Grant Carlton might be the best of the lot.

"Ugh!" she groaned disdainfully.

She was starting to sound like a rancher choosing horses from a herd. It was disgusting. Sound body, good teeth, gentle ride! That was no way to choose a husband, a mate for life. She refused to fall into that trap. She knew it distressed Juana, maybe even her father, but she was going to look for something else. What exactly that something else was she wasn't sure, but she hoped and prayed she would know it when it came along.

"Oh, Lord, please help me to *know*. Help me to find the right man." Then Lucie stamped her foot in frustration. She wasn't looking for a husband! So she added to her prayer, "Or better still, Lord, help everyone else just to leave me be. I only want a husband if that's what you want for me. And if you find him, I know he will be as perfect as all your wonderful gifts."

Vaguely she thought of the other recent prayer she had prayed, the one for the outlaw. Then she laughed. Even God is not that ironic, she thought ruefully. Then remembering her place as hostess, she hurried out in time to wave good-bye to her guests.

Five

MICAH TOOK OFF his hat and wiped a sleeve across his sweaty brow, then coughed when a cloud of dust caught him just as he inhaled a miscalculated breath. Who said stealing was easy money? He hadn't worked so hard in months.

When he had finally caught up to his cohorts, half a day after rustling the mustangs, he'd had to work along with the others to drive the small herd to Harvey's box canyon. After two days of swallowing dust and eating dirt on the trail, the work of changing the brands had come. There were only thirty-five head, but they were wild, not cooperative at all.

Then Harvey had the hairbrained idea of partially breaking the animals. Said they'd fetch a better price that way. All in all, it was nearly a week before they started on the way to Laredo.

"Hey, Micah!" Jed edged his mount near enough so he could be heard. "I been thinking—"

"Tell me later, Jed. This dust'll choke us if we talk." He and Jed were riding drag on the herd, and even with bandannas pulled up over their mouths, it was miserable.

"I gotta tell you now, in case something happens." Jed's voice was muffled under the red cloth. "Micah, I feel powerful bad I didn't come back for you when them Injuns attacked."

"Forget it, Jed." Jed had been apologizing for this all week. It was wearing thin in Micah's ears.

"I shoulda. But I was mighty scarit, though I'm ashamed to admit it. I was so scarit!"

"Listen here!" Micah said sharply, with impatience. "I'm telling you for the last time, you would have been a fool to come back. You hear? It would have been a dumb, stupid, crazy thing to do. And I don't ever want to hear such foolishness from you again."

"You mean you forgive me?"

Micah rolled his eyes again. "You got the thickest skull I ever seen, Jed! I want you to give me your word you'll never even think of doing something like that again."

"Well . . ."

"Do it. Now!"

"All right. I'd swear on a stack of Bibles, if I had 'em."

Micah snorted, then coughed as he inhaled grit up his nose and into the back of his throat. "If you're gonna swear, do it on something useful—like your gun."

"If it makes you feel better, Micah." Jed let go of his rein with his right hand and laid it on the butt of his pistol. "I swear by this here gun that you yourself gave me!" Jed grinned, or at least there was a gap in his bandanna where his lips were.

Micah grinned, too, then his lips tensed as Jed added, "What you got against the Bible, Micah? I remember my ma and pa set much store by it."

"Nothing," Micah answered shortly. "Now get back to work before Harvey chews you out."

He purposefully edged his mount several feet away from Jed to discourage further conversation. But Jed was obviously bored with driving horses, especially when there were so few it hardly took four men to do the job. He maneuvered within earshot again.

"Can I ask one more thing?" Jed asked.

Micah shrugged. He supposed he was bored, too. "Just as long as it ain't got nothing to do with Bibles and such truck."

"Nah, ain't nothing like that. I was wondering if you'd tell me again about that gal you rescued?"

All the men had been interested in that. They had wanted detailed descriptions, too, almost as if he'd done more with her than catch her as she fainted. Micah pitied the poor women in Laredo when these outlaws arrived.

"Well, she was a pretty little thing." Micah supposed he, too, liked remembering that soft, smiling female creature. "Even if she was dressed nigh like a man."

"Did she have on trousers?"

Though Jed well knew the answer, Micah provided it anyway.

"No, course not! But she had on a leather vest and flat-brimmed sombrero, just like a vaquero. She mounted a horse like an expert."

"Astride?"

"She was a lady, you fool!" Micah surprised himself with his quick defense of the girl's honor. He knew nothing at all about her, not even her name. No, wait, someone had called her Miss Maccallum. He just realized it. She was a gringo, further establishing his fear they had raided a Texan herd. Anyway, he had no idea if she was a true lady. For all he knew she might be some camp follower.

No. Not that one. Tender innocence had glowed from her, along with a strength that even now made his breath catch in his throat. Instinctively he knew she was not the kind of woman they would be hunting in Laredo. She was the kind of woman men like him could not even dream of.

But they did. He guessed that's really where Jed and the others' interest had sprung from. They weren't just starved for women. They hungered for the kind of gentility, even civility, women represented. Good women, decent women—not the bawdy house kind. They craved the mere sight of a woman in calico stirring a pot of stew in a humble log cabin. A woman of soft-spoken delicacy, tender-eyed, just the kind of woman who would probably faint dead away at the sight of a bunch of grubby outlaws.

He smiled. The gal on the drive had fainted upon sight of him, though he figured it was more due to the ordeal of almost becoming a Comanche captive.

"I ain't so bad, am I, Jed?" Micah asked suddenly.

"What'd you mean?"

"You think a real lady might take a fancy to a man like me?"

Jed laughed his usual snorting croak, oddly dulled by the bandanna. "Thinking of settling down, Micah?" he taunted.

"No! Last thing in the world I want."

"But you gotta settle down for a lady."

"What do you know?" Micah derided his friend harshly to cover his own discomfiture at his idiotic words. "You ain't nothing but an addlepated kid. Ya ain't got the brains you was born with."

"I know that."

Jed's solemnity cut like ire through Micah.

"I know I'm stupid. Can't help it, Micah."

"Aw!" Micah gave a disgruntled shake of his head. "Don't mind me." He smacked the side of his head with his hand. "I'm the fool. I know less than you about anything, especially women."

"Naw, that ain't—"

But Jed's words were cut off by the sharp crack of a gunshot. Twisting in his saddle, Micah saw a half dozen or more riders in the distance, not within rifle range but closing the distance behind them. They weren't Mexicans either. But why would they just start shooting? Could they be rustlers?

"What'll we do, Harv?" Micah shouted up ahead.

"Outrun 'em!"

They'd lose the herd if they did that, but then again, Micah sure didn't want to die protecting a measly thirty-five mustangs. There had to be a better way. Micah dug his heels into the flanks of the big chestnut until he was abreast of Harvey.

"We can't outrun them," he shouted after tearing off his bandanna. "And they outgun us. Maybe we can parlay with 'em."

"Can't. They're rangers."

"How can you tell that?"

"Joe recognized one of the mounts. He's almost certain it's Big Foot Wallace's mule."

Micah glanced back once more. If those riders were indeed rangers, then their only choice was to try to outrun them and forget the herd. Micah slowed to allow Jed to catch up, then relayed the news to him.

"Rangers! Oh, Micah—"

"Don't worry, Jed. We'll get away."

But Micah had far less confidence than his words indicated. The riders—he could see now there were at least ten of them—were gaining fast. He spurred his mount into a full-out gallop. The chestnut was a very good animal and would have no difficulty getting away. Glancing back, he saw Jed's mount was also striding at a gallop now. The herd was running, too, and scattering.

"Hah!" Micah lashed the chestnut's flanks with the ends of his reins, his confidence growing by the minute, especially as there was no more shooting. The pursuers would not be able to shoot during the chase. That first shot must have just been a warning, as if the rangers—if they were rangers—thought that would stop the outlaws.

Harvey and Joe were well ahead. Jed was several lengths behind. Micah twisted his head. "Come on, Jed!"

At that moment Jed's horse stumbled, and Jed was thrown over the top. Micah cursed, then slowed enough to turn the chestnut. He reached the place where Jed was sprawled over a low mesquite bush and leaped from his horse before it had come to a full stop.

"Jed! Jed!"

Micah dragged Jed's body to solid ground, then dropped to his knees next to the boy and gave his shoulders a hard shake. Jed groaned, but Micah had no time to feel relief that his friend was at least alive. The riders were within gun range, and Micah quickly drew his pistol and fired, clipping one in the shoulder. Grabbing Jed's pistol from his belt, Micah fired again. He missed, but he hadn't been aiming to kill. The last thing he wanted was to kill rangers. Still, his gunfire had the hoped-for effect. It divided the force. Half continued in pursuit of Harvey and Joe, while the other half dismounted, taking cover behind rocks and brush, then returned fire. Micah also took cover behind a rock, tugging Jed along with him as best he could.

There were several volleys of shots after that, then one of the riders yelled across the distance.

"You best give it up!" The voice was vaguely familiar. "We're rangers."

"What're you shooting at us for?" Micah called back, taking the defensive. Perhaps they would believe it if he claimed he ran because he'd thought they were rustlers.

"We just wanted to get your attention. No one asked you to run."

"How were we supposed to know that?"

"Why don't you surrender, then we'll talk some 'bout it."

Micah was considering what other options he might have when Jed groaned again. His arm was twisted grotesquely, and his head was bleeding. He was hurt, maybe badly, and needed help. Micah might have decided to shoot it out if he had been alone. He figured he could pick off half of those rangers, then maybe the remaining ones would think twice about capturing him and would retreat. But what about Jed? He might die if he didn't get some doctoring. If he surrendered, the rangers would see to it that Jed got help— that is, if they didn't decide to string them both up here and now. Glancing quickly around, Micah was gratified to note there were no hanging trees nearby.

"Do you give your word you'll hear me out?" Micah asked. "And that you'll see my friend gets help?"

"You got my word. Now throw out them guns."

Micah complied, then very carefully moved to stand out in the open, his hands in the air.

"Easy, boys," warned the same man who had spoken before. An instant later he, too, stepped out from his cover.

In a few moments all the rangers had come out and were approaching Micah. Before he knew what was happening, one grabbed Micah's arms and tied them behind his back.

"I thought you was gonna hear me out!" Micah protested.

"Reckon you can still talk with your hands tied—" The speaker stopped abruptly and gasped. "Well, I'll be! Micah Sinclair! That really you?"

Micah peered more closely at his captor. That voice had been familiar. The man was sporting whiskers now, but there was no doubt just who he was.

"Yeah, it's me." For some reason Micah could not explain, he felt a twinge of shame as he made the admission.

"You remember me?"

"Yeah. Tom, ain't it?"

Micah looked the man up and down, from the top of his slightly tattered slouch hat to the tips of his worn, dusty boots. The man's teeth were just as yellow and rotten as Micah remembered. And his skin looked even more like an old boot than when Micah had last seen the man—that is, what skin could be discerned under the thick growth of brown-gray whiskers. This man, this ranger, was clearly the same fellow who had rescued Micah's family years ago. It was old Tom Fife.

Micah didn't know whether to be relieved or even more worried about this unexpected encounter.

"So you're a ranger now, Tom?" he said, cautiously feeling the man out. Was he a hard-nosed lawman now or the same easygoing character who had been so kind to Micah years ago?

"Reckon so." There was a sheepish quality in Tom's tone, as if the admission was somehow embarrassing. "And you are. . . ?" He paused, his eyes, which seemed to have a permanent squint in them, giving Micah an incisive appraisal.

"What're you up to, Micah?"

Before Micah could answer, another ranger approached, leading the chestnut by the reins. "Look here, Tom. This horse fits Pete Barnes' description. And see this—" he moved his hand to the animal's rump. "The brand's been tampered with."

"Looks that way," Tom said noncommittally.

"Besides that, this here fella fits the description—yellow hair, baby face."

"Whadd'ya got to say to that?" Tom asked, an inscrutable expression on his grizzled face.

"Nothing," Micah said, trying to affect his own inscrutable look.

"I reckon I'm gonna have to take you in," Fife said.

"Guess you gotta do what you feel is right."

Fife shook his head slowly and, Micah thought, rather regretfully. Micah felt confident that at least he'd have the benefit of a trial before they hanged him.

Six

MICAH LAY ON A COT in a San Antonio jail cell, his eyes scanning the ceiling for the hundredth time. He was coming to know intimately all the cracks and holes where the adobe had chipped away completely, revealing the rough, crumbling insides of the bricks. Old as this place was, he had no doubt it was solid. The oak door of the cell was several inches thick.

Escape was out of the question. He'd already tried it once on the trail when the rangers were taking him in and had received a lead ball in the thigh for his efforts. Well, it had only grazed his leg, but it hurt like the dickens. Tom, who had fired the shot, had been mighty sorry about it and hoped Micah understood he'd had no choice.

Micah rubbed the place on his leg now covered with a thick bandage. He couldn't figure out Tom Fife. Everything about the man indicated he didn't like having to arrest Micah, yet he seemed in no way disposed to looking the other way for a few moments in order to give him a bit of a break. Guess the man had indeed grown hard-nosed, taking his job as a ranger a bit too seriously.

At least he had gotten help for Jed, though it had been a grueling three-day ride to San Antonio and Jed had suffered mightily. Micah still had no idea if the doctor had been able to help the kid. He'd been in jail two days now, and there'd been no word about anything. It seemed that Fife had dumped him in jail, then forgotten about him.

Micah's gaze was diverted to the far side of his cell where a cockroach the size of a walnut was making its way across the soiled wall. Micah took off his boot and gave it a hard toss. *Thwack!* The critter fell to the floor, either stunned or dead, but it didn't move.

This had been Micah's chief amusement the last couple of days. The floor was littered with carcasses of dead varmints. This complemented his mood perfectly.

Since coming to jail he'd been having frequent nightmares. He was almost afraid to sleep anymore. He was starting to wonder if all this was his comeuppance for an evil life. After six years he still could not shake all that religious prattle from his mind. He'd always sensed God was an angry God with an appetite for retribution. Well, now He would get His full measure.

Maybe I deserve it, Micah thought.

At twenty, Micah had already seen and spilled so much blood that he felt certain he deserved the nightmares as well. He thought he had lived through hell but wondered if surviving was something to brag about. He certainly had not escaped without scars and soul-deep wounds that still were not healed.

———

After a few early skirmishes in the war, Micah and his Uncle Haden had been sent to the presidio of La Bahia near Goliad to join General Fannin, who was rebuilding the fortress that he had renamed Fort Defiance. Eventually four hundred twenty men gathered at the fort.

Fourteen-year-old Micah had observed this fighting force with skepticism. "Uncle Haden, some of them men don't even have guns."

"Or shoes either," Haden replied. "And I hear Fannin is low on supplies himself."

Micah wanted to leave. This motley group did not represent glorious warfare as he'd imagined it. But Haden said they were bound to get in some fighting soon. Rumor had it that a call for reinforcements had come from Travis at the Alamo. Haden promised Micah that they would be the first to join up with these reinforcements. But Fannin would not release any troops to aid Travis. Some said he couldn't make up his mind what to do, others said what passed for a revolutionary government in Texas was sending Fannin a stream of contradictory orders. At any rate, Fannin's army lolled away at the fort in frustration and boredom while a war passed them by.

Finally Fannin organized a relief force, but en route supply wagons kept breaking down, delaying the army. Then news came that the Mexican

General Urrea was closing in on Goliad. Fannin ordered the ill-fated force back to the fortress. Not long after, word came that the Alamo had fallen. In response to this defeat, Houston ordered Fannin to blow up the fort and retreat.

"Ain't we ever gonna fight, Uncle Haden?" Micah had complained. He hadn't gotten to shoot anyone yet and was growing bored with this whole idea of war.

At last, however, they met the enemy in battle, if the minor skirmish outside La Bahia counted as such. Fifteen hundred Mexican troops against Fannin's paltry force. Micah was in the rear and didn't get a chance to fight. But his efforts would have hardly mattered. With nine dead, sixty wounded, and overwhelming odds, Fannin surrendered, and his army was led back, captive, to the fortress. The prisoners were told they would be paroled to New Orleans. They wanted to believe that more than the rumors of vast executions of Texans by the Mexican army. When a week later they were told they would be marched out the next day and taken to ships bound for New Orleans, Micah figured his fighting days were over before they had really begun.

That last night in the fortress the men were in good spirits. Some had heard the Mexicans would allow them to stop on the way to the sea to say farewells to their families. And New Orleans wasn't such a bad place. Eventually they would make it back to Texas, hopefully before the war ended.

Micah lay back on the bare ground, using his blanket as a pillow, and gazed up at the stars. Uncle Haden was sitting beside him smoking a cheroot. They had become quite close in the last months. Though neither talked about it much, they both shared the deep pain of the loss of Micah's mother. Haden understood Micah as his father never had.

"Uncle Haden, you ever been to New Orleans?"

"Yes, a time or two. It's a beautiful city."

"I was there once on my way to Texas." Micah didn't like to think of those dreary times, but for some reason he had an urge to speak of them now. "We didn't really go into the city. Pa called it an especially godless place, the Devil's playground. So we mostly kept to the harbor some miles south."

"I forget you've done some traveling yourself, Micah. You're getting to be quite a worldly fellow." Haden smiled that grin of his that made his eyes twinkle and made anyone who saw it want to grin in return.

"Guess I got my pa to thank for that," Micah said dryly.

Haden laughed heartily. "He was good for something, then, I reckon."

Micah only replied with a loud "Harrumph!"

"Too bad you couldn't have known your pa when he and I were younger," Haden said. "He was quite a rascal, that one."

"My pa?"

"He ever tell you about the time we set the parson's barn on fire?" When Micah shook his head, Haden added ruefully, "Oh no, he wouldn't. Well, we didn't mean to do it. We had hid in the barn during a picnic in order to smoke a couple of Wilfred Miller's big stogies we had found— actually, we had found them in the pocket of the man's coat, which he had laid over a chair while he played horseshoes. Anyway, our pa came in the barn looking for us, and we knew we'd catch it if we were caught. Ben grabbed both stogies and stuck them in a pile of hay. Not too smart, your pa!" Haden laughed, not in a derogatory way, but rather as if at a pleasant memory. "You can guess what happened after that. We were lucky the house and the entire town didn't go up in flames. Our pa blistered our bottoms so bad we couldn't sit for a week." Haden sighed, then crushed out the stub of his smoke. "Religion spoiled your pa."

"That's why I'm gonna stay as far away from it as I can," Micah said firmly.

"Can't say as I blame you, boy. But I wish . . ." Pausing, Haden glanced over at Micah, sadness replacing his earlier humor. "Your pa ain't all bad. Fact is, I heard he'd changed since Rebekah's death. Fella told me he'd come before his parishioners recently real humbled and talked about how he'd been wrong in some of his notions about God. I saw something, too, Micah, when he came after you last month. Maybe . . . maybe he ought to get another chance."

"Not after what he did to Ma." Micah's tone deepened to that of a steely man, not a boy. "He don't deserve to wreck everyone's lives, then say he's changed and expect to be forgiven."

"Maybe not."

"Would you, Uncle Haden? Would you forgive him?"

Haden drew up his knees, rested his folded arms on them, and was silent for a long while before answering. "I ain't quite ready to forgive him either, but if I live through this war, I might go and talk to him at least."

But Haden did not live past the next day. In the morning the prisoners were marched out of the fortress in four separate groups, each heading in slightly different directions. When they were halted a half mile from the fort, some began to realize what was going to happen, but it was too late for anything but a defiant shout.

"Hurrah for Texas!" the doomed men cried.

Within seconds the shooting began. Micah saw his uncle gunned down before he obeyed the man's order—or was it a plea?—to run. The sight of the massacre of Haden and the others would be etched in Micah's mind forever, both waking and sleeping. Only a handful of the four hundred and twenty men, Micah among them, escaped.

Wounded, weaponless, and starving, Micah had spent a harrowing five days on the run before he caught up with Houston's army. Lying in the brush with nothing but a growling stomach for company, Micah had thought only of avenging his uncle and the others. When one of Houston's men gave him a rifle, his fingers had truly itched to use it. It had been hard not to shoot at some of the Mexicans fighting with the Texans. There was a distinction in Texas, and always would be, between good Mexicans and bad Mexicans—meaning those who fought with Texas and those who didn't. Fourteen-year-old Micah found that distinction extremely hard to fathom. He still did.

Adding to his frustration was the fact that Houston kept retreating from the Mexicans. They called the retreat of the army and the settlers from the path of Santa Anna the "runaway scrape," and it was quickly causing Houston to lose face with his army. Hundreds deserted, mostly to aid their families, who had become refugees in the face of the enemy's advance. But in the end Houston led the army to San Jacinto.

In all the time of the retreating, Micah's bloodthirst had not abated. He fought bravely, if savagely, on the battlefield of San Jacinto. He only vaguely remembered the first man he ever killed, a Mexican private. It had happened quickly, and the heat of battle did not allow him to think much about it, especially as many more fell by his hand after that. But Micah remembered too clearly the last man he had killed in the war. He still had nightmares about it.

The battle was mostly over. Victory belonged to the Texans. The Mexicans had dropped their weapons in surrender, and that's when Micah realized he was not the only one still longing for vengeance.

A yell ripped through the battlefield. "Take prisoners like the Mexicans do!"

Even Houston could not stay the hand of slaughter. The Texans fell on their prisoners, stabbing, slashing, and clubbing them mercilessly.

Cries of "Remember the Alamo!" "Remember Goliad!" mingled with the screams of the victims.

Those screams would sear Micah's memory, but he had joined in the slaughter. For once Scripture stood him well. "An eye for an eye, and a tooth for a tooth." But instead of the killing quenching his thirst for revenge, it only seemed to whet it more. Near the end, he chased a Mexican soldier, pinning him up against the bank of the bayou. The man fell on his knees before Micah, hands clasped beseechingly, tears oozing down his battle-stained face.

"Have mercy, por favor!" the man begged.

Micah stared into those pleading eyes, leveled his pistol, and fired.

———

Holy retribution? Yes, Micah had no doubt he was in for a strong dose of it. He could almost hear his father's voice quivering with fervent zeal.

" 'And now also the axe is laid unto the root of the trees: therefore every tree which bringeth not forth good fruit is hewn down, and cast into the fire.' "

Micah smiled as he realized he himself had spoken the oft-heard words out loud. For good measure, like a sword thrust, he added, "Matthew chapter three, verse ten."

How Micah hated that he knew all this. But it had nearly been rammed down his throat. He'd been forced to memorize half the Bible! He'd like to exercise it from his brain, but no matter how much he tried to forget, a sneaky little verse would invade his mind at the most inopportune moment before he had a chance to do anything about it.

At any rate, Micah was headed for the fire for certain now. He wished he didn't believe in heaven and hell. Well, he wasn't so sure about heaven, but he knew without a doubt there was a hell. He'd lived in it for years now.

Seven

SOUNDS OUT IN THE CORRIDOR captured Micah's attention. He'd just had supper, so it couldn't be that. Maybe a new tenant was arriving. The distinct sound of a key in a lock proved this was probably true. Then a door opened with a groan and a moment later creaked shut again. Footsteps thudded in the corridor again, and then there was silence.

"Micah, you there?" came Jed's voice.

Micah jumped from his cot and with a single stride, though limping slightly on his one bare foot, went to his cell door.

"Jed? You okay?" he called out the small barred opening in the door.

"Yeah. My arm pains me still, but my head feels better."

Micah hated to admit how good it was to hear a friendly voice and to know this particular friend was all right. Funny, but he hadn't given near as much thought to Harvey or Joe.

"You break your arm or something?" Micah asked, just to keep up the welcome flow of conversation.

"Don't know for certain. The doctor said he had to 'locate' it. But I could see my arm was there the entire time. Don't know what he meant."

Micah could almost picture his friend's bemused look.

"But that locating business hurt worse than that time I sat on a cactus! The doc liquored me up good but still I about passed out. Now he's got it all trussed up in a sling. Said it'd be better in a few days."

"Glad to hear that, Jed. Did you hear about anything else? Did they bring in Harvey and Joe?"

"Not as I know of."

There was a long pause. Micah tried to think of another topic for discussion but could think of nothing besides their fate, and he didn't really want to consider that at the moment.

It was Jed who brought it up. "What's gonna happen to us now, Micah?"

"I was told we'd stand before a judge soon, but they didn't say nothing else."

"What about that fella you seemed to know? Maybe he'll get us out."

Micah shook his head as if Jed could see. "Don't know."

"He came to see me at the doc's. Just to see if I was okay. Maybe he'll help us."

The hopefulness in Jed's voice was a little pathetic, even desperate. Micah cursed himself, as he had done continuously since his arrest, for getting Jed involved.

"I told him how you were a good man, and how you wouldn't have got caught 'cept that you came back for me. Maybe it'll help."

"Maybe." Micah spoke tonelessly, knowing even that much was a dream.

"Micah?"

"Yeah, Jed?"

"Why'd you do it?"

"Do what?"

"Why'd you come back for me? You told me it'd be a stupid, dumb thing to do—"

"Well, I never said I was any smarter than you!"

"You're lots smarter," Jed replied so matter-of-factly that it made Micah's stomach clench. He knew Jed practically worshiped him, and he hated it. Hated the burden of responsibility, hated knowing it was the most misplaced worship ever bestowed upon a miserable creature.

Micah returned to his cot and plopped down, making the flimsy wooden structure creak and sway. "I want to get some shut-eye," he said. "It's late."

———

In the morning Micah and Jed were brought before the town magistrate. Because the evidence was overwhelmingly against them, they were easily convicted of horse thieving and sentenced to hang. Jed cried. Micah stood like a stone, not even blinking at the words of the judge. When the execution was scheduled to take place in three days, Micah's stomach quivered, but no one could see that.

Back in his cell he killed a couple more cockroaches, and when the midday meal came, he ate every scrap of it, though his insides felt like a big knot. He'd give no man the satisfaction of seeing him regret anything about his life.

Jed tried to talk to him, but Micah answered tersely, then told his friend to shut up. It was cruel, because he knew Jed was scared and needed to talk about it. But Micah was scared, too, and he needed to be silent. Despite the fact that he'd always suspected his end would come in this manner, he'd believed it would wait a few years. He wasn't even going to see his twenty-first birthday in a few weeks. But he was not going to whimper about the thing. What was done was done. He'd accept it like a man, and when the moment came ... well, he just hoped he'd be able to take that like a man, too.

He'd chosen his path a long time ago. Maybe not consciously, but he'd always known he would take whatever route was the exact opposite of his father's. He had made that decision one dark night as he sat by a campfire and watched his mother die. No one had said much to him, and certainly no one had explained why he and his sisters found themselves many miles from home with their uncle and their mother, but not with their father. No one had *said* their father had driven them away. No one had *said* his mother was dying because she had chosen to travel in a delicate condition instead of enduring another moment with that monster Micah must call "Father."

No one said anything.

But Micah was twelve years old at the time, and he perceived far more than anyone had given him credit for. He knew his mother had been a long-suffering saint while his father was demanding, harsh, self-righteous. And when his mother had breathed her last, Micah had silently sworn to himself that he would hate his father and all that he stood for as long as he lived.

He had never thought his father would outlive him. In a way, though, that was rather a sweet irony. At least it gave Micah a small satisfaction in his inglorious death. For that religious hypocrite to know his son had hung for horse-stealing, well, there was a certain beauty in that.

Footsteps in the corridor intruded into Micah's grim musings. Glancing at the small barred window high up near the ceiling on the wall opposite of where he lay, he saw it was full dark out, and he had not even noticed the growing darkness in his cell. He did not move from his cot even when he heard a key twist in the lock of his door, nor did he glance toward the door.

"Micah, you ain't asleep, are you?"

The voice belonged to Tom Fife. He was holding a lighted candle that illuminated his face in an eerie orange glow.

Micah only grunted in reply.

Fife stepped around so as to see Micah better, and probably so Micah, who remained still, could see him.

"I'd like a word with you, if I might." He set the candle on the table near the cot.

"I'm locked in here. I don't got a choice," Micah muttered.

"True . . ." Fife drew out the word as he laced his fingers through his beard. "I got a proposition for you."

Micah's eyes, almost against his will, flickered toward the ranger. He hated demonstrating even the slightest interest or curiosity. But "propositions" for a man in his position couldn't mean too many things. More'n likely they wanted him to give up Harvey and Joe in exchange for some concession. But Micah had never yet said so much as a word about the others. And he wouldn't either.

"Make it fast, Tom," Micah said as if he didn't care. "It's late, and I want some sleep."

"Well, since your sentencing today, I been talking myself blue in the face trying to get you some kind of lighter sentence. I just been two hours with Captain Hays trying to convince him you are worth saving—"

"Sorry you wasted your breath, Tom."

"It wasn't wasted."

Micah's heart did a double beat. What did that mean? Was he going to get off? No way would he turn in his friends. He said nothing, however, continuing with his stoic indifference.

"Why, you knuckleheaded, impudent, thick-skulled, addlepated, foolish little brat!" Fife suddenly raved.

This forced Micah's attention. Fife's face was turning beet red, his fists were clenched, and he looked about two breaths away from murder. In fact, in the next instant Fife's fists swung into motion and grabbed Micah's shirtfront, dragging Micah into a sitting position.

"You ornery little twit!" Fife continued to yell. "I know you got better manners than that. You look at me when I talk to you!"

Micah licked his lips. He was thirsty, that's all. But his eyes shot up to meet Fife's fiery gaze. "Calm yourself, Tom," he said in a tone barely above a squeak.

"Do you realize you are gonna die in three days, boy? Is that what you want?"

Tom's gaze bore into Micah like a knife, only this hurt far worse than a stab with any blade. Though his gaze was sharp and furious, there was no hatred in it. Though the man's voice shook, it was filled with something that finally penetrated Micah's senses. Tom Fife was scared. Scared for Micah.

"N-no." That realization made Micah's voice tremble. And, God help him, moisture rose in his eyes. He turned his face away. He didn't care if Tom smacked him. He couldn't let the man see him cry.

"Boy?" Fife said softly, loosening his grip on Micah's shirt.

"I ain't a boy no more." Micah wiped a sleeve across his face, eyes still averted from the ranger's.

"I want to help you."

"I won't give away any of my friends."

"Didn't think you would. And I never thought to ask." Fife sat on the foot of the cot. "You want to hear my proposition?"

Micah swallowed and blinked back the brimming moisture. Then he nodded. He supposed it wouldn't hurt to listen. He really didn't want to die.

"Well, I convinced Captain Hays that in view of your tender years—"

"I said I ain't no boy—"

Tom held up his hand. "I know . . . I know. But it wouldn't be so bad to be thought a kid if it'd save your life, now, would it?" Without giving Micah a chance to respond, he went on. "Besides, I think he was more impressed when I told him you was also a hero of San Jacinto. He wondered why you was stealing horses instead of working your land allotment. I wonder the same thing. What happened to your land grants? You should have got six hundred forty acres, and another six hundred forty as your uncle's heir. That could have set you up real good, Micah."

"Are you gonna lecture me, or are you gonna tell me about this all-important proposition of yours?" Micah asked, risking only a mild sneer in his voice.

"All right." Tom sighed resignedly. "Captain Hays figures that maybe you deserve another chance. He's prepared to release you into my custody for a probationary period of one year, during which you will serve the Republic of Texas as a ranger. If you conduct yourself in an honorable manner in that time, he reckons to commute your sentence."

Micah stared, disbelieving. All he could manage to say was "A ranger?"

"That's right."

"A lawman?"

"Not exactly . . ." Tom scratched his head. "But close enough."

"You mean to tell me that this here captain of yours is willing to take a thief and make him into a lawman? Don't make no sense. . . ." Micah leaned against the wall, shaking his head. "No sense at all."

"I spoke up for you, Micah."

"What'd you tell him? You don't know me." He studied the ranger more carefully. Tom was looking at him, but what did he see? A frightened kid clinging to his mother's skirts, ripped from the home he loved and forced to endure hardships of a life in a rough, strange land? Or perhaps a boy smeared with gunpowder and blood and the stench of death, fighting battles meant for men? He surely did not see the man Micah had become: at best, a thief; at worst, well, at worst a man who did deserve to hang.

"It has been a long time," Fife admitted. "But I'm willing to take that risk."

"Why?"

"I seen lots of men in my time, Micah. And I know when a man's bad to the core, and you ain't one of those. Leastways, I'm willing to stake my reputation on it. Now, are you gonna accept my proposition or not? You ain't got a lot of time."

"What about Jed?"

"Huh?"

Micah jerked his head toward the next cell. "My friend. He get the same proposition?"

"Aw, now Micah, it'd be pushing it mightily just to get it for you." Tom lurched to his feet and paced across the cell. "We can't be letting every horse thief loose."

"What about Jed's tender years? 'Sides, he's even younger than he looks. His mind ain't quite all there, you know."

"I thought maybe he was a mite slow."

"And he don't deserve to hang, even more than me."

Tom turned and faced Micah. "The captain won't go for it." He chewed his mustache and shook his head. "I'm truly sorry."

"Don't matter," Micah said imperturbably. "I wasn't gonna take your offer anyway. I don't want to be a ranger."

As Tom left the cell, Micah experienced a twinge of regret. This rangering business might not be too bad. In fact, it might offer him all the excitement and adventure he'd found riding with Harvey Tate without the constant threat of, well, of where he was right now. He'd heard of the exploits of the rangers since they had been officially recruited just after the war. They mostly fought Indians and Mexicans, protecting the borders of the new republic. Imagine that! He'd be able to fight all the Mexicans he wanted, and it would be perfectly legal.

But there was no way he'd let Jed hang alone. It was his fault Jed was in this position, and Micah might be a lot of unsavory things, but he wasn't the kind to desert his friends.

Eight

TWO UNEXPECTED VISITORS came to see Micah the day before his hanging. He was eating his midday meal when the first one arrived. He wasn't much interested in the beans on the tin plate and the hunk of bread. He and Jed had had lengthy discussions that morning about food because they had been told that for supper they'd be able to have anything they wanted since it would be their last meal. Jed couldn't decide between ham and fried chicken. He was very definite about what he wanted for dessert—pecan pie. And not just a slice, but the whole thing!

Micah moved the beans around on his plate with his spoon, the only eating implement his jailers trusted him with. He wondered if he'd have an appetite for anything when supper came. Then he heard the noise of someone approaching. With a defiant flourish he scooped up some beans and stuffed them into his mouth, following that with a huge bite of corn bread. When his cell door opened, he nearly choked on the food.

"Hello, Micah."

He just stared at the figure nearly filling the doorway, his mouth and throat working desperately to swallow the food that had suddenly become as dry as sawdust. But even without the food, he would not have known what to say. In fact, he wasn't certain he'd say anything. He'd finished talking to this man six years ago ... no, long before that. He'd quit having anything to say to his father the day he had dragged his family from their home in Boston.

Benjamin Sinclair ducked under the door lintel and stepped fully into the cell as the jailer closed and locked the door behind him. Micah continued to stare silently. But silence wasn't going to make the man go away. His father filled the small cell with that presence he'd always had, some inner force that made people listen to him, fear him, and hate him. His preaching had often driven people to tears. His recriminations had made them tremble. Micah himself had trembled often in the man's presence. There had been a time when he was a very young boy that he had even regarded the man with awe. Micah had thought that the fiery Almighty whom Reverend Sinclair had so eloquently preached about had actually been his father and that if he worshiped his father, his father would love him, but if he fell short, that same father would condemn him to hell. Then Micah had grown older and wiser, realizing there was nothing he could do to please either father—the one in heaven or the man now standing before him.

"Say something, son," Benjamin said in a tone of soft entreaty.

It reminded Micah of how his father had claimed to have changed after his mother's death. He had behaved kind of differently then, but the changes had come too late. For Micah, at least.

"What're you doing here?" Micah could barely speak. The food was gone, but his throat still felt constricted.

"Tom got word to me about what happened. I . . . had to see you, Micah."

"Why?"

"W-why?" The man now returned the same gaping expression his son was wearing. "You're my son!"

"You figure to take one last chance to save my soul?" Micah taunted.

"I don't know what I figure to do. I haven't seen you in over six years, had no way to find you. I guess when I heard you'd finally . . . well, lighted in one place, I just came."

Benjamin continued to stand, towering over Micah. His legs were slightly apart, his hands clasped behind his back like a soldier at ease. He looked like he could and would stand there forever.

Micah resisted the urge to squirm. But he could not deny the inner sense of being an errant child awaiting deserved discipline.

He knew if he stood, he'd be just as tall as his father. He knew if he wanted, he could engage in a physical battle with this man and win. Yet he wouldn't. And he had no idea why. But he would not hurt this man, at least physically. Still, he grasped his spoon as if it were a weapon.

"I don't want to talk to you," Micah said stiffly.

"I've come a long ways to see you."

"No one asked you to."

Benjamin's jaw began to work spasmodically, and a brief flicker of something like fire glinted from his eyes. Micah had seen that look before. It had usually come just before a particularly painful beating.

But Benjamin continued to stand like a statue. Finally he spoke, tightly at first, then seemingly gaining control of his ire, his tone relaxed. "Tom Fife tells me they have offered you a way out of this mess. I guess it wouldn't help if I encouraged you to take his offer."

The corner of Micah's mouth quirked slightly into a hint of amusement.

Benjamin shook his head. "So you'll let them hang you just to spite me?"

"Don't flatter yourself, Pa. I got my reasons, and they don't have nothing to do with you." Deliberately, Micah laid down his spoon and pushed aside his tray, which was on his bed.

"Don't be so stubborn, son!"

"You ain't got no right to tell me how to be or what to do," Micah rejoined.

"No ... I suppose I don't." He paused, his eyes blue like the summer sky, blue like Micah's, searching his son. "I know you'll never believe it, but I have changed. I've made mistakes—I still make mistakes—but I've learned that God sees only a man's heart, and I am trying to do that as well. Not always successfully, I admit. But..."

The fire was gone now from those incisive pools, replaced by something Micah could not read ... or did not want to.

"Son, I know I am to blame for the parts of your heart that are dark and painful. But I know, too, that your heart is not all dark. I know that because, even more than me, your mother had a great influence upon you. Her love and her tender spirit are in you as well. And just maybe they are even stronger than my part. I think that is what Tom Fife sees, and that is why he is willing to take such a risk for you. I ask you—not for me but for your mother's sake—to stay alive."

"My mother is dead." Somehow Micah's flat monotone managed to convey volumes of scorn.

Then the statue of the man moved. Benjamin lifted a hand and raked it through his hair, blond like Micah's.

"You know what I mean." A desperate quality suffused his voice.

"Well, just remember this. If I live or die, it has nothing to do with you." Micah's voice rang clear and confident, though in his heart he feared the fate he chose would have everything to do with this man.

"I know."

The pain in those two words made Micah's stomach twist. "Now leave me alone," Micah said.

Benjamin turned toward the cell door, then paused. "Do you care to know how your sisters and brother are, and my wife?"

Micah shrugged.

Benjamin, apparently taking that for assent, continued. "You've got a half brother and half sister now. The youngest was born a few months ago. The whole family is well. Isabel is growing into a pretty young lady. She wanted to come with me and told me to tell you she misses you—"

"Do they know about me?" Micah cut in, not really understanding the sudden concern rising in him.

"They don't hear as much news as I, so I doubt it. I would never tell them."

Micah shrugged as if he didn't care, then said with the most sincerity in his tone that he'd yet used, "Well, tell Issy I miss her, too. And the other kids. And Elise." He thought briefly of his father's second wife. She'd been kind to him, and he hoped she didn't one day suffer the same fate as Rebekah Sinclair had.

"I'll do that, Micah." Benjamin put his face close to the barred opening in the door. "Guard, I'm ready."

His voice held a hesitancy, as if he truly was not ready, as if he had more to say. But he remained silent as he waited. Micah did the same.

It seemed to take forever for the guard to come. Micah did not realize he was holding his breath until the door creaked open, and he expelled a sharp burst of air.

"Good-bye, Micah," Benjamin said in a tone that seemed rough and brittle, then he paused a moment before stepping outside.

If he had been waiting for parting words from his son, Micah disappointed him, remaining silent. The door then clanked shut, and Micah was left alone.

The next visit came just before sunset. Micah thought it would be Tom with one last plea. And Micah wondered what his response would be, desperately wanting a way out but believing that would not be possible.

When the door opened, it wasn't Fife who stepped inside, but a dream. At least he wondered if he was dreaming while still wide awake. He'd had this dream several times since the Comanche attack, and it had been a welcome respite from his Goliad and San Jacinto nightmares. He'd dreamed of a beautiful, genteel girl with a smile that could melt stone or turn a dry riverbed into a rushing stream of water, dancing and sparkling in the desert sun. He'd dreamed that smile was meant for him, only him. And he'd wake with a gnawing ache, knowing he would only see such a smile in the netherworld of sleep.

That's why Micah rubbed his eyes and stared, half expecting the vision to suddenly dissolve. But she was still standing there, all feminine in cornflower blue, her dark hair escaping the confines of her lace bonnet and falling around her lovely face.

The spell was broken by Tom Fife's discordant voice. "Got a visitor for you, Micah." Then he added, "I'll be right outside here, miss."

Before Micah could say a thing or give his leave, the door shut.

This time, however, Tom did not lock it.

She smiled that smile, and Micah realized he remembered it perfectly from their last meeting.

"I hope you don't mind my coming unannounced," she said.

Mind? Micah could have been ready to die that minute just with the sight of her, feeling his life had been complete.

"Naw, I don't mind," he said casually. "It gets kind of boring in here." Then remembering his manners, he jumped up. All at once he became acutely aware of himself and his surroundings.

He was still wearing the same dirty clothes he'd been wearing the day of the Comanche attack. And, of course, he hadn't had a bath in all that time either. Nothing unusual about that. Not enough water on the trail earlier, and now no one cared to waste the effort if he was just gonna die in a day. He smelled like rotten onions, and his week's growth of beard made his face look like he'd been kissing dirt. He didn't have much of a beard, but what he had was darker and ruddier than his hair. Instinctively his hand shot up to his chin, then he grimaced, and instead of welcoming this visit, he decided that before he died tomorrow, he would kill Tom Fife.

"I don't have a chair to offer you," he said, as if this admission could account for everything else.

"I don't mind standing."

The corners of her lips twitched, and he realized she was just as nervous as he. She held her hands in front of her, twisting them together.

"Didn't figure I'd ever see you again," Micah said.

"I heard you'd been arrested, and I felt so bad, I just couldn't stay away."

Her dark eyes were like lumps of obsidian, only fluid and expressive. They glittered now with what Micah dared to hope was sadness.

"I don't hold nothing against you," Micah replied with just a hint of magnanimity in his tone. He thought about holding her that day when she had fainted and decided the experience was well worth arrest, maybe even hanging. "You had to tell the law what I done."

"Please don't think that!" The obsidian now flashed with passion. "I would never have turned you in after what you did for me. I prayed they would never find you. But it was Pete's best horse you took, and, well, he was pretty upset."

"I'm sorry I did that, and not just because of ... well, what's gonna happen tomorrow." Micah shifted nervously on his feet. In truth, he wasn't entirely sorry, but he couldn't have her know that. "I didn't know you was Texans, and ... I wouldn't have done it if it had been his only horse." That, at least, was true. "Anyway, I am sorry."

"I came to town to tell the constable about what you did for me, how you might have escaped free and clear with no one able to identify you if you hadn't come back to see to me—"

"You shouldn't have done that," he broke in, horrified on several different levels, most of which he could barely define. But for certain he hated the thought that she had come merely out of pity.

"You rescued me at your own peril," she insisted.

"I also took you hostage—"

"Pooh!" She gave a dismissive wave of her hand. "You never would have harmed me."

"How do you know that?"

"I just do."

Completely abashed, Micah said rather helplessly, "Well, at any rate, you shouldn't have come here, because you'd likely ruin your reputation if folks believed you had any truck with a man like me."

"I don't care what people think. I owe you my life, Mr. Sinclair."

"Still ... it ain't right."

She then bestowed upon him such a look—part smile, part admiration, part impish rebellion—that it made him suck in a breath of shock.

"My father would have a conniption if he knew I was here." A curl fell in her eyes, and that impish look had full reign for a moment before she lifted a hand and flicked the silken wave back into place.

She was the most beautiful thing Micah had ever seen.

She continued. "But I learned something about you the day you saved me, Mr. Sinclair, that no one else knows."

"Y-you did?" He silently cursed the flustered squeak in his voice.

"You are a decent man, Mr. Sinclair. I know that and ... and I can't bear the thought of..." Her own voice broke with emotion. "Goodness! I didn't think I'd..." She fumbled with the reticule that hung from her twisting hands and withdrew a handkerchief.

"Miss! You..." But as much as Micah knew he should say something, he was speechless. This beautiful girl, this vision of sweet dreams, was weeping ... for him! He didn't even think how this would be the ideal opportunity to hold her once again, just to comfort her, of course. Instead, he just stood there, gaping woodenly.

She dabbed her eyes daintily. "I'm so sorry for carrying on this way."

"You oughtn't cry, not over me," he finally said.

"But ... but ..." her tears kept flowing.

"Tom! Tom!" Micah yelled, not knowing what else to do.

The door flew open, and Tom leaped into the cell like an avenging knight. "What's going on?"

"It ain't my fault!" Micah declared preemptively.

"No, Mr. Fife, it isn't Mr. Sinclair's fault." She sniffed and her words trembled. "I just don't want to see him ... I can't even say it! And I am to blame!"

"No you ain't, miss."

Tom reached out and did what Micah had been hungering to do. He put an arm around the weeping girl. But at the same time Tom made this gentle gesture, he turned blazing eyes on Micah.

"What'd you say to her, boy!" he accused more than asked.

"N-nothing!" But Micah knew in his heart he was totally the cause of her distress. Yet he was helpless to do a thing about it.

"He was a perfect gentleman," she said through her tears.

How could she defend him? He'd stolen from her, held her hostage, and put her through emotional distress.

"I'm taking you out now, miss," Tom said. "Your pa would

kill me if he knew I'd let you in here. And now look at you!" He nudged her toward the door. Pausing only for a backward glance at Micah, he added threateningly, "I'll be back to talk to you later."

Nine

TOM DID NOT RETURN for two hours, during which time Micah fretted as if worse could happen to him than already was going to happen tomorrow.

That girl should never have come to his cell. It had been pure foolishness! And Micah would chew Tom out good for allowing it to happen. What had the man been thinking, letting a decent girl into a depraved man's jail cell to see a condemned criminal? Even Micah would have known that a girl's delicate sensibilities could have been upset by such a thing.

Then he thought about those tears, erupting from obsidian, coursing down pure ivory, and all for him. It should have disturbed him to have a gal like that pity him so, yet as he mulled over the visit in his mind, Micah began to sense that there had not been anything like pity in her response. Maybe it was just wishful thinking on his part, but it might be true that her sorrow sprang from something else entirely.

What that might be, he dared not think about. It was no use anyway. He was going to die tomorrow.

But if there was a way to avoid the inevitable, well, he might just take it. He could stand being a ranger if it meant pleasing a gal like Miss Maccallum. If it meant he could dispel those tears and the distress in those lovely eyes.

"Hey, Micah!" Jed called.

With a jolt Micah remembered why he would never see those eyes smile again.

"What!" Micah snapped. But it really wasn't Jed's fault. Micah had gotten Jed into this mess, and he was going to stick by him till the end. That was that. A bit more gently he added, "Haven't heard much from you today, Jed. What's going on?"

"You sure have had a slug of visitors. I saw a pretty female in the hall."

"Yeah. Of all things, Jed, it was the gal from the trail drive."

"The one whose horses we stole?"

"The same. She was crying because of me."

"You don't say!" Jed gave a low whistle. "She sure was pretty."

Micah shrugged, then swung his legs off his cot and stood. Striding to the door, he added, "When do you suppose supper is gonna come? I'm starved." He didn't want to talk about Miss Maccallum. He didn't want to be reminded about all he was losing.

The outer door opened, and Tom stepped into the corridor. Micah took it as a good sign that the man seemed to have calmed since his earlier visit.

"Hey, Tom, when's supper?"

"Yeah," Jed put in. "I'm gonna get ham and fried chicken, right?"

"I got more important things to discuss than your stomachs." Tom came to Micah's cell, opened it, and stepped inside.

Micah immediately noted the door was kept unlocked and slightly ajar. But no doubt the outer office was filled with rangers armed to the teeth. Micah knew escape was impossible, but he could not prevent himself from thinking about it.

Snapping the door shut behind him, Tom ordered, "You! Sit down and listen to me!"

He took a step toward Micah, who retreated until he was at the edge of the cot and forced to sit anyway.

"Tom, you're not still mad at me, are you?" Micah hated having to look up at the ranger, again feeling like a naughty kid.

"That girl was still crying when she left here," Tom went on in a tone so even it was frightening.

"I swear I didn't do nothing to her!"

"Shut up and listen to me! You're gonna take my proposition." When Micah opened his mouth to protest, Tom added firmly, "No ifs, ands, or buts about it! I ain't gonna watch that girl's heart break over a low-down, no-account, sidewinder like you. You're gonna become a ranger. No arguments."

"I can't do it," Micah said, his own conviction floundering as he

thought of the miserable girl and his own demise. "You know why
. . . and I just can't."

"Aw, shoot!" Tom practically shouted. "You're both gonna have
to become rangers, then."

"Both?" Micah was certain he had not heard right. "You mean
Jed, too?"

"Yeah, him too. I'll live to regret this, I'm sure. You'll both likely
drive me to an early grave—"

But Micah had jumped to his feet and, nearly knocking Tom
over, was at the door. "Jed, you hear that? We ain't gonna hang!"

"What?" Jed said, several steps behind everyone else as usual.

"I'm telling you we ain't gonna die. Tom's made us a deal. All
we have to do is become rangers."

"Huh?"

Remembering the door was unlocked, Micah flung it open and
strode down the corridor to Jed's cell. "I'm telling you, do you want
to be a ranger?"

"A ranger?"

"It won't be much different from what we've been doing 'cept
we'll get paid for it, and"—he added this last part quickly as Tom
approached—"of course we can't steal no more."

"And we don't have to hang tomorrow?" Jed asked, still bemused.

"Nope," Tom answered. "But don't think you're gonna get off
easy. I'm gonna make you work your tails off. You're both gonna
be the best durned rangers in this here republic, or I'll want to
know the reason why. I ain't risking my own neck just to have a
couple of poor malcontents hanging around my neck. Got it?"

"You don't have to worry about us," Micah said. "We won't let
you down." And oddly enough, he meant it. He suddenly glanced
at Tom and felt a peculiar tightening in his chest. He wanted to
tell him thanks but couldn't get the words out.

"Does this mean I don't get no pecan pie?" Jed asked.

Fife rolled his eyes. "Saints preserve me! What have I gone and
done!"

"Angry? That does not begin to describe what I'm feeling right now."

"But, Papa, I had to do what I felt was right." Lucie hated to have her father upset at her. She looked at him now, his face more florid than usual, and searched in her mind for something to say that would ease him. "Papa, you taught me yourself to follow my heart—"

"I did not teach you to consort with criminals, nor to defy me!" Reid gasped a breath and sat down at the table in the kitchen.

It had been a silent ride in the back of the carriage as one of the hands drove them home from San Antonio. Lucie knew her father was fuming and feared anything she might say would set off fireworks. She was still upset as well, her eyes red and puffy, and she continued to be on the verge of tears. Deciding it was best to let matters cool a bit, she had gone to the kitchen to fix some tea. She'd offered her father a cup, but declining, he had retreated to his office.

That had been two hours ago. Finally her father had come from his study, finding Lucie still in the kitchen moping over her now cold tea. She had asked him if he was still angry and learned that, though he had calmed, he indeed continued to be irritated.

"Would you like some tea? The kettle is warm." She started to rise, but he laid a restraining hand on hers.

"Forget the tea, Lucie. We need to talk this out."

"Yes, Papa, I know."

"Tell me, whatever got into your head to go into that jail?"

She sighed. "It was the right thing to do—at least speaking in the man's defense was. As far as going to see him . . . I don't know. Maybe it was not wise." She bit her lip as sudden emotion threatened her again. "Oh, Papa! He is a nice boy, I just know it! And I didn't help him after all. Tomorrow . . . tomorrow . . ." A hiccough escaped her lips.

"Now, now, Lucie, baby . . . you mustn't fret so."

As if she had intended it, her tears were softening her father. She found the effect of a woman's tears on a man to be astounding, and though she dared not use such power brazenly, it was rather comforting to know she did have some small recourse as a woman. However, it hadn't helped in the case of Micah Sinclair. Her tears had not softened the heart of that ranger captain. They would not save the young horse thief.

"Papa, it just isn't right that a man with so much life to live, so much promise, should have it all end in such a way. He is not a hardened criminal, I am certain. Surely something awful must have happened to him that set him on the wrong path. He was very kind to me. And I felt I had to let him know someone cared." She sniffed and her father handed her his handkerchief. She wiped her eyes and blew her nose. "Can you imagine having to die all alone? And, Papa, he turned down a chance to avoid his sentence. They were going to let him become a ranger—"

"I know. That is the most outlandish thing I ever heard. And I told the captain so," Reid said.

"One of the rangers cared enough to take him in hand..."

"There you go! He did have someone else who cared for him." A satisfied looked spread across Reid's face.

"Well, it doesn't matter anyway," Lucie said with just a hint of disrespectful ire. "Micah refused the offer because he would not let his friend hang alone."

"Sounds like pure foolishness to me."

"Oh, Papa, you can't fool me. You know as well as I that it was an act of grand courage and honor."

Reid looked down at the table, fumbling nervously with the handle of the teapot. Finally he looked up at his daughter, a smile teasing the corners of his lips. "Well, maybe it was at that."

"I think you would like him, Papa. I think you would like him a lot." For a brief moment Lucie nearly forgot her father would never meet the young man, thinking instead she might actually see that handsomely boyish face again. Then reality struck her, and a sob broke through her lips. "Papa, even prayer did not help him."

"You don't know that, sweetheart." He grasped her hand in his. "We can never know what God intends."

"It seems so hopeless!"

"Well, I kind of think it's in hopeless situations where God shines most. Now, don't fret, all right? You leave the lad in God's hands, eh?"

She nodded tearfully.

Then Reid rose. "Maybe I would like some of that tea. You just stay put. I'll get it."

She watched her father lumber to the stove and lift the kettle from the iron surface. It had been a trying day for him as well. The two-hour drive to and from San Antonio alone was taxing. In addition to that he'd had his own business to attend to. Maybe it had been selfish for Lucie to insist upon going and being allowed to speak to the ranger captain, and then to slip away and visit the jail while her father was at the bank. Maybe she should have thought before putting her father through such an unnecessary ordeal. Maybe she should have put his well-being before that of a stranger.

Yet she knew a large portion of her father's surly response was only out of concern for her. She knew he would be the first one to insist upon justice and fairness and mercy. Had she not been involved, Lucie felt certain Reid Maccallum would have been the first man to stand up for Micah Sinclair.

Juana came in just then. "Señor Maccallum, let me get that." She reached for the teakettle as he brought it to the table.

"I've got it, Juana," Reid said. "Sit and join us."

"When there is work to be done? You know me better than that, señor." She chuckled, adroitly taking possession of the kettle as she did so.

Shrugging his surrender, Reid resumed his seat and let Juana continue the task. She filled the teapot with the hot water, took the kettle back to the stove, and returned with a dish of biscuits and a pot of butter.

"So how was your trip to San Antonio?" she asked.

"Tiring," Reid said.

"Frustrating," Lucie added.

"I want you both to stay home for a good long time now. No more trips to San Antonio or anywhere." She lifted the teapot and refilled the cups.

Lucie shrugged, in no mood to argue. In truth, she felt little desire to leave home at the moment. And she had no desire to go to town for a good while, because she did not want to hear stories of what had already occurred or what would occur on the morrow.

Lucie and her father were sipping their tea in silence while Juana was mixing bread dough when a knock came at the kitchen door. Juana let in Pete.

"I just got back from town," he said. "Thought you might want to hear the news."

"Come on in and sit down," Reid said.

"Thanks, but I only got a minute. I need to see to my horse—I came right here." He glanced at Lucie. "Looks like you're gonna get your wish, miss."

Lucie could not tell from his expression if this was a good thing or bad. At least Pete did not seem to be bubbling with happiness.

"My wish?" Lucie asked.

"That kid in jail that you was so worried about? Looks like he isn't gonna hang after all."

"Pete! Really?"

Now Pete let escape a hint of his personal view in the matter. A slight grimace twisted his broad tanned face. "He got a reprieve for being so young and for being a hero of San Jacinto. Same with the other kid. I reckon now everyone who was even close to San Jacinto will take this as leave to rob this here country dry."

But Lucie heard little of the foreman's diatribe. Micah Sinclair was going to live! Maybe, just maybe, her words had done him some good after all! She wanted to jump up and dance around the room. She wanted to kiss her father and maybe even that old leathery foreman.

Suddenly she thought of something else. Maybe she would see Micah again. When she glanced up from her joyous musings, she noticed both men were staring at her. Only then was she aware of the wide grin on her face.

Ten

"TRY THIS FOR SIZE." Tom held out the pistol.

Micah turned the weapon over in his hand. He'd heard of these but had never seen one, much less held one in his hand. A Paterson Colt single-action revolving handgun. A five-shot .40 caliber affair.

"Five shots, no reloading," Micah murmured. "Hard to believe."

"Give it a try," Tom said. The gun was already loaded because Tom had demonstrated how to do it a few minutes before. He had also given a couple of pointers about using the Colt.

They were in a field near the area where a group of rangers were camped on the edge of town. A few other rangers had gathered around to have a look at the newcomers. Micah noted such luminaries as Big Foot Wallace and Sam Walker. There were also a couple Mexicans; in fact, the ranger company had several Mexicans. But these were from the good families, the ones that had fought with Houston.

Tom had set several rocks in a line on the ground in the center of the mesquite- and sagebrush-covered field. Micah positioned himself just within gun range of the rocks. With a quick glance at Tom, as if still uncertain that he might actually have this privilege, he took a breath and raised the gun. He felt oddly calm in the august presence of so many veterans. But shooting was one thing he felt confident about. Biting the inside of his lip, a habit he'd picked up from his uncle, he cocked the pistol to release the trigger, then squeezed it nice and easy. A rock skipped into the air, shattering into pieces. He repeated the process four more times, never missing.

"Mighty fine shooting," Wallace said in his Virginia drawl.

Micah shrugged at the big lumbering ranger. "Ain't nothing to shoot at rocks."

"Yeah," put in one of the other men, "just wait till he's got a dozen Comanches breathing down his neck."

"My boy could take on more than that, no sweat," bragged Tom like a proud parent.

Micah rolled his eyes, uncomfortable with the attention, yet a certain part of him basking in the praise. He handed the Colt to Jed.

"We gonna get one of these?" Jed asked in awe.

"Only if you got about forty dollars to spare," said Walker, who was the resident expert on the weapon since he had gone back East to tour Samuel Colt's New Jersey factory and had offered suggestions on making improvements in the weapon. It was, in fact, Walker's Colt they were now trying out.

"I hear tell Captain Hays is trying to work out a deal with navy ordnance to get some Colts they have and ain't gonna use since they have been decommissioned," Wallace said. "I'm thinking, though, that we do just as well with our flintlocks and percussion caps." He paused, taking his flintlock pistol from where he had tucked it into his belt. "Truth be told, that Paterson is just a bit too tender for me."

"Well, you gotta keep the grit out, or it gets touchy," Walker said, "but these Colts will take over the West one day. You just wait until Sam Colt makes his improvements."

"So, Jed, you ready to give it a try?" Tom asked. "You remember how to load it, don't you?"

"Sure, it's easy." Jed took the powder pouch and poured a measure into each chamber. Tom had told them not to put in too much powder or the recoil might, in his words, "Wrench your arm out of its socket." But Tom now looked on approvingly at Jed's technique. When the powder was in, Jed set a ball on each chamber opening, tamping them down in turn.

"You'll get faster loading as you get more practice," Tom encouraged.

Micah had jogged out to the middle of the field and put up a row of new rocks, then he stepped aside and gave Jed the go-ahead. Jed hit three out of five.

Wallace nodded at the display. "Well, Tom, your horse-thieves-turned-rangers might just work out after all."

That was high praise indeed coming from the famous Texan. Micah felt like grinning as Jed was now doing, but he was already suffering under the greenhorn, new-recruit stigma, so he merely gave the man a cool nod.

The rangers were careful not to waste powder and lead, and soon the shooting demonstration ended, the men dispersing about to their own business. Supplies and finances were a constant burr in the rangers' skin. Though theoretically each ranger was to receive a monthly stipend of around twenty-five dollars, few ever saw any money. Sometimes the government came up with the cash months after the ranger's term of service was completed, but usually not at all. Sometimes they received land for compensation— one commodity Texas had plenty of. But basically these men simply were not in it for the money. Sheer thirst for adventure or a sense of duty to their country drove them. This was not a job for any man who cared for the comforts of life. Their living quarters consisted of the sky for a roof, the dirt as a floor, and the brush for walls.

They were expected to provide their own equipment and fill their own bellies. However, when there was no pay coming, this became a serious problem, especially when they were too busy scouting and such to hunt. For some time Captain Hays had been keeping the men from his own pocket, thus far, to the tune of some three thousand dollars.

Though Micah was officially a ranger, not much had changed for him. He still had the same clothes, though he had allowed himself the luxury of a bath. He wore no badge or other insignia. But for all the poverty of the other rangers, Micah was much worse off because he lacked the most essential tool of a ranger—a good mount. Or for that matter, any mount. At least Jed had his horse and saddle, though he almost lost it when he nearly admitted to having stolen the beast a few years before. Only a sharp jab in the ribs from Micah prevented that costly error.

Rangers were required to have a horse worth at least a hundred dollars. Many had fine-blooded animals from Kentucky. Their horses were their most important piece of equipment. They often lived or died as much by the skill and stamina of their mounts as by their own. The vast open plains of Texas, often with neither road nor trail, required a good mount. And it was frivolous to even consider facing the mounted Comanches or Mexicans any other way. Micah worried over his lack of a mount, wondering also how he would afford one of those fine revolving pistols.

"You don't need much besides a horse and a good gun," Tom assured him. "Rangers travel light, living off the land when we can, starving when we can't."

"Just what we been doing for years, huh, Micah?" Jed said.

"That still don't solve my biggest problem," Micah said. Without a horse he might just as well be without a leg or an arm. And a hundred-dollar horse? That was easily four months' salary, when the impoverished republic could afford to pay salaries.

Sometimes the rangers had a small remuda of captured horses, but their supply was rather depleted at the moment. The best of the handful of beasts was a broken-down old Comanche pinto that had seen better days some twenty years ago. After the discouraging experience of examining the remuda, Micah, Jed, and Tom went to a cantina in town to slake their thirst. Both Micah and Jed were dragging a bit after a day of firing practice and the other drills Tom felt necessary to get the two new rangers up to par with the others in the company.

Micah was lifting a glass of beer to his lips when a fellow about his own age stepped inside the door that had been left open to let in what little afternoon breeze was there.

"I was told there might be a Micah Sinclair in here," he said.

Micah swallowed, glancing nervously at his companions. He supposed it would take more than a couple days to shake that apprehension at being singled out, which came naturally with criminal behavior. Tom was suppressing a grin, making Micah feel all the more foolish.

"That'd be me," Micah finally answered.

"I got something for you."

"What is it?"

"You gotta come outside."

Micah studied the young man closely. He didn't appear to be

looking for trouble. With a shrug, Micah strode toward the door.

The stranger had gone to a hitching post, loosened the reins of one of the horses tied there, and was leading it toward the sidewalk in front of the cantina. "This here is yours," he said simply.

"Whadd'ya mean? I ain't got no horse."

"You do now. You're supposed to look at the note in the saddle-bag." The stranger thrust the reins once more at Micah.

Instead of taking the reins, Micah walked down the step of the sidewalk and circled the animal, finally lifting the flap to the bag. Inside he found the paper, which he took out. "Who's this from?" he asked as he tore open the seal.

"I reckon the paper will tell all you need to know. I brought the horse from the Maccallum place."

Micah scanned the few lines on the page written in the fine script of a female hand.

Dear Mr. Sinclair,
   I realize nothing can ever properly repay you for all I owe you in saving my life, but please take the gift of this horse as a small gesture of my appreciation.
                              Yours sincerely,
                              Miss Lucie Maccallum

Below this was an addendum: *This is an official transfer of ownership of this buckskin gelding to Micah Sinclair. R. Maccallum.*

Deliberately, Micah folded the paper and replaced it in the saddlebag. Saying nothing, he continued to stand, now on the street, and contemplate the animal. It was indeed a fine-looking buckskin with a light tan coat and silky black tail and mane. It looked powerfully built, too, though sleek as well, as if it had been built specifically for the needs of a ranger desiring both stamina and speed. And it had a good Mexican saddle on it, too, not new by any means, but broken in nicely. The whole lot was worth far more than a hundred dollars.

By now Jed and Tom had come outside. "Whadd'ya got there?" Tom asked.

"Its from that Maccallum girl," Micah replied darkly, no gratitude apparent in his tone. "She had a mind to give it to me."

"Hey! That's great!" Jed said.

"No, it ain't great at all." Suddenly Micah sprang to life. He grabbed the reins from the stranger and swung up into the saddle.

"Where you going?" asked both Jed and Tom.

"I'm taking this horse back, that's where." Micah started to urge the animal forward.

"Wait one minute!" Tom called. "Don't do anything without thinking first, Micah. You need a horse."

"Not this horse."

"What's wrong with that horse?"

"I'm not taking no gift from a woman, for one thing."

Tom rubbed his whiskered chin. "I see your point. But you still need a horse."

"I'll get me a horse myself!" Micah didn't know where his sudden ire was coming from, but he knew it was indeed anger surging through him now.

"Okay, but how you gonna get back to town once you leave off that animal?"

Micah grimaced at Tom's practicality, then quickly solved the problem. "Jed, get your horse. You're coming with me."

Eleven

THE TWO-HOUR RIDE to the Maccallum ranch impressed upon Micah the probable folly of returning the horse. The buckskin was a better mount than even its looks had indicated. It had taken to a new rider admirably, showing its intelligence and even temper. In fact, as they neared the ranch, Micah could not believe how comfortable he felt on the buckskin. It was almost as if they had been meant for each other. And though Jed's sorrel was a fairly good mount, Micah found he had to check the buckskin's pace to let Jed keep up.

By the time they came within sight of the ranch buildings, Micah knew he was making a mistake giving up the horse. But he had also had time to solidify his ambiguous emotions in the matter. He knew a large part of his anger stemmed from the fact that since leaving his parents' home six years earlier, he had pretty much lived for himself, answering to no one. Yes, Harvey Tate had made demands, but Micah had always had the choice of walking out of the gang.

Now all of a sudden it seemed as if Micah's freewheeling world was closing in on him. First, he was all but owned by the rangers, at least for a year. All he had to do was mind his p's and q's. It would be like being in prison for a year, or worse, being home under the thumb of his father.

If that weren't bad enough, now Lucie Maccallum was ... well, what *was* she trying to do? He couldn't quite put his finger on it, but the giving of that horse made him mighty jumpy. She said it was a gift for saving her life, but in his mind gifts, no matter what the reason for them, just made a body beholden to the giver. And why would she feel the need to gift him anyway? Had she forgotten he had stolen nearly thirty-five of her mustangs? Maybe it didn't

91

count because he was no longer in possession of the animals, but they were still gone.

He couldn't explain it. But he was certain she must have some motive. One didn't give away fine animals just like that.

He rode into the yard of the ranch. A quick glance behind indicated Jed had fallen back quite a bit since Micah had spurred the buckskin into a gallop as he had neared the ranch. Now he slowed, not so much for Jed's sake as because a female figure was walking across the yard toward him.

He came to a halt a few feet from her and dismounted. "Good afternoon, miss," he said, tipping his hat politely.

"Hello, Mr. Sinclair. This is a pleasant surprise," Lucie Maccallum said. An afternoon breeze had sprung up and it was blowing wisps of her hair into her face, and she lifted a hand to push them back, revealing lips parted in a warm, welcoming smile.

He didn't want to be reminded of how pretty she was, but how could he not be when she was standing so close that he could smell her fragrance, an oddly heady mix of hay and horseflesh and rosewater. Her dark eyes, too, were sparkling in the afternoon sun. And her riding dress, a brown color that perfectly matched her eyes, seemed to emphasize the clear glow of her skin, which had the aspect of tanned ivory. His throat suddenly went dry and his anger was forgotten, as was his reason for coming to the ranch.

He stood there staring dumbly.

"Mr. Sinclair..." she prompted.

"Miss Maccallum..." He swallowed, finding no moisture in his mouth. The afternoon heat was as debilitating as this beautiful young woman's presence.

"You've no doubt had a long ride," she said. "May I invite you in and offer you a cold drink?"

It was the offer of yet another gift that snapped Micah back to himself. "No, miss." He remembered the buckskin's reins gripped in his hands. "I ... uh ... I've come to bring back your horse."

"I don't understand. I gave him to you." She looked truly perplexed.

"I can't accept him."

"But—"

Micah's resolve gathered back around him with each word. "I know you probably meant well, but I can't take him. I don't want, nor do I deserve, a gift for what I did."

"Are you saying my life isn't worth a gift?"

"Yes—I mean no! Confound it! That ain't what I mean at all. It's just . . ." Pausing, he saw how her eyes were searching him, seeking to understand. And all he could respond with was a jumble of half-formed emotions. "It's not right. Don't you see?" Micah tried once more to explain, yet it was difficult since he wished to avoid the issue of the stolen horses. "I did what anyone would have done in the same place. And to take something in return . . . it doesn't set well with me. And no matter how you put it, giving me such a fine gift makes me beholden to you."

"I respect your sense of honor in the matter," she responded, "but try to look at it from my viewpoint. I am indebted to you for my very life. The gift helps me to not feel so beholden to you."

"Is that why you gave it to me?" Instinctively, he thought differently.

The way she ducked her head, glancing sheepishly at her toes, indicated his instincts had been correct. "I gave you Jose—"

"Jose?"

"The buckskin," she amplified, then at his nod to continue, she did so. "Anyway, I gave you Jose because you needed a horse, and I wanted to do that for you. It is as simple as that."

Somehow he didn't think it was that simple at all, but he knew she was telling the truth. He gave a deep sigh, then said, "And I can't take it . . . simple as that."

"I told you he wouldn't take it, Lucie," interjected a new voice.

Micah looked around to see a big redheaded man approach. Micah had never met Lucie's father, but he was certain this must be he. In addition to a certain family resemblance, the man carried himself like the owner of one of the largest ranches in Texas. Micah was six feet tall himself, but this man seemed to tower over him by several inches. He was one of the biggest men Micah had ever seen. And his size was only emphasized by his husky girth—not fat by any means, simply *big*—and by his shock of thick hair that was truly as red as a carrot.

Lucie's voice drew Micah's attention from the awesome figure. "Papa, you said if he was worth his salt, he wouldn't take the horse."

"That's right, I did." There was a touch of smugness in the man's tone. Then he turned fully toward Micah. "I'm Reid Maccallum, Lucie's father." He held out his hand.

Micah took it and, remembering a lesson from his youth, gripped the man's hand firmly. "Micah Sinclair."

"I am happy to meet the man who saved my daughter's life." For some reason Micah could not fathom, Maccallum's tone was taut, lacking the ebullience his words might have called for. No doubt he wouldn't forget the loss of his mustangs as easily as his daughter appeared to have done.

"As I was trying to tell your daughter," Micah said as he let go of the huge meaty hand, "I don't expect no payment for what I did."

"I myself did not think you deserved any," Maccallum said flatly.

These words were unexpected. Micah opened his mouth to respond to what he had expected, then snapped his lips closed, nonplussed.

A tight smile twitched upon Maccallum's lips. "My daughter forgets that the men you were with got away with a fair number of my horses."

"I expect, then, you might have preferred that I hang," Micah replied dryly.

"I have always believed hanging a bit harsh for the crime of horse stealing, especially considering the murder of human beings often goes with a far lesser punishment. But that aside, I only know my daughter would have been extremely unhappy at your demise, Mr. Sinclair."

Maccallum glanced his daughter's way, and Micah noted a hint of tenderness flicker across the man's stern visage.

"And that, sir, I could not abide," he concluded.

Micah remembered something. "Mr. Maccallum, if I recall rightly, your signature was on that transfer for the horse."

"Yes, Lucie prevailed upon me." Glancing over the heads of

both his companions as if embarrassed, Reid added, "I have been told I tend to be an overly indulgent father."

"At any rate, sir," Micah said, "I won't be taking the horse."

"Yet you need a horse in order to fulfill the terms of your release from jail, do you not?"

"I'll find one somehow."

"Somehow?" The man's hazel eyes squinted with a touch of reproach.

"Not by stealing, sir!"

"You have the money to buy a horse?"

"Not exactly . . ."

"He don't have one red cent," put in Jed, who had by then rode up and, though still mounted, was listening to the exchange.

"And who might you be?" Maccallum inquired, giving Jed a careful appraisal.

"That's my friend Jed Wilkes," Micah answered. Things were getting complicated enough without the added element of Jed, who, if true to form, would only confuse matters more. "He was in jail with me."

"Ah . . . yes," Maccallum said. "My daughter mentioned him." Maccallum paused, rubbing his clean-shaven chin. "As I said, you no doubt plan to purchase a mount. But having no ready cash, you might find this difficult unless you buy on credit."

"Credit?" Micah knew what this was, of course, and didn't like the sound of it.

"I wouldn't speak so skeptically of this method, Mr. Sinclair. The entire Republic of Texas has made extensive use of credit for its survival and is no worse for it—well, at least it is surviving because of it. No doubt if the republic intends to pay you for your services as a ranger, it will do so by loans it has received from other nations and such. There is no reason, then, why you shouldn't purchase a horse—a desperately needed horse, I might add—by the same method."

"Who would give me credit? I don't have any collateral or nothing." Micah knew there would be a ready answer for his query or Maccallum wouldn't have brought up the subject.

"I'll extend credit to you for this buckskin. If it weren't for my daughter, you would be dead now and thus in no need of a horse, so I feel rather obligated to make the situation right."

Micah restrained a smile at the man's rather twisted logic. Part of Micah knew Maccallum was simply attempting to make the giving of the horse tolerable to Micah's sense of honor. Thus he still wanted to refuse the offer. But it was such a fine horse. And how else was Micah to get a horse? He'd considered going out to the open prairie and catching a wild mustang, but that would take considerable time. Credit seemed to be the only practical way. So why not arrange some credit with Maccallum? Glancing at Lucie, Micah could think of many reasons against an arrangement that would tie him yet closer to her, but he could also think of a few good reasons for doing so. One of which was that her feelings would be terribly hurt if he didn't. And the last thing he wanted to do was hurt her.

"I guess since you put it that way..." Micah said thoughtfully. "I suppose we could work out a deal."

"Come on into my study," Maccallum said, "and we will discuss it further."

Micah glanced up at the lowering sun. He didn't want to refuse the man's invitation, but as it was, it would be nearly dark by the time they returned to town.

"I don't mean to be unsociable, sir, but I'd like to get back to town before it gets dark."

Maccallum nodded, understanding. "Of course. Well, the matter is simple enough. Let's say the horse and saddle is worth one hundred fifty dollars. You can pay me in monthly installments of say, five dollars."

Micah did some quick ciphering in his head. "That would take nearly two and a half years, sir!"

"If you should come by a windfall and would like to pay the debt sooner, I would have no problem with that."

"I might not get a salary for months on end," Micah said practically.

"I will take that into account, since it would be through no fault of your own."

"What about interest?" Micah might be giving in to his better judgment, but at least he wanted to be businesslike about it.

"I do not hold with the setting of usury." Maccallum appeared firm about this, so Micah made no argument.

"All right, then," Micah agreed. "If you make up a contract, I will sign it."

"I believe a man's handshake is better than any piece of paper." Maccallum thrust out his hand.

A bit bemused, Micah took it. They shook firmly. He glanced at the buckskin as if to remind himself again what this was all about.

"He is yours now, Mr. Sinclair," Lucie said. Micah had almost forgotten her presence, caught as he had been in the wake of Reid Maccallum's *presence*.

"I thank you kindly," he said rather dumbly. He had made a business deal with Maccallum, yet he still felt beholden to these people. He shook away the vague sense of unrest over this. He needed that horse. Well, he needed a horse. He *wanted* that horse. "We best be on our way." He swung up into the saddle of the buckskin named Jose.

"Good-bye, Mr. Sinclair," Lucie said.

Glancing back at her, something strange happened inside him. His heart felt like a fist had grabbed it and shoved it up into his throat. He couldn't speak. He could only lift a hand and wave in response. It was all he could do to ride away at an easy canter, when what he really wanted to do was ride like the Devil himself was nipping at his heels. He was more scared now than when he used to hear his father's sermons about hell and brimstone. Lucie Maccallum was more frightening than that.

"You are looking quite smug, Lucinda Maria Bonny Maccallum," Reid said, thick arms crossed in front of him as he gazed quizzically down at his daughter.

"We have done a good thing just now, Papa." She gazed off into the distance at the rapidly disappearing riders. "We have helped set a man upon a path of . . . good, or even righteousness."

"Lucie, it is a mistake to try to change men."

"Don't you think men can change? That God can change men?"

"Let's get in out of this heat," Reid said and started walking toward the house. Lucie caught up as he continued. "Men change, but it is folly to try to effect changes, especially for women to try to change men they have an eye for—"

"Papa! Really, I have no—"

"I hope and pray you don't, sweetheart." They reached the kitchen door, and Reid opened it, stepping back to allow Lucie to enter first.

It was hardly any cooler in the kitchen with the stove going in preparation of supper. After a brief greeting to Juana, the pair exited the room and continued back to Reid's study. Inside, they found their favorite seats. Reid, the big leather chair behind the desk, and Lucie, the big upholstered chair opposite. By silent agreement, they both seemed to realize their conversation was not finished.

Staring into her lap and toying with the tassel at the end of her belt, Lucie spoke reluctantly. "Why do you pray not, Papa?"

He knew what she meant without further elaboration. "He's a wild one."

"But weren't you impressed by his returning the buckskin?" Her tone reflected her hopefulness at having her father's approval.

"I'm not saying he's a bad sort, even though we came into his acquaintance through his criminal behavior." He smiled. "Half the men in Texas are horse and cattle thieves. That's how many of the ranchers around here got their starts."

"You, Papa?"

"Harrumph." Reid made the characteristic rumbling sound deep in his throat that usually indicated he was rattled or slightly abashed. "No men are perfect, no matter how much you want them to be, Lucie," he hedged. "I expect from what you've said and from what I've heard that this Sinclair fellow has some good solid values and just fell into thieving as a means of survival."

"I am almost certain of it, Papa!"

"But some men just got wild hearts, even if they aren't basically bad. And I am afraid you'll end up hurt if you try to tame this fellow."

Chewing rather disconsolately on her lower lip, Lucie lifted her eyes to meet her father's gaze. "I'll try not to, Papa."

"I think you already have," he replied gently without rebuke. "That's what the horse was all about, wasn't it? You figured if he had a horse, he'd stick with this rangering job and keep away from crime."

A shaky sigh escaped her lips as emotion sprang into her chest. "You helped him, too, didn't you?"

"A foolish thing for me to do, but ... if your heart's going to be lost to such a wild one, I at least hope to keep him on the straight and narrow."

Reid leaned forward, his eyes turned to pools, and Lucie felt certain he was feeling a bit of emotion himself.

"Lucie, can you try not to fall in love with him?"

"I ... I'll try." Her voice was small and uncertain. What was this young man she hardly knew doing to her? She was not in love with Micah Sinclair, was she? But what did she know of love? Did it have anything at all to do with the way her insides trembled when he was near? Or with how her thoughts were never far from him? Or how he figured into many of her dreams, both waking and sleeping?

No, she was not in love with Micah.

But her father was smiling a rather peculiar smile, wise and sad and full of resolve but with little humor.

When she spoke again, she forced a firmness she didn't quite feel into her tone. "Don't worry, Papa."

But his smile looked worried.

PART TWO

—✦—

Late Summer 1842

Twelve

MICAH'S FIRST ASSIGNMENT as a ranger came within days of receiving the buckskin. The company, usually consisting of around two dozen men when Captain Hays could recruit that many, was sent to patrol along the Nueces, where increased Comanche activity had been reported. After a week with no enemy sightings, half the company returned to town while the remaining half was to make one more sweep of the area and then also return to San Antonio.

Micah was with this half, and he wasn't the only one getting itchy for some action. But it looked like any Comanches previously sighted had cleared out long ago. There weren't any fresh signs. Tired, mostly from boredom, the men made camp late one afternoon, an hour earlier than usual. A hunting expedition brought back two plump turkeys to feast upon for supper.

While a couple of men cooked up the meat, Micah set about cleaning his rifle, wondering if he was ever going to get the chance to use it. The last thing he expected as he began taking apart the weapon was to look up and see a woman standing like an apparition in the late afternoon light. He blinked once, but when she was still standing there, he laid aside his gun and jumped up.

"Hello, ma'am," he said softly. He noted now that she was ragged and battered and looked as skittish as a colt eyeing a rattler.

"It . . . can't be . . ." she rasped.

Seeing that she was about to collapse, Micah rushed forward, catching her as she crumbled. "Tom! Come quick!" Micah yelled to his friend, who happened to be nearby.

Tom came running as Micah was laying the woman down on the grass. Several others joined him.

"What you got there, Micah?" Tom asked.

"She just appeared out of the brush . . . just like that."

"She looks half dead," Bill McBroome said.

"Jed, get some water," Micah ordered. Then he said to the woman, "Ma'am, what's happened to you?"

"Indians!" she said. "They have my baby—" Her voice rose shrilly, then disintegrated into a wracking cough.

Just then Jed returned with a canteen, and Micah set it to her swollen and parched lips. As the water touched them, her tongue flicked out, catching some of the drips. Micah let a bit more drip from the canteen, and she lapped this up eagerly.

"Easy now," Micah said.

The water seemed to revive her a bit, at least giving her strength to speak again, though still with great difficulty. "I thought if I could escape, I could get help. Please . . . save my baby!"

She poured out her story in fits and starts, often incoherently. Micah tried to get her to stop and rest, but she seemed to have a need to tell it. Her name was Martha Hornsby. Apparently she, her husband, her ten-year-old son, and her infant son were traveling by wagon to their new homestead south of Austin when they were attacked. The husband and ten-year-old were killed, and she and the baby were taken captive. That had been, by her best guess, some four days ago, though she had been unconscious some of that time, so her estimation of time passage was not completely reliable.

She was in bad shape. Dehydration and malnutrition were the least of her problems. The worst was a wound in her head and one in her leg from which she had lost much blood.

As one of the men who had some skill with doctoring tried to clean her up and tend her wounds, Micah tried to get details from her that would aid them in tracking the Indians. Yet it seemed it might be a hopeless pursuit. The woman had managed to escape from her captors two days ago, giving the Indians a good head start.

"Find my baby!" Martha Hornsby gasped again, nearly spent now. "They had him wrapped in hides and tied to a gray mule. That's . . . what you . . . should look for. . . ."

"We'll find him, Mrs. Hornsby," Micah said with confidence.

Only a quick glance at Tom indicated he wasn't as confident as his words sounded.

Leaving four men behind to stay with the woman and guard the camp, the rest, eight in all, departed without waiting for supper. They didn't want to waste the daylight left to them. Jed was told to stay behind, and Micah was certain he also would be one of the unlucky ones to be stuck in camp. But the others felt that since he had found the woman, so to speak, he should have the privilege of joining the search for the child. He was thrilled and excited as he hurriedly put his rifle back together, loaded it and his brace of pistols, and mounted the buckskin.

It wasn't until the next afternoon that they located fresh tracks. Apparently the Indians had spent some time trying to find their missing captive. They also did not appear to be in a great hurry, nor were they exercising much caution, which no doubt explained how the woman had escaped.. Perhaps they felt enough time had passed that they were safe from pursuit. Or they might simply feel confident in their numbers, which Big Foot estimated at about twenty. Nevertheless, Micah was frustrated when the rangers had to halt for the night so as not to destroy the signs in the darkness.

Two hours after sunrise the next morning, the rangers located the Comanche camp on the edge of a dense cedar break. The Indians were only beginning to break camp. Indeed, they seemed as relaxed and unconcerned as if they were on a Sunday picnic. Only when they heard the approach of the rangers did they spring into action, grabbing weapons and horses, leaving all else behind, and dashing for the cedar. The Comanches weren't about to make a stand against the obviously better armed and better mounted rangers.

Micah dug his heels into the buckskin's flanks. They would lose their prey if they reached the trees. Before realizing it, he was several lengths ahead of his comrades. In another minute, he was in the midst of the Comanche camp where the braves were still running helter-skelter in a frenzied escape attempt. Several had already reached the trees. They were on foot, since horses would be of little use in the dense wood. One Indian paused and fired at Micah. The ball from the Indian's ancient musket tore Micah's hat from his head. Micah jumped from his mount and fired back but only grazed a tree as the Indian took off running.

Micah fired again at the retreating Comanche with his second pistol, bringing him down. He quickly reloaded and was about to continue pursuit when someone yelled his name.

"Micah!"

He spun around in time to see a warrior bearing down on him with a drawn knife. Micah pulled the trigger, but his pistol jammed. The Comanche leaped for a final attack, but a shot from behind stopped him. Micah saw it was Bill McBroome who had come to his aid. He didn't have time for more than a nod of thanks because the Comanche Bill shot was only wounded and was now dashing for cover. Micah also raced toward the trees.

But he was too late. The Comanches were quickly disappearing into the cover of the break. It would be useless to attempt to engage them in the thick woods, but it was a hard reality to accept. Only one dead Indian for the rangers' efforts. And no baby. Discouraged, Micah joined the others in search for booty, mostly horses that the retreating Indians had not had a chance to take. Four horses and two mules.

"A gray mule!" Micah yelled.

He found his reward carefully wrapped in several layers of hides. The squirming, wailing baby was definitely white and seemed no worse for his ordeal.

A few minutes later Big Foot Wallace came up to Micah with another unexpected reward. "Reckon you got the only kill of the day, so you earned this." He held out a bloody swath of black hair.

It wasn't the first scalp Micah had ever seen and would surely not be his last, but he'd never get used to them, to the blood, the gore, and the gruesome kind of victory they represented. He only took the thing and tied it to his saddle because he thought it might give Mrs. Hornsby some comfort knowing at least a small price had been exacted for her loss.

But the screaming child made him quickly forget all this. Tom was holding the baby, but completely bewildered, he handed it off to Bill, who grimaced as if he'd just been handed a rattler. He held the child out at arm's length, looking desperately around for rescue.

Micah took the baby almost instinctively, though it had been years since he'd been around children. "He's wet," Micah announced. "Anyone got a spare shirt in their saddlebag? I don't have a spare, or I'd use it."

Tom found a shirt and gave it to Micah. "What'd you need that for?"

"You'll see. In the meantime, someone get a fire going and boil up some water with a couple pieces of jerky in it." Almost in spite of himself, Micah began warming to the task. It brought back many memories. Most were unwelcome, but not everything about his growing up had been unpleasant. Like any normal boy, he hadn't liked helping his mother care for his siblings, yet there had been something nice about the companionship of his mother and sisters. These tasks had formed a bond among them. A bond that had excluded his father.

Micah stripped off the baby's diaper, a mere rag that looked as if it hadn't been changed for days. The smell caused tears to sting his eyes. The other men stepped back with various noises of disgust. Micah cleaned the boy, who appeared to be about eight months old, with the damp ends of the old diaper, which he then laid aside.

As he positioned Tom's shirt under the squirming child who was fully exercising his healthy lungs, Tom leaned in closer to see what was to become of his shirt. At just that moment, the baby decided to release more than tears. A stream of urine struck poor Tom right between the eyes.

"What the—" he sputtered, then jumped away, looking like he'd have rather been shot.

The other men howled.

Bill was nearly doubled over with laughter. "That kid's got a better aim than Micah!"

Then, as if Tom's humiliation wasn't complete, he began to perceive exactly to what use his shirt was being put when Micah wrapped the main part of the shirt around the baby's bottom, circling the sleeves around his middle to fasten it all together.

"That's my best shirt!" Tom protested.

"It'll wash up fine," Micah assured him.

"I ain't wearin' no shirt that's been fouled by a kid's innards!"

"You'll smell better'n ya do now," taunted Bill.

Tom was sputtering, trying to think of a retort, when Micah picked up the old diaper and thrust it out. "Here, Bill, go wash this out in the stream."

Bill jumped back, hands raised, obviously appalled. "I ain't touching that!"

Micah marveled that men who thought nothing of lifting a human scalp were so repulsed at a little child's mess.

"Do I gotta do everything?" he railed. "This baby has to eat. Now one of you sorry varmints take care of this rag. We'll need a spare, unless someone has another shirt . . ."

With a curse, Bill picked up the offensive item and marched off to the stream. Micah lifted the child against his shoulder, and at last the baby's wails began to subside a little. He walked around the camp patting the boy's back and cooing softly. Soon the broth was ready. After it had cooled some, he took off his bandanna, loosely knotting one end, and dipped it into the broth. He brought the sodden knot to the infant's lips and the baby sucked hungrily at it.

"Well, I'll be!" said Big Foot. "Looks like our horse-thieving ranger is also a baby's nurse. Wonders will never cease!"

"Where'd you learn all this stuff?" one of the other men asked.

"I was the oldest of four," Micah replied casually. "I've changed my share of diapers and such."

"Well, I was from a big family, too," said one of the men, "and I never learned all that. My pa made sure women's work was done by the women."

My pa didn't give a hang, Micah thought but said nothing out loud because he didn't care to open his personal life to everyone. He did allow himself a private grin when he remembered those days his father had suffered so, right after his mother had died. Benjamin had been in way over his head trying to care for the newborn, in addition to the other children. Micah had taken special pleasure in making the task as hard on his father as he could, never volunteering information and helping only when it seemed that to do otherwise might be harmful to the children.

"Well, Micah," said Big Foot, "I'd start to wonder about you if'n you wasn't so good with a gun."

Micah responded with a disgruntled snort, then gave the baby another taste of broth.

———

When they returned to the camp where they had left the child's mother, they learned that Mrs. Hornsby had died hours earlier.

"Well, boy," Micah said gently to his little charge, "I'm sorry for you. You poor kid." He ran a finger over the child's downy soft yellow curls. "You don't even have a name," he murmured. "Ain't right that you have no family and no name either." He smiled into the limpid brown eyes. "When my brother was born, I wanted to name him for my uncle, but my pa would have none of that. I think I'll call you Haden . . . just so I don't have to keep calling you kid."

He held the child a little closer, rocking him gently. He'd had sole responsibility for the baby on the ride back, and now it looked as if he'd have to continue to do so until they got to San Antonio. He'd gotten a couple of the others, Tom included, to help some, but it seemed the baby was most content when Micah had him. Sometimes as he rocked the baby, humming little snippets of tunes he remembered from his childhood, he'd find his thoughts wandering to Lucie Maccallum. That amazed him more than anything. It gave him a kind of warmth all over, a sensation he hadn't felt in many years. But he knew it was a dangerous sensation to feel, much less enjoy.

———

They arrived in San Antonio four days later on a Sunday afternoon. As the rangers rode past the new Protestant church, Micah decided the service must have just recently concluded because the members were still milling around outside visiting. He saw the big redheaded figure of Reid Maccallum, then quickly jerked his head away before his eyes made contact with Lucie, who he knew would be somewhere near her father. He wanted to see her, to talk to her again. But he knew it wouldn't be a good idea.

He and Tom took the baby to the constable's office so they could discuss what was to be done about the boy. Once apprised of the situation, the constable sent his deputy over to the church to see if any of the women could help out. In the meantime one of the other men found some milk to feed the child. Micah warmed the milk and fed the boy while the child's future was being decided.

"I'm pretty sure Martha and Ned Hornsby had family up around Austin," the constable said.

"Then they'll take him," Micah said hopefully. He himself was growing much too attached to this kid. The sooner he was rid of him, the sooner he could get back to an existence he understood.

"It'll take time to reach them, of course."

"Well, surely one of the women here will take him until then."

"No doubt."

About fifteen minutes later, a woman did come to the constable's office. Lucie Maccallum. Micah was alone with the baby. Tom and the constable had gone to see how the deputy was doing finding a temporary home for the child.

"I heard about what happened," she said softly, lowering her voice even more when she saw the baby was asleep.

"Poor fella," Micah said. "It's a rotten thing to happen to an innocent kid."

"Yes. To lose his mother like that ... it makes me sick." She gingerly lifted the corner of the blanket, Micah's trail blanket he'd torn in half to use for the child. "But he seems awfully content now."

She lifted her eyes from the baby, focusing fully on Micah. He felt like squirming under her gaze but willed himself to keep still. So as not to disturb the boy, he told himself. He didn't know why his heart seemed to stop moving as well.

"Th-the constable says he's got other family up north, so that's good." Micah's voice squeaked nervously over the words.

"Mrs. Wendell at church said she'd take the boy until his family can be found."

"Well, where is she?"

"Are you going to be able to let him go?" She smiled, her eyes twinkling, but not in a taunting way. "Tom explained how you've cared for the baby since he was found. He said you had a special knack—"

"That fool Tom!" Micah exclaimed, his raised voice causing little Haden to move and whimper in his arms.

"What's wrong with that?"

"I just did what had to be done."

"Like when you rescued me?" Her smile broadened and now contained a trace of smugness.

"Oh, that's—" But Micah was cut off as the door opened.

Mr. and Mrs. Wendell, accompanied by the constable and his deputy, entered. Micah was never so relieved and so unhappy about seeing anyone. Micah told himself the child needed a woman's care. As for himself, he had Indians to hunt and Mexicans to kill. He had a job to do that held no room in it for babies and such.

Yet when it came time to relinquish the boy, Micah found it difficult to release him. But he wasn't about to let it show. With a grunt and loud sigh of relief, he deposited Haden into the woman's outstretched arms.

"Thank goodness you finally got here," he said. "This kid was about to drive me crazy."

Micah hurried from the office the first chance he could, choosing a moment when Lucie was occupied in conversation with Mrs. Wendell. He raced outside, gasping in air as soon as he'd exited. His throat felt constricted, and his eyes were burning.

He gulped deep breaths. How could he have let that kid get to him so?

Then Lucie was there at his side. She'd gotten to him, too! And it scared him.

But he couldn't resist looking at her. Now that his arms felt so achingly empty from the departure of the child, he thought it would be so easy to fill them with Lucie's soft, inviting form.

"I must see to my father," she said, her words not quite breaking the spell but at least keeping him from doing something very foolish.

"Give him my regards."

"I will." She gave him a parting smile, turned, then paused and turned back. "Mr. Sinclair, I was wondering if you knew about the ball to be held here in town next weekend? You might enjoy it, and if you attended, I would love to save a dance for you."

"Well, I . . ." He stared at her, incredulous. He had never been to a dance in his life, and he certainly had never been promised a dance with a beautiful, genteel lady such as she. It smacked of civilization, and coming as it did on the heels of the unsettling experience with the baby, it frightened the life out of him. But in an odd way, it enticed him, too. He knew he should tell her "no thanks."

Babies and dances and genteel ladies were not for men like him.

"I'll see if I can make it," he heard himself say.

Thirteen

MICAH DECIDED NOT TO go to the dance. He didn't know why. It just seemed like a good idea to avoid such vestiges of civilization. He had gone out on another patrol with several rangers, and he had hoped that would have kept him away, but as ill-luck would have it, they returned to town Saturday morning.

"Plenty of time to get yourself spruced up for that dance," Tom suggested as they tended their horses.

"And how am I supposed to do that, Tom?" Micah groused. He was tired and ill tempered. The patrol had not gone well. He had been sent off to investigate some tracks leading to a ravine and had gotten turned around and lost his way back to the main force. When he finally did catch up to the company, the men had ridiculed him unmercifully, all in good nature, of course, for days after.

"A bath would be in order first," Tom replied, wrinkling his nose.

"You smell like a coyote yourself, Tom, so don't go making fun of me!"

But Micah did smell, and his beard was stubbly and itchy, and his hair was plastered down against his scalp with sweat and grime. However, these drawbacks could be easily repaired. What he could do nothing about was his clothing. He had no change of clothes, and there was no way he'd take more charity. Even if he was of a mind to go to the dance, he could not do so in dusty, worn dungarees and a matching shirt. The worst of it was, if he attempted to launder these items one more time, they would probably fall apart.

"Anyway, how'd you know about that dance?" Micah asked.

"Jed mentioned it."

Micah glared at Jed, whose lips were curved into a smirk. "I ain't

113

never seen no one with a bigger mouth!" Micah rebuked his friend.

"He also told me as how that pretty little Maccallum gal wanted to dance with you," Tom added.

"So what?"

"You're at an age where you ought to be thinking of settling down." This seemed a peculiar statement coming from the grizzled bachelor.

"What are you? My mother?" Micah sneered.

Tom grunted a couple of unkind remarks, then returned his attention to his horse, loosening the bindings and removing the saddle.

They were in the field near the edge of town where the rangers had staked out their camp while off duty. One of the men had built a fire and was cooking a late breakfast. Others were grooming their mounts after the stint on the trail and others were heading to the river for baths in what little water there was so late in summer.

"If I had a gal like that who wanted me," Jed declared, "I sure wouldn't refuse."

"Then take her," Micah muttered.

Jed only snickered and snorted in response. "But, Micah, you got things turned around, don't ya? First you got the baby, then you got the gal, and you ain't even got married yet." He laughed even harder at his humor.

Cursing at his friend, Micah turned to tending his buckskin. Even if he had botched this most recent mission, Jose had performed admirably. As Micah unhitched the saddle, his thoughts turned to the woman who had given him the horse, though he truly wanted *not* to think of her. He wondered what it would be like to dance with her, to take her dainty little hand in his, to see her smile and glow with the exertion of the rousing music. He'd heard of a dance called a waltz where couples actually held each other. It wouldn't be as close as he'd held her when she had fainted, but close enough, he supposed.

What was he thinking? He couldn't even dance, for heaven's sake! He would trip over his own feet and hers as well. Was civilized dancing the same as he'd done in cantinas and bawdy houses? He'd learned a few things about dancing from those gals. But it couldn't be the same, could it?

"Hey, Tom," Micah said, "you think they dance the same at a respectable ball as they do in a saloon?"

"Ain't as much holding on to the gals as you might do in a saloon," Tom answered thoughtfully.

"So you've been to a ball like the one tonight?"

"Once or twice," Tom replied rather shortly, then turned his back to Micah.

Micah had the feeling Tom was holding back. Not that he was the most ebullient of men, but it seemed as if he was leaving something very important unsaid. Micah also sensed from Tom's suddenly solemn demeanor that it was best not to probe further.

Jed, not as sensitive to subtle changes in temperament, started laughing once again. "You, Tom?" He snorted. "Show us, Tom! Show us how they dance respectable like."

"Micah's right!" Tom growled, "you got a mouth bigger than the Palo Duro Canyon. Now shut it up!"

Still laughing, Jed urged, "Come on, Tom, you're supposed to be our teacher. Teach Micah to dance!"

In a mere blink of Jed's eyes, Tom snatched his Bowie knife from its scabbard and held it threateningly before Jed's face, which had paled a shade or two in response to the sudden action.

"Shut up, or I'll ram this down your throat!" Tom growled.

Jed backed up a step. It was clear the usually mild-mannered ranger had a dangerous side that Jed had seriously stirred.

"All right, all right," Jed muttered, "I was just funning. Can't no one have no fun!" He stalked away with his head jutted forward, still muttering as he went.

Tom sheathed his knife, tied his horse, then said, "I'm going to the river."

Securing Jose, Micah followed Tom. He still saw no way he could attend the dance, but he needed a bath nonetheless. On the way they met a couple dripping rangers.

"Reckon you got the water all muddy for the rest of us," Tom grumbled.

"What's got into you?" asked one of the men.

"None of your business!"

The rangers just rolled their eyes and continued on. Micah caught up to Tom. He knew it was risky, but he asked, "What'd Jed do to set you off, Tom?"

"Nothing."

They reached the water's edge and stripped down to their long johns. There were already two or three men splashing around in the water. Micah and Tom joined them. The water was muddy but cool in the summer heat. One of the other swimmers offered the use of a hunk of lye soap. Micah lathered up his hair, and as he ducked under the water to rinse he thought he would smell like lye, but at least he'd be clean. But why did it matter? He wasn't going anywhere.

A few minutes later he sloshed out of the water and onto the shore to dry in the sun before donning his clothes. Tom came up the bank a couple minutes later.

"Can't go to no dance in these," Micah said, picking up his shirt with two fingers and giving it a shake, sending a cloud of dust all around.

"Yeah, they do look pretty sorry," Tom offered.

"Maybe they can stand one more wash."

"Won't help." Tom gave his shaggy wet hair a shake, sending a spray of water to join the dust. "I'm sorry 'bout what I said to Jed," he added.

"Don't tell me. Tell him."

"I'm also sorry for needling you about going to that dance." Tom sat down on a rock, stretching his legs out before him. "I nearly forgot something that happened to me a long time ago. When it come to my mind, Jed's words were just like rubbing a raw nerve."

"What happened?"

"I been to only one dance, so I ain't that much of an expert. It was just before I come to Texas." He scraped a hand over his chin. "Actually, it was kind of your fault I went. I was pretty content hunting and trapping and living on my own, but when I seen your family and especially you and your little sister when I guided y'all to Natches . . . well, it just put a hankering in me to have a family of my own. I was only thirty years old, so I figured I wasn't over the hill yet."

Micah gaped openmouthed at his friend. "You was only thirty years old! I remember thinking you was an old man."

Tom snorted a laugh. "Thirty looks a lot older when you are twelve than when you are twenty-one, I suppose. Anyway, I figured to find myself a wife. I didn't fancy a squaw or a hurdy-gurdy woman, so when I heard about a respectable dance in town, I gussied myself up and went down from the hills to attend. There was a gal there who gave me a sweet smile, and I thought for sure she might take a shine to me." Pausing, his eyes glassed over momentarily, as if it were no longer Micah's grubby face before him but rather that of a pretty freckle-faced, blue-eyed dream. "I asked her to dance, and we did okay while the music was slow and easy. I didn't know the steps but could keep up, just tramping on her toes once or twice. Then the band struck up a fast reel. I got overconfident, forgetting I was just a clumsy mountain man. Somehow my feet got tangled up, and I went flying to the ground. Out of pure reflex I grabbed on to her, and we both went stumbling and tripping. I tore her dress in a most immodest way. She screamed and cried and started hitting me. Then her pa got in the act and began beating me up. I barely got out of there with my life. Swore I'd never go to another dance again."

The two men fell silent. The hot sun felt good baking on Micah's face and wet body. His underwear was drying out quickly. His hair was also dry, and to keep the glare of the sun from his eyes, he grabbed his hat from his pile of clothes and pressed it on his head. In the moody quiet that hovered over him and Tom, Micah considered the older man's sad story. His friend's experience seemed as good a reason as any to keep away from places where one did not belong, and Micah instinctively knew he would be as out of place at the dance tonight as Tom had been at his. Micah had lived wild for too many years to consider mixing with decent folks now.

"I'm glad you told me that story," he said at length. "You probably kept me from making a first-class fool of myself."

"That's not why I told you about my experience," Tom said. "I just thought you ought to know why I was acting the way I was. Just 'cause I made an ignoramus of myself don't mean you'd do the same."

"I don't get it. You still saying I should go to that dance?"

"I ain't saying nothing, you dunderhead!" Tom snapped. "Make up your own mind."

"Well, maybe I would go if I had decent clothes."

Tom jumped up and strode to the pile of clothes. He picked up an item between two fingers as if it were diseased. "It'll take another wash. And you won't look half bad once it's clean."

"I don't want no wife," Micah suddenly declared.

Tom stared at him, then laughed. "First things first, boy." He dropped the garment back into the dusty heap. "Who knows? Maybe she don't want no husband."

"Isn't that what all respectable women want?"

Tom shrugged. "Going to a dance isn't a marriage proposal. But I'm thinking a man ought to go to at least one dance in his life. I figure it has more in the way of making a man out of you than killing Comanches."

"Maybe. If it turns out the way your dance did." Micah smiled as he thought again of Tom's story. When Tom allowed himself a smile, Micah knew the tension was dispersed. "Give me a Comanche attack any day!"

"Go wash these duds of yours." Tom picked up the pile and tossed them in Micah's face.

Laughing, Micah gathered the clothing in his arms, rose, and marched resignedly to the river. He didn't know what he was doing or why. Even as he knelt by the water and began scrubbing his shirt, he still hadn't made up his mind about the dance.

Fourteen

BILL MCBROOME HAD A bottle of toilet water stashed among his belongings. In a moment of extreme stupidity, Micah let the man convince him to splash some on himself. Now as he strode toward the hall where the dance was to be held, Micah was certain he smelled like a bordello.

Music emanated through the open doors and windows of the place. Inside, it looked very festive, with garlands hanging from the ceilings and candles and lanterns lit all around the room. The hall was crowded with at least a hundred people. It was hard not to be self-conscious of his shabby appearance, since almost everyone was dressed in their Sunday best. There were a few other rangers present, and some of them looked no better than Micah. A couple of them were sharing a suit jacket between them, taking it in turns to dance when they had the jacket.

At least Micah had shaved, and one of the Mexican rangers who had been a barber before joining up had trimmed his shaggy hair. He was also wearing his buckskin coat, the one made for him by his stepmother shortly before he left home. It was probably the only reminder he had kept of his home, and he told himself he only kept it because good coats were hard to come by. It was stifling hot in the coat, but it was the nicest thing he owned, and it somewhat camouflaged his other worn garments.

He headed toward the punch table, where a couple of rangers were standing. He tried not to scan the crowd for the face of Lucie Maccallum. In fact, he was trying so hard to keep his eyes fixed on the punch bowl ahead as he skirted the edge of the dance floor that he failed to maneuver around a dancing couple. It was a reel, and they were moving fast. The woman slammed forcefully into him.

"Ugh!" he grunted.

"Oh, I am so sorry," she said.

"Watch where you are going, fellow!" her partner said.

"I'm sorry. It was my fault," Micah said when he gathered his wits about him.

Only then did he see he had bumped into Lucie. Visions of Tom's debacle jumped into his head.

"Why, Mr. Sinclair, you did come!" She seemed not in the least disturbed by his clumsiness.

"Yeah, I did," he said obviously enough.

"Who might this be?" asked the gentleman a bit unsociably.

"This is Micah Sinclair. He's a ranger." Then to Micah, "This is Grant Carlton, a local rancher."

The two men nodded, and Micah sensed immediate hostility from Carlton. They did not shake hands.

"Come, Lucie, let's finish the reel." Carlton put an arm around Lucie and nudged her back to the disrupted reel.

Micah thought Carlton acted rather possessive toward Lucie. Fleetingly he thought about leaving right then. But with a dogged determination he could not explain, he instead headed to the punch table. So Lucie had a beau. Well, that pretty much let him off the hook. Why didn't he feel relieved, then?

He ladled himself a glass of punch and frowned when he realized the sweet concoction had not even a drop of wine in it. He could use something a little stronger right now. But he gulped the punch, realizing as the liquid slid down his throat that his mouth was as dry as sand—from nerves, not exertion. He casually watched the dancers and, he thought just as casually, let his gaze rest upon Lucie. She was wearing a frock of a deep red wine color, and now that he had let himself observe her, she was all that he could see except for her partner, whom he was forced to take note of as well.

He was a handsome man, Micah supposed, in his fancy suit and black cutaway coat with its velvet collar and his striped silk vest. He complemented the lovely Miss Maccallum quite nicely. And they danced well together, too. Lucie was smiling and laughing while Carlton's hand took every opportunity it could to rest upon her trim waist. Micah's throat got even dryer as he watched. He gulped another swallow of punch.

Bill McBroome sidled up to him. "Ya want a little fortification in that punch?"

"I'd like more than a little," Micah said wistfully.

McBroome took a flask from his pocket and poured a measure into Micah's glass. Micah never expected his wish to be fulfilled, but he grinned his appreciation. Several glasses of Bill's punch later, Micah was emboldened to stride onto the dance floor, right up to Lucie and her partner.

"Ahem!" he said politely, tapping a finger on the fine fabric stretched over Carlton's shoulders, for indeed it was Carlton dancing again with Lucie.

Carlton ignored him, but much to Micah's pleasure, Lucie didn't.

"Mr. Sinclair, are you ready for that dance I promised you?"

"I reckon so."

Carlton glared at him as Lucie stepped between the two men. "You have been monopolizing me, Grant."

So *Grant*, was it?

"People will talk, you know," she added.

"I wouldn't mind that, Lucie, *my dear*."

The way Carlton emphasized "my dear" set Micah's teeth on edge.

Lucie gave Grant a rather coquettish smile, then grabbed Micah's hand. "Come, they are starting up a new reel."

As they moved deeper onto the dance floor, Micah drawled quietly, "I ain't the best dancer."

"Just follow my lead and watch the other men. You'll catch on."

He did as she instructed and managed quite well. All the while, though, he kept track of his own feet. No way would he trip and tear her pretty dress.

Lucie was glad to be rid of Grant Carlton, but she knew that accounted for only part of her joy at the moment. Micah had decided to come to the ball! And he had mustered the courage to ask her to dance. She well appreciated it must indeed have taken some courage to break in on another man and risk refusal. But he had done it, and now they were hand-in-hand, stepping to a lively

Virginia reel. He was a bit awkward on his feet and had stepped on her slipper more than once, but she supposed he had not been to many balls such as this. At any rate he was picking up the rhythm and the steps well. He seemed to be enjoying himself if the smile on his face was any indication.

Too soon the music stopped, but the leader of the musicians had an announcement to make. "We're gonna try something new. A waltz. I heard several of you know the steps. Everyone else can watch and learn."

"Shall we give it a try, Micah?"

"Sure."

Glancing around, she saw Grant heading toward them. Quickly she placed a hand on Micah's shoulder, drawing him close. Then the music began, and it was too late for Grant.

"Put your hand here." She took his hand and placed it on her waist.

"Whoa!" Micah breathed. "They allow this sort of thing?"

Lucie giggled. "It is currently very popular. Now listen to the beat of the music. One, two, three . . . one, two, three." She moved her free hand in an approximation of the rhythm. "Let me have your other hand."

Free hands clasped, she nudged him into step with the music. His boot nicked her slipper once or twice, but she bit back a cry of pain even though it did hurt some. It was easy to overlook pain when she concentrated on his nearness. His hand on her waist was warm and oddly secure. The touch of his other hand in hers sent a tingle through her entire body.

"D-do you like it?" she asked, her voice cracking a little as she looked up at him. They were barely an arm's length apart.

"Yes," he replied.

Lucie sensed he wasn't talking only about the dance. The way he was looking at her made her knees rather weak. He was so handsome, but not in the polished, slick way of Grant Carlton. She could tell he had spruced himself up for the dance, but there was still something very rough-cut about him. And thinking in those terms, she thought of an uncut gem. That's what Micah Sinclair was. Wild, her father had said, but even he had to admit there was something solid beneath the untamed exterior. Remembering his tenderness with that orphaned baby only reinforced her conclusion. And that was the difference between Micah and Grant. Grant was a diamond, cut in all its glory. But what shined on the surface was all there was to him. She thought of the quote she'd read in *The Merchant of Venice*: "All that glitters is not gold." How true in this case. Lucie was certain the real gold dwelt beneath worn cotton and denim, not serge wool and silk.

"I'm glad you came to the dance," she murmured.

"So am I." There was a very slight tremor to his voice. But his gaze was so steady, almost boring into her like a shaft of blue light. His hand tightened on her waist, and she thought he had eased her ever so slightly closer to him.

Neither of them noticed when the music had stopped. Lucie was certain it was several heartbeats before that fact penetrated. He dropped his hand first and stepped back, obviously flustered.

"That was nice," she said dreamily.

"I gotta go now."

"What?"

He turned and all but fled the dance floor. In another moment he had disappeared among the crowd. She strained to see over the heads of those pressing in about her and thought she caught a glimpse of him exiting the building. She would have gone after him, but Grant came up to her.

"That was rude of him to leave you standing here like that," he sneered.

"He . . . he . . ." She didn't know what to say or what to make of Micah's surprising behavior.

"What more can you expect from trash like that," Grant droned on. "As I waited for the dance to finish, I was told by one of the gentlemen that he was a horse thief who barely escaped hanging by joining up with the rangers. Had I known that, I would never have let you in his company."

"I . . . I think I need to freshen up." She was feeling a trifle flushed and warm, but it wasn't really the seclusion of the ladies' parlor that she wanted.

Without waiting for a response, she headed across the room in the direction of the parlor, passing her father on the way. She smiled at him—at least she offered a thin disguise of a smile—then continued on her way. She stepped into the corridor that ran at the rear of the ballroom and, seeing a woman exit a door, noted the location of the parlor. But Lucie went down the corridor, past the parlor door to the end, where she found another door she knew led to the outside. This she opened and plunged into the cool night air.

Indeed it was a warm evening, but the air was fresh and pleasant after the crowded, stuffy atmosphere indoors. It seemed Micah felt the same way. He was leaning against the sidewalk rail in front of the building next door. His hands gripped the rough wood of the rail, and he was gulping in air as if he had just risen from being buried alive.

Lucie had never chased after a man in her life. Her father's words came back to her with alarming clarity. "Lucie, can you try not to fall in love with him?" Perhaps it was too late.

"Micah," she said, coming up behind him.

He jerked around, truly startled. "What're you doing out here?" he asked sharply.

"I . . . I was afraid you might be ill. You left so suddenly."

"Go on back inside. It's not right for you to be here all alone."

"I don't like people telling me what to do."

He rolled his eyes with just a hint of humor. "I surely feel sorry for your pa, then."

"Yes, I am a sore trial to him." Her lips twitched with uncertainty at how her attempt at humor might be received.

"You ain't worried about your reputation at all?"

"I suppose I am a little." She moved up beside him and leaned her back against the rail so as to face him. He turned back to the way he had been standing before, hands on the rail, looking into the now quiet street instead of her probing eyes. "I was having a nice time dancing with you and didn't want you to leave," she added.

"Well, it ain't right, that's all!"

She gazed at him. He could have meant so many things with that statement, and perhaps he meant them all.

"Why did you leave?"

"If I'd have stayed..." He loosened his grip on the rail long enough to run a hand through his thick pale hair. It hung in waves to the top of his collar and curled slightly around his ears. He wasn't wearing his hat. Maybe he had planned to return to the dance after all.

"I was afraid I might have ... kissed you!" He swung around now, facing her full on. "Right there in front of everyone."

"Oh ..." She hadn't expected that response, but now that he'd said it, she understood that the feelings she had been experiencing on the dance floor had been mutual. It pleased her, though she knew it ought to frighten her as well.

"I still want to."

His eyes were riveted upon her and her heart nearly stopped with anticipation. But he made no move toward her.

"Oh my." She could think of absolutely nothing else to say.

"Go back inside, Lucie, before—"

"Before what?"

His eyes, now pools of confusion and something else she could not quite define, raked over her in a manner that caused her to wince.

"You don't belong with me, and I don't belong with you. Simple as that," he said.

"That's the most ridiculous thing I have ever heard!" she replied crisply to hide her quelling insides.

"You are a God-fearing woman, aren't you? Churchgoing and such?"

Perplexed, she answered, "Yes."

"There you go!" There was a triumph in his tone, as if that settled everything. "You ain't supposed to be unequally yoked."

"Are you a heathen?"

"Look at me!" he practically yelled. "What do you think?"

"I do not judge people on surfaces. Neither does God."

"Don't tell me what God does. I know all about it. And believe me, God turned His back on me long ago. I'm a reprobate, a sinner—"

"We are all sinners, Micah."

He cursed under his breath, almost with humor. "Oh yeah. I forgot that. But you know as well as I that churchgoing sinners smell a mite sweeter than horse-thieving, gun-toting, carousing sinners like me."

She laughed in spite of herself. "Where'd you get ideas like that?"

"My pa is a preacher." He ground out the words, leaving no doubt that he believed this was a heinous admission indeed.

"You?"

Now he laughed. Bitterly, this time. "A real shocker, huh?"

It was, but Lucie didn't want to admit it, so she said casually, "And your pa told you these things?"

"More like he bludgeoned them into my head."

A silence fell between them. Again he had left her speechless. Part of her knew that at least some of what he had said was true. She did not wish to be "yoked" to a heathen. But now she was more certain than ever that Micah was far from a heathen. He had grown up in a religious home and no doubt knew the Bible better than she. That didn't necessarily make him a Christian man, of course, but she knew now why she had sensed there was so much more to Micah than the surface presented. He had an intimate knowledge of God, no doubt, and for some reason was deeply bitter—toward God perhaps, but most especially toward his father. She wanted to know why. She wanted to know what lay in the deepest parts of Micah's heart. And because of that, she could not let go. And probably because of that, as well, she did not *want* to let go. There was a diamond beneath that rough, tarnished exterior. She was certain of it now. And she had to see it chipped and polished into being.

"Maybe some of those things are true," she said quietly. "I don't know everything. I only know how I feel, Micah. And I feel something toward you."

"Don't say that!"

"It's too late."

"I'll bring you nothing but grief."

She nodded, feeling the sting of tears rise to her eyes. "I know."

"You are a foolish woman."

"And you are a wild man. What a pair we make—" she began glibly.

But he broke in fiercely. "We are not a pair!" Then, as if to belie his words, he grabbed her.

She gasped as his arms violently encircled her, tightly, nearly choking the air from her. Then his lips pressed down upon hers, hard, savagely as his arms drew tighter and tighter about her. She didn't fight him and even tilted her head ever so slightly to better accommodate him. She'd never been kissed before and anticipated the sweet sensation of tender lips touching. But this wasn't like that at all. This was rough, aggressive, punishing. She tensed in his arms, feeling the power of his strength, the awesomeness of her helplessness. She was lost, and the worst of it was that part of her *wanted* to be lost forever in that embrace.

But not like this.

Her resistance increased. She wrenched her head around, knowing all the while that her paltry strength was no match for his had he chosen to press home his assault. But the vicelike grip of his arms loosened. He was breathing hard as he let go, but no harder than she was herself.

He mastered his wits first. "Don't ever get involved with a man who would kiss you like that," he said.

Then he walked away.

"Micah!"

He didn't turn back.

He had hurt her. Not so much physically, though her lips burned and throbbed, but he had hurt her by not giving her credit for having a brain. Didn't he realize she'd see through his puny attempt to frighten her? Oh, she was frightened, to be sure, but not in the way he had intended. His very attempt to do so had only made her see another facet of Micah Sinclair. He was a good man. She knew it.

Fifteen

MICAH AND ABOUT A dozen men of Hays' ranger company were patrolling along Cutter Creek where they'd received word that Joaquin Viegas, with at least two dozen of his banditos, had been spotted.

Since the invasion of Texas by Mexico in March and the subsequent occupation of San Antonio, the rangers were being especially vigilant. The occupation by Santa Anna's army lasted only a few days, but it was nevertheless harrowing for the residents. They did not want a repeat. In the months that followed, rumors flew rampant in the area, the most persistent being that the gangs of banditos threatening Texan borders were actually in the pay of the Mexican government, and their purpose was to disrupt Texan life enough to give Mexico another chance to invade.

The rangers had been tracking Viegas's gang for two days before finally coming upon the outlaws' camp. Unfortunately, the Mexicans saw the rangers approach and opened fire.

The rangers quickly dismounted and returned fire. Micah killed two bandits in the opening volley of shots and only then realized the Mexican shooters in the front line were providing cover while the main force was escaping.

"Hey, they're getting away!" Micah shouted.

By then the others saw the ploy. They also saw there were far more than a mere twenty-four bandits—more like fifty! Hays ordered pursuit but emphasized caution because of the disparity of numbers. More shots were exchanged, then Micah detected the pungent odor of smoke in the air. The Mexicans had fired the grass, and the wind, as well as the smoke, was heading directly for the rangers.

Cursing rose from the ranks of the rangers to join the blinding smoke. Micah pulled a bandanna over his nose, but it didn't help much.

"Sneaky greasers!" he muttered.

The rangers had to pull back.

"Take defensive positions!" ordered Hays. The captain feared the fire was merely a cover for a full-scale attack.

Coughing and grumbling, the men obeyed, gripping their rifles. Eyes burning and watering, throats on fire, they waited. Micah tried to peer through the smoke, but it was too dense to make out anything. He hated just sitting there when Mexicans were so close he could smell them. Well, he could have if the acrid stench of smoke wasn't numbing his nose! He'd only killed two, and he knew he could get more if given half a chance.

But when the smoke finally dissipated, Micah saw he'd lost his opportunity. The banditos were gone.

Determining that the Mexicans couldn't have gone far, Hays decided to track them. Micah welcomed not only the chance for vindication, but also the opportunity to hone his tracking skills. He didn't think about what might happen if the rangers actually did catch up to the banditos. A dozen against fifty could be a bloodbath. But he'd seen these rangers in action now for some time, and he had every confidence in them. He also had no little confidence in his own prowess, despite a few mistakes he'd made in the beginning. Even Tom had told him he was coming along fine.

———

Lucie was happy to be back home in familiar surroundings. The time in San Antonio, especially after the events of the ball, had been trying. To make it worse, her father had grown ill after church the Sunday following the ball, forcing them to remain in town with friends for a few extra days. He was better now, at least not so frightfully sallow and breathless, but the doctor had strongly admonished him to keep indoors and to his bed whenever possible.

Lucie had nursed him faithfully, though he accepted her ministrations grudgingly. Until this morning, that is. Then he had lost his patience completely and told her to quit hovering about him like a fly on raw meat. He ordered her to go out and get some fresh air. So she did, leaving Juana in charge of the recalcitrant patient.

She saddled her piebald mare and rode away. The men had long since ceased arguing with her about riding alone, and she was glad of that because she especially needed to be alone now. She had hardly had a moment since the ball to mull over all that had occurred.

But first, she just wanted to appreciate the wide outdoors. Since her return from Mexico, she had been out riding only a few times, and then not far from the ranch for fear of her father needing her. She didn't know what was different about today, but she wanted, perhaps even needed, to feel the open, empty vastness of the prairie around her. She sucked in a breath of the air, pungent with the scents of grass and earth and cow dung. Even in the summer heat there was a crispness in the atmosphere carried by the dry prairie wind.

She loved this land, hot and alive, dangerous and inviting. Not unlike the man who had been haunting her dreams and thoughts. The man whose kiss still burned upon her lips. The man who sought to push her away with actions that only made her desire him more. Both he and her father had warned her she would be hurt, but wasn't that always a risk where the heart was involved? She knew so little of love, perhaps she should listen to them. To what purpose, then? To be safe and marry the likes of Grant Carlton?

If the Texas settlers had thought that way, they would have been denied the exquisite joy and yes, also the pain, of this wonderful magical land.

She rode south for about two hours and knew she was on the farthest reaches of her father's ranch. She really should begin to think about turning back toward home. The sun had passed its zenith, the time further evidenced by the growling of Lucie's stomach. She had brought a bit of food in her saddlebags and was looking about for a pleasant place to stop for a snack when she heard the gunshots.

She paused her mount's easy canter and listened. They could not be more than a mile away. Sound traveled oddly on the prairie, but the shots seemed to be coming from north of her. Was it just vaqueros and ranch hands showing off? Or banditos? Or Comanches? If it was either of the latter two and they were involved in a skirmish of some kind, they might well soon be heading south toward the border. Right past her!

It was definitely unwise to head for home now. Nor could she hope to outrun them. Perhaps her best course would be to find some cover and wait it out. The stream, a branch of Cutter Creek that bordered the ranch, was not far. She had smelled the moist, muddy proximity of water. There would be shelter there.

"Come on, Belle," she said to the mare, speaking mostly for the comfort of hearing something besides her pounding heart.

The shots had ceased by the time she reached the creek. It had probably been nothing after all. But just as she had begun to be successful in convincing herself of this, she saw a plume of smoke rise toward the sky from the direction of the gunshots. Now what? Did this have something to do with the shots?

No matter what it was, whether a mere prairie fire caused by careless travelers or an attack, the creek was still her safest refuge. Easing down the creek bank among a stand of cottonwoods, she forced her racing heart to calm.

"It's nothing," she murmured.

Where the trees stood thickest, she dismounted. She tied Belle to a low branch, took her saddlebag of food, the musket she always brought when riding alone, and found a place to sit where she was as secluded as possible. It was an outcropping of rock set into the bank with a few boulders around it for good measure. Convinced now that she had blown the disturbance out of proportion, she relaxed, opened the bag, and took out a cloth in which some jerky and a biscuit were carefully wrapped.

She had barely finished the meal and settled back for a bit of a nap when the sound of pounding hooves shattered her solace. She froze. They were coming near, almost certainly heading for the creek. Scooting farther back behind the cover of the rocks, she clutched her rifle and held her breath. Quickly she loaded the weapon.

Her heart began thumping wildly when she heard the scramble

of horses descending the creek bank.

"*Alto, amigos!*" came a man's voice. "I think we have lost them." He spoke in Spanish, which Lucie understood as well as English.

"That was close, Joaquin."

Joaquin? Now Lucie's heart skipped a beat. Could it be he? Joaquin Viegas, he called himself. The famous bandito. She had to find out. She had to know. Gripping her rifle, she crept as stealthily as possible from her hiding place to the edge of the farthest boulder. She could see forty or fifty riders, all Mexican, all heavily armed. Her gaze focused on one in particular, mounted on a fine black stallion with one white sock. This man was taller than his companions, swarthy skinned, broad shouldered, lean and strong. He wore a sombrero, but she knew the crop of hair beneath the hat would be brown, not black, and much lighter than her own.

She studied him closely, forgetting all else. He sported a thick mustache now, something that had been absent the last time she had seen him. Other than that, he was not much changed.

"Why did we run, Joaquin?" asked one of the men. "We outnumbered them."

"There is no point in taking unnecessary risks, especially when we have nothing to show for it." Joaquin answered. "Besides, they were rangers, Gustavo."

The tall bandito lifted a canteen from his saddle, took a long swig, then inclined his head, apparently listening. Lucie could not take her eyes from him. She took in his every movement as if she were imbibing a drop of water on a desert and it would be many miles till the next watering hole. She had forgotten the musket in her hand, and when her arm went slack, the weapon clanked against the rock.

"*¿Qué es?*" one of the banditos said.

Before she could do anything about it, her presence was revealed. Only vaguely did she realize that she had probably wanted to be seen.

Joaquin's eyes met hers. Though his gaze flashed, the rest of his features remained passive. "What is this?" he said.

"Señor Viegas," she quietly acknowledged him.

"Come out from behind that rock. Let me see you," he ordered.

Licking her dry lips, she obeyed.

"Drop the rifle," Viegas said.

She did so. Then they stared at each other for such a long time the horses grew restive, snorting, twitching, prancing.

"Joaquin, we must go," urged the bandito named Gustavo.

"I must go," Joaquin said to her in a soft, almost apologetic manner.

"I know," Lucie replied.

"Can we leave her?" Gustavo asked. "She will give us away."

Joaquin's mustache twitched, and though it was hard to discern beneath the thick growth, he might have been smiling.

"Can we leave you, señorita?"

"*Sí*, Joaquin, you can."

"I thought so." To his men Joaquin added, "*Vaquamos los hombres!*"

The banditos needed no more command than this and in a few moments were heading toward the creek. But Viegas paused and looked back.

"Joaquin," Lucie called, "Papa has not been well."

The bandito leader nodded. "I am sorry to hear that."

"He would like to see you."

"Would he?"

"Yes, he would." It was a small lie, Lucie knew, but she could not help herself.

"I must go now," the bandito said, then urged his mount across the creek.

Lucie watched his retreat. He rode with such assurance as he caught up with his men, tall in the saddle, shoulders square, completely in command. He had shown no sense of panic over the fact that the law was breathing down his neck. Nevertheless, the pace of the banditos increased considerably after they ascended the far bank and reached more level ground. They were out of sight in a matter of minutes.

Several minutes later the noise of riders coming from the other direction pulled Lucie from her reverie. That would be the rangers. In a mere moment Lucie decided what she must do. Quickly she scooped up a handful of dirt, which she smeared on her clothes and swiped across her face, and knocked her hat to the ground as well. A kind of calm stealing over her despite her thudding heart, she sat down on the ground, arranging herself in as much disarray as she could.

Her heart had calmed by the time the rangers crested the bank, but it flipped again when she saw that one of the men was Micah. In that moment she feared she could not proceed with her plan. But she had to. She must help the banditos get as much distance between them and the rangers as possible.

"Lucie!" Micah called when he saw her lying in the dirt. He was off his horse the instant it finished scrambling down the bank. "What happened?" The clear distress in his tone made her nearly quell again at her deception.

There were half a dozen rangers with Micah. Tom Fife, Jed, and three others Lucie did not know. She laid the back of her hand against her forehead and shook her head as if faint.

"You okay?" Micah knelt down beside her. "Was it the banditos?" The look in his eyes as he spoke made Lucie shiver. It contained far more than mere distress. For a brief instant, there was pure murder in his eyes.

"No . . . I'm all right. . . ." The lies did not come easily, but she was too motivated to fail now. "I fell and twisted my ankle."

"Did them banditos hurt you?" Tom asked, a look of consternation on his face also but far less intense than Micah's.

"No, it wasn't them," she said firmly. She did not want to make it worse for the outlaws. Suddenly she almost smiled as she thought of the irony of her being in yet another situation in which she must defend an outlaw. "I saw them and was running in the opposite direction so they wouldn't see me when I tripped. They hardly even noticed me as they rode by."

"Which way did they go, miss?" Tom asked.

"I was so dizzy . . ." What an awful lie! She hated sounding like a simpering female. But she went on, stuck now with her resolve. "I . . . I hardly noticed. Maybe that way." She lifted a limp hand and pointed vaguely in the right direction. These were rangers, after all. They would easily pick up the trail, so lying would hardly help.

"How long?"

"I've lost track of time. Seems like forever, but perhaps fifteen or twenty minutes."

"We best get moving," urged one of the other rangers.

"Hold on, Bill," Tom said. "We can't just leave Miss Maccallum." Tom took off his hat and scratched his head, then said, "Micah, you see the lady home. The rest of us will continue the pursuit."

"But Tom—" Micah protested.

"Ain't nothing else for it."

Lucie was more than a little disappointed that Micah appeared less than eager to be with her. Yet she had come between him and his work, his duty, and thus she ought to consider it a good sign that he had such a sense of responsibility toward this new job of his. She hoped that was the cause, at least.

"We'll be going, then," Tom said. "Micah, you may as well head on back to San Antonio when you're finished. I don't reckon we'll keep tracking them hombres if they cross the border."

"Mr. Fife," Lucie said quickly, searching in her mind for something else that might delay the pursuit, "I don't mean to interrupt your work, but if you brought me my horse and helped me to mount, I am certain I could get home on my own."

"Not in a million years!" declared Tom. "Anyway, what you doing out here alone?"

Oh, this was good! It always took time for men to browbeat her for her independence. The banditos would easily get across the border now.

"Well, Mr. Fife," she began thoughtfully *and* slowly, "I just hate to impose. . . ."

"Shouldn't you get going, Tom?" Micah urged.

Lucie restrained a smirk at his untimely intercession.

"Yeah, of course. Miss, if you'll pardon us . . ." Tom tipped his hat then gave his mount a crisp "Geeup!" The others followed.

Well, she had done the best she could. Joaquin Viegas would have to do the rest. She relaxed and blew out a deep sigh.

"Something wrong?" Micah asked, concerned.

"No, it has just been a trying day."

"I'll get you home right away."

"Could you let me have a drink of water first?" Now that she no longer had to worry over the banditos, she was in no particular hurry to go home, especially since she had Micah Sinclair all to herself.

Sixteen

LUCIE WATCHED MICAH as he went to his horse, removed his canteen, and brought it to her.

"Where's your horse?" he asked as he returned. Kneeling beside her, he handed her the canteen.

She jerked her head toward the trees. "In the shade." She uncorked the waterskin and took a long swallow.

"You sure had a close call with those banditos," he said. "We're pretty sure that was Joaquin Viegas himself we were chasing."

"Really! Oh my!" She swayed, raising her hand to her head again. She better not drop her ruse too quickly, or it might arouse suspicions. To her surprise and delight, Micah's arms went quickly around her. He grabbed the canteen from her hands and splashed a dollop in her face. "Bah!" she sputtered. She hadn't expected that.

"I thought you was gonna faint," he said in obvious distress.

"I assure you, I wasn't." She gave her head a shake, sending a spray of water in his direction. Then she smiled. "That was kind of you . . . holding me, protecting me."

He glanced down and seemed to fully realize that she was indeed in his arms. He wrenched them from her so quickly she nearly fell into the dirt. But she caught herself, remaining in a sitting position. He scooted away from her.

"You don't make it easy . . ." he said. "Protecting you, that is. You might have been in serious trouble if them banditos had taken a mind to hurt you."

"I don't think they would have harmed me. They weren't even interested."

"You are mighty thickheaded, ain't you?"

She shrugged, then changed the topic. "Do you think the rangers will catch the bandits?"

139

"I doubt it. They got too much of a head start. But we'll get them eventually." Micah's tone was as hard edged as the rocks surrounding them.

"What will happen to Viegas if he's caught?"

"I wouldn't think even you'd have to ask that."

No, she didn't have to ask, but there was still a naïve part of her that hoped for justice. "I suspect he will be tried and . . . punished."

"Tried?" Micah snorted derisively. "Ain't no way he'd make it back to San Antonio alive. If the rangers don't hang him on the spot, he'll likely get shot while *escaping*." He spoke that final word with relish.

Lucie was certain Micah hoped to be the one to bring down the famous bandito. This was definitely a side of Micah she hadn't glimpsed before, and she didn't much like it. She wondered how deep the hidden diamond inside him was.

"Every man deserves a fair trial," she replied.

"You ever seen four hundred unarmed men gunned down without benefit of a trial, fair or otherwise?"

Beneath his harsh gaze she saw a flicker of pain.

"No, Lucie. You won't find me giving no Mexican a fair trial."

"All Mexicans, Micah?"

He shrugged, obviously uncomfortable with the direction of the discussion. "Soon as you're feeling up to it, we'll be on our way." His initial concern had faded, and now he spoke woodenly, like a man hiding something behind a flimsy facade.

"Micah?" Lucie reached out to touch the hand he had resting in the dirt to support himself as he sat.

He inched a bit farther away from her.

"We haven't talked since the dance."

"Nothing to talk about, is there?"

"Are you afraid of me?" She glanced down at his hand so near hers, though she had restrained from actually touching him after his reaction.

"Tarnation, lady! I'm scared to death of you!" He jumped up and spoke as if ranting, or at the very least, flustered. "You're dangerous, you hear? Very dangerous! Sitting there looking so helpless, yet I think you could take on Santa Anna's entire army if you wanted to with just a flap of those eyelashes of yours or a shake of hair that looks every bit like an earthy mountain full of copper when it catches the light of the sun. I've faced vicious enemies and wild animals, and I've looked death in the face more than once, but none of it compares to the bone-chilling fear you put in me." Micah paused, breathing hard, and she thought perhaps she did note fear in his remarkable blue eyes.

"What is it you fear most?" she asked quietly, in sharp contrast to his own frenzied response.

He snatched off his hat and ran a hand through his red-flecked hair. "I told you at the dance."

"And you tried to make me afraid, but it didn't work." She gazed up at him, and the flutters in her heart grew more pronounced.

"You're a stubborn woman," he said.

She nodded.

"You should be very afraid, Lucie." His tone was steady now, so serious it made her tremble as nothing else had.

"When I see you talk about your enemies," she said, "it does scare me a little. But something in me says there is much more to you than that."

"I keep trying to tell you—"

"Sit down, Micah, and tell me about yourself."

He gaped at her sudden change of tact, and she knew she sounded like she was inviting him to tea. Here they were in the middle of the wild, empty prairie, outlaws in the near vicinity, and she had the audacity to request a social conversation. It was rather outlandish, if not downright ridiculous.

She giggled lightly. "We do manage to meet in the oddest places. But I always say to seize opportunity when it knocks. Who knows when I will see you again? And even if everyone may be right about us being mismatched, couldn't we at least be friends?"

He shook his head, still nonplussed about the oddity of the situation. Then he plopped down beside her, however at a safe distance.

"So what'd you want to know?" He was serious, yet he had

allowed a small hint of amusement to trifle with the cool blue of his eyes.

She scratched her chin thoughtfully. "How did you come to be an outlaw?"

"Now, there's a nice neutral subject to start with," he said dryly. "Anyway, there isn't much to tell about it. After the war I was kind of aimless. I was fourteen. I needed to survive somehow, and I just took the easy way."

"You fought in the war?"

"Yeah."

"What was that like?"

"Next question," he said flatly.

She did not press, for she didn't want to spoil this time. It occurred to her that after all they had been through together in such a short time, this was the first chance they'd had to really talk. She was liking it very much.

"Were you born in Texas?" she asked. This was a nice safe query.

But he scowled in response, the blue of his eyes darkening like a cloud passing over a sparkling stream.

"No," he said evenly.

She could tell it took effort to talk about his past.

"I was born in Boston. Came here when I was twelve."

"Do your parents still live here?"

"I don't want to talk about my parents."

"Is there anything you do want to talk about, Micah?" she asked, unable to completely hide her frustration. Altering her tone a bit, she added, "Maybe you should just tell me what you want me to know."

He was silent for a long time, and she feared the conversation had ended before it had had much of a chance. Finally he spoke.

"My ma died about seven years ago. My pa . . . is still here."

He turned upon her intently, the blue in his eyes still dark, but not shadowed. Just very, very dark.

"Okay. I'll tell you about my pa." It was almost as if he were answering a challenge. "He killed my ma—not directly, of course. He killed her by dragging her out here from Boston, then leaving her high and dry while he went about God's work. He rode a circuit up north near Cooksburg that was more important to him than anything, especially his family. After a while Ma just couldn't take the loneliness anymore—leastways, that's how I see it, though I was just a kid then, and no one really told me anything. One day while my pa was gone, my uncle came to visit, and she got him to take her and us kids back to Boston. She was in a family way, and we didn't get too far before she gave birth and died."

"And you blame your father?" Lucie asked softly. She had sensed he was a man who had known pain, but to have it laid before her like this so clearly, so coolly, almost like it wasn't a deep wound in his heart, was disconcerting. She sensed Micah was a man who had grown quite expert at shielding his true feelings.

He snorted a sharp, hard laugh. "Who else should I blame? He has even admitted to it."

"He admits it?"

"Yeah. After my ma died, he acted like it grieved him terribly. He said it changed him."

"People do change." The hopefulness in her tone sprang from more than just trying to convince *him*.

"I don't care. Even if he did, it was too late. He killed her. He ruined our lives. A person just can't do that and expect forgiveness."

"Maybe you are being a bit hard on him," she ventured.

"Oh yeah!" he retorted. "Guess all you religious fanatics got to stick together."

She blinked, shocked at the venom in his response.

He added a little more gently, "You didn't deserve that, I guess."

"I didn't mean to defend your father, Micah. But I think all the hate you seem to be storing inside is hurting you more than it's hurting him. Hate is a double-edged blade."

"What do you know about hate?"

He was studying her closely. Then, to her amazement, a small smile played upon the corners of his lips.

"You've never hated a soul in your life, have you, Lucie?"

"I don't think so. I have never had reason to, I suppose."

"I fear you'll one day come to hate me," he said, no humor now in his aspect.

"My mother and father had a little pact between them," she replied. "They said they would never let the sun set upon their anger. I think hatred comes from anger that is allowed to fester."

"Many suns have set on my anger," he said grimly.

"My parents would give their anger to God."

"I think . . . I hate God as well."

"Oh, Micah!" She wanted to weep for him.

"I wish I could be like my Uncle Haden. He didn't even believe in God. But unfortunately, I believe."

"Who is the God you believe in?"

"He looks a lot like my father."

Her barely checked tears now erupted at the vast emptiness in his tone. She reached out to touch his hand because she simply could not leave him there so alone, so empty. Her hand brushed his, and scarcely had contact been made when his arms came up and gathered her to him. He held her fiercely, but not like he had at the dance. Now there was a desperation in him, as if he might crumble without her to keep him intact. She felt the grate of his day's growth of beard in her hair as he pressed his cheek hard to her head. She thought he was trembling a bit, but perhaps it was her own quaking she felt.

This was different than before, not a physical need, but a need that went to the heart, the very soul.

"It's been so long," he murmured. "So long . . ."

Lucie wasn't certain what he meant, but she had a feeling he had not held a woman out of sheer emotional need since the death of his mother so many years ago. She wondered if anyone had held him, loved him since then. She encircled him with her own arms, patting his back, cooing comforting words.

Still holding her, he moved his head and looked into her eyes. "I knew you were dangerous. You are so decent, so sweet. . . . Oh, God . . ."

"I love you, Micah!"

"Don't say that."

"Why won't you let yourself love a little?" she entreated. "Maybe it will chase away some of the hatred."

"I'm not sure I'd know how. It's been a long time." He ran his finger along her cheek. All the shadows had fled from his eyes. They were the purest of blue now. "I could love you, Lucie."

"That's enough for now, then." She smiled, though she knew she was lying. She would never be satisfied until his love was as complete as hers. "I won't ask for more." She was telling herself as much as him.

He bent closer and his lips touched hers. The kiss was as gentle and tender as the last kiss had been heated and passionate. He knew as well as she that what was happening now far surpassed anything physical.

"We better go back," he said, his grip on her loosening.

She nodded. She did not know what would happen now. She only knew a line had been crossed, one she couldn't turn back from. She loved this man. She prayed God would understand.

He rose, but she did not see the hand he had extended to help her as she jumped to her feet.

"Looks like your ankle is better," he said matter-of-factly.

"Oh ... uh ... yes, it is." She remembered her deception and felt all the worse for it after what they had just shared.

Seventeen

THE SUN WAS LOWERING in the west as they rode up to the ranch. The sky was a dusky shade of orange and red with a deeper purple near the horizon. Micah and Lucie had been silent for most of the two-hour ride. There was so much more to be said, yet already they each had as much as they could handle to consider.

Micah could hardly fathom what had passed between them. Lucie had said she loved him. Even now, to remember her profound declaration made his chest constrict. He had not realized until that moment sitting there on the creek bank how desperately empty of things like love he had been. Until Lucie had come along, it had been easy to shrug off this need, and he knew it was indeed a need.

She had said maybe a little love would help wash away some of the hate. But he had lived with hate for so long that maybe it was too deeply a part of him. Maybe hate had made him the man he was. If he gave it up, it might be relinquishing too much. Yet that little touch of love he'd felt from her had been so sweet. And as he'd felt it, he realized just how much he'd missed it.

He glanced over at her. The lowering sun was shimmering in her dark hair like flames. She was so beautiful he could hardly believe she had reached inside him and touched something that had so very little to do with physical attraction. If he believed in God, or rather, if he acknowledged the God he knew was there, he'd feel certain she could be the answer to a man's prayers.

She smiled, catching his open appraisal of her. "We're almost at the ranch. Won't you stay for supper?"

He could see the house and outbuildings on the horizon. He wondered what it would be like to sit to supper with these decent folks. That scared him as much as anything.

147

"I don't know," he hedged. "It's getting late."

"When was the last time you had a home-cooked meal?"

"A coon's age, I reckon. You doing the cooking?"

She laughed. "Not tonight. But I do cook, if that's what you're getting at."

He didn't know at all if that's what he'd meant. He was afraid of her thinking of him as a man evaluating the qualifications of a prospective wife. He shook away the thought. What was he thinking? He knew she was a dangerous woman.

They rode into the yard, and as they brought their horses into the stable, several of the men offered Lucie friendly greetings. For Micah they only offered cautious stares. Instead of being offended, he was glad these men felt a protectiveness toward her. He wanted her protected, cared for. He just didn't know if he was the man for the job.

Once in the house, Lucie ushered him into a parlor. "Why don't you make yourself comfortable while I tell Juana there will be one more for dinner?"

He didn't recall actually telling her he'd stay, but he made no protests. Micah wanted this as much as he feared it. He simply could not remember the last time he'd been in a family home. Once or twice when he and Jed had been youngsters and wandering around, a couple of folks had kindly taken them into their homes and given them meals. But for the most part he lived under the sky, with occasional visits to bawdy houses or maybe even a hotel when he had some money in his pockets. He'd never been in a simple cabin with a family, a woman in calico, children toddling about, the fragrance of bread in the air.

Not since his own home. And oddly, when he thought of home, it was the dingy Texas cabin that came to mind, not the fine frame house in Boston. For all the misery he'd known there, that cabin had represented something he now sorely missed. A certain cohesiveness, even security. Especially after his stepmother had come and brought a bit of happiness to the place. Not that Micah had ever been able to embrace that happiness. But if he had . . .

Micah shut out such thoughts. They were confusing, and the last thing he needed was more confusion. Instead, he wandered around the Maccallum parlor. It was a nice room, tastefully but expensively furnished. A far cry from the simple Sinclair cabin. The furnishings were made of dark-stained wood of Spanish design. Micah imagined they were old. No doubt Reid Maccallum had purchased them from former residents. Though of course he could have had them shipped from Spain or Mexico City, but the man did not appear the type to indulge in such tastes. In fact, Micah was rather surprised to find such fancy things in his home at all. Lucie had said her ma had died two years ago, so this might well be her influence. Still, most frontier women tended to ship household items from the States, not Mexico.

Micah ambled aimlessly over to the fireplace. This was made of good Texas stone. No fire burned on this warm summer day. Above the hearth was a large portrait of a woman, a beautiful woman. A Mexican woman. She was dressed in a deep red gown, stylishly designed and obviously expensive. On her head was a veil of the kind Mexican women wore for special occasions, which Micah had heard called a *mantilla*. It was of black lace and blended with her dark hair, piled fetchingly under the mantilla. She was probably thirty years old, but her creamy tan skin was flawless, and Micah thought this was more her natural appearance than the strokes of a skillful artist.

He stepped back from the portrait to get a better look. He didn't know why it captured him so. Probably because out on the frontier one seldom saw fine works of art. Yet there was something else about this particular painting. Something vaguely familiar. Something—

"It's beautiful, isn't it?" came Lucie's soft, almost reverent, voice from over his shoulder.

"Who is it?" His voice held a bit of reverence as well, though at the same time a small knot began to form in his stomach.

"My mother."

His mouth went suddenly dry, and he could not speak. Perhaps he should have known all along. Her rich dark hair and eyes, her skin tanned—he'd thought from the sun. But maybe he hadn't wanted to see, to know what now was so unavoidably true. Lucie was Mexican.

"Y-you never said anything," he said hoarsely, with some accusation.

"I didn't think it mattered."

He spun around to face her. What he saw was the absolute truth of her heritage. He also knew she was lying. She had known it might matter. She must have faced prejudices from whites before. And he knew without doubt he was prejudiced. Unlike some, he could not separate loyal Texan Mexicans from those who had murdered his uncle.

"I don't know what to say," he breathed, hardly able to speak the words because he knew they would cut him off from what his heart desired.

"I'm disappointed in you, Micah."

"Me? How about you?" his voice rose with both defensiveness and accusation. "Why did you hide it, Lucie? Are you ashamed?"

"I am proud of who I am!"

With her chin jutted out and her eyes flashing, he had to believe her.

"I said nothing because it never occurred to me that there was any reason to stand and shout, 'I am Mexican!' And I didn't believe you could be so petty until this afternoon when we were talking about the banditos. I glimpsed a bit of it then. Maybe I should have run when I saw it."

"Maybe you should have."

"I wanted to believe there was more to you, that the hate was only a small part that could be eased away with enough love. I see now it is bigger than I thought." Her voice shook, but it was cold, too, especially as she spoke those last words. "You are just a bigoted fool!" She spat her final words.

"And I've got every right to be!" he spat back. "And it's not just bigotry. It's founded in solid facts. I watched while your people slaughtered hundreds of men, my uncle among them. Slaughtered them! Gunned them down when they were unarmed and couldn't fight back. And then when they were dead, them Mexicans just kept shooting and shooting. I swore I'd hate and kill as many as I could. That ain't being a bigot. It's pure revenge."

"It is bigotry," Lucie retorted. "I wasn't one of those murderers, and neither were many others. Yet you lump us all together."

"It ain't that simple."

"Like hating your father isn't simple?"

He could tell she knew her words would hurt.

"I think you just thrive on hatred, any way you can get it," she added.

"I ain't listening to this! You lied to me. You deceived me. So you don't have any cause to get righteous with me!"

"Leave this house immediately!" she practically screamed.

"Oh, I'm leaving all right! I'm leaving right now!"

As he quickly saddled his horse and rode away, Micah didn't know why he kept thinking she would come after him. And he certainly didn't know why he actually *wanted* her to. She represented everything he hated. He didn't go around gunning down every Mexican he encountered in the streets, though part of him wanted to. Maybe not women and children, 'cause he wasn't an animal. But he held no great affection even for them. In San Antonio, ninety percent of the population was Mexican, so it was hard to avoid them. But he tried.

Even he had to admit, however, that it was wrong to lump them all together. He rode with a couple of Mexicans in Hays' company of rangers. And there was an entire company of Mexican rangers run by Antonio Perez. They were good men. They had covered his back on numerous occasions. But he knew he consciously tried not to think of them as Mexican. Contrary to what Lucie had implied, he didn't walk around with hate just oozing from him. He could be tolerant. But that didn't mean he'd be squeamish about killing Mexicans when they deserved it.

Micah could be tolerant of Lucie as well. Question was, did he want more than a relationship of mere tolerance? And no matter what he felt, she had told him she loved him. He had repaid those extraordinary words by accusing her of deception and defaming her heritage. Being Mexican didn't really change who she was, and it shouldn't change what he thought of her. Maybe if he could find it in himself to accept this about her, it might go toward diffusing some of the hate inside him, just like she'd said.

He truly didn't want to be so wrought up with hate, especially if it was going to prevent him from having any good come into his life. He was due for some good, wasn't he?

"I reckon I can be man enough to let go of some of it. . . ." he murmured into the wind. "Just a little for now, then see what happens. Maybe I'll die without it to sustain me. But just maybe I'll actually like it."

He reached out a hand, smoothing it over the buckskin's dark mane. "What do you say, Jose? Do ya think I should give it a try?" He smiled. "You're Mexican, ain't you, boy? You've done all right by me."

Shrugging, he nudged the buckskin to turn around and headed back to the Maccallum ranch.

———

Lucie was shaking as she sat on the velvet divan in the parlor. At first her gaze remained fixed on the place where Micah had been standing, as if he might reappear and the entire scene could be replayed and maybe changed. But as much as she wished the fiasco hadn't happened, she was still angry. The things he'd said angered her, but even more, she was furious at the fact that she'd been so wrong about Micah.

Perhaps it was a good thing all this had taken place now, before she'd become any more entangled with the man. She could deal with their differences in faith because she'd felt so certain God could and would change him. She could accept his wild nature because she'd known there was a gentle side to him as well. But add bigotry to the mess, and it was too much. Too many barriers to overcome. Too many differences.

Lucie, some things just aren't meant to be, she told herself, trying to feel pragmatic about it, even though she felt her heart was being ripped from her chest. She had told him she loved him, and she had meant it. But now she feared what her father, and even Micah, had said. Love wasn't enough. But neither could love be turned off so easily. She knew she would hurt for a long time, but it was still better this way. She could not be with a man who disdained the very blood that coursed through her body. The one thing that could never be changed.

It was better this way.

Wasn't it?

"God, I fear I have imposed too much of my own desire in this situation. I had hoped you were in it, but I didn't wait to see. I blinded myself to good advice and blundered ahead, thinking I could perform miracles. I could not have been more foolish. I think I know better now. Miracles are your business, not mine. But is it wrong to still hope? I cannot help myself. I still believe Micah Sinclair is worth hoping for. And I believe you think so, too. I guess I just must be patient and wait to see what you will do with him."

She smiled. Patience was not her best virtue. Yet she was indeed willing to wait on God. She only prayed He would let her know when to stop waiting and move on with her life.

Feeling a bit restored, she rose and went down the hall to look in on her father. As she passed the kitchen, she saw Juana busy with supper preparations. She should tell her their guest had left, but she couldn't face that just yet. She continued on to the back. Quietly she turned the latch on her father's door and opened it. He was snoring peacefully. She was glad the heated conversation earlier in the parlor hadn't disturbed him.

Lucie returned to the kitchen and was about to tell Juana about their absent guest when she heard a tapping at the front door. Her heart jumped, thinking it might be Micah. Well, she wasn't going to change overnight, she thought ruefully.

"I'll get it, Juana," she said and retraced her steps down the hall, trying to walk in a deliberate, sedate fashion, ignoring the urge within her to run.

She opened the door to find one of the stableboys. "Señorita Lucie," the lad said, "I have a message for you."

"Who is it from?" Again her heart raced.

"I was out a ways from the stable walking the newly shod mare when a man came up out of the shadows and called to me. He was a stranger."

"What did he want?"

"He said I must tell you, and only you, to meet with him out by the mesquite tree, the big one that was split by lightning some years ago. Do you know this place, señorita?"

"It happened before you were born, Pedro, but I think I know the place." What Lucie did not know was how Micah knew about it. "Is that all he said?"

"Only that you should come alone and as soon as possible."

Why was Micah acting so mysteriously? He certainly couldn't be afraid to come directly to the house. And she just did not see him as trying to entice her into some romantic rendezvous.

"Thank you, Pedro."

"I will go with you, Señorita." The lad squared his shoulders in a sweet attempt to look older than his twelve years.

"I'll be fine." She smiled confidently. "It's just a friend of mine playing games. Now run along and don't worry."

She saddled Belle as she fended off inquiries from the men in the stable. She told them she and her friend were just going on a moonlight ride. Questions of being properly chaperoned were broached, but she handily ignored them. Anyway, it was just sundown, hardly midnight. There was nothing improper about riding with a *friend*.

It was about a quarter of a mile to the tree on mostly level ground. She knew the way. As she went, she continued to puzzle over the oddity of Micah's behavior. She also tried *not* to puzzle over her own swift response to his request. But she couldn't ignore him, could she? Just because she had decided to give God full reign in the situation didn't mean she was to cut herself off from Micah completely. Did it? What if he did apologize and recant all his harsh words? She simply did not know how she would or should respond to that.

Then she remembered something her mother had always said: "When in doubt, pray."

So Lucie did just that as she drew close to the rangy old mesquite tree. Though the sun was down, there was still enough light for the tangled, gnarled branches to stand out a stark black against the faintly lighted sky. The tree looked quite pretty, even if most residents considered mesquite more a pest than a marvel.

"Lucinda!" came a soft call.

She gasped, the sound taking her by surprise. Only then did she wonder why Micah was using her given name. She did not think he knew it.

Eighteen

LUCIE GASPED AS A man stepped out of the shadows. A man, tall and lean, but not Micah.

"Joaquin!" Lucie breathed. "Oh, Joaquin, you came."

"Hola, Lucinda. I wondered if you would remember the tree." He spoke in Spanish.

"How could I not?" She also replied in Spanish as she dismounted. She knew he had his reasons for not speaking English, and she did not wish to offend him, at least this soon in the meeting. "I remember many races to this tree."

"I always won," he replied, his tone as soft as the gathering dusk.

"Yes."

"But you never stopped racing me."

"I loved you all the more, Joaquin, because you never pandered to my inexperience and femininity." She smiled at the thought of those long-ago memories. "You were my friend as well as my brother."

"Sometimes I could weep at the crazy hand life has dealt us."

His face was drawn and hard, in no way indicating a man given to tears. Yet she remembered when she had seen him slip in unobtrusively among the crowd gathered at their mother's graveside two years ago. Tears had erupted from the hard black surface of his eyes then. Tears only she had seen, for he had disappeared before even Reid had noticed his presence.

"I am so glad you have come," she said.

"I could not stay away. I am a fool for doing so, but . . ." He shrugged as if to complete his sentence.

"But what, Joaquin?" she pressed. "Are you a fool for wanting to see your father before he dies? Are you a fool for not wanting to

155

be cheated like you were two years ago?"

"I did not say I would see our father." He shifted on his feet and chewed on his mustache. "But the few minutes today just was not enough."

"You won't see Papa?" Lucie's voice rose. "Then why come at all?"

"At least I can see you—"

"I'm not dying," she cut in fiercely. "I am not lying in bed aching inside because I fear I will not have one last chance to see my son before I die. You are so selfish! I thought you were better than that."

"I am a bandit!" He retorted, his eyes flashing now. "I am better than nothing! I prey on others, especially you Texans. I have a price on my head—a large price. If I am ever caught, I will be executed on the spot. Is it selfish to guard my skin? I would like to live to a ripe old age, but I doubt I will. Yet, still I come . . ." He shook his head harshly. "No, you are right. I am selfish *because* I have come."

"I don't understand."

"I hoped at least Papa would."

"Tell me why you don't come, Joaquin," she implored, more gently now.

"Think about it," he said. "If your association with me is discovered, it could bring you and Papa both down. Papa could lose everything if he is thought to be a spy for the Mexicans. I have seen it happen to others. You have also, I know. And it could happen to a gringo as well as a Mexican. Don't fool yourself. Things are happening now, politically, that would make such an association even more dangerous. It is far too risky for me to come any closer than this to the ranch."

"But why even come this close? It is Papa you need to see."

"How bad is he?"

"He had a bad spell a few days ago and has been confined to his bed. We won't be able to keep him down much longer." Her lips twitched as she thought of the big Scot chomping at the bit like a racehorse hitched to a freight wagon. "It is hard for him to accept his illness."

"I can well imagine."

Joaquin's gaze shifted up toward the dark sky. Lucie recognized the ploy as a way to hide emotion.

"Does he hate me much for not coming?"

"He loves you, Joaquin!" she said emphatically. "As you well know, at first he resented the fact that you sided with ... the enemy."

"Mexico was never my enemy," he replied ironically.

Yes, she and her bother had always been caught in the middle. She was younger and more sheltered by her parents, so it was easier for her, Lucie supposed. And even though she had darker hair, Joaquin looked far more Mexican, aided by the fact that he maintained a more Mexican persona. He dressed in Mexican clothes, spoke Spanish almost exclusively, and he practiced the Catholic faith. As a boy he'd been frequently mocked for his heritage by neighboring Texans, even when he tried to look as American as they did. Then in his adolescence, he reacted by rebelling. He took on Mexican ways in open defiance of those arrogant Texans who, in his mind, thought they could come swaggering into the land of Mexico and rudely denigrate all the traditions of that land.

When the war broke out Reid had not been surprised, though it had sickened him, when his son joined Santa Anna. Lucie remembered finding her father in tears the day after Joaquin had left. Reid's disappointment only deepened when after the war Joaquin had turned to outlawry in defiance of the new republic. At least he had protected his father's name and even that of his Mexican grandfather by taking an alias for a surname. Nevertheless, Lucie hadn't fully understood it all. She had never felt anything but Texan. Maybe, she thought bitterly, she would have thought differently if she'd encountered more people like Micah. Maybe that would have stripped away her loyalty. But she didn't want to think of Micah now, for she was confused enough being confronted by her brother after so long.

"I cannot stay much longer," Joaquin said suddenly.

In desperation, Lucie grasped his arm. "Don't let Papa die like Mama did without seeing you one last time."

"Do you think I wanted her to go that way?" He turned away from her, sighing, the tension almost visible in his broad, strong shoulders. "I tried to get back, but I was spotted as I crossed the border. Two of my men were killed."

When he turned back to face her, she saw the pain he had suffered, both then and now. She knew he had wanted her to see it, and only for that reason had he revealed it.

"All I could do in the end was to creep like an interloper at my own mother's grave! It is one more score against the gringos who have forced such a life upon me."

For an instant he sounded far too much like Micah. Had her heart not been wrenched by the similarities and the irony, she might have smiled.

"You can make up for it now," she suggested.

"It is a bad time now. More dangerous than ever." He paused, seeming to carefully consider his next words. "Lucinda, things will soon be happening . . . and you will want to distance yourself more than ever from me."

"What things?"

"Ah, you never could just accept things, could you, dear one?"

His mustache twitched, and she wanted to believe he had allowed himself the luxury of a smile. She remembered that even when they were children, her brother had seldom smiled.

"At any rate, I cannot tell you more. Only that you should keep away from San Antonio for a while."

She asked no further questions. She didn't want to know more. How she hated being in the middle. She always had.

Joaquin continued, "Tell Papa I love him and explain why I could not come to see him. Tell him I hope he understands. Tell him also that I have taken a wife and have a child on the way—"

"A wife! A child!" Lucie exclaimed. Then impulsively she threw her arms around her big brother. She was tired of conceding to his reserve. "When?"

"The child should come by Christmas. My wife is in Mexico, of course, near Saltillo."

"What's her name?"

"Pilar."

For a moment his features softened, and Lucie was comforted to know her brother had found love.

"She is a gentle, sweet woman. But she doesn't like me to be away so much."

"I shouldn't wonder!" Lucie smiled, already feeling a kinship to the sister-in-law she might never meet.

"Someday I will stay home with her for good. When all the trouble ends, when there is peace between our two countries."

"Let us pray for peace, then."

"I must go," he said reluctantly.

"Try to find a way to tell us when your baby is born. Papa will be a grandpa, and I will be an aunt. We want to know when that happens." And though she had wanted to be brave, she could not prevent the tears from spilling out of her eyes. She threw her arms around him again.

She felt a deep fervency in his returned embrace. He kissed the top of her head.

"*Adios!*" he said finally, letting go of her reluctantly.

He retreated to the far side of the tree where Lucie now saw he had carefully concealed his horse. Adios! She tried to reply but could not get words past her constricted throat. She lifted a hand instead in mute farewell.

Oh, God, let him come back! Please let him come back!

————

Micah had seen Lucie ride out to the big misshapen mesquite tree. He would have called to her, but he didn't know why he kept silent. She had been riding with such purpose that he was reticent to stop her. He didn't know what to make of her riding out like that so near dark and all alone. Is that what she did when she was angry? Then all the more reason not to approach her, even to apologize. He didn't want to face her anger again. It had hurt him more than he cared to admit. It had hurt to have such a wedge driven through the sweet things that had happened between them such a short time before.

He decided to just keep an eye on her for a few minutes to gauge if it was safe to go to her. He reined his buckskin up sharply when she dismounted at the tree and a man stepped out. Micah pulled his pistol, ready to kill the man if he tried to harm Lucie, but it quickly became obvious this was no chance meeting.

Micah dismounted Jose, tied him to a branch of one of the few other trees nearby, then crept in closer to the pair. He wanted to make certain Lucie was not in trouble, but if she wasn't, if this was some friendly meeting, well, he wanted to know about that, too!

Circling the mesquite tree, Micah found the man's mount. It looked vaguely familiar. Where had he seen such a horse? It had been recently. A sleek black stallion with one white sock.

He made his way back to where he had a view of Lucie and her ... friend? He was still too far to hear their conversation, though he could discern it was in Spanish. And it was obvious that, though it was impassioned at times, it was not hostile. Who was this man? One of the vaqueros? Surely he was Mexican. Then Micah remembered. It had only been this morning, though so much had happened since to cloud his memory, that he had chased just such a stallion.

Joaquin Viegas rode a black mount with one white sock.

Then Micah's breath caught painfully as Lucie threw her arms around this man, not once, but twice! And that embrace had been filled with passion. What was she up to? What kind of game was she playing? What kind of fool was she playing Micah for? Here he had come back ready to apologize for his harsh words, ready to accept her heritage or at least to tolerate it. And what was she doing? Having some kind of romantic rendezvous, not only with a man, but with a notorious Mexican outlaw!

Sweet Lucie? It couldn't be.

But there was the proof before his eyes.

Then Viegas—it had to be him!—rode away. He headed south, so Micah was not in danger of being discovered. But he knew he was, nevertheless, in very great danger. And he had worried about hurting *her*! He had to be the worst kind of fool. And like the fool he surely was, he was not about to just slither away, leaving her to her machinations. She was not going to get away with it. So intent was he on confronting Lucie, it didn't occur to him he was missing a prime opportunity to catch the outlaw.

He jumped up from his hiding place and fairly charged into the clearing by the deformed tree. He saw her race to her horse and was afraid she was going to get away. But he quickly saw escape was not on her mind. He screeched to a halt, looking down the barrel of the rifle she had suddenly drawn from her saddle scabbard.

"Stop there or I'll shoot!" she cried.

"Lucie, it's me."

"Micah?"

"Yeah. Put that rifle down!"

She lowered the weapon but did not replace it in its scabbard. "What are you doing here?"

"Maybe I could ask you the same question," he accused. "I came back to apologize, only to find you in the arms of another man."

"What are you talking about?"

Even in the deepening darkness he could see the bewilderment on her face. "I saw, Lucie. I saw him." It surprised him how wounded he felt. Ever since he met her, he had been trying to push her away. He should be glad she wasn't interested in him. But the white-hot anger he now felt proved otherwise. And the fury was even greater than when he'd seen her with that Carlton fellow. Probably because since then she had made empty confessions of love to Micah. It certainly wasn't because the man was a Mexican, an enemy.

Lucie sighed. "You have it all wrong, Micah."

"I saw you two embrace."

"And what should that matter to you, anyway?" she said, her temper flaring. "A little while ago you walked out on me—"

"You told me to leave."

"Only because you insulted me."

Micah cursed in his frustration.

"And don't you curse at me either!" she warned.

Micah sucked in a steadying breath. "Who was that man?"

"I don't have to tell you anything!"

"He was Joaquin Viegas, wasn't he?"

She drew her lips taut, as if she feared what might escape them. Then she, too, took a breath. "Go away," she said tightly, "before we . . . before things get out of hand."

"What were you doing having a secret rendezvous with a low-down, traitorous outlaw?"

"Who said it was secret?"

He rolled his eyes. "Come on!"

"I am not saying another word!"

"Lucie, this is serious." Only then did the full import of the situation truly strike him. "If it wasn't a romantic tryst . . ." Please let it not be that, he silently prayed! "If not that, then the only other conclusion that can be drawn is that you are somehow in league with Viegas's band."

"That's ridiculous."

Micah tried to rein in his anger. This was serious, more so than he at first thought. It went far beyond his bruised feelings.

"Listen," he said with forced control, "you are courting disaster here. You better consider yourself lucky it was me who found you—"

"What? And not some narrow-minded bigot?" she rejoined snidely. Then she gasped, obviously sorry about what she had said.

They both fell silent, a silence filled with tension and confusion. Staring at each other, Micah knew she was probably thinking the same as he. How could they get out of the corner they had backed into? How could their harsh words be unsaid? And more importantly, who would make the first move toward conciliation?

It wasn't going to be him. He still wasn't certain he'd done anything wrong. Well, maybe not now, but he had been wrong before, back at her house when he had accused her of deception. Or had he been wrong after all? He had just found her with a Mexican bandit.

"Ah, Lucie . . ." he breathed, not even realizing he'd voiced his dismay. But now that he'd started, it was easier to continue. "We've made a real mess, haven't we?"

"I guess so," she replied tightly.

"It's my fault." At first he'd thought to be magnanimous by taking the blame, but as he said the words, he knew the full truth of them. "It was wrong of me to accuse you of deception before. You have the purest heart of anyone I know. I, of all people, had no right. As for what happened now . . . I have no hold on you. For heaven's sake, I have done all I could to discourage you. I'm a real jackass for making accusations. I—"

162

She raised a finger and set it against his lips. "Joaquin Viegas is my brother," she said quietly.

"Your what?" he gasped. This was more stunning than any surprise he'd had thus far.

"I hope you can understand why my family has kept this secret. I didn't mean to deceive you."

"How can this be?" He had been thrown seriously off balance by this and was trying desperately to make sense of it. One of the worst enemies of the Republic of Texas was Lucie Maccallum's brother. The man whom it was Micah's sworn duty to hunt down, capture, and most likely kill was Lucie's brother. It suddenly seemed this was the final blow to fantasies he'd only barely let himself have about this sweet, decent gal.

"Joaquin had his reasons to throw in with Mexico," she said.

"No one knows about this?"

"Papa has one or two loyal friends who may know, but for the most part, it has been a fairly well-kept secret. Most folk think my brother just went to live in Mexico or the States or perhaps even died." She paused.

He now noticed her lip was trembling. He wanted to hold her and comfort her, but that would only compound all the mistakes he'd made that day.

"Lucie, today by the creek bank—"

"Yes, I tried to distract you and the other rangers to give him time to get away. What else could I do? He's my brother!" Tears welled in her eyes.

He thought he could handle her anger better than her misery, though he'd made a poor job of that as well. "Folks might not see it that way," he said lamely as he tried to figure out what *he* thought about it. She wasn't going to give him a break, though.

"What do you think?" she asked incisively.

"It don't matter what I think—"

"Yes, it does! It matters to me! Do you think I am in league with the notorious outlaw? That perhaps I am his spy?"

"Shoot!" He kicked at the dirt. He hated being in this position. Maybe he could lie. But she was too smart to fall for lies. "I don't know what to think. Your loyalties are torn. I can see that."

"I love Texas. I am not a traitor."

"Maybe without even realizing it—"

"No!" she shouted. "I am not a traitor."

"Your pa—"

"Don't even say it, Micah!" Her eyes flashed like a lion protecting her young. "My father is a hero of San Jacinto. He fought against Santa Anna when he knew his only son was in the army of the enemy. No one had better *ever* question his loyalty!"

"People will talk."

"Not if they never find out." Her words were a clear challenge.

"Unless I find any clear evidence against you, I won't say anything, Lucie. I swear to God."

"To God, Micah?"

"I guess that's a pretty empty oath coming from me, but what else would convince you I mean it?"

"I'll just take your word for it." Her tone had grown cold.

He hated himself for asking, "Is everything spoiled now, Lucie?"

The smile that slanted upon her lips was as cold as her voice, and her eyes—her beautiful, warm, dear eyes—stared at him now like a chill frost. And he knew he had lost something he'd not even had the courage to grasp.

"I'd like to be left alone now," she said.

He nodded. "Sure ... I ... uh ... will go, then." He paused, not knowing why, just hoping. But she did not stop him. "I'll see you."

"I don't think so. You were right, Micah. We are too different."

When he didn't move, she turned and walked to her horse, mounted, and rode away.

Micah watched. He remembered only one other time he'd felt emptier. The day his mother had died.

———

Young Pedro waited until the gringo rode off before making his own way back to the ranch. He knew it was wrong to eavesdrop, but who could blame him for being too afraid to make his presence known? Señorita Lucie had just been talking to two very dangerous-looking men. One, the gringo, Pedro had seen before at the ranch and knew to be a ranger. But the other, could it be possible he was really Joaquin Viegas?

Pedro had been near enough to hear much of the conversation except when the wind carried away the sound before it reached his ears. Hearing was one thing, however. Understanding was a different matter. One thing was clear, the *patrón*'s daughter was closely related to Joaquin Viegas.

What to do about this matter now plagued Pedro as he returned to the ranch, running all the way. Only as he saw Pete Barnes walking from the stable to the bunkhouse did he decide.

"Señor Pete!" he called, jogging up to the foreman.

"What is it, Pedro? You look all in a lather."

"Señor, I have seen something." Pedro paused and glanced nervously around. "I must talk to you alone." There was no one in the yard at the moment, but it might not remain so.

"Let's go to the springhouse," Pete said.

Once at the springhouse, Pedro launched into his recent experience. "Pete, I saw him! She was talking to him, not a quarter of a mile from here—"

"Saw who, boy?"

"The bandito—I am certain it was him. Joaquin Viegas himself!"

"What's this?" Pete leveled narrow, incisive eyes at the boy.

Pedro would have trembled at the foreman's look had he not just survived being a stone's throw away from a notorious outlaw. Besides, though Pete could be tough, he had always been good to Pedro. Trying to remain calm and speak clearly, Pedro related what he had seen and heard of the conversation between Lucie and Joaquin. Pedro did not mention the gringo, only because it did not seem important beside the incredible encounter with Viegas.

"That's a mighty tall tale," Pete said when the boy was finished.

"I swear it is the truth!"

"Well, seeing as how you and I share the same name, and you have always been a good boy, I'm gonna take you at your word."

Pedro sighed with relief, not only that his story was believed, but also because he did not like carrying something like this alone. "What should we do?"

"You think a lot of the *patrón* and his daughter, don't you, Pedro?" When the boy nodded emphatically, Pete continued, "Well, then, the best we can do for them is to forget all about this. Don't sound like the *patrón* is involved at all, and with him ailing and all, it just wouldn't do to worry him over this."

"*Sí*, Señor Pete!" The last thing Pedro wanted was to bring more grief on the family that had been so kind to him over the years.

"So you won't say a word to anyone, right?"

Again the boy nodded.

He really didn't think it counted when a few days later he was bragging to that bully stableboy over at the Carlton place and let slip about having seen the infamous bandito.

Nineteen

TENSIONS WERE MOUNTING in San Antonio, rumors flying as thickly as Texas dust. It was believed that the Mexican general Adrian Woll had a force camped on the left bank of the Rio Grande and was poised to invade Texas.

Over the summer Congress had approved the raising of new ranger companies to defend against such encroachment. President Houston, a major proponent of statehood for Texas, knew that as long as Mexico was such a threat to the republic, the United States would drag their feet regarding admission. But little had come of the recruitment efforts.

"I can barely keep the men I have," Hays complained one hot morning at the beginning of September.

"It ain't that you haven't tried," offered Tom.

They were seated in a cantina trying to fight the heat with a tall beer. But Hays' rising frustration wasn't helping to dissipate the effects of the temperature.

"The men are practically destitute." Hays shook his head dismally. "How many who have lost horses in battle have been able to replace them? Precious few."

"Or they are forced to ride them rangy, sickly Indian ponies we capture. It's pathetic. We all live in fear of getting our horses shot out from under us—maybe even more than getting killed ourselves."

"It's a sad state of affairs."

Micah, Jed, and Big Foot Wallace walked in just then and joined the two men.

"Well, how did that inventory of supplies go?" Hays asked, though the look on his face indicated he already knew it wasn't going to be good news.

"Pathetic," said Wallace, who pulled out a chair and sat straddling it. "Jed, get us some beer. I'm parched."

Jed, always eager to serve his ranger companions and never taking offense at his status as "kid," went to the bar. In a couple of moments he returned juggling three glasses of beer.

"The barkeeper still giving us credit?" Big Foot asked.

"He wasn't too happy about it," said Jed, "but he did . . . 'this time,' he said."

Micah brought the conversation back to the earlier topic. "Captain, I hate to mention this, but any word yet on when we're gonna get some pay? Look at this—" He held out his leg, displaying the knee of his trousers where even the patch was worn through. "And you should see my backside. It's getting indecent."

"I'm sorry, boy," Hays said.

Micah had to smile at the captain's words, since he was only a handful of years older than Micah himself.

"What about the other supplies?" Hays continued.

"In a terrible state," said Wallace, taking a gulp of his drink. "Powder and lead are so low we couldn't fight a passel of Sunday school teachers. And there's something else—" Wallace glanced around, then leaned forward. "I been in these parts long enough to know just about every face and name there is. Well, I been seeing a lot of strange Mexicans in town lately. I don't like the look of it."

"All right, Wallace, I'm going to have to send you up to Austin to try and scare us up some powder and lead and whatever other supplies you can lay your hands on. Take Jed here with you. I got a little money in the budget you can have. Use credit if you have to."

After finishing their drinks, the men dispersed. Micah and Tom walked with Wallace and Jed to the livery stable and helped them get off on their journey to Austin. Jed was obviously quite pleased with himself, going off on his own with the redoubtable Big Foot Wallace on a vitally important mission.

"Just don't get yourself killed," Tom admonished Jed.

"Better yet, don't get *me* killed!" put in Wallace.

"I'm gonna do good," Jed assured, his grin taking some of the edge off his earnestness. "Just you see!"

Micah slapped his friend on the shoulder. "While you're at it, see if you can scare me up some new trousers."

"I won't leave that town without some," Jed promised.

"Let's move!" Wallace ordered.

Micah watched the two ride off with a sense of despair he couldn't quite identify. He supposed it had to do with the probable futility of the Wallace mission. The chances were quite slim they would find enough powder to hold off the Mexican army. And if they did, would they get back in time? Though it was all still speculation, Micah had a funny feeling in his gut that trouble was near. He thought about what Wallace had said about all the strange Mexicans in town. He thought about Lucie's covert meeting with Viegas. Her brother? He hoped that was all it was. But it was just too coincidental that the impending trouble had come so close on the heels of that meeting. If it had been anyone else but Viegas, he might have let the matter drop. Yet he had given his word to her to keep quiet about the meeting. She would truly despise him if the matter became known and she discovered it was he who had turned her in.

And as rocky as their relationship had been lately, the last thing he wanted was her ire upon him. Even if it turned out that she was indeed a spy . . . well, he didn't know what he'd do about that.

"Tom," Micah asked as casually as possible, "you think Joaquin Viegas is really working for the Mexicans?"

"No doubt about it. Why do you ask?"

"Just wondering. Guess that's why he's been spotted so much lately in the area."

"True," said Tom. "If there's gonna be an invasion, you can bet Viegas has been laying the groundwork by keeping these parts in turmoil."

"You think he's working alone? I mean, could he have some locals spying for him?"

"I wouldn't be surprised." Tom paused, then gave Micah a careful appraisal. "You know something, boy?"

"No," he answered, probably too quickly. "I'm just curious, is all."

Just then Hays approached, cutting off any response Tom might have made. "I can't believe the people around here," he said without preamble. "The town leaders are afraid of panic among the citizens, so they are trying to go about business as usual. I just pray that all we are looking at are rumors. God help us if there's anything to them."

Indeed, for the next few days nothing unusual happened, and life settled once more into a dull routine. Then Antonio Perez, captain of a Mexican ranger company, confided to the mayor of San Antonio that a force of fifteen hundred Mexican troops had crossed the border. A meeting was held that included a hundred native citizens and not quite that many Anglos. When one of the men reported seeing a hundred mounted riders in the vicinity, everyone seemed content to believe the invasion rumors had overblown the danger, and the townsfolk felt confident in their ability to hold off such marauders. Nevertheless, Hays was commissioned to take his men and patrol the area.

Micah was glad to do something. He'd be happy to prove once and for all that there was no threat of invasion. If it should be proved otherwise, he would be just as happy to fight. He felt he was going soft lately, thinking too much of romance and such nonsense, too little of settling old scores and righting old wrongs. Lucie had said he ought to let a little love disperse some of his hate, but he wasn't ready for that, and he needed a good fight to remind him of that fact.

The rangers patrolled south along the Laredo road, the most likely approach of a Mexican army. They turned up nothing, and two days later returned to San Antonio. Upon reaching the outskirts of town, they were astonished to find it was occupied by General Woll's army. Apparently while the rangers were scouting to the south, Woll, with well over a thousand soldiers, had slipped around to the north and invaded from that direction.

Hays took his men and retreated to Seguin, about thirty miles northeast of San Antonio. There, several days later, they met with Wallace and Jed, who luckily had stopped there to get feed for their horses before going on to San Antonio. Wallace had a keg of powder, and Jed had a box of lead balls and some percussion caps.

"We ran into Comanches," Jed said.

They were seated around a campfire on the edge of town eating stewed rabbit Micah had shot and exchanging news.

"Jed killed one," added Wallace.

"Good thing they didn't get either of you," Hays said. "We're gonna need every man we can get now."

"I still can't believe that old varmint Woll slipped into San Antonio like that," Wallace said.

"I wouldn't be surprised if someone didn't let him know just when we'd be gone on patrol," Tom said.

Micah squirmed uncomfortably. Lucie could not have had anything to do with that, but still, sitting on his secret was wearing away at him.

"I don't reckon it would have done any good if we'd been there," Micah said. "A couple dozen against a thousand?"

"Only took a hundred twenty-five men to take San Antonio from the Mexicans back in '35," Tom said. "Caldwell down in Gonzales has at least that many mobilized and will march when he doubles that number."

"I've sent couriers all over," said Hays. "We'll raise an army now that Woll has made his move." He didn't add that it was too bad it took an invasion to rally an army, though all were thinking it.

Then Jed jumped up. "I nearly forgot!" He went to his saddlebag and took out a small bundle that he then held out to Micah.

"What's this?" Micah asked.

"What you asked for."

Micah unfolded the brown bundle, revealing a pair of trousers, slightly used, but still in fairly good condition.

"Where'd you get them?" asked Wallace. "I didn't see you buy nothing in the store."

"I bought them from a woman who was hanging out her laundry." Jed's reply was edged with defensiveness.

"Where'd you get the money?" asked Tom. It was understandable the man would be concerned, since Jed was his responsibility and still on probation.

"Well . . . I . . . didn't—"

Jed, suddenly flustered at the negative attention, glanced at Micah as if asking his friend to get him out of this mess as he usually did. But this was a rare time when the two had been apart, and Micah didn't know what to say in Jed's defense.

But he couldn't remain silent. "Hey, you got no right accusing Jed like that!"

Tom softened his tone. "It's just that . . . well, Jed, we know you meant well. But what else are we supposed to think? You ain't got no money, and you wouldn't be the first man to lift an item from some housewife's clothesline."

"I didn't! Honest!" Jed exclaimed.

"Least you can do is believe one of your own men," Micah said, growing more and more perturbed, especially since this had all been started because of him. "Jed's covered your behind more than once, Tom."

"We all get tempted occasionally," Hays said in a placating tone. "But I expect my men to be above reproach."

Micah snorted snidely, but a sharp look from Tom made him think again about showing disrespect toward his captain. "Well," his own tone altered slightly, "I ain't met a ranger yet who could pass for an angel."

"That may be true," Hays said.

"I'm thinking it's more important that we stick together," Micah added, and if he would have listened closely to himself, he would have noted a self-righteousness in his tone that sounded hauntingly like his father. "We ought to back each other up instead of thinking the worst and accusing—"

"All right, Micah," Tom cut in. He obviously was not happy about the way the matter had disintegrated. They had bigger problems to solve. "Jed, I apologize for what I said and what I thought."

"I reckon I do, too," said Big Foot.

"Thank you kindly," Jed said sincerely. "Just so's you know," he added, "I helped that woman carry a couple of tubs of water up from the creek—that was while you was in the cantina, Big Foot. Remember, I went for a walk around town. Well, that lady said she wished she could pay me for my help, but she didn't have no extra money. I asked if she had a spare pair of trousers her husband might not miss. That's how I got 'em."

"Let's see how they fit," Micah said, glad for an opportunity to further disperse the tension in the air. Quickly, and with Jed's help, he tugged off his boots. Then he slipped off his old pants and put on the new ones. They were a pretty good fit. A bit short, but otherwise could have been made for him.

He looked at Jed. "It's been a long time since I had a new pair of pants."

"They ain't new," Jed said almost apologetically.

"New enough." Micah ran a hand along the slightly worn fabric, feeling a touch of emotion. He didn't appreciate Jed's friendship enough and was going to have to find a way to make it up to him.

The other men, mostly for Jed's sake, added their own compliments. Captain Hays even commended Jed on his resourcefulness, saying that was a prime ranger attribute and proved Jed was coming into his own as a ranger. That made Jed forget all about the previous altercation.

Twenty

THE SOUND OF HORSES clamoring into the yard drew Lucie to the front door. Opening it and stepping outside, she saw several riders, perhaps a half dozen. They were familiar faces, her neighbors. The lowering late afternoon sun set them into a shadowed relief, making dark expressions seem even darker.

"Your pa around?" asked Axel Carlton without so much as a howdy-do.

"He's not well," she replied. "What can I do for you?" There was not a friendly face among the lot of them.

"If your pa can walk, he best come out here and see us," Carlton ordered.

"I'm sorry." She wasn't sorry at all and made that clear in her tone. Lucie didn't like his attitude. "My father isn't leaving his sickbed, so you best tell me what the matter is."

"Never you mind, Lucie," Reid said from just over her shoulder.

"Papa, I'll take care of this—"

"Maccallum!" Carlton broke in harshly. "You got some explaining to do."

"Yeah, Reid," said one of the other men, the foreman out at the Samson ranch. "We been hearing things—"

"And we want to know just what is going on!" Axel finished, with a sneer on his face. He had obviously wanted to be the spokesman in the group. "We hear your daughter's been meeting secretly with Joaquin Viegas."

Reid had come up beside Lucie, and now he gave her a quick unreadable glance before facing Axel. "What are you implying, Carlton?"

"It's pretty obvious!"

"Of all the nerve!" Lucie piped up, desperate to shoulder the load of these accusations for her father. "Where have you heard such lies?"

"Don't matter where I heard them," said Carlton, with no intention of backing down. "You sure they are lies?"

"If my daughter says they are, Carlton, then that's all anyone needs to hear." Reid put a protective arm around Lucie.

It felt so good, and she needed his support so much. She hated lying, but what else could she do?

"We got a witness who says she met with Viegas just a few nights before the Mexicans took San Antonio," Carlton said. "This witness says Viegas is her brother, and there's just no reason he'd make this up. What do you say to that?"

"We have been your neighbors for years, Mr. Carlton," Lucie began.

But Reid stopped her, laying a hand on her shoulder. "I am a loyal Texan, Axel." His tone was weary but somehow managed to be forceful as well. "As is my daughter. I fought with Houston, and I'll not listen to anyone who calls our loyalty into question. But I will not lie to you—I am tired of secrets and lies. Joaquin Viegas is my son—"

Startled gasps from the group of still-mounted riders interrupted Reid. Lucie noted an ugly look of triumph on Carlton's face. She was a little gratified to see that Grant Carlton, mounted next to his father, wore an expression of supreme discomfort. Maybe he had a redeeming quality after all, but she would still have a hard time forgiving him for even being present at this obvious witchhunt.

"So you have been lying," Axel said.

"When my son went off to fight with the Mexican army in '36, I wasn't proud, to be sure. I disowned him." Reid's lips trembled slightly over the words, and Lucie knew he was barely keeping his emotions in check. For six years he'd swallowed his pain over his son's actions, and he was not about to reveal any of it now, especially not in front of the hostile men who used to be his friends. "When folks got the idea he'd returned instead to my relatives in the States, I let them think it. None of you people had accepted him much anyway, and you sure didn't miss him. Soon he was forgotten. I let it happen. But *I* never forgot him. When I heard what he was doing and who he was . . . what was I supposed to do? What would any of you do?" Lucie felt her father lean more heavily upon her. Now she placed a supportive arm around him.

"Papa, let me take you in."

"Not yet, Lucie. It's time these things were said." He took a labored breath. "I am a dying man," he said, and no one could deny that at the moment, "and God help me, but I want to see my son once before I die. I don't care what he's done or who he is. I haven't seen him in six years, but if he should come, I will see him."

"What about your daughter?" Lloyd Samson asked.

"No one will say anything against my daughter!" Reid growled, momentarily gaining some of his old vigor. "You try that and there *will* be trouble here."

"You need some help, boss?" called Pete Barnes.

Lucie glanced beyond the riders and now saw all the Maccallum ranch hands had taken defensive positions, encircling the riders. They were on foot, but each man carried a rifle. She wanted to cheer but only let a small smirk tilt her lips.

"Thanks, Pete, but I got it under control," Reid said. "These gents were about to leave."

The riders, too, had noted their precarious position.

Carlton still refused to act defeated. "Because you are a gringo, Maccallum, I'm going to give you the benefit of the doubt. But I don't know about . . . anybody else. If Viegas comes here, it is your duty to report it."

"Don't you dare tell me my duty, Carlton. Now get off my land!"

There followed a tense moment when it was unclear if the riders would obey. The Maccallum ranch hands raised their rifles as if to add emphasis to Reid's words. Then Carlton turned his horse and rode away. The other riders followed suit. Grant was the last to leave. Just before he caught up with the others, he threw a look back at Lucie. She didn't know what to make of it. Maybe it was regret, but she didn't care.

She turned her attention to her father. He was practically hanging onto her, barely keeping to his feet.

"Pete!" she called.

The foreman hurried forward to give a hand. It showed the extent of Reid's fatigue in that he did not protest such assistance, especially within sight of his men. He let them help him to his room and to a seat on the edge of his bed. Even then, however, he refused to lie down like an invalid in the presence of his foreman.

"Thanks, Pete," Reid said, "I mean for what you did out there. Tell the men, too. I just thank God it didn't erupt into something ugly."

"They had no right saying the things they did," Pete said.

"Even if they were true? At least about Viegas being my . . . son."

"They had no call to question your loyalty."

"I appreciate *your* loyalty. To me." Reid clasped his foreman's hand. "You're a good man. Now I think I want some rest."

"All right, boss. I'll go talk to the men."

When Pete left, Reid lifted his feet onto the bed. As he lay back on it, he said to his daughter, "We're alone now, Lucie. . . . You got something to tell me?"

"Don't you think you should rest, Papa?"

"Ain't no way I'll rest proper until you tell me. Did you see my son?"

Lucie tried to stall by fussing over her father. She drew a blanket up over him and straightened his pillows. She poured him a glass of water from the pitcher at his bedside.

"Lucie . . . ?"

Sighing, she plopped down with defeat into the chair at his bedside. "Papa, I didn't tell you because I thought it would only cause you more anguish . . . knowing he was so close but had not tried to see you. He had his reasons."

"Does he still believe I want nothing to do with him?"

"No, I am sure he doesn't. He understands. He only stays away because he wanted to prevent just what happened today."

"Bah!" Reid shifted in his bed, which creaked with his weight. "I don't give a hang what those people think any longer. That they would turn on us so quickly at the word of—I wonder who it was anyway, informing on us like that."

Lucie played with the lace on her shawl. "I think I know." She didn't let her eyes meet her father's for fear he'd see the anguish this caused in her.

"Who is the rascal?"

"It doesn't matter, Papa." Then she hurried on to shift the direction of the conversation. "Papa, Joaquin told me he is married now and has a child on the way."

"A child . . ." Reid smiled for the first time that day. "I'll be a grandfather . . . though I'll never see the child."

"Who knows, Papa? They live near Saltillo. It is not a horribly long journey."

"Even if I live that long, he is still an outlaw, and he would be taking too much of a risk to come see me. And I could never make such a trip. With the trouble now between our two countries, I couldn't make it even if I were healthy." He reached out a hand, and Lucie took it. "Ah, Lucie, it is a lost cause. But I am happy you saw him. Tell me some more about him. What does he look like? What does he sound like . . . ?"

Lucie spent the next hour, until her father drifted off into sleep, telling him every detail she could about Joaquin . . . Maccallum.

She left his room and ate a quiet supper with Juana, neither having the heart to wake Reid for the meal. Juana was more silent than usual. She was the only one outside of family who had known about Joaquin, so all that had transpired came as no surprise to her. She made it clear that her silence had more to do with grief over the family's plight than with disapproval. She may as well have been a member of the family, for all her deep bond with them.

Lucie went to her room right after supper. It was dark by then, and there seemed nothing else to do but get some sleep. However, sleep eluded her. All she could think about was how Micah had broken his promise. She tried to defend him, thinking that it was too much to ask, especially of a lawman, to keep such a secret about an outlaw. Yet she had believed him. She had trusted him. She had wanted to trust him.

And he had betrayed her.

It always came back to that. And she could not prevent her rising anger and hurt. It wouldn't have killed him to keep silent. He knew she could not have had anything to do with the invasion. But even if he had believed her to be a spy, why not face her himself rather than take such a cowardly way out?

She had thought better of him, and perhaps that's what hurt the most.

But wasn't it best she discover all this now before she did something really stupid? It was bad enough she had declared her love. How much more foolish could she be!

Lucie squeezed her eyes shut. She wanted sleep. She wanted to force all thoughts of Micah Sinclair from her mind. She wanted the impossible.

Twenty-One

THE RANGERS HAD BEEN keeping busy since Woll's invasion, making frequent sweeps around San Antonio, watching the Mexicans' movements to ensure they did not go farther east. There was no time to hunt, and they had little other food supplies, so the men were all but starving. When it was decided to make a more determined strike against the Mexicans, Micah was the first to volunteer. Hays only wanted the men with the best horses, and Micah's buckskin, even on low rations, was just that.

Micah tried not to think about whether Hays' plan was a good one. It might be foolhardy, but at least it was doing something. Thirty-eight of the best mounted men of the two hundred now gathered near San Antonio were to approach the Alamo fortress near the town where the main force of Mexicans was encamped. There Hays and his men would act as a decoy to draw out the Mexican army. For the most part they hoped to use the enemy for a bit of target practice. If they could get some away from the fort, they'd lead them into an ambush Hays set up near the banks of the Salado. If they could get at least part of the enemy there, they might well knock down the formidable odds of eight to one against the Texans.

Gesturing and taunting loudly, the Texans challenged the Mexicans to come out and fight. The ploy worked. But instead of a mere forty or fifty soldiers emerging from the fort as they had expected, six hundred mounted Mexicans poured from the gates of the Alamo.

"Retreat!" Hays screamed, and it almost seemed as if he were truly in a panic and not merely feigning as the plan required.

The Texans took off at a full gallop. Micah's buckskin performed admirably. Under a barrage of Mexican fire, the Texans led a merry four-mile chase. But the Mexicans were too well trained to be lured into the ambush. Still, Hays' scouts were able to hold off the enemy until Caldwell's two hundred arrived to reinforce them.

The Texans had good cover and knew the terrain. The enemy sustained heavy casualties, while the Texans had one dead and several wounded. The skirmish forced Woll to send four hundred more of his men from the town to aid the army in the field.

The next morning Micah was sent to scout out the town. He returned with good news.

"The Mexicans are definitely leaving town," he said.

"What about prisoners?" Hays asked.

"I'm pretty sure I saw some gringo captives."

"Then we'll maintain pursuit."

Micah knew for a fact there were a handful of rangers among the captives in town, those who had been left to aid in the defense of San Antonio when Hays had made that first scout just before the invasion. He was now determined to get his men back.

An opportunity arose at the Hondo River. Hays encouraged the other commanders to strike the Mexicans before they crossed the river, but they were reluctant to face Woll's cannons. Hays responded that if he had a hundred men on good horses, he'd capture the artillery first. By then the ranks of the Texans had swelled by a few more hundred, and the commanders were then emboldened to commit two hundred to reinforce Hays once the cannon was taken.

At sunrise the next day, Hays, his rangers, and almost a hundred Texans charged Woll's front line. The Mexican artillery fired wildly, overshooting Hays' men and giving them the chance to draw close enough to make lethal use of their rifles and pistols. McBroome's horse was killed and several men were wounded, but they broke through the Mexican artillery. But when Hays looked about for the promised reinforcements, he saw nothing.

"Micah," Hays yelled, "ride back and see what's keeping those reinforcements. Tell 'em to get their sorry behinds up here pronto!" Hays' eyes flashed darkly. He was a mild-mannered type until riled, then he well earned the name the Indians had for him, Devil Jack.

Micah wheeled around and, flanking the artillery that was quickly regrouping, made it down the hill to the camp. Caldwell's men were nowhere near to being ready for an attack. Micah set upon the first man he saw.

"Where's Caldwell?" he barked. Micah had escaped the charge unscathed, but his buckskin had been grazed in the neck and, though not hurt mortally, was suffering more than Micah cared to see. He was furious to find that no one was even making an attempt to aid Hays.

The man whirled around. "How am I supposed—" But he stopped abruptly as both men locked eyes and recognized each other.

The man whose gaze was now just as sharp as it had been on the dance floor back in San Antonio was Lucie's escort that evening. Grant ... someone. Micah had seen him before during the last weeks with the army but had managed to avoid him. He thought it odd that there should be such antagonism between them, but there was no denying it. It had been there the night of the dance, and it was no less present now.

But there was no time to consider personal affairs. His comrades would not be able to stand for long against Woll's army if help did not soon arrive.

"Why aren't you men preparing to advance?" Micah demanded. "Captain Hays is gonna be slaughtered up there."

"We have received no orders," Grant said.

"Well, I'm ordering you to mount up and move it."

A sardonic grin slipped across Grant's finely chiseled face. "You and who else?"

Micah knew he had little authority, but he put as much bluff and bravado as he could behind that little he had. "I'm authorized by Captain Hays, and his orders are for you to move."

By now many of the men had gathered around. Grant's eyes swept the group. "Anyone here see Hays?" Of course no one did, and none of them were going to take orders from anyone lesser. "We ain't taking orders from you, Sinclair."

Micah wanted to leap from his horse and strangle the man, not only for his personal agenda but because Grant's blatant unconcern for his endangered comrades inflamed him beyond reason. Then he made the mistake of glancing again at Grant's sneering, superior face, and reason left him completely.

"You low-down snake!" Micah growled as he vaulted from his mount.

He smashed into Grant with enough force to practically knock the air from both of them. He backed up the force of his body with a well-aimed fist, and Micah could not remember anything feeling so good as the sound of the crunching cartilage of that smug face.

Blood spurted from Grant's patrician nose. He touched his face, then looked with horror at his bloodied hand. Grant was about to make a counterattack when a gruff voice stopped him short.

"What's going on here?" It was Caldwell himself.

Micah pulled his attention from Grant, for though his hands itched to do more damage, he knew he had larger things to consider.

"Where's the reinforcements?" Micah asked, his voice shaking. He didn't care if this was the commander of the Texan army. He'd pound him, too, if he tried to wheedle out of his responsibility.

"You're one of Hays' rangers, aren't you?"

"That's right. We broke through the artillery, but it was no use because there was no one to back us up. We're getting torn to pieces!" Micah didn't even try to curb his accusing tone.

"The ground is too boggy, and our mounts are simply too exhausted to make a go of it," Caldwell replied, somewhat defensively. "It'll be in my report."

"Hang your report!" railed Micah. "What about Captain Hays?"

But Caldwell was spared, for the moment at least, as Big Foot Wallace on his stout mule galloped into camp with the news that Hays was in retreat.

"Anyone killed?" Micah asked.

"None that I know of."

Micah shot a glance at Grant as if he would have been held personally responsible had any of Micah's comrades been dead.

"You want to finish what you started," dared Grant, "I'm ready."

Micah advanced, but Wallace, who had dismounted, sized up the situation and stepped between the two.

"Hold on there," he said. "We have too many problems without adding fighting among ourselves to 'em."

Micah swallowed his rage. He knew it was unfounded. This man was nothing to him, certainly not a rival for the affections of a girl he could never have. And as far as Hays' failed attack, Grant could not even be fairly blamed for that. He was just following orders.

"I guess I overreacted," Micah admitted, though through gritted teeth.

Grant touched his nose again. Blood was beginning to congeal and crust, and the skin was turning an ugly shade of black. "Wallace is right. There's more important things to see to right now. But I owe you, Sinclair—for a lot."

"What'd you mean by that?"

"No one takes what's mine. That's what I mean. Not that you *could* take what belongs to me, but I'm not forgiving you for trying."

Micah snorted derisively. "That's ridiculous. If you're talking about Lucie Maccallum, I don't believe she belongs to anyone—me or you. She's her own woman. But aside from that, unless you've a mind to marry her, I got just as much right to pay her attention as you."

"I'm merely protecting her from scum—"

Micah made another menacing move, but Big Foot intervened again. "Carlton, this is the last time I'm gonna stop my friend. Next unsavory remark from your mouth, and I'm gonna let him at you—and believe me, you don't want that. I've seen Comanches fall before his fists, and I don't reckon you're anywhere near as tough as a Comanche."

Grant's inner debate was obvious on his face. Finally he took a breath and spoke. "You can't blame a man for desiring to protect a woman's honor."

"Well, go do it someplace else," Wallace said.

Grant stalked away, very obviously not in defeat but mollified for the time being. There were other battles to be fought. They both knew that.

When they were alone, Micah turned to Wallace. "Big Foot, I ain't never fought a Comanche with my fists."

"Never?"

Micah shook his head.

"Well," Wallace said, an easy grin bending his lips, "I reckon you'd be pretty fierce if you ever did."

"Thanks, Big Foot."

"Now let's go see to our men."

Hays' company had by now ridden into camp. Thankfully, they had but one horse killed and five men wounded. But they were as ready as Micah had been to vent their fury upon Caldwell's army. Hays barely held them in check. Tensions, however, rode high in camp that night and weren't helped when they woke in the morning to find that Woll's army had slipped away during the night.

Reinforcements from Bastrop and La Grange brought the numbers of Texans to nearly five hundred. After several more successful engagements, Woll's army fell into a full retreat. When the Mexicans reached the border, the Texan commanders argued to end the pursuit. There was a small contingent of dissenters, but the majority won out. There were too many practical considerations. The army was worn out from long marches and little food, and most of the horses had reached their physical limits. Ammunition supplies were also low.

Micah's first taste of real battle since San Jacinto proved not to be as satisfying as he would have hoped. Most of the time he was off scouting, and the encounters he did participate in were far too few and too brief. He hated letting Woll escape across the border and was hardly mollified at the promise that the Texans would regroup in a month, after men and supplies were bolstered, to continue the pursuit.

Regardless of how disgruntled he was, he had to admit that at least this battle had not left a legacy of nightmares. He decided he had finally grown out of all that.

Twenty-Two

SEVERAL WEEKS AFTER the dust of battle settled, as November made its appearance, Lucie made a point to go into town. Even her father did not protest. He knew as well as she the importance of being seen standing proud among their neighbors.

Manuel Ruiz, the shopkeeper, kept his eyes averted as he spoke to Lucie. "You have a long list, Señorita Lucie."

She nodded, trying with her own eyes to get him to look at her, but he kept staring at the paper she'd written on. "We ran low on many things during the fighting," she said to the bald spot on the top of Ruiz's head.

"Supplies are low here as well, but merchandise has started coming in. Flour, yes," he said referring to the list. "But no sugar. And I can give you a pound of coffee, no more. I may have a few buttons—white, not black."

"That will have to do, then."

Ruiz hurried to the back storeroom as if fleeing the Evil One himself. Ruiz had been a family friend, drawn closer because he and Lucie were among the few Mexican Protestants in the area. He attended her church, a small assembly that had sprung up since the revolution. But she tried not to blame him for his reticence now. He had himself to protect.

Some Mexican citizens of San Antonio had departed the town with General Woll. Among them were Juan Seguin and Antonio Perez, two prominent citizens. Those who left would never be trusted again. Those who remained were not officially reprimanded in any way, yet a pall of suspicion would hang perpetually over them, perhaps forever. They would have to work harder than ever to prove their loyalty. They would have to studiously avoid suspicious associations, such as with the sister of a notorious Mexican outlaw. Lucie understood this. She understood that the only reason she was able to remain north of the Rio Grande at all was because her father was an Anglo, and no one who knew him could honestly reproach his loyalty.

Many white males had taken Mexican wives and could thus be held suspect, and in fact, many were. But this alone could not condemn a man. Reid was probably the only one who also had for a son a man who was an outlaw and most assuredly an agent for Santa Anna. Yet Reid had many friends, including Sam Houston himself. It would take more than the likes of Axel Carlton and his handful of cohorts to discredit Reid.

Lucie wandered idly around the store as she waited for Ruiz to fill her order. She was looking through a small crate of books, the only books to be found in the store, when the front door creaked open. Glancing up from the volume she held open in her hand, she saw Micah Sinclair.

Framed in the open door with the glaring afternoon sun behind him, he looked as if he were some kind of ethereal creature, illuminated by a hallowed glow. For a moment Lucie forgot all about her animosity toward this man who had betrayed her. She saw only the handsome boyish face of the man who had saved her life, tenderly holding her, risking his freedom for her. She remembered how vulnerable and dear he had been with the orphaned baby, and how hard he had tried to camouflage the soft core of his heart.

Micah took off his hat as he entered the store, perhaps out of habit in the presence of a lady. His hair, seeming more golden than ever with the sun glancing off its tangled strands, had grown since she had last seen him, curling about his collar, the long side strands tucked haphazardly behind his ears. His complexion was quite ruddy from long hours in the sun, and his chin and jaw were covered with reddish stubble.

"Ma'am," he began casually, then he took more than casual note of the woman in the store. "Lucie!" he said with soft intensity. For a moment his eyes glittered with blue warmth, and a smile invaded his lips.

Lucie tried not to think of the touch of those lips upon hers, or that even now, in spite of everything, she longed to be held by him again. But even as her heart skipped a beat or two, even as her body reacted hungrily to the sight of him, she remembered his betrayal. And she steeled herself against her own betraying body and heart.

"Mr. Sinclair," she said stiffly, formally.

"How you been doing?" He stepped fully into the store, letting the door slam closed behind him. Though his tone was casual, she sensed a forced quality to it. From guilt?

"Fine." She snapped shut the book in her hands. "Just waiting while Señor Ruiz fills my order."

"I'm here to pick up a few supplies as well." He shifted uncomfortably on his feet. "Won't be long before the army invades Mexico."

"Are you sure you should be telling me that?" she asked coldly.

"It's common knowledge."

"Good. I wouldn't want you to reveal any state secrets. I may tell Santa Anna, you know."

He squinted at her, perplexed, then shook his head. "I know you ain't gonna do that."

"Do you?"

"Of course I do!"

The certainty of his tone made Lucie momentarily doubt herself. Yet no one else had known of her meeting that night with her brother. How desperately she wanted to believe that Micah was innocent, but the facts of the matter were too clear to be denied.

"Then why did you inform on me, Micah?"

"What're you talking about?"

"The whole county knows about Joaquin being my brother!"

"Well, they didn't hear from me!"

"Who else?"

"Never mind, Lucie," he cut in sharply. "You believe what you want to believe."

He turned away from her and wandered over to a barrel of apples. He gave these his attention, pawing through the contents, lifting out one apple, then another, as if searching for the perfect one. He finally found a likely candidate, plucked it out, and wiped it against the sleeve of his shirt, a peculiar action since his sleeve had to be dirtier than any apple skin.

Thoughtfully, as if he'd gained some wisdom in the apple search, he said, "Listen, if it got out about Viegas, I reckon it's only natural you'd think I was the one who told. I didn't, but I'll allow the way it must look."

"Well . . ." she tried hard to be as magnanimous as he, "I shouldn't really blame you for doing your duty as a ranger. It was wrong of me to place you in such a compromising position."

"Except I didn't do it." A tense silence fell between them. Micah continued to rub the apple against his sleeve as if polishing silver. Finally he spoke again. "We just can't cut a break, can we?" The regret was clear in his tone, clearer in the darkly blue surface of his eyes. "I won't deny there is something powerful between us, something I can't explain. But whatever it is, even you've got to admit it has been doomed from the beginning."

"It hasn't been given much of a chance," she allowed.

"*Doomed*, Lucie," Micah said with more emphasis. "You said it that last night. We are too different, and there are just too many things going against us. You made the right decision when you said we shouldn't see each other again."

"I know I did," she softly, reluctantly admitted. "I was right, but—"

He gave his head a dismissive shake. "But nothing, Lucie! A polecat and a prairie flower ain't never gonna mix."

"A polecat and a prairie flower?" She permitted a touch of amusement into her voice. "Who is the polecat, Micah?"

"This ain't no time to jest."

"If only there had been more jesting between us, more fun. Have I ever seen you smile, Micah, really smile? Dear me, how I would have liked that."

"I never smile much," he said flatly.

She had a sudden urge, despite the pain of the words spoken between them, to do something outrageous—a flying somersault, or perhaps take that mop rag and perch it upon her head—anything to draw one raucous belly laugh from her solemn ranger. But it wouldn't happen. Not now. It was too late.

"You see it, too, don't you?" he said dismally.

"Yes, but I don't have to like it."

"I hope then we can part on good terms—that is, with you not thinking I would betray you."

She sighed with the hopelessness of it all. "Even if you had betrayed me, Micah, I don't think I would have stayed mad at you long."

"And I would not have cared about you being Mexican—" he broke off with an apologetic bent to his mouth. "I don't mean that in any demeaning way. I guess I just mean that there are some things that can be accepted and others than can't."

"We have too many that can't."

"That's the problem."

Sighing, she replaced the book in the crate and turned toward the front counter. "I wonder what's keeping the shopkeeper?"

"I'll be on my way, Lucie."

"What about your supplies?"

"I'll come back later. Ruiz is busy now anyway." He turned to go, opened the door, then paused.

The light again glinted in his hair, and the sight caused a lump in Lucie's throat.

"Like I said before, the army will be departing soon. Can't say how long we'll be gone or what will come of it—" he stopped, a rueful, humorless twist to his lips. "Guess that don't matter, though. I mean, you and I . . . we won't be seeing each other again anyway."

"Maybe occasionally, in the store like this," she said, unable to mask the longing in her tone.

"Maybe. But . . . well, good-bye, Lucie."

"Good-bye, Micah."

When he left, closing the door behind him, it was truly as if light, glorious, sweet light, had been cut off. Lucie wondered about what fools they both were. Fools for loving the unattainable. Fools for succumbing so easily to barriers. Fools for setting themselves up in the first place for what had been destined to fail.

But how could she be a fool if she had done the right thing, the only thing possible in ending this relationship with Micah?

Why did she feel such loss now, not only for what they'd had but also for what she had once been so certain they could have had? She had loved the man Micah was, but perhaps even more, she had loved the man she had believed him destined to become. Maybe that had been wrong, as her father warned her. And for that reason, she had said that "good-bye" a few moments ago. Yet it did not wipe out the love she still felt, and it did not make her believe in Micah any less.

"Dear God, I just don't know what is right or wrong anymore. I only know I still love him. I am willing to let him go—" she snorted a dry laugh—"well, I hardly had a choice." But even as she murmured the words, she realized she indeed had very much of a choice. She knew Micah felt something for her, and thus it would have been quite easy to use her feminine wiles to bend him to her will.

But it wasn't her will she wanted.

"God, I can't turn off my feelings for Micah. I'm not completely sure if some of them, at least, aren't from you. But I am willing to place those feelings into your hands. Take them away from me, Lord, if it is your will. But if you would have us together, then change the situation between us—his prejudices about my blood, my fears about his life-style, his fears about losing his freedom, but most especially, his bitterness toward you. Bridge the gaps between us, Lord. If you can do that, then I will know it is a match made in heaven."

Twenty-Three

RAIN DRIPPED DOWN Micah's neck. His hat sat like a pathetic, wilted flower on his head. Even his buckskin coat was soaked, weighing down on his shoulders like the burden of a failed life.

"This can't go on much longer," he muttered to no one in particular.

"I seen bogs like this go on for miles," Tom said. "We could be mucking through here for days."

"Days!" groaned Jed. He was afoot, leading his lame mount.

"We got Somervell to thank for this," Tom said.

"I heard he decided to abandon the Laredo Road and go cross-country in order to flank Laredo," Micah said, wiping fresh drips of rain from his eyes.

"Hogwash! He says that now to cover up the fact that he don't know squat 'bout what he's doing." Tom hocked and spit his disdain into the wet air.

He was not the only disgruntled member of the hapless Texan army. It was now nearly the end of November. The army had sat idle for weeks, waiting for orders to begin an invasion of Mexico. In that time, the army that had swelled to a thousand was now down to less than eight hundred. Men had simply grown tired of waiting. Most were not soldiers and had left farms and families to join the army. But even this might not have stood in the way had there been better leadership. Somervell, commander of the militia, was perhaps the essence of incompetence. He wasted time with frivolous training and never indicated if he had a plan in mind for an invasion of Mexico. No wonder few believed it when he said this stumbling into a bog had not been entirely by accident.

"I gotta admit I had my doubts," Micah said, "when we waited for that cannon to arrive—"

"Two weeks! Two whole weeks we waited for that cursed cannon," Tom erupted. "And then the blaggard decided not to take it!"

"We ever gonna fight, Tom?" Jed asked.

"There's been plenty of fighting among ourselves," Micah answered.

"And Somervell could prevent that, too, if he'd take a stand one way or another."

Tom was no doubt referring to a confusion of command between Captain Hays' ranger unit and Captain Bogart and his sixty Washington County men. The two small units had been combined to form a company, but there was no agreement as to who should be in command. Somervell had come up with a cockeyed plan for splitting the duties.

"Any stupid idiot knows you can't have two chiefs," Tom declared.

"What if it's Bogart that leads instead of Hays?"

"Why, that would be pure nonsense. Hays is the best man!"

And so the friction within the company continued, but that was only a small picture of what was plaguing the entire army.

For three days the men slogged through the bog, rain, and cold, chilled to the bone. Tom's horse broke his leg and had to be shot. Micah, seeking to spare his buckskin, took to walking ankle-deep and sometimes knee-deep in mud.

By December snow and sleet dogged the army, but they had finally come within sight of Laredo. Desperately needed supplies were requisitioned from the town, which, though Mexican, was not overly hostile toward the Texans. Then about sixty Texans decided the supplies received weren't enough, and on their own volition, they raided the Mexican town, plundering and looting what supplies were left. Though these men were severely reprimanded by Somervell, their actions turned the heretofore cooperative Mexicans against the invaders. And it gave more proof than ever that the commander had little control over his army.

When an order was issued by the adjutant general on December 19 for the army to return to Gonzales and disband, it was enough to further split the disintegrating army. Half the army was ready to go home, while the remaining force wanted to ignore the order and continue with the invasion of Mexico.

Several of the rangers discussed the matter as they sat around a campfire, barely flickering a small flame because only damp wood could be found with which to build a fire. Even the rangers were divided over the issue raised by the general's order.

"We came to fight," Big Foot Wallace said. "So far all we've done is scare the dickens out of a couple of Mexican villages."

"What's the point anymore?" Tom mused. "We ran Woll's army out of San Antonio and out of Texas. And it's pretty clear they had no intention of really taking Texas in the first place. They were just gauging our forces. What tactical purpose would there be in invading Mexico?"

"A show of force," said Bill McBroome. "If we don't hit back hard, they will just make further attempts until they succeed."

"Well, we don't have enough of an army to hit anything hard," argued Tom. "Why, if the political situation weren't so shaky and disorganized in Mexico City, I doubt we'd have gotten this far."

"Ain't like you, Tom, to give up like this," observed Micah.

"I'm cold and wet. My shoes got holes in 'em big enough to drive a wagon through. I ain't giving up. I'm just being practical. We can't fight with an army that's half dead already."

"Does that mean you ain't gonna stay?" Jed asked.

Instead of answering directly, Tom turned to his captain. "What're you gonna do, Jack?" he asked Hays. "I'll go along with whatever you decide."

Hays held his hands over the paltry flame and gave them a thoughtful rub before responding. "First off, I give you men leave to decide for yourself. But let me tell you what I told Fisher, who plans to lead the new invasion enterprise. I was scouting down Mier way, and I heard the Mexican army was gathering a large force to oppose us. I recommended to Fisher that he abandon his plan because we do not have the resources to meet such a force. I don't like turning back, but I believe it is the prudent thing to do."

"Even if it means following Somervell?" asked Wallace.

"I don't like following that man," Tom said, "but I don't like a lost cause either."

"Some would have said Texas back in '36 was a lost cause."

The debate continued for some time. But in the end the majority of rangers, including Tom, decided to follow Hays and return to Texas. Wallace, McBroome, and a handful of others would remain with Fisher.

"What about you, Micah?" Tom asked after most of the men had abandoned the sickly fire for their damp bedrolls, leaving only Tom, Micah, and Jed to siphon off the last bit of heat from the dying flames.

"I came to fight Mexicans," Micah replied.

"Yeah. That still a burning desire of yours?"

"Of course it is." But Micah sensed that his friend had probably guessed before even he realized it that his vendetta against his old enemies had dulled in the last weeks. Maybe Tom had also guessed that the reason for this was a certain half-Mexican gal, a gal Micah could not get out from under his skin even after such a firm good-bye.

But the Mexicans were still the enemy, even if Micah was coming to see for the first time in years that the enmity he held did not have to extend to an entire people. Maybe he could actually accept that there were good Mexicans and bad Mexicans. Yet what good was such a conclusion now, now that he'd lost the whole reason for coming to it in the first place? It seemed all he had left were his old enmities. At least continuing with the invasion would give him some purpose and would keep his mind from plaguing thoughts of what he'd lost.

"I reckon I'll go on with Fisher," he said finally. "I been wanting to fight Mexicans for years, and it would be pure stupidity to give up the chance just for . . . for something that don't exist anyway."

"Then I guess we'll be parting company in the morning," Tom said.

"What about our probation?"

"Aw, that ain't necessary no more. You proved yourself many times over. I'm sure Hays would agree."

Micah grabbed a twig and tossed it on the last ember of the fire. Avoiding the sudden discomfort he felt at the prospect of parting from his friend, Micah turned to Jed, "What about you? You gonna stay or leave?"

"I'm doing whatever you do, Micah. We always stick together, don't we?"

Micah scowled, not liking the sudden burden this seemed to place upon him. He didn't like the uneasiness he felt even more. Maybe he should follow Jed's lead and stick with his friend and mentor, Tom. Yet it was hard to let go of a passion that had driven him for so long, even if that passion seemed not to fit very well anymore.

Micah did not let himself nurse regrets in the disastrous days that followed. He'd made his decision, chosen his path. But it was a path paved with blood.

The first and only engagement of the Texan invasion force occurred near the Mexican town of Mier. Numbering only three hundred, the Texans managed to prevail, causing the blood of their enemies to practically flow in the streets of the town. The rampaging Texans looked too much like images from Micah's nightmares. Yet this was what he wanted. This was what he'd sought. Wasn't it?

When the fortunes of war turned against the Texans, Micah refused to philosophize about it. It began when Fisher was wounded, leaving a serious gap in command. Sick and unsure of himself, Fisher listened to rumors that Mexican reinforcements were on the way. Short on supplies, as usual, and barely maintaining order, he believed his army would not withstand another battle. He surrendered to the Mexicans after receiving a guarantee that his men would be treated as prisoners of war and kept near the northern border.

Instead they were marched inland to Monterrey. Micah and his comrades were tossed into a Mexican prison, where Micah would come to entertain new nightmares.

Twenty-Four

TOM FIFE LOOKED AS out of place in the Maccallum parlor as another younger ranger had so many months ago. Tom twisted his battered hat in his hands as he sat on the edge of the upholstered divan. At least he'd bathed for this visit, his hair was slicked back, and his clothes were clean. He hadn't groomed his beard, and the tangled mass, streaked with gray—salt and pepper, Lucie's father would have called it—was bristly and made his face appear grimy despite his scrubbing.

But Lucie was less concerned with his appearance than she was with the news he bore. Micah had been captured in battle.

"But he is alive?" she asked hopefully.

"I believe so, miss. But—" he stopped, scraped a hand against his chin, then continued with resolve. "He is! I know it. I feel it here."

He thumped himself, and Lucie could not tell if he'd intended to indicate his heart or his gut, maybe both.

"But it is not certain?"

"Miss, nothing's ever certain in battle. Reports are confused and such. We just gotta hope."

She nodded but could say no more.

"President Houston is trying to get to the bottom of the matter," Tom added. "We'll soon have a list of all the prisoners."

"What will . . ." She tried to force the words out. She had said good-bye to Micah. They had both realized the futility of their relationship. Why, then, did she still feel as if she'd been kicked in the stomach? As if Micah had been something to her? She made herself speak. "What will become of the prisoners?"

"It's hard to say. I imagine Houston will negotiate for their release."

"I know about Mexican prisons."

"Don't think about that, miss." He licked his lips and turned his hat. "I ain't a churchgoing man, Miss Lucie. Why, I don't even pray regular-like. But I do believe in God, and I believe He kind of has His eye out for us all down here. I figure He's got His eye out for Micah, too, even if that boy tries to talk disrespectful 'bout God."

Lucie could not repress a small sad smile at the tenderness in the man's voice.

Tom went on. "I get the impression you have a strong faith, stronger than mine, for certain! Anyway, I think your prayers'll be mighty powerful right now."

"Thank you for reminding me, Mr. Fife."

"He's a good boy, Miss Lucie." Tom's lip trembled a bit beneath his whiskers. "He's been like a son to me these past months."

Lucie reached out and patted Tom's rough, gnarled hand. "I am so happy he has a friend like you."

"You been a good friend to him, too."

She shook her head. "I'm afraid I have only caused him grief—"

"Don't say that!" Tom laid his other hand on top of Lucie's in a mutual gesture of comfort. "I think you saved him. If you hadn't come visit him way back when he was in jail, I doubt he'd of ever listened to me. Miss Lucie, you have shown him that life can be good, real sweetlike, you know. Oh, he's got a hard head and may fight it longer than is good for him, but I don't think he'll fight forever because he knows now, because of you, there is something better out there."

"I pray that is true." She looked down into her lap, a bit ashamed of her last meeting with Micah. "I am afraid we said good-bye to each other just before he left with the army. Good-bye forever."

"You young people got no idea about that word 'forever.'" Tom's whiskered lip twitched with amusement. "When you get old like me, you realize nothing's forever. Things happen. Things change. They just have to be given a bit of time. Patience, ya know?"

"I was never much good with patience."

"Most young folk aren't. But take it from an old codger, you and Micah have plenty of time." He gave her hand a final squeeze, then rose. "I best not be keeping you any longer, miss. Thank you for seeing me."

"It was my pleasure, Mr. Fife, despite your awful news." She made herself smile, imbuing the gesture with all the warmth she felt for Micah's friend. "Come and visit anytime. Perhaps next time my father will feel up to receiving you."

"That'd be nice. Now you take care, and I'll keep you informed about Micah."

Lucie walked him to the door and watched him ride away. It was surprisingly hard to let the man go. He was a part of Micah, and she wanted to keep him there to talk more about Micah, to get him to tell her all he knew about Micah. She expected they had spent many hours together as they ranged the countryside. They probably talked about many things. Oh, the things Tom Fife must know about Micah! The little things—what he liked to eat, his favorite color, his birthday. Goodness! Lucie thought dismally, she did not even know Micah's birthday.

But with even more dismay, she wondered if she would ever learn those things. Even if it was true what Tom had said about nothing being forever, Micah was gone now. Would he return?

"Dear God, please protect him! Bring him back. Not just for me, but because I feel so certain you still have special things to do with Micah."

Not relishing the idea of being alone just then, Lucie wandered into her father's room. His eyes were closed as he lay in bed, so Lucie turned to leave, not wishing to disturb his sleep.

"That you, Lucie?" he called softly from his bed.

"I didn't mean to wake you, Papa."

"I can sleep anytime, sweetheart, and these days it seems to be *all* the time. Come sit with me." He patted the edge of the bed.

There was a chair at Reid's bedside, but Lucie sat on the bed itself, and needing only the further encouragement of her father's outstretched arm, she bent down and hugged him. His arms went firmly around her, and he kissed the top of her head.

"What is it, Lucie? What's wrong?" It took only those tenderly spoken words to bring Lucie's emotion fully to the surface.

"Tom Fife, the ranger was here. . . ." She paused, interrupted by a sob. "The . . . the army that went into Mexico surrendered and was taken captive. There's no word yet which men survived the battle." Sobs and tears prevented her from saying more.

"There . . . there . . ." soothed Reid, patting her head.

He held her thus for several minutes, just cooing words of comfort and gently caressing her. How good it felt. How desperately she needed her papa! What would she do if she lost him on top of Micah? She would not be able to bear it.

"The last time I saw Micah," she said at length, her words muffled because her face was still buried in her father's chest, "I told him good-bye, that I couldn't see him again."

"I'm sorry," Reid said.

"Are you, Papa?"

She lifted her head just enough to see his face and see him sadly shake his head.

"I'm sorry it hurt you so," he went on, his voice husky with the difficult truth. "But you know how I felt about the boy. It could not have worked."

"Yes . . . I saw that, but . . . oh, Papa! Why does it still hurt so? Why do I still care?"

"You are a caring young woman. You don't give your affections recklessly." He paused for a long while, then added, "Lucie, don't confuse caring with pity."

"Is that all I felt? Pity?" She didn't want to think so, yet maybe that was the answer. Maybe it hadn't been love at all she'd felt. Maybe it wasn't love now tearing her heart wide open.

"You mentioned that he was all alone," Reid said. "He has no family?"

"His father is alive."

"Is he. . . ?"

"They are estranged."

Reid nodded grimly. He knew all about that kind of thing, of course.

"So I pitied Micah." She let the words roll around in her mouth, as if trying them out. They didn't ring true.

"It is possible."

Her father wanted her to believe it as much as she wanted to. He gave her hand a gentle squeeze.

"All I want is for you to be happy, Lucie. When I die, which I fear will not be too far in the future, I want to know you will go on living a full and contented life."

"I want you to have peace about these things, too, Papa." She hated thinking about him being gone, but it was no use denying that possibility would be sooner rather than later. She could tell he needed to talk about it, and she had to admit she needed to prepare herself. "What can I do?" she asked plaintively. "How can I help you have peace? If I were safely married, you'd feel better, wouldn't you?"

His slight hesitation told her more than his words. "Only if you were happy."

"Yes . . . of course."

"We can't second-guess the future, my dear." His pale lips curved into a gentle smile. "Only God knows what is best for either of us. So let's just wait on Him."

"That's not always easy."

"You know, Lucie, there is something you can do. Not so much for me, but for another father . . . Micah's father. Perhaps you can write him about his son. If they are estranged, he probably knows nothing of his son's plight. If I were in his position, I would want to know."

She wondered only a moment at his sudden change in the direction of their conversation. Maybe he also didn't want to think about the realities his illness was forcing upon them. They would both have to eventually, perhaps even soon, but she was happy he hadn't pressed it just yet.

"That's a good idea, Papa. I think I will go do that now, so it will be ready for Pete to post next time he goes to town." She bent down and kissed her father's forehead. "I feel so much better talking to you." He probably knew as well as she that it wasn't the entire truth, but it wasn't a complete lie either. She did feel a bit better now that she had at least a small thing to do.

She went into her father's study, took paper and pen, and

composed a letter to Reverend Sinclair. She kept it simple, trying to convey her concern for Micah while toning it down at the same time. No need to open her full heart to this man, a stranger. Besides, for all she knew, the Reverend Sinclair might burn the letter the moment he saw it was regarding his son. Micah had indicated how he felt about his father, but he had never said much about how his father felt about him. The minister might have disowned his son to the point of complete animosity. He was a man of the cloth, and Micah had lived a wild and sinful life. Thus, such a reaction would not be surprising.

Lucie sealed the letter, addressed it to the town where Micah had mentioned his father lived, and took it to the kitchen. Juana was busy as usual. Lucie set the letter on the table, then took up a dish towel in order to help out by drying and putting away the breakfast dishes.

"Juana, if Pete comes by, would you let him know I have a letter to post next time he goes to town?"

"Sí, Lucie." Juana paused in kneading bread dough and glanced over at the folded paper. "Who do you know in Cooksburg? That's quite a ways north of here, isn't it?"

"The letter is to Micah Sinclair's father, informing him of what has happened."

"Micah is the ranger who came calling a while back, isn't he?" Juana picked up the dough, which was still a bit sticky, and sprinkled a handful of flour on the board. "What has happened to the boy?" There was real concern in her tone, though she had shown disapproval of Micah in the past.

"He was captured by the Mexicans."

"That is too bad."

Lucie carried a stack of dried crockery to a cupboard. "Do you truly think so?"

Juana looked hurt at the words. "I did not approve of him as a suitor for you, Lucie, but he seemed a good boy, and he was trying to defend Texas."

"I'm sorry, Juana." Lucie sighed. "It's just that . . ." She picked up her papa's coffee cup and absently began drying it. "I had a talk with Papa. He won't come right out and say it, but I know he wants me to marry soon. He says he wants me happy, but I don't think I can have both."

"Because the young ranger is in a Mexican prison?"

"Even if he weren't in prison, I don't think we could have a future together." As she set down the cup and picked up another, she saw a flicker of relief in Juana's eyes. It made an anger flare within Lucie that she did not realize was in her. "Well, maybe you have a better marriage choice for me!" she snapped. "You keep nagging me about getting married. Perhaps you would have me choose Grant Carlton."

"Him!" Juana snorted derisively. "I can't believe I once thought him a suitable match. But after what he and the other ranchers did . . ." She pounded a fist into her dough, leaving no doubt as to what she thought of the actions of those men.

"Then that eliminates half the men in the county and their sons as possible suitors," Lucie said.

"It doesn't mean you have to settle for that wild ranger."

"Settle . . ." Lucie shook her head. She knew that was definitely not the case with Micah. But how could she explain what she felt, when she was not even certain herself? How could she get Juana and her father to see Micah through her eyes, eyes that saw to the heart of the man? But it didn't matter if she could. No matter what was in Micah's heart, there were still too many marks against both of them for a match to succeed.

"There is Levi Jessup's son," Juana was saying. "What's his name? No matter. He is your age, and the Jessups did not turn against your father."

Lucie didn't want to point out that Darnel Jessup was six inches shorter than she and weighed a good hundred and fifty pounds more. She didn't want to believe she was that concerned with physical appearances, but she'd tried having a conversation with Darnel once. He could neither read nor write and could only talk about cows and crops.

She looked askance at the housekeeper, then said snidely, "Why don't you just line up all the prospects, and I'll go, 'eenie, meenie, miney, moe,' and choose one. If I don't marry for love, it really doesn't matter."

"Don't get smart with me, miss!" Juana's tone was as hurt as it was miffed. "I may be only the housekeeper, but I love you just the same and want only the best for you."

Knowing full well she deserved the rebuke, Lucie wrung the dish towel in her hands. "I'm sorry, Juana." Abandoning her task, Lucie plopped down in a chair by the table where Juana worked. "I'm just so confused and afraid."

Juana lifted a hand to gently caress Lucie, then drew it back when she appeared to remember it was covered with flour. She smiled sadly instead.

"I am also sorry, Lucie dear. I am worried and afraid as well— for both you and your papa. You should marry for love, but your papa should also be able to die in the peace of knowing you will be well cared for. I fear that neither will be possible."

"Juana, I don't think I need to marry in order to be happy or well cared for." Lucie looked at the housekeeper, expecting to see shock at her unorthodox statement.

Juana's smile only broadened. "Oh yes. I forgot what an independent soul you are. And I half believe you could find contentment without marriage. You could probably run this ranch better than any man. I've no doubt you could do whatever you set your mind to."

"But?"

"But, *mi pequeña,* is that truly what your mind is set upon? To be alone, to never have babies of your own to love and care for?"

"I think I'd rather have that than be bound to a man I didn't love."

Juana sighed. "And you love this wild ranger of yours?"

Lucie's cheeks burned at the directness of the question. She opened her mouth to respond, though she had no idea what she would say. She was spared by the sound of booted footsteps on the front porch, followed by a knocking at the door.

"I'll get it," she said, relieved the uncomfortable conversation had been interrupted.

Twenty-Five

LUCIE'S RELIEF FLED entirely when she saw the caller was Grant Carlton. She fought an urge to slam the door in his face.

"Good afternoon, Mr. Carlton." Her polite words came through gritted teeth.

"Miss Lucie." He doffed his hat and gave a polite bow.

"What can I do for you?" she asked coldly.

"I've just come calling."

"Well, you do have nerve, Grant Carlton!" she said. "Seems the last time you called, it was with a gang of others ready to all but tar and feather us."

"Now, Lucie—"

"*Miss* Lucie, if you please. Or better still, Miss Maccallum!"

"All right, *Miss* Lucie. I can explain myself, if you'd let me."

Lucie crossed her arms and nodded. "Go on."

"Right here on your doorstep?"

"I'm certainly not inviting you in until I am assured your intentions are friendly."

He shifted uncomfortably on his feet with his eyes focused on the hat in his hands. It was a hat of black felt, the brim new and crisp-edged still. Lucie found herself contrasting it with the grubby hat of Tom Fife earlier. And that made her think of Micah, who had probably never owned a new crisp hat. Micah, who, despite what Tom had said, was lost to her forever. Micah, who she feared still owned her heart.

"Won't you give me a chance?" Grant finally said. His tone was contrite, but when he lifted his eyes to meet hers, there was something lacking in them. They weren't burning with blue passion. They weren't blue at all.

"Come in, then," Lucie said. Despite everything, she had to think of her father.

True, Reid would probably have a fit if he knew she was letting a Carlton into their home, but if Grant could answer for himself.... Lucie had sensed before that he hadn't been fully behind Axel Carlton. She supposed he deserved one chance. If he couldn't satisfactorily defend himself, she'd happily toss him out on his ear.

She led him to the parlor and motioned for him to sit on the divan. She took an adjacent chair. She did not offer refreshment.

"Lu—I mean, Miss Lucie," Grant began. "First off, I have to say I never supported the other ranchers."

"What kind of person are you, then, Mr. Carlton," Lucie said harshly, "that you would silently stand by while innocent folks are abused?"

"What could I do? It was my father, after all!"

"And why has it taken you this long to answer for yourself? It has been three months."

"I was fighting with the army, don't you know."

"I didn't know that." But instead of being impressed, Lucie could only wonder if he had fought with Micah. And would he be able to tell her anything of the ranger? But she couldn't ask, of course.

"We had a rough time of it, and I came down with the ague and have been recuperating since returning to the ranch."

What must Micah have suffered? And knowing him, he had probably been at the forefront of the most dangerous battles. Her lip quivered as she thought of him wounded and suffering.

"I'm all right now," Grant said tenderly.

Lucie realized he had noted her flicker of emotion and taken it quite wrong. "I'm glad to hear that." She couldn't very well tell him what was really in her thoughts.

"And this is the first chance I've had to come tell you how wrong I was about what happened a while back."

He seemed sincere.

"We should never have questioned yours or your father's loyalty. But you know how these things get out of hand. And you've got to admit how it looks, Joaquin Viegas being your close relation and all."

"Have the other ranchers changed their minds as well?"

"I can't speak for them. It wouldn't be right. Just as it wasn't right for me to let them speak for me before."

It sounded reasonable enough. Lucie could easily see how a young man could be so torn in his loyalties. It was no easy thing to stand against one's own father. Again she thought of Micah. For good or ill, he *had* stood against his father. Instead of submitting to the man's beliefs, Micah had left home. It was probably more complex than that, but still, in comparison with Grant, it was clear that Micah was the more principled of the two.

But she had to stop comparing them! It served no purpose. She'd said good-bye to Micah. She must accept that. And perhaps she also had to accept the reality that she must go on with her life. For her father's sake, she must!

"I suppose so," she said halfheartedly.

"Confound it, Lucie!" Grant blurted, then jerked to his feet. "How long you going to make me suffer for one mistake?" He strode across the room, agitated.

"It was a serious matter, Grant."

In three strides, he returned to her, grabbed her arm, and tugged her to her feet. "What I feel is a serious matter, too!" He pulled her into his arms.

She struggled, but his hold was firm. "Mr. Carlton!"

"I've about lost patience with your teasing and your fickle behavior," he said. "It's time you accepted what is bound to happen."

"Bound—?" she gasped hotly, but he cut her off.

"Yes! I'm willing to accept plenty about you," he said.

"No one has asked you to accept anything!"

"You are not going to find better than me." He dodged her remark. "I'll be able to give you all you need and deserve. And together our two ranches will make us the most powerful family in Texas—"

"What? I thought it was me you wanted."

"Of course I do. But it doesn't hurt that land and power will be thrown into the deal."

She made the mistake of looking into his eyes just then. Now there was passion in them, but she sensed it came less from her than from the prospect of riches and power.

She pulled away from him. "I don't consider marriage some kind of *deal*."

"Everything is a deal, Lucie. But have no fear. I want you just for you. I want you so much I am, as I have said, willing to overlook the fact that you are half Mexican and that your brother is a notorious bandit. I want you so much I am willing to defy my father to have you. I should think for that some recompense is due me."

Her mouth fell open. "Due you?"

"Be reasonable," he said. "You shall have security, protection, and the love of a good man. Your father will have peace of mind. I will gain a beautiful wife who is the heir of a fine ranch. We shall both benefit mutually. That's what makes this such a perfect match."

Aside from the fact that his words made her skin prickle, she had to admit the truth of them. Hadn't she said as much to Juana just a few minutes ago? She would never marry for love. So why not consider all the other beneficial elements? Grant was a cool, calculating man but he wasn't vicious. He wouldn't hurt her. He might even love her to some extent, probably more than she would ever love him in return. He had much to offer her—why shouldn't he expect something in return?

She must be calculating as well, and there was more to think of than her own desires. Still, she could not make herself capitulate entirely to necessity.

"I don't know, Grant," she hedged. "I suppose it all does make sense."

"Of course it does!" He drew her once again into his arms.

She tensed but not because of the forwardness of his actions. It was hard to accept the fact that she felt nothing in his arms, or that, if Grant had been captured by the enemy and she did not know whether he was alive or dead, she would be alarmed but would not feel the wrenching loss she'd felt when Tom Fife had given her the news about Micah.

"I must have time to think, Grant," she said.

"I'm willing to allow you some time." His arms tightened about her. "But not too much."

"Ow! That hurts, Grant."

"I'm so sorry. I just got carried away with my affection." He grinned. "I've waited a long time for you, Lucie. I can wait a little longer for you to be mine."

Lucie wasn't sure she liked the way he intoned that final word, "mine." It made her already shaky resolve even shakier.

"It doesn't bother you that I don't love you?" she asked, not knowing why she felt the need for such destructive honesty. Yet she knew exactly why. For her father's sake, she would consider Grant. But if he withdrew his interest, she would be freed of responsibility.

"It is not as if you love another," he said tightly.

She did not refute him. What was the use?

Then he grinned again. "You will come to love me. I have no doubt of it." His fingers pinched her arm possessively. "I will see to it," he added.

She backed away. "When my father is feeling better, I will speak to him."

"I think I should speak to him."

"All in good time." She tried to smile in a coquettish manner but could only manage a glib twist of her lips.

"I will consider that we now have an understanding, Lucie."

"I only said I would think about it."

He dropped his hand from her arm and plucked up his hat from where he had set it on the divan. "I must go. Why don't I come to dinner tomorrow night? Make sure your father is there."

He then strode from the parlor, leaving Lucie with her mouth gaping, her head practically spinning. What had she done? An understanding? What did that mean? And whatever it meant, could she go through with it? Could she marry a man in a cold, calculating manner for "mutual benefits"? Could she marry one man while she loved another? Did her father expect it?

Of one thing Lucie was certain, her father must never know of her sacrifice. If she did this thing, no one would ever know how she really felt.

If. . . ?

Then all of her doubts and questions and fears spilled over her like a summer downpour. And the imagined wetness turned real as tears once again coursed from her eyes. Tears for what her life was suddenly becoming—out of control like a spooked stallion careening wildly across the prairie. Would only crashing over the beckoning cliff stop it? Or was there some other way?

She sank down on the divan, wringing her hands and looking helplessly about for a handkerchief. But she had none with her. She caught the flow of tears with the back of her hand, then simply covered her face with her hands.

That's how Juana found her.

"Lucie, what is the matter?" The housekeeper sat beside Lucie and put an arm about her heaving shoulders.

Lucie succumbed to the embrace and cried into the woman's shoulder. "Everything is so confusing."

"I saw Señor Carlton leave. Did he do something. . . ?"

"He wants to marry me."

"But you do not cry tears of happiness, do you?" cooed the housekeeper.

"Oh, Mama—I mean, Juana!"

"I wish your mama was here for you now, sweetheart." Juana gently stroked Lucie's hair.

"I do, too, but you are almost as good—I mean—oh, you know what I mean, don't you? I am so thankful for you, Juana!" Lucie sniffed but still could not stop the tears.

"There, there. Somehow we will work out your problems." Lucie felt Juana shrug. "I don't know how, but we will."

Lucie didn't know how either, and at the moment she had little hope that the solution would make her or anyone happy.

Twenty-Six

A FEW DAYS LATER Lucie was doing her chores in the stable. She'd always had her share of work to do on the ranch because neither she nor her father believed anything was gained by her learning to be a pampered belle. But since the trouble with Mexico, with all but a few of their hands going off to join the army, her labors had been more than a matter of principle. Neither Pete nor her father had permitted her to go beyond the immediate ranch compound during the worst of the trouble, so she, with the help of young Pedro, had almost complete responsibility for the stables. Though the trouble was over and the men had returned, she kept up most of her duties. She was still needed and, in truth, needed the distraction of work.

She was forking fresh hay into the stalls when Pedro called her. "Señorita Lucie, there is a stranger in the yard asking for you."

"A stranger? For me?" She straightened her back in time to see the object of her query appear at Pedro's back.

"I thought he wanted me to follow him," the man explained with an apologetic smile.

He was a tall, sturdily built man with pale hair and striking blue eyes. He appeared to be in his early forties. He was handsome and vaguely familiar, though Lucie was almost certain she'd never met him.

"I don't usually receive visitors in our stable," Lucie said. "Please excuse me."

Though the man was dressed simply in twill work trousers and a brown cotton shirt with a homemade leather coat, there was something rather formal in his bearing that made Lucie acutely aware of her coarse woolen work skirt and smudged muslin blouse. She had no doubt her face was smudged as well, and her hair had escaped the confines of her chignon and was trailing in her eyes. She brushed a strand away with her gloved hand, and then noticed the stained leather glove. She probably smelled like horses, too.

"Forgive me for coming unannounced," he said. His eyes, so blue, so vivid, emanated a warmth that immediately put her at ease. "Let me introduce myself. Benjamin Sinclair.".

"Oh my!" She couldn't help gaping. If she had ever imagined meeting Micah's father, she was certain she would have come face-to-face with a monster. This man was hardly that. But perhaps looks could be deceiving. Perhaps she was deluded by his now obvious striking similarities to Micah.

"I see you never expected your letter to prompt a personal visit."

"I . . . I don't know what I expected." Then remembering herself, she added, "I am pleased to meet you, Reverend Sinclair." She held out her hand, saw the glove, and quickly removed it.

He took her hand politely and bowed with a formality that conveyed at least one thing that set him apart from his son.

"I am very happy to meet you," he said.

His deep resonant voice was full of earnestness. She caught hints of Micah in the timbre of his voice, but Reverend Sinclair's was far more practiced and refined. He was either a born preacher, or he had spent much effort honing his voice to reflect that calling.

"And I you, Reverend." She meant her words, too, with all sincerity. No, she hadn't expected her letter would have brought the man himself to her doorstep, yet now she was pleased that this had been the result, if for no other reason than that his presence seemed to bring her closer to Micah. That is, she would be pleased if his visit didn't indicate something was wrong. "I must know, Reverend Sinclair, is . . . is Micah all right?"

"As far as I know, yes. I spoke with President Houston two days ago. I thought you might be interested in my news."

"I am!" She tried to subdue her relief, but it was difficult when she only now realized what a burden she had been carrying in her fear for Micah. She set the pitchfork she had been holding in her other hand against the wall, then removed her second glove, laying both on the ledge of the stall.

"Please, won't you come to the house," she said. "I'll fix something to drink. I'm sure you have had a long ride to get here."

"I'd like that," he said. "I am rather parched."

She led him to the house and bid him to settle in the parlor while she excused herself to get refreshments, to clean up a bit, and to see if her father felt up to joining them. Juana took care of refreshments while Lucie went to her room and quickly changed her clothes and repaired her unruly hair. Then she spoke to her father, who seemed to perk up more than usual when he heard about the visitor.

"Yes, I want to meet that man!" he said enthusiastically.

Lucie laid out his clothes for him, then left while he dressed. These days he usually only rose from his bed for meals, insisting that he'd rue the day when he had to eat in bed. Two or three times a week he'd go to his office to do paper work, and on rare occasions he would venture to the stables to check on his favorite horse and simply inhale what he felt was the best perfume around. He seldom received visitors—not that there had been many since the trouble with Mexico. He had reluctantly joined Lucie and Grant for dinner the other evening and just as reluctantly let go of his animosity to give Grant permission to court his daughter, and that only because Lucie didn't protest.

There was no reluctance now as he prepared to meet Reverend Sinclair. He was just as curious as Lucie had been.

Lucie was pouring tea for her guest when Reid came to the parlor. Lucie introduced the two men, and as they clasped hands, she noted how they appeared to size each other up, not in a hostile manner, but in the way of men gauging another's merits and faults. She couldn't tell for certain, but when they dropped hands, they both seemed satisfied with what they saw. At least they both relaxed and spoke in a friendly manner to each other.

"I hope your visit doesn't indicate bad tidings, Reverend Sinclair," Reid said as he took a seat in a chair opposite Benjamin.

"Not entirely," answered Benjamin. "I was able to set your daughter's mind at ease about that. I saw the official list of prisoners, and Micah's name was on it. However, Micah and the other prisoners aren't out of the woods yet, I'm afraid. They were initially marched to Matamoros, then to Monterrey. Now word has come that they are being marched once again to Saltillo, deeper into Mexico and further out of reach of help."

"Not that Texas can mount a rescue expedition anytime soon," Reid added.

"I am afraid not. President Houston is trying to use diplomatic channels. The United States and Britain have both made attempts to reason with Santa Anna."

"They can't keep them in prison forever, can they?" Lucie asked.

Reid and Reverend Sinclair exchanged looks. Lucie had seen such expressions often, though seldom from her father. They seemed to say, "This isn't a matter for feminine sensibilities." It must be ominous if even her father was reluctant to discuss it in her presence.

"What will they do with the prisoners?" she persisted.

"We must pray for their release," Reid said.

"I have been praying." Lucie didn't much like being put off, but she relented because she suddenly was afraid to know more.

"Then you are doing the best thing possible for Micah and the others," said Reverend Sinclair, who paused, though obviously he had more to say and was wondering how to proceed. After a few moments he spoke. "I want to say, Miss Maccallum, that I was most heartened when I received your letter. Over the years I have worried considerably about my son, so I was most pleased to see he had such a caring friend—a friend I now see is also a fine woman of faith. I want to thank you for reaching out to him."

Lucie's cheeks flushed but not so much at the compliment as because she knew her involvement with Micah went so much deeper than his father could imagine.

"Reverend Sinclair," she replied, "it was no difficulty at all for me to . . . befriend Micah. He's . . ." she paused, her cheeks heating even more. "He is a fine man. A good man. A . . . a . . ."

"Micah?" Benjamin's brow arched.

It suddenly struck Lucie that both father and son must have perceptions of each other completely differing from reality. Micah saw his father as an unbending fanatic, a hard, unfeeling monster, while Reverend Sinclair seemed to see his son as a bad seed, an amoral rebel. The irony of it made Lucie's heart ache for both of them.

Forgetting her previous embarrassment at her barely concealed feelings for Micah, Lucie lifted her eyes to meet the reverend's gaze. "Micah is a man with a tender heart, Reverend, a gentle soul. That's what I see, what I know is there despite how he tries to hide it under his swaggering, uncouth demeanor. Do you know he saved my life once? That is how we met. He was in the process of stealing my father's horses, but he risked his escape to safety in order to rescue me from attacking Comanches. He was always kind to me and gentle and honorable." She paused as a lump rose in her throat. And she was courting another because she'd lost her faith in him, perhaps even lost faith in the belief that God could and would claim him.

A long silence followed. The only sound was of the clock on the mantel ticking and Reid shifting in his chair. Lucie and Reverend Sinclair were both as still as a windless day. Lucie dropped her gaze to focus on the safer territory of her hands folded in her lap. She could not face Micah's father. She did not want to confront his denial of her words. She did not want to think he had given up on his son. As she had?

"Miss Maccallum," Benjamin said finally. "I can't ... that is ..."

Lucie could not help risking a look at the man. His expression was a confusion of emotions. The muscles of his jaw twitched along with his lips, helpless, it appeared, to form the words he wanted to say. He released a ragged sigh.

"Dear God! I always knew in my heart Micah could not be lost completely. But I ... I have seen Micah once in the six years since he left home, and that was only a few months ago when he was in jail—I believe it was for stealing your father's horses. Over the years I have heard things, distressing things. I could never know how deeply his unsavory actions went to his heart. I tried never to give up hope, but I could never *know*. I suppose in six years I should have made a more concerted effort to find him and bring him to his senses. But a large part of me was afraid to find him, afraid that my worst fears would be realized, that my son was beyond help. When he was home, he was filled with such anger. I just did not know if that anger had finally consumed him."

Benjamin stretched out his hands in front of him, gazing thoughtfully at his fingers. They were large hands, brown and work worn, with nails broken and perpetually stained with earth. They seemed to conflict with the refined formality of the man's bearing, just as the man himself conflicted with all Lucie had heard about him from Micah.

Shaking his head, Reverend Sinclair continued. "I am afraid part of me gave up on him. Oh, I prayed for him and hoped he would turn around, but I was too afraid to believe. Yet here you are, a mere friend, and you have faith in Micah—"

"Please, Reverend Sinclair, I..." Lucie forced herself to look into the man's eyes. "I gave up on him, too. Before he went to fight, I told him I could not see him again."

"But you saw to the core of him and found him to be a good person?"

"Yes, I did. I still do. I don't know what happened. I suppose I gave up on God as well."

Benjamin returned a sympathetic look. He seemed to know exactly how she felt.

"It must not have been easy for you to maintain a friendship with one of differing beliefs"—he gave a dry chuckle—"with little or no beliefs at all, if I have a clear perception of my son's spiritual values."

"I was uncertain if I should," Lucie said. "But I feel strongly that Micah has not completely abandoned God. It's just that—" she stopped. How could she tell the truth, that Micah's faith had been trampled by his own father?

Sinclair shook his head, a sad smile on his lips. "I know, Miss Maccallum. I know I destroyed my son's faith." The man's pain was palpable, despite the fact that Lucie sensed this was not a man to bear his inner soul to strangers. It spoke more than anything else about the true nature of this man, Micah's father.

"I'm so sorry," Lucie said gently.

"As am I."

Reid shifted once again in his chair. Sensing he wished to speak, Lucie turned toward him.

"I, too, have had difficulty with my son," Reid said, catching Benjamin's gaze and holding it. "Fathers and sons are such strange animals. Fathers tend to invest their hearts and souls in their sons, perhaps more so than with daughters, because they feel so much more is required of them. Sons, for their part, want to worship their fathers. Both are doomed to fail in attaining the other's expectations. Accepting or laying blame is pretty futile in such a situation. It helps neither party." He paused and took a breath.

Lucie could tell such a long speech was taxing him. But he continued.

"I have come to believe it is the heart of a man that matters. Certainly it is only the heart that God himself sees. How many times do we want only good for our children, and yet our actions to achieve this blow up in our faces like a touchy musket? And the worst of it is that our children are the last to credit our good intentions."

"My father used to tell me, 'Boy, the road to nowhere is paved with good intentions,'" Benjamin said.

"Ah yes..." Reid smiled. "But the road to perdition is paved with evil intentions. I would choose the former. And I would keep hoping that one of those good intentions would get me on a path to *somewhere*. Life, and especially child rearing, is essentially a guessing game. Just when you think you have the rules figured out, they change, or your children change on you. If we do the best we can, how can we do more?"

"I only wish I would have known these things when my son was young," Benjamin said. "Unfortunately, I made rules for my children and my family, and the rules were like iron—no bending at all. Of course, something had to break if the rules would not. What broke was my son's heart, his spirit, I suppose. He has every right to resent me, even if I have changed now." Pausing, he glanced back and forth between Reid and Lucie. "I do not expect I will be the one to reach my son. Yet my faith has been greatly renewed by you folks. God has clearly shown that He is faithful to my prayers and to my son. He has brought you good people into Micah's life, and that restores my hope."

Lucie smiled. "My hope has also been restored, Reverend—by

you! From all Micah has told me of you, I fully expected to meet a ... uh ..."

"A monster, Miss Maccallum?" Benjamin's tone revealed a hint of wry amusement.

Lucie's smile relaxed. "Yes, if you'll forgive me for thinking such a thing. But I find that is not true at all. I doubt it ever was, even if you might have been a strict parent. I know now you always loved Micah, though he might not have perceived it. And because of that, I know with more certainty than ever that there is indeed hope for Micah."

An hour later while Reverend Sinclair was washing up, Lucie went to the kitchen to help with supper preparations. Sinclair would sup with them and bide the night at Reid's invitation. As Lucie cut up vegetables for Juana's delectable rosemary stew, she felt absolutely buoyant. As never before, she had an assurance that Micah would be all right, spiritually at least. With a man like Benjamin Sinclair for a father and with friends like her and her father, Micah must eventually come to see the love of God.

There was still much uncertainty about her own relationship with Micah. But she knew she could not give up quite yet. How she would break the news to Grant, she did not know. But she did know she would not marry him now or ever. The visit with Reverend Sinclair had helped her understand her own father a bit better, and Lucie was now sure he would never ask or expect her to make such a sacrifice.

Still, Micah's captivity created a pall over Lucie's renewed spirit. Anything could happen to him in Mexico. Reverend Sinclair had not said as much, but Lucie had heard rumors that Santa Anna wanted to execute all the prisoners. That could not happen. She would not accept the possibility. God had plans for Micah. She knew it. Plans that did not include an early death in a Mexican prison.

Twenty-Seven

THE LAND BETWEEN Saltillo and the Rio Grande was a desert so barren, so desolate, it might have been forsaken by God as well as man.

The captives had known that much, but none had ever traversed it, so they imagined it could not be any worse than other deserts they had seen. At any rate, they had chosen to risk the unknown rather than suffer further at the hands of their Mexican captors. When the opportunity for escape had arisen, they had taken it. That chance had come in the spring of 1843 when they were to be moved from Monterey to Saltillo. They managed to overpower their guards on the road, capture some weapons and ammunition stores, and make a break. They had lost five men in the process, and only God knew how many more they would lose before they set eyes upon Texas again.

Jed stumbled over a rock and crumbled to his knees. Instead of pulling himself back up, he just sat on the dry, crusted ground, letting his head drop into his hands.

"That's it for me," he mumbled thickly.

Micah shuffled to a stop beside him. "What you talking about?" he said a bit gruffly, but who could tell with his throat parched and raw and his tongue so thick he could not keep his mouth shut.

"I tell ya, I ain't moving. I've had it!"

Micah sank down beside him. "All right, you said we're sticking together, so guess I've had it, too."

"Get out of here! I don't know how ya do it, but you got miles left in you."

Micah shook his head. "What difference does it make if I die here or in a couple of miles?"

They had already spent days in this desert. They had abandoned the road, hoping to elude pursuit, but had become hopelessly lost instead. No one had any idea, not even Big Foot, how far it was to the Rio Grande. They had no food and had long since tossed aside their weapons to spare the weight, so they couldn't hunt, not that they'd have the strength to do so anyway. They had tried eating insects and snakes when they could be caught with their knives. But there had been no way to cook anything. Micah had become violently ill trying to choke down a grasshopper.

There hadn't been a watering hole in two days, and the last one, if the moist hole in the ground could be called that, had provided enough only for the men to dampen their tongues. Some had tried drinking their own urine, but the results had been disastrous. Several men had been lost thus far on the desperate trek. There were now fewer than two hundred prisoners left. A look at the ragged line of stumbling men stretching out over the desert said there would be fewer than that by tomorrow.

"You gotta keep going, Micah," Jed was saying. "You got your gal waiting for you back home."

"I ain't got no gal," Micah insisted with as much force as he could muster. "Lucie and I . . . well, she ain't my gal, that's all. But don't you have no reason to live, Jed?"

Jed shrugged. "Sometimes . . . I don't know . . . I get tired of it all."

Suddenly he looked old and even wise, not at all like the boy Micah knew.

"Sometimes I get a strong hankering to see my ma and pa again."

Some of the other men had come up and dropped to the ground as well, this seeming as good a time as any to take a rest.

"There you go," Bill McBroome said. "You got your folks to go home to." McBroome was faring better than many of the men. He'd lived on insects and wet dirt before, years ago when he'd been a captive of the Comanches. He'd survived once before and knew he could again.

"Jed's parents are dead," Micah said.

"Oh, didn't know that," McBroome said.

"Guess I'd have to go to heaven to be with them."

"That what you want, Jed?" Micah asked.

"No, but I don't want to get up neither!" Jed took off his hat and wiped a hand across his face. He was so dehydrated he was no longer even sweating. "I might if I had a pretty gal like Miss Lucie to get to."

"Who is this Lucie?" Big Foot asked.

"Micah's gal."

"No, she ain't," Micah said.

"Tell us about her, Micah," Big Foot said.

Micah would have refused because the last thing he wanted to think of then was Lucie Maccallum and all he'd never have with her. Even if he made it back to Texas, she would never be his. Why, he wouldn't be surprised if by now she was married off to that Grant Carlton. But as he looked around at his companions, he realized they needed to be reminded of home. They needed to be reminded about why they were suffering so to get back.

"She's the prettiest gal there ever was," Micah began. He closed his eyes, and it wasn't hard at all to conjure an image of the sweet and beautiful Lucie Maccallum. He almost thought he caught a whiff of rosewater instead of the stink of filthy men. "She's got hair like black silk caught on fire—"

"Silk caught on fire?" questioned McBroome. "That don't sound pleasant at all."

Jed amended, "That's his way of saying her hair is dark, nearly black, but with lots of red in it."

Micah rolled his eyes. "You want me to tell y'all about her? Or maybe you could do a better job of telling me."

"You're doing a fine job," encouraged Big Foot. "Go on."

"Well, there ain't much more to tell. She's just pretty, that's all. And sweet. And when she laughs . . ." Micah's chest clenched as the memories were released. He should never have gotten started. "Hey, Charlie," he said to one of the other men, "you got a sweetheart, don't ya? Tell about her."

Dreamily, Charlie complied. "She's pretty, too, of course. 'Cept her hair's yella', like gold. No fire, just shining gold. . . ."

Soon everyone was telling about someone special back home,

and in a half hour they all found the strength to rise to their feet and trod on.

Into the heat, into the blinding sun, into the stinging wind. They ate sand and grit when they longed for an apple pie baked by a sweet woman of their dreams. They swallowed thick saliva when their mouths ached for a cup of springwater from a slim, smooth hand.

Time slipped away until even the rising and setting of the sun meant little to them. When the Mexican army finally caught up with them, they could not have fought them even if they'd had weapons. As it was, some considered it more rescue than capture.

———

Santa Anna had enough of his own problems just trying to stay in power, without dealing with those pesky Texans. He was fed up with them and prepared to execute the lot of the prisoners. But when the ministers from both America and Britain learned of his decree, they raised such a protest that Santa Anna had to back down. He could never win a war against both Britain and America.

Instead, the Mexican president decided to deal with the prisoners in the Latino way. Every tenth one would be shot, to be decided by a simple lottery. The commander of the prison would place one hundred fifty-nine white beans and seventeen black beans, representing the number of the remaining prisoners, into a jar. Each prisoner would then draw a bean. Those drawing a black bean would die.

Word of the decision reached the prisoners, causing varying degrees of dismay, disbelief, and anger. But practical men that they were, they realized seventeen dead was far better than nearly two hundred. So they awaited their fate with stoicism mixed with enough fear to prove they were only human.

Micah was certain he would draw a black bean. He'd cheated death too many times lately to have any confidence he'd do so again. He was scared of the prospect, to be sure, but there was also a kind of comfort in his certainty about his fate.

A few sheets of paper were passed among the men along with a pen and ink. Those who could write were permitted to leave notes.

Micah took some paper, and when he had a turn at the pen, he chewed on the tip and wondered what he would write. But what perplexed him more was who he would write to. He thought of Lucie, but there seemed no sense in that. They'd made a break. It was over. Best for her if it stayed that way.

He thought of writing to his father or, if not him, perhaps his stepmother or his sisters and brother. Oddly enough, the thought of writing, even to his father, did not bother him as much as it should. Perhaps the desert had burned some of the hatred from him. Perhaps the nearness of death was making him more pragmatic. Or maybe, just maybe, his problems with his father had been to some extent his own fault. At the very least, it might well be that Benjamin Sinclair was as much a victim of circumstance as anyone. The man had made some mistakes, some very serious ones, but then, hadn't everyone made mistakes? In the last months, Micah had seen more clearly than ever how easy it was to blunder even with the best intentions.

This revelation came as an enormous surprise to Micah. Until just a few moments before he would have been certain his hatred for the man was fully entrenched in his heart. Now he didn't know what to think. He dipped the pen in the ink jar, then set the tip to the paper.

Dear Pa, he wrote. *I guess I'm finally gonna die. Don't figure it would do any good to go to my grave filled with hate....* The pen paused. He tried to write the words "I forgive you," but simply could not make his hand do it. It was one thing not to hate but something else entirely to put it all behind you by forgiveness. He knew about forgiveness, and he knew what his father's perception was of forgiveness. It was an act of sublime acceptance, and Micah could not do it.

Perturbed with himself, he drew an *X* through the words. He thought a moment, then decided upon another, far easier and more comfortable, path.

To Whom It May Concern,
    I have some land coming to me from my service at San Jacinto and from an inheritance left to me by my Uncle Haden Sinclair. I hereby will all that land to one Jed Wilkes. He's a mite slow in the

brain, but I know he will do right by the land. Anyhow, since I have served the Republic of Texas honorably and am now about to give my life for Texas, I figure you are bound to follow my last wish.

He signed the letter and got two men who could write to witness it, then he turned to Jed, who was curled up on the ground in their crowded cell trying to sleep.

"Hey, Jed." He gave his friend's arm a push.

Jed grunted and rolled over. "Micah? I was dreaming. I saw my ma. I was powerful happy to see her." He gave his body a stretch. "What'd you want?"

"I want to give you my last will and testament."

"Huh? You want to give me a test? Aw, Micah, you know I ain't good with schooling. Can't read or write. You know that."

"No, Jed." Micah thrust the paper at his friend. "This is my will. It says what to do with my possessions after I die—"

"What you talking 'bout?" Jed sat up and became fully alert. "You ain't gonna die."

"How can you say that? Seventeen of us are going to die tomorrow. I am certain I'll be one of them. I got a premonition."

"A prema—what?"

"Never mind," Micah said impatiently. "This paper says you are to get my land allotments. Put it in your pocket and keep it safe. I won't be around to take care of you no more, Jed. It will be important for you to have this land so's you can make a living. You can't go back to stealing and such, or even rangering."

"I can't be no farmer. I don't know nothing about it."

"You can, Jed. I know you can. I know lots of men without learning who make good farmers. You gotta take this land and make a life for yourself." Micah stuffed the paper into Jed's pocket. "Maybe Tom will help you. I had the feeling when we last saw him that he was ready to settle down."

"Maybe you should give the land to him."

"I want you to have it."

Tom had land, and if not, he had the wits to fend for himself. Jed would need all the help he could get. Even with the land, Micah was afraid of what would become of Jed when he was left all alone.

He couldn't do anything about it now. He hoped the land would be enough. It would sure do more good than some lame letter to his father with foolish words of forgiveness.

The next morning the prisoners were gathered in the courtyard of the prison. Each man stepped forward and dipped into the jar. Bill McBroome drew the first black bean. A grim smirk twisted his lips as he defiantly flicked the damning bean in the direction of the commander.

As Big Foot's turn came he commented to Micah and Jed, who would draw after him, "Them black beans are on top, so dig deep." He drew a white bean.

Micah's turn came and he hardly gave it a thought as he thrust his hand into the jar. He didn't even look at the bean he drew but simply headed to where the unlucky black bean holders had gathered.

"Look at what you got!" Big Foot yelled.

Micah glanced at his hand and was shocked to see he held a white bean. He wanted to whoop but didn't because there were still men who were going to die that day.

Jed came next. He dipped into the jar. Micah watched casually. Then he felt as if the hard earth of the prison yard had been suddenly yanked out from under him. His knees trembled, but he remained on his feet. He rubbed his eyes, but that did not change what he saw. Jed drew a black bean. Jed was no less shocked as he glanced at his death warrant. He looked at Micah beseeching, as if asking his friend to get him out of this mess. Micah wanted to run forward and exchange beans with his friend. He would have, too. He made the move, but Big Foot's big hand stopped him.

"Micah, they won't allow it," the ranger said, as if reading Micah's thoughts.

"They can't! He—"

"He took his chances with the rest of us. He's smarter than we give him credit for."

"But ... but ..." How could Micah make them understand? It was supposed to be him. He was supposed to die that day, not Jed. What had gone wrong?

"You let him die like a man," Big Foot said. "That's all you can do for him now."

Micah thought of the worthless paper in Jed's pocket, his lame attempt to help his friend. But Micah had been so preoccupied with himself, his stupid fears, he had not even thought to give Jed a chance to talk about his own fears. What had Jed been going through last night? What was he going through now? Micah would never know. He opened his hand and looked disdainfully at the white bean still clutched in his fist. He dropped it to the ground and smashed it with the heel of his boot.

"Jed . . . I'm sorry . . . I . . . can't help you," he intoned miserably.

"It's all right, Micah," Jed said, the shock beginning to clear from his face. "You done good by me, Micah. I wouldn't have made it this long without you." His lip trembled a little, but he bit down on it firmly.

Bill McBroome stepped from the growing group of doomed men. He put an arm around Jed and nudged him into the group. "Jed, you are gonna see your ma and pa soon."

Jed visibly brightened. "That's right! Ya hear that, Micah? It's what I been wanting. Remember? I dreamed it. Don't worry 'bout me no more. My ma will look after me now."

If Micah had not been forced to watch the executions, he probably would have hid in his cell, burrowing into the deepest, darkest corner he could find. That is exactly what he did afterward—figuratively, since it was not always possible to do so literally. For weeks he retreated within himself, becoming dark and glum. And the nightmares he thought he had finally escaped returned in full force. There was not a night that passed undisturbed by visions of death and violence.

PART THREE

---✦---

Spring 1844

Twenty-Eight

IT HAD BEEN A long trail from Mexico City. A hungry trail, a thirsty trail, a lonely trail.

Most of the time Micah wondered if he'd ever see Texas again. Sometimes he thought it might be best if he never went back. Too much water under the bridge, as it's said. Life had been too hard and grim in the last year since his capture. The filth and privations of prison, the struggle to survive were enough to change any man. Add to that the last couple of months since he and a handful of others had finally made good an escape.

This time they had hoped to increase their chances of getting home by splitting up. But it had been hard going trekking alone on foot through wild lands where, if there were people, he was the enemy. And because he was a fugitive, he often had to hide from danger or fight his way from place to place.

He didn't make directly for home because at first he hadn't been certain if he wanted to return to Texas at all. He had nothing there, nothing but failure and sour memories. So Micah wandered aimlessly about the Mexican countryside, and if he appeared to be heading north, it was only unconsciously, until finally the loneliness became more crushing than his fears about home. Tom was there, and the rangers. They had been like a family to him and could be again. They would accept what he had become. Many of them had suffered similarly.

Funny, though, when he thought of going home and what he would do there, it never occurred to him to return to his former life of crime. Well, the idea might have flickered across his mind briefly, but he'd never risk seeing the inside of a prison again if he could help it.

Yet even with a purpose, it was difficult getting to the Rio

Grande. He had no money and no weapons, except a knife he had stolen along the way. If he had to justify that act, he reminded himself that he was in enemy territory, and anything he took to survive was merely contraband. He became quite adept at stalking animals and killing them with only a knife. He also had been without a horse for much of the time. Only in Laredo was he accepted enough to be able to find a steady job sweeping and cleaning up in a cantina. He stayed only until he had earned enough to buy a few supplies. He got some clothes, used but in far better shape than the rags he'd been wearing since prison. They were mostly Mexican, including a sombrero and a striped serape. But more importantly he was able to purchase a cheap pistol and a mount and tack.

Micah let a bitter smile slip across his brown weathered face. It wasn't rightly a horse he ended up with, but rather a mule, and a poor excuse for one at that. He was the color of the blasted desert earth, and Micah called the beast Stew, because once when the animal was being particularly obstinate, Micah had yelled, "You mangy, no-good churn-head. Ya ain't good for nothing but a pot of stew!"

It indicated the extremity of Micah's solitary condition when he began to converse with Stew often and even started to take a liking to the creature. At least when he didn't want to kill the mule. Micah figured they deserved each other, and if there was a God, He was surely feeling mighty pleased at the circumstances.

The blast of a gunshot interrupted Micah's thoughts. Instinct alone made him dig his heels into Stew's flanks. He forgot about the tender place in Stew's stomach where the beast had once, before Micah's ownership, been mauled by a cougar. The crazy animal reared, and Micah fought to get him under control as another shot split the air several feet away. If he could get to some cover, he could dismount and make use of his pistol. But the land surrounding him was pretty open, tall grass and nary a tree in sight. As the mule sprang into a very reluctant gallop, Micah ventured a quick glance back. There were three riders, and they appeared to be gringos. They might be rangers, but why would they be shooting at him without cause? Then he remembered his appearance. If they were looking for banditos, he certainly looked the part.

"Hah, Stew!" he yelled over the heavy beating of the mule's hooves. Though the animal was stubborn and mean spirited at times, he could be fast when he wanted, and with shots blasting in his ears, he definitely wanted to now!

Micah led a good chase. He broadened the distance between himself and his pursuers so that they no longer took shots at him. A dry riverbed spread out before him, and he scrambled down its moderately steep bank. He quickly jumped from the mule and took up a position near some rocks, the only cover to be found. When the riders crested the rise, he fired over their heads.

He'd chosen his spot well for making his stand, because the lowering sun was in the pursuers' eyes at the top of the bank, and by the time they oriented themselves as to the direction of the shot, Micah had reloaded. As he took aim, he got a better look at the three riders.

"My pistol's aimed right for your heart, Tom Fife!" Micah shouted. "I sure don't want to kill you the first time I seen you in over a year."

"Mercy me! I sure recognize that voice," Tom said.

"It's me, you dunderhead! Micah Sinclair. Promise ya won't shoot, and I'll give ya a look."

"Go ahead," agreed Tom.

Cautiously Micah stepped out into the open, flicking off his sombrero as he did so. Tom's grin made him drop all further cautions. He strode up to the three. Jack Hays and Ben McCulloch were riding with Tom. They all dismounted. Tom crushed Micah into a breath-stealing bear hug. The others slapped his shoulder until he was sure he'd be bruised. But if he'd had doubts before about returning home, they were gone now. He did indeed have friends.

"What you doing traipsing around looking like a bandito?" Tom asked.

"Don't be too hard on him," Hays said. "If he was a bandito, we'd be done for now. I'm glad to see prison hasn't dulled your edge, Micah."

"I got plenty of edges. And as for the clothes, I had to take what I could get."

"You coming back to San Antonio?" Tom asked.

"That was in my mind."

"Well, we can use you," said Ben. He glanced at Hays. "That right, Jack?"

"No doubt about it," Hays concurred. "Say, I think we have earned a bit of a rest. Let's sit a spell and talk."

There were cottonwoods on the other side of the riverbed that provided some shade, so the men let their horses graze while they sat beneath the boughs of the trees. Stew wandered back and joined the horses.

The men broke out jerked venison and hardtack from their packs, sharing what they had with Micah, whose supplies had run low since Laredo. As they ate, Micah related briefly about his escape and trek across Mexico. He omitted much detail, and the others seemed to understand because they asked few questions. On the other hand, he freely quizzed them on their activities in the last year, and they were just as free to talk.

"Had quite a time keeping the rangers together all year," Hays said. "Funds, as usual, were low. Sometimes there was as few as fifteen of us to patrol the entire Nueces–Rio Grande region. As much as Houston wants to make the borders safe from raids by Mexicans, he also wants to keep a lid on us raiding them. He wants peace so as to help his efforts to join up with the United States."

"Things did quiet down a mite last year," Tom said. "A few Indian raids and some harassing by banditos, but it could've been worse. The final two months of last year we were out of action completely."

"Jack even took a vacation," McCulloch said.

"He went a-courting, is what he did!" Tom added with a grin.

Steely-eyed Jack Hays, "Devil Jack" as the Comanches called him, looked about as close to blushing as he ever would. "Well, a man's got a right to a vacation once in a while, now, don't he?" he sputtered gruffly to hide his embarrassment.

Everyone laughed, even Jack. And Micah realized what these men meant to him. He was laughing, really laughing, for the first time in a year. He was truly with amigos, and he had forgotten what that meant.

When the joke had played itself out, Micah asked, "Well, since you are out on patrol again, are things better?"

"In February Congress authorized the formation of another ranger company," Hays said.

"And for the first time ever, they did it right!" added Tom. "They specifically designated Jack to be the commander, not that we wouldn't have voted for him anyway, but they finally are giving credit where credit is due. We voted for Ben here to be lieutenant. They allowed for forty rangers in the company. We up to that yet, Jack?"

"Nearly, but we got room for you, Micah."

"Count me in, Captain. I'd be honored to serve." In one sense Micah was growing tired of fighting and violence, but stronger than this was the sense that he didn't know what he'd do without the rangers right now. He needed them, if only because he had nothing else to turn to.

"Pay's fairly regular, too. Thirty dollars a month, paid every two months." Hays glanced at the grazing horses. "Looks like you got a good mount."

Micah shrugged. "He's learning, if mules *can* learn. But he did outrun you fellows." Then he remembered another important piece of equipment he was lacking. "I only got this here beat-up old flint-lock pistol."

"We'll fix you up," Hays said.

"We have finally been issued Colt revolvers," Tom said with a gleam of delight in his squinty eyes. "I know it don't matter much to a crack shot like you, Micah, but for the rest of us, them revolvers are pure heaven."

The men talked for a few more minutes, then mounted up. After three hours they joined up with the rest of the company, then Hays told Micah to go on back to San Antonio so he could get his equipment squared away before officially joining the company. Tom was to go with him.

It was a two-day ride back to town. Neither he nor Tom were great talkers, but it was hard to avoid all conversation. Not that Micah wanted to, but he knew that with Tom alone, talk might get more personal. He was right.

"I still can't believe it about Jed," Tom said as they rode the next morning. "It was hard on you, wasn't it, Micah?"

"It was a heck of a lot harder on him," Micah said glibly.

"You know what I mean. You two was close, like brothers."

Micah nodded. His chest tightened. He still could not think about Jed without deep emotion, much less talk about him.

"I liked that boy, annoying laugh, slow wits, and all!" Tom said. "Wish there was some way to make them Mexicans pay."

"I reckon it won't bring Jed or the others back."

Tom's brow arched. "Don't sound like you, Micah." He peered more closely at his friend. "You've changed some, haven't you?"

Micah sighed heavily. "I guess I have, but mostly ... I don't know ... mostly I'm just too tired to hate right now. Maybe later it'll come back to me."

"Maybe it won't, and that'd be good. The hate was eating you up."

Micah thought of the last person who had expressed a similar sentiment to him. It wasn't the first time this past year he had thought of her, though he had tried mighty hard not to. But Lucie Maccallum had always been the sweetest, most pure thing in his life, and it had been especially true in the last year. Thinking of her had been both agony and delight. Sometimes he had needed delight so badly he had been willing to risk pain and agony to find it.

"So, Tom ..." he tried to sound casual, but he could think of no way to broach the subject that was on his heart in an offhand or casual way. "You ever catch that Joaquin Viegas?"

Tom gave Micah a skeptical glance, then a slow smile inched across his whiskered face. "No, but it was him we was chasing yesterday when we ran into you. But I don't reckon you want to know about him as much as about his sister."

Micah shrugged. "How is she?"

"Last I heard she is fine. Her pa is still ailing, hardly leaves his bed is what I've heard."

"He's no doubt glad she is securely married."

"Married? Where you hear that?"

Micah took off his hat and wiped a sleeve across his sweaty

brow. "I assumed she would have married that young Carlton fellow by now."

"Ha!" Tom spit into the dirt. "She'd have nothing to do with him. Why, it was his pa that fired up the ranchers against them after the invasion."

"That so?" Micah tried not to think anything of this news, yet his thumping heart betrayed him. Lucie was free! But he harshly reminded himself that free or not, they had said good-bye over a year ago, and for very good reasons—reasons that he clearly knew had not changed. He was wilder than ever and far less fit for a woman like that.

"You ought to go see her," Tom said.

Micah almost laughed at that. "Look at me, Tom! You said I'd changed, and I have, but not all for the good—very little, in fact. I've got scars inside me that a gal like that just should never have to look at."

"I'll bet that gal has a real knack at fixing wounds and such."

"Not mine. They're too deep. I'm just too far gone and wild."

The conversation waned, much to Micah's relief, as they came to a stream and had to concentrate on crossing it. The water was deep with spring runoff, and Stew was in no mind for a swim that day. A distaste for water was another of the critter's faults and now he fairly screeched to a stop and refused to move. Finally Micah was forced to blindfold the creature before he'd test the water. Once they reached the other side, as the sun beat down upon their wet bodies, warming and drying them, Tom spoke again.

"Micah, you don't know much about women," he said as he removed his bandanna and squeezed the water from it.

"And I suppose you are gonna teach me? You, who's been a confirmed bachelor all your life!"

"I know a sight more'n you give me credit for! I know that women were made for taming men. It is the natural way of things. The men come west to fight, to hunt, to raise Cain. And the women come with the cookstoves and the china and the pretty calico to make curtains on the log cabin windows. And we're glad they do, too, even if we complain about getting tied down, because down deep, part of us wants peace as much as them. We want it, but we only know the way of violence to get it unless the womenfolk show us another way. Oh, I reckon it ain't as simple as all that 'cause I ain't one of them philosophers. But it is still the basic truth that women want to tame men, and men want to be tamed—by women at least."

Micah looked away, but there was only grass ahead, and it was a poor distraction.

"I don't know, Tom," he said finally.

"If I could find a woman that'd have me, I'd jump at it." Tom looked ahead as well, but there was a dreamy quality to his voice. "Yes . . . I wouldn't mind it at all. A by-the-hearth kind of life. Do a little farming, raise a few young'uns."

"Ain't you too old to have kids, Tom?" Micah asked in an attempt to redirect the conversation.

"That ain't the point!" Tom answered crisply, not to be deterred.

"I know . . ."

"You won't regret letting her tame you, Micah."

"I know, but I'm afraid she'd regret trying."

Twenty-Nine

"YOU GO BACK for the others. I'll keep on the trail." Micah gazed ahead. There was no sign of riders, but they could not have passed that way more than a couple of hours ago.

"There's a half dozen of them," Tom said. "Ain't worth the risk. Besides"—Tom peered up into the darkening sky—"there's a storm coming. We don't want to get caught in it."

"The storm's a long way off," Micah countered. "And Viegas could be one of them bandits. It's worth the risk."

Micah had been back at the job a couple of weeks and was now on patrol tracking the banditos responsible for raiding a couple of ranches. An hour ago, Tom and Micah had picked up the trail of two riders. They were definitely not Indian, and by the look of the tracks, could well be Mexican. These tracks were the first bit of luck any of the rangers had come across. Now those tracks had met up with several more. There was no way Micah intended to lose them.

"All right," Tom said, "you go back. I'll keep—"

"Uh-uh!" Micah said firmly. "I saw the tracks first. You know my eyes are better than yours, and I got a better chance of sticking with them."

"But it's me giving the orders!"

Micah glanced up at the sky. The sun, when clouds weren't obscuring it, was directly overhead. The day was slipping away. "Be reasonable, Tom. I am the better tracker."

"I taught you all you know."

"Then you know I am good."

Tom cursed under his breath. "I knew I'd regret taking you in."

"Let's get moving. Time's a-wasting."

"You leave clear sign of where you're heading."

"I will. I will!"

Micah watched Tom turn around and head back in the direction from which they had come, then he urged his mount forward.

An hour later, he felt he was gaining on the bandits. The tracks
were fresher, but he still saw no riders, which was just as well because neither did he wish to be seen by them. He just hoped Tom
and the others caught up to him soon, or he'd have to give up the
chase. The wind was steadily increasing, and Stew was getting restive. The temperature was dropping so Micah took his buckskin
coat from his saddlebag and slipped it on.

He wondered if it was Viegas's gang he was following. What
would he do if he caught up with the outlaw, Lucie's brother? He
had no doubt Viegas would rather die than be caught, and Micah
also had little doubt that he himself would kill the man if given
cause. He hoped he wasn't placed in such a position, but Viegas
was the enemy, and he, as much as any Mexican national, was responsible for Jed's death.

No, he'd have no qualms about killing Lucie's brother. But
then, it shouldn't matter where he and Lucie were concerned because there was no "he and Lucie." Why he kept thinking of her he
didn't know. It wasn't healthy, that was for sure, not the way his
guts twisted every time thoughts of her came into his mind.

Squinting ahead, he forced his mind back to business. He
thought he spotted a small stirring of dust. Maybe it was just the
wind, or maybe he was getting too close to his quarry. Then he felt
a prickly sensation on the back of his neck. He jerked his head
around. Small black spots on the horizon behind him were definitely approaching riders. Could they be the rangers? The cloud of
dust surrounding them indicated they were gaining fast on Micah.
There were three riders. The mounts did not look familiar. Tom's
gray was definitely not among them. In another couple of minutes
they would be within rifle range.

"Hah, Stew!" Micah slapped the mule's flanks with his reins.
The mule skittered, then started at a reluctant trot. "Hah, you stupid beast!" Micah yelled. This time he purposefully dug his heels
into Stew's middle, knowing it always made the mule mad and
probably hurt like the dickens, but sometimes it was the only way
to get him moving. Stew skittered again, bucked a little, snorted,

then shot into motion. Micah made no apology to his less-than-faithful mount, for just then the riders started shooting. The shots made on horseback were not very accurate, but they were close enough to worry Micah.

In the flurry of his escape, Micah forgot about that cloud of dust he'd seen in front of him earlier. But now his error was deadly plain. The cloud was three more riders coming right at him. He thought of his bravado with Tom before. A better tracker! Ha! The banditos had no doubt spotted him an hour ago, then split up to catch him in a trap. And he had accommodated them beautifully.

His only chance now was to surrender and hope they were more interested in taking a prisoner than in killing one. That at least would give him time to think of another way out of this mess or give the other rangers a chance to catch up to him. He reined in Stew, then tossed his rifle to the ground and thrust his hands high into the air. Then he waited for the inevitable slug of lead to his heart.

Though he hoped to be spared, he was no less shocked when the bandits rode up to him and did not shoot.

"Your other weapons," one of the bandits ordered.

There were six banditos, all with weapons trained on Micah. He quickly obeyed the order, tossing down his brace of pistols and, with just a slight hesitation, also throwing down his new Colt .44 revolver. He had only had the weapon for a week, and he had come to like it a lot. He doubted Hays would issue him another one soon.

"The Bowie knife, too, eh?" said the bandit.

Micah complied. He was now completely disarmed except for the small knife he kept in his boot, not that it would do him any good in this situation. It was as he dropped the Bowie knife that he saw the rattler coiled up near a rock. Its head was raised as it contemplated this disturbance of its afternoon nap. Micah's captors had not seen the snake, and Micah wondered how he could use it to his advantage.

"So ... I think we have found ourselves a ranger," the bandit said.

Micah said nothing.

Another bandit spoke in Spanish, "Gustavo, he must have *compadres* close. Kill him and let's go."

Micah had learned enough Spanish in Mexico to understand what was said.

The one called Gustavo said in English to Micah, "Where are the other rangers? You surely did not come after us all alone."

Again in Spanish the second bandit said, "I know this one. He is dangerous. We must kill him."

Micah knew his time was running out. Yet any escape he could think of would be suicidal. Still, even a futile attempt would be better than being gunned down like a sitting duck. Then it occurred to him how he could use the rattler. Ornery as his mule was, Micah didn't like endangering Stew, yet there seemed no other way.

Surreptitiously Micah pressed his heel into the tender place on the mule's midriff, not hard, but enough to cause discomfort. The mule, already nervous, snorted and skittered. Micah, appearing to rein him, instead edged him closer to the snake.

"Keep that mule under control," ordered Gustavo. Then to one of the other bandits he added, "Rodrigo, get those weapons and tie his hands."

The rattler, now in the mule's line of sight, moved. Stew saw and reacted predictably. He neighed shrilly and gave a panicked buck, encouraged by another prodigious jab in the stomach by Micah. Stew reared, causing a frenzied chain of events.

Rodrigo's mount, which was closest to Micah, was spooked either by Stew's behavior or by the snake. It also reared, and Rodrigo, who had been in the process of dismounting, spilled to the ground with a sickening thud. He lay still on the ground, but Micah could not pause to wonder about him. Micah could barely keep Stew under control as the rattler lurched. When he was thrown from the mule, it was only partly by design, however, he hit the ground fully prepared and made sure he rolled toward his discarded weapons.

"The ranger!" someone yelled.

By now all the horses were spooked, and their riders were having their own problems keeping them under control. One—Micah hoped it wasn't Stew—screamed as only a panicked horse can, and Micah was almost certain it must have been struck by the rattler.

But he did not let himself dwell on this either. His full concentration was on the pile of weapons. His hand grasped one as a gunshot zinged past his ear. He rolled to the left toward the only cover he could find, a rock no larger than a tree stump. Flattening out behind it, he took quick aim and fired. A yell told him he had hit his mark before he saw the dead bandit with his own eyes.

Another slug whizzed over Micah's head, taking off his hat. He fired again, thankful his desperate plunge into the pile of weapons had been rewarded with the Colt. It had been fully loaded. His second shot took down another bandit. He had three shots left and there were three bandits remaining, not counting the one who had been thrown from his horse and was still unconscious. All Micah's spare ammunition and his powder horn were in his saddlebag, but even if he could have reached it, Stew had bolted.

The bandits had dismounted and taken cover behind the fallen horse, which must have been injured by snakebite or some other cause. The bandits might have made an attempt to ride off, even though they risked getting shot down in the attempt. They probably figured they had a better chance in a standoff. The odds were in their favor. He was only one man with three shots. But he had already killed two of them and caused another to be injured. This was his first real gunfight since coming back from Mexico. His first chance to avenge Jed and the others.

Another shot from the bandits grazed Micah's rock, sending a stinging spray of rock fragments into his face. Eyes burning, he fired back, but the shot only struck the dead horse. He cursed his foolishness. He couldn't afford any wild shots. Patience. And for the first time in a long time, he thought of when his Uncle Haden had taught him to shoot.

"Patience, boy, is the first and most important rule," he'd said often. "And always take time to sight your target."

Micah took a steadying breath and waited. There were three bandits behind that horse, and one was going to make a mistake sooner or later, hopefully before Micah did so himself.

"Listen to me, hombre," said the bandit called Gustavo, "you have two shots left. You don't have a chance. Give up."

"So you can kill me?"

"I would take you to see *mi jefe*. Perhaps he'll make a deal with you—information for your life, eh?"

"I'll take my chances with my two shots."

"You are a fool. There are three of us."

"And only one of you is gonna come out alive, so I'd suggest you discuss which of you it will be."

Micah knew his words were mere bravado, yet he had already made it further than he could have expected. Maybe the thirst for vengeance had finally returned to him.

The scraping sound behind him was so faint he might have mistaken it for the wind, yet something made him turn. He fired practically in the same instant he saw the figure approaching from behind. Micah did not pause to watch the man fall, nor to ascertain if his shot had been fatal. He knew it had been. He also knew the man had circled behind him in order to create a diversion. And in the next instant, Micah spun around.

A lead ball grazed his right shoulder before he could get his shot off; another shot blasted within an inch of his ear. But that was the bandits' mistake. They were not carrying revolvers. He noted that one now had to pause to reload. The other lifted his second pistol to fire, but Micah was faster. He fired and the man—Micah noted it was the one named Gustavo—fell forward, blood splurting from his head. Now only one bandit remained. But Micah's Colt was empty.

He and the last bandit exchanged looks of desperation. In that exchange, he saw in the bandit's eyes that there was no possibility of a truce. This was the same man who had wanted to kill him in the first place. But Micah had killed four of them. Four! Vengeance is mine, he thought. If he died now, he could do so vindicated. But why didn't it feel better? Why were his insides suddenly quaking? He'd killed four men. Mexicans. The enemy. For Jed.

But this was no time for thinking!

Micah knew he had only a moment before the remaining bandit reloaded. Swallowing rising bile in his throat, he made a dive for his discarded weapons still lying on the ground in the middle of the small battlefield. Ignoring the throbbing ache in his gun hand from his wounded shoulder, ignoring the wrenching of his guts, Micah laid his hand on the butt of one of his pistols.

He was too late. The bandit had reloaded.

The man fired and, amazingly, missed! But the shot struck the earth close to where Micah was lying on the ground, and it sent more dirt and grit into his eyes. Though momentarily blinded, he knew if he didn't do something quickly, the bandit would reload and finish him off. This was survival, not vengeance, he told himself. He raised his pistol, but his eyes were blurred.

"Always take time to sight your target..." his uncle's words echoed in his benumbed mind.

Why hadn't he asked his uncle what to do if you were blind?

The enemy's weapon should be loaded by now. He'd be taking aim. Micah raised his pistol, not aiming, not thinking, allowing pure instinct to guide him. He fired. He felt like an animal attacking an enemy, acting and reacting instinctively. What would the animal do now that all his options were used up? Micah groped around for the other weapons, all the while waiting for that final fatal shot, the one that would at last end his miserable life. But nothing came. He heard no more shots. He lifted himself up. Through the blur of his vision he saw that the last bandit was sprawled over the carcass of the dead horse. Were they all dead, then?

Micah sat there for some time, too spent to feel even relief. He just sat listening to himself breathe, amazed that he *was* breathing. Then he heard the sound of stirring. He vaguely realized it must be the unconscious bandit finally coming to. A sudden fear, a kind of dread, washed over Micah. He knew he wasn't afraid of dying. But what was it?

"*¡Madre de Dios!*" exclaimed the bandit as he struggled to his knees and surveyed the battlefield. He then focused wild eyes upon Micah, as if he were looking upon evil incarnate.

Only then was Micah fully aware of the scene surrounding him. A dead horse. Five bodies. Blood. Death. And there must still be more death. He knew then that this was the cause of his dread. He would have to kill yet again. But his body seemed to be functioning completely apart from his appalled mind. In a flash, before he had even given conscious impetus to the action, Micah had the other pistol in his hand. There was a single split second when the thought flickered on the edge of Micah's mind that he didn't have to kill this man. The bandit was reaching for his pistol, but there could not be time for him to draw it. Yet it all transpired in the space of a single heartbeat—the stray thought and Micah's trigger finger twitching faster than his mental ability to grasp the thought. His gun blasted, and the last bandit fell.

Suddenly Micah's hand began trembling so badly that the gun fell to the ground. His stomach roiled and heaved, and before he could even turn his head aside, he vomited all over himself. His legs had turned to mush, and he could not stand. He sat and stared, but everywhere he looked there were bodies.

What had he done?

The sound of galloping horses thundered through the afternoon air, heavy with the silence of death. Within five minutes Micah was surrounded by his friends.

"You all right?" Tom asked with concern. It seemed a silly question to Micah. He was alive. There were six dead men. How could he be all right?

"You done well, Micah," Hays said.

Micah stared at him, uncomprehending. "They're all dead," he said. He tried to force himself to stand, but the ground seemed to be buckling underneath him, and he had to stay put. He looked at Tom. "They . . . are . . . dead. . . ."

"You did what you had to do," Tom said, as he kneeled next to Micah and made an attempt to tend his wounds.

"What shooting!" exclaimed Bert Long. "How many weapons did you have?"

Micah gaped at the unabashed awe in the man's voice. Then his stomach betrayed him again. This time he turned aside and emptied its contents onto the dirt. But his insides kept heaving.

"This ain't the first time you've killed, Micah," Tom said. "What's wrong, boy?" His eyes carefully scanned Micah's body again, looking for hidden wounds.

"N-nothing," Micah rasped, his voice as thin and empty as his stomach.

Micah remembered the first time he killed a man. San Jacinto.

He hadn't been sick at all. He'd been fourteen and had not felt even a twinge. He'd joined the slaughter with relish. Now he was a man who had been in many battles, killed many times. What was happening to him?

"H-help me up, Tom," he said. He saw Tom and Hays exchange worried looks. "I gotta get out of here!"

"Soon as we find that mule of yours."

Micah struggled on his own to gain his feet. Tom, apparently seeing the futility of trying to get him to stay put, gave him a hand. His knees were shaky, but he willed himself to be steady.

"Let me take your horse, Tom."

"We'll all be heading back together soon enough," Tom argued.

Micah leveled a look at his friend that he knew was filled with desperation. He didn't know where the feeling was coming from. He did not understand any of it. All he knew was he had to get away from this place of blood and death. The men would want to do something about the bodies. But he could not stay.

"Tom!" Micah came as close to pleading as he ever had in his life.

Hays stepped forward. "Let him go, Tom. He just needs some time to himself."

"Take my horse," Tom said. "But take this as well." He held out his revolver.

Micah recoiled from the weapon, shaking his head. "Don't you see, Tom?"

"No, I don't see at all!"

Dismally, Micah said, "Neither do I."

He mounted Tom's gray gelding and rode away. Just *away*. He had no place to go *to*.

Thirty

THE RAIN CAME AS IT only can on the Texas prairie, hard and heavy. The wind from the south drove the rain, mixed liberally with hail, into Micah's face. Lightning flashed, ragged and blinding in the night sky, followed by cracks of ear-splitting thunder. Tom's gray winced occasionally. Stew would have bolted and run for it by now.

Micah was soaked to the skin, all the blood and dirt and stomach contents washed away. But he still felt dirty. He'd killed six men. And was Jed truly avenged? Had any amount of killing ever given him peace about his uncle's death? Would he have to keep killing forever and ever?

Would he never feel clean and at peace?

Through the rain and darkness, he saw a light ahead. He steered toward it. He wasn't surprised by the light, though why he expected lamps to still be burning this late, he didn't know. He only knew that an hour ago he had begun to veer toward the Maccallum ranch. In a way, his direction had been as involuntary as that last shot in the gunfight had been. Some reflex had driven him to kill. Another reflex was driving him toward the exact opposite. The only thing Micah knew for certain was that just then he needed to find for himself, killer that he was, something completely pure and good. And Lucie was the only thing like that he'd ever known.

No one stirred at the ranch. The light he'd seen was coming from the bunkhouse. A dog barked. He rode toward the house, dismounted, and climbed the step to the porch. It took almost as much courage, or audacity, to raise his hand and knock on the door of the darkened house as it had to gun down six bandits.

For a few moments there was no response, then the light of a lantern shone through the front window.

"Who is it?" came Lucie's voice.

Just that sound made his heart do such strange things. How he needed her!

"Me," he said, foolishly thinking that she'd recognize his voice after more than a year. But his lips were trembling with cold and fear and such a longing ache that he could say no more.

He heard the metal latch being thrown back. Then the door opened, and there she was. Lucie. Real flesh and blood. Not a dream. His throat was too tight and dry to speak.

"Micah!" She was dressed in a long white nightgown with a wool shawl drawn closely around her. Her hair hung loose about her shoulders. He'd never seen it loose before. He wanted desperately to plunge his face into the mass of dark curls.

He tried to speak instead. "L-Lucie, I . . . I . . . I killed six banditos." The words spilled out before he could stop them. He wanted comfort, but part of him must have wanted punishment as well.

Her hand went to her lips. "Joaquin!" she gasped.

"No."

She sagged visibly with relief.

"Lucie," called Reid Maccallum's voice from the back of the house, "is something wrong?"

"No, Papa." Her eyes scanned Micah, pausing briefly where the buckskin of his jacket was rent and his wound gaped through. "It's nothing, Papa. Go back to sleep." She reached a hand toward Micah's shoulder. Quietly, she said, "You're hurt."

"I had to see you."

"Just a moment." She turned back into the house, closing the door. In five minutes she returned, wearing a hooded cloak over her nightgown and carrying a basket. "Let's go to the stable. I can't see you in the house. Papa has such a hard time sleeping."

He followed her, pausing only to take the gray's reins and lead him also. "It's Tom's horse," he mumbled. "Can't let anything happen to it. I don't have good luck with horses. I . . . I lost the buckskin in the war."

In the stable Lucie lit a lantern while Micah put the gray in an empty stall that Lucie directed him to. As he unsaddled the horse,

Lucie gave the animal some fresh straw.

Then she said, "Now for you, Micah." She took his hand and led him to a stool. "Sit and take off your jacket and shirt. I've got some medicine here and some bandages." He sat and she kneeled on the hay-strewn floor at his feet.

He shrugged out of his jacket, then noticed the hole. "Look . . ." He fingered the tattered hole, stained with blood and gunpowder. "I . . . can't have nothing fine," he mumbled.

"Your shirt, Micah? So I can see your wound," she prompted.

"I don't care about that," he said. "It doesn't bother me."

"The rain has probably cleaned it out pretty well, but it could fester. Let me have a look at it."

Because he wanted only to hold her, to smell the fragrance of her hair, feel her lips on his, he obeyed her command. He couldn't touch her. He shouldn't touch her. He wouldn't touch her.

Lucie still could hardly believe that after more than a year, Micah had turned up on her doorstep. Wet, disheveled, and obviously distraught, but there he was, the reality of her dreams. Forbidden dreams, but ones she could not prevent in sleep.

Unable to put her thoughts in a proper frame, she clung to the practical. "The wound is deep, but the lead did not penetrate."

"It grazed me, is all."

His voice was distracted, almost dull, yet there was an intensity in his eyes that made the cool of the blue seem almost on fire.

She poured a couple drops of liquid from a brown bottle onto a cloth, a concoction of balm of Gilead buds mixed with rum that Juana swore by for open wounds. Micah winced as she dabbed it on his shoulder. "The alcohol burns a little."

A whole year and all she could talk about was his wound. No, there was much she wanted to say, but they had said good-bye. Yet he had just told her he had to see her. What had he meant? More to the point, what had it meant when her heart had leaped upon seeing him and she had wanted only to throw herself into his arms?

"How long have you been back?" she asked as she placed a clean bandage on his wound.

"A couple of weeks." His eyes briefly flickered toward her, then he jerked them away. He was afraid to look at her, yet there was yearning in his eyes. "I know I shouldn't have come. We said good-bye."

"Micah, what happened?" She, too, focused her eyes elsewhere, on her work. She wrapped the bandage under his arm and back over the wound. "You said you've been in a . . . a gunfight?"

He nodded, still staring somewhere over the top of her head. "Six banditos took me prisoner, but I got away."

"You killed them all? By yourself?"

"It was them or me," he said defensively.

"Oh, Micah!"

"I didn't want to!"

She lifted her eyes, but still he looked away.

"Jed was executed in Mexico, you know that? He and sixteen others were shot down, and for what?" He shook his head, the muscles in his jaw and neck twitching violently.

"So you got your revenge." She could not help the words.

Micah started to jump up, but she laid a restraining hand on his other shoulder so she could finish the bandage. He glanced down at her hand, and only then did she realize she was touching his bare chest. She jerked her hand away as if from a hot iron, and he jerked to his feet. He paced a few steps away from her, then turned. She could not read the expression on his face.

"It made me sick, and I don't know why," he said plaintively.

"You killed six men, Micah!" It seemed so obvious to her.

"I've killed before."

"Vengeance wasn't as sweet as you hoped it would be."

"Lucie, I'm scared!"

She could tell he had never admitted such a thing before.

Rising, she went to him and took his hands into hers. They were rough, coarse hands, hands that had just taken six lives. Lethal hands, deadly hands. She brought them to her lips.

"Don't be frightened," she said as she kissed his palms. "Your reaction is a good thing. You are not a killer in your heart. Maybe at last your heart is trying to tell you that."

"Being a ranger is the only life I have," he said miserably. "If I can't . . . use my gun, I don't have nothing."

"Micah, are you afraid because you might not be able to kill anymore?" She could not prevent the slight rancor in her tone. She dropped his hands.

"What else have I?"

"Micah!" she exclaimed in frustration. Then she turned her back to him and walked to a nearby stall. Looking over the top of the low wall, she saw the gray gelding munching placidly on hay. She felt Micah come up behind her and stop when he was so close she could feel the heat of his body nearly sear into her back.

He spoke softly. "I knew when that last bandit fell today that it wasn't gonna help cure my anger. Maybe that's what made me sick. All the Mexicans I've killed over the years trying to heal the wounds from Goliad, and now with Jed, too—suddenly I saw no matter how many I killed, it wouldn't help. It had never helped, but maybe I'd hoped there'd be a magic number that would finally clean my filthy soul. But there isn't. The hate is there, the loss is there, the hurt is there, and nothing will stop it."

"That's not true, Micah. There is one thing that will stop it."

"I don't want to hear it."

"But it's God you are really afraid of. And so to avoid Him, you will let yourself continue to wallow in your hate and pain."

He sighed, the puff of breath stirring the top of her head. "Yes, I think you may be right. But I won't hear of God."

She turned sharply, finding herself within an inch of him. She leveled her gaze at him, forcing him to return the look. "This isn't about your uncle or Jed and their killers. It is about your father. Why don't you kill him? He killed your mother, didn't he?"

"He's my father!"

"But you want to kill him, don't you?"

"No!"

"Instead you kill Mexicans."

"You are getting this all twisted up, Lucie."

"Maybe I am." She slipped past him. He had been way too close. She couldn't think straight. Her thoughts were all jumbled. Yet she knew all the hate in Micah stemmed from his father. She knew that was the key to everything. She sat on the stool. Maybe he wouldn't get so close to her then.

"All I came here for was—"

"What *did* you come here for?" she shot back accusingly. "Did you want some kind of absolution for what you did?"

"I just needed . . ." He dropped down in front of her, taking her shoulders in his hands. "You are the only good thing in my life. I thought if I was with you, it might make me forget who and what I am. Lucie . . . please . . ."

She remembered how in the past she'd felt his desperate need for love. It was there now. He needed so to be loved. And she did love him, but though she could not deny it to herself, she must deny her feelings to him.

His hands were trembling as they gripped her. She tried to ease from him, but he held her firm. Then his hands suddenly moved until he had pulled her fully into his arms. Plying her with kisses, he half carried, half dragged her to the floor, loosening her cape and casting it away.

"No, Micah!" She fought him, but he was heavy and too wrought to respond.

His kisses grew more and more intense, painfully intense.

"I need you so," he murmured. "I need your love."

"This isn't love—"

"No more preaching. No more talk. Hold me, Lucie. Please!" But he wasn't really asking, nor did he wait for a reply.

"Will you drag me down into that pit of hatred with you? Is that it?" She fought him even harder, especially as her own body began to betray her. How easily she could let herself succumb to him, for she loved him so. Yet she could not capitulate to her desires. It would hurt them both too deeply. Still, it was clear she couldn't fight him except with words. "Admit it, Micah, I am only another Mexican you will hurt today." She tried to spit the words out forcefully but could barely get them out because of his nearness.

"What? No! It's not—" Suddenly he stopped what he was doing. He pulled away, a look of utter horror on his face.

She thought he might be sick again, as he said he had been after his gunfight when he viewed the death in its wake.

He lurched to his feet and, saying nothing, grabbed his wet

jacket and shirt. Slipping into the shirt, he went to the stall and saddled the gray.

"Micah, it's raining." He had nearly forced himself upon her, yet still she cared. She knew he had not acted out of spite or malice or evil.

He led the gray from the stall. "I'm sorry, Lucie. You don't have to worry about me bothering you ever again."

He walked out, and through the open door she watched him mount and ride away, rain and wind pelting him, darkness swallowing him.

Thirty-One

THE PERSISTENT THREAT of invasion from Mexico continued to hang over Texas. Internal political problems in Mexico spared the republic from a major confrontation, but there was still raiding along the border, and Hays had to take seriously any rumors of danger. One such rumor arrived while he and several other rangers were sick with fever. With forces low, he sent only four to scout it out: Tom, Micah, and two new men, Baker and Lowe.

In the weeks after Micah's shoot-out with the bandits, he had continued on as a ranger. He had no place else to go, and truth be told, he liked the work for the most part. He liked being needed and useful, although it irked him to no end when the men held him up as some kind of hero for that gunfight. It was worse when regular citizens did the same as tales of his feat spread.

At least in all that time he had yet to be in another gunfight. Mercifully, Hays had mostly used Micah as a courier to carry government dispatches to Washington-on-the-Brazos, the new capital of the republic since Austin had been abandoned during the invasion of 1842. Micah received extra pay for this and practically had the buckskin paid off. He made the payments by depositing them directly into Reid Maccallum's account at the bank. There was no need for any personal contact. No need at all.

Except where his heart was concerned. But he did not let himself think of that. If there had ever been a chance to win Lucie, he had destroyed it that night of the shoot-out. How could he have been so stupid? He'd been blinded, he supposed, by his own aching need. She'd been so right. It had nothing to do with love. Or so he told himself whenever a thought of Lucie would creep past his defenses and haunt his mind.

Bandits had been reported along Carrow Creek near the Nueces. And that's where the four rangers were headed. Micah dreaded the prospect of encountering more bandits. He hadn't killed Joaquin Viegas that last time, but he felt he was doomed to confront and kill the bandit sooner or later. In a life filled with irony and disaster, that would surely be the greatest of all.

Toward the end of the day the rangers made camp. Tom wanted to stop on high ground so they could have a better vantage, but the others convinced him to camp by the creek. It had been a blistering hot day for the end of May, and they wanted a swim.

Baker and Lowe stripped and were in the water while Micah was bringing the horses down to the creek to water them. Tom was up on the bank getting a fire going. A dozen Comanches were upon the rangers almost before they heard the war cries. Tom had grabbed his revolver and was firing, but an arrow struck him and he fell. The last Micah saw him, he was crawling toward the cover of a bush. Micah heard splashing in the water but did not have time to turn to see what Baker and Lowe were doing.

Snatching his revolver from his belt, he managed to get off a round and wound one of the Indians. Then an arrow penetrated his right arm, jolting his weapon from his hand. The arrow went out the other side, but the pain nearly took his breath away. He grabbed his pistol, also in his belt, then took a shot with his left hand that went wild. Another arrow struck him in the side, and while he managed to pull the arrow out through his back, the pain and sudden loss of blood brought him to his knees. He tried to see what had become of Tom, but he could not see his friend and could only hope he had managed to reach the cover of a nearby mesquite bush. Baker and Lowe were also nowhere to be seen.

Micah tried to reload his pistol, but his hand was shaking too much, and his powder horn fell to the ground. As he fumbled around for it, swaying on his knees, a final arrow struck him in the head, and he fell back into the dirt. He thought about finishing himself off before the Comanches got to him. He drew his Bowie knife and brought it to the vicinity of his heart, heedless of the obvious fact that at the moment he didn't have enough strength to plunge it into his chest. But before he could make the attempt, blackness engulfed him.

When he came to, all was quiet except for some low voices not far away.

"Them Comanches are gonna come back. Let's get out of here!" That was Lowe.

"We can't just leave them," Baker replied.

"They're dead, I tell you!"

"But—"

"Lowe ... Baker ..." Micah rasped from where he lay. He tried to move to give some sign that he was still alive.

"You ain't dead?" said Lowe.

Micah couldn't tell if that was surprise or disappointment in the man's voice.

"Tom?" Micah breathed, barely able to form words.

"Dead," Baker said.

Micah's vision was blurred by blood and pain, but he saw that Lowe and Baker were both dressed now and appeared fairly unscathed. They had probably managed to find cover during the battle.

"Those Indians will be back," Lowe said. "We gotta go."

"Horses...?" Micah said.

"Only one left. The rest run off or the Indians got them."

"We ain't all gonna make it," Baker added, and to his credit, he seemed miserable about it.

"Sinclair, I think you know you are a goner. If we try to take you, we'll all get killed," Lowe said. He looked more afraid for himself than concerned about Micah.

Micah didn't blame him. It was just the practicality of the frontier. He was mortally wounded. He could feel the life drain from him as the blood flowed from his wounds. Words stuck in his throat, and he could only shake his head. Let them make of that what they wanted. He wasn't going to beg for his life.

They carried him to the other side of the creek and left him with a rifle. They mounted the horse and rode off, but Micah did not watch them. He couldn't keep his eyes open. He had cheated death way too often and knew his time had finally come.

When he didn't die immediately, however, Micah knew he couldn't just lie there and wait for it to happen. He crawled to the water's edge and took a couple handfuls of mud and leaves and packed his wounds in an attempt to staunch the flow of blood.

About a half hour later, the Indians returned. Micah had covered himself with branches and other debris, and the Comanches either did not see him or did not think him worth the effort of even scalping. They rode away.

Though the day had been hot, the night was freezing, at least it felt so to Micah, whose blood loss left little to insulate him from the cold. He dozed off a couple of times but knew he could not sleep or he'd never wake. When dawn came he took the rifle and, using it as a crutch, rose and started walking. He hated the thought of leaving Tom's body to the vultures, but he had no strength to do anything about it. Half the time he merely crawled, but he kept on the move without sleep or food except for a few mesquite beans and cactus apples. He was fortunate enough to encounter occasional watering holes to sustain him on the way.

Micah headed north. San Antonio was a hundred miles away, and he was certain he didn't have a chance of ever getting that far. He had resigned himself to the fact that he would soon die. He just knew he could not lie still and wait for that to happen. He could only travel a few miles at a time, then usually collapsed before he could decide for himself when to stop. A couple of times he merely passed out.

He kept this up for four days. When he had the capacity to think, which wasn't often, he wondered why he was doing this at all. He had no reason to go on. Lucie was lost to him. His friends were dead. Tom! Even Tom. The thought sliced through him worse than the pain of his wounds. Tom had been the only one left whom Micah cared about, and more to the point, the only one who Micah believed cared about him. Now there was no one. He was alone.

Why then was he struggling so to live?

Thankfully he blacked out once more, preventing further rumination. When he came to, the sun was beating down relentlessly upon him, and all he could think of was finding a drink of water. He crawled over miles of rocky earth and was so thoroughly scratched and cut, he appeared to be one large wound. He envisioned a swim in a cool, wet river, the water washing over every part of his scorched and bleeding body. He imagined the prickles of icy moisture getting into his mouth—cool, refreshing drops. He worked his thick, dry tongue over his lips but found only a cracked and swollen surface. No water.

Why wasn't he dead?

They're all dead. Jed, Tom. Uncle Haden. Mama . . .

Why not me? I killed them all.

"The wages of sin is death . . ."

Yes . . . I am a sinner . . . rotten . . . dirty . . .

"What do you want from me, boy! I admit I killed your mother. I am everything you believe me to be. I am a rotten, dirty sinner! I am the worst reprobate . . . a hypocrite. I deserve your hatred. But I need help. . . ."

I won't help you, Pa, but I can't kill you either. I can't . . . kill . . .

"Don't be frightened, Micah. This is a good thing. You are not a killer in your heart."

You are not a killer . . . Pa, you are not a killer.

Micah shut his eyes against the image of his father's agonized face, as he always had. But behind his closed eyes that image would not fade. Instead, the face changed subtly into his own! Tears oozed from the eyes—his father's tears, his own eyes. Or were they his own tears also? He could no longer tell.

"You're going loco, Micah, plumb loco!" he rasped, shocked that any sound at all could come from his dry, constricted throat.

Using the rifle once more as a crutch, he distracted himself by trying to rise and walk. He took a couple of steps, but the world spun around, and he crumbled back to the ground.

"Die, you ornery critter!" he groaned.

But he dragged himself several feet more. He didn't know why.

Another night passed. He still did not let himself sleep if he could help it. But sleeping and waking had become blurred. Dreams or reality, he could no longer tell. He spoke to his mother, and he thought he truly had finally died. But something told him his wounds would not hurt as they did if he were dead. His father's face came often, but Micah shut it out when he could, yet too often he simply had no control over it.

The best times were when Lucie came to him. Sometimes he was able to forget that he had no right to dream of her. Sometimes he imagined they had a little farm and children and love, so much love.

On the sixth day, Micah found a watering hole. It was small and muddy, but he buried his face in it and drank as if it were a crisp mountain spring. Then he passed out.

He awoke to an odd sensation, like a feather gently brushing his face.

"Mama," he murmured, not knowing why he thought of his mother just then except that the feather was soft and comforting.

His eyes were swollen and stuck shut with discharge so that he could barely open them. But he struggled to do so, because if he was finally dead, if this was the comfort he'd sought for so many years, he wanted to look upon it. He parted his eyelids just enough to see a vague image hovering over him. Not his mother, but he still figured he must be dreaming.

"Stew!"

The mule nudged Micah's cheek with his nose.

"Ya ol' churnhead," Micah croaked. "Ya ain't as worthless as I thought."

Maybe it was a dream, but what did it matter? This was a dream to be grasped. Yet the struggle he had to mount the mule was proof it was real enough. He began to think it would have been easier to continue crawling on hands and knees. He passed out twice during the excruciating process, but each time that mule prodded him back to consciousness. Finally, making one concerted effort that nearly was the death of him, Micah straddled the animal. He tried to sit straight, but everything spun so horribly that he nearly fell off again. Leaning forward, he circled his arms around Stew's neck and laid his head against the animal's head. In that way, with occasional direction from Micah, the mule carried Micah back to San Antonio, less than a two-day ride. Incredibly, Micah had already traversed over fifty miles of the journey on foot.

When he came to the outskirts of the town, he tried to sit upright in the saddle. Some crazy pride made him not wish to ride into his town pitifully half dead. But the exercise was misplaced.

The world spun, and Micah slipped from the saddle as the ground careened up to meet him.

"Pride goeth before a fall...."

The words came to him as he hit the dirt.

Thirty-Two

DEATH WAS MORE PLEASANT than Micah had imagined it would be, especially when he'd always been fairly certain he'd end up in hell. But here he was lying on something soft as a cloud, clean and white, too. Just as he'd imagined heaven to be.

He opened one eye, a little afraid at what he'd find. If this wasn't heaven, if he wasn't dead, then he'd have to keep on facing life, and he just didn't feel strong enough to do that. But his vision was blurry, and he could not tell much with only one eye, so he opened the other. What he saw were the rough wood beams of a ceiling. There was a cobweb in one corner. He'd bet money there were no cobwebs in heaven. He tried to move, and the sharp pain from several different places in his body quickly proved his fears.

He was alive.

"Hey!" he called, but he could not get his voice to rise above a whisper.

In a moment the door, which the bed faced, opened, and he thought if he wasn't dead he must still be dreaming, for the figure stepping into the room was garbed in checkered green calico and had hair like the night caught on fire.

"Lucie . . ." he breathed.

"You're awake," she said, her voice causing an ache inside him that had nothing to do with his wounds.

"What are you doing here?"

"I live here. This is my house."

"Then . . . what am I doing here?"

She smiled and drew closer to the bed. He noticed now that she was holding a small basin and a towel. She set these on the bedside table.

"I had them bring you here," she said. "The trip was risky from town, but Mr. Paschel had his hands full with so many down with fever. And he's not a doctor. He'd given you up for dead. And..." She lowered her eyes to gaze directly into his.

Her expression was not one of revulsion, which he knew she had every right to feel after what he'd tried to do to her that night in the stable. A lump formed in his throat.

"I told him I would nurse you, and you would not die."

"Why...?"

Ignoring his question, she opened a drawer and removed a few items. "I was about to change your bandages. Let me just lift the blanket."

"How long have I been here?" he asked, unable to recall anything since riding into San Antonio, clinging to Stew's neck.

"You've been back for four days now and in my house for nearly all of it. I happened to be in town the day you got there, and that's when I heard what had happened. Now let me get to work and clean your wounds. There's still a chance of them festering, and you have been feverish, so you aren't out of the woods yet." She put her hands on her hips and directed a stern don't-argue-with-me gaze at him.

"Why can't Juana do it?" he asked, not sure he wanted Lucie doing that unpleasant job.

"Well, if you'd rather she care for you—"

"No!" he said quickly. He couldn't believe he had nearly rejected her again. But what good could come of it? Nevertheless, he was simply too weak—and not just physically weak—to give up the prospect of her tender care. And he knew it would be tender despite who or what he was. "I ... I haven't said thank you yet ... for taking me in. I expect I'd be dead now if you hadn't."

"We're even, then." She smiled.

Micah knew he was powerless against that smile, and he might have been afraid for both of them if he didn't feel so downright good just then.

"Let me have a look at your wounds," she added.

He lifted his arm from under the covers. It was quite weak, and he had difficulty moving it. He wondered if he'd ever be able to shoot again. He forgot all about that when Lucie took his arm and helped him. There was a bandage wrapped around the fleshy part of the upper arm where the arrow had penetrated. Lucie removed the bandage, swabbed some creamy concoction over the wound, then put on a new bandage. She did the same to his head. Luckily, the arrow hadn't penetrated his skull, but it had made a deep gash four inches long over his left ear.

"Juana stitched up your head wound," Lucie said. "I think she did a nice job. It'll scar, but your hair will cover it eventually. Thank goodness you've got a hard head."

Then she lifted the lower part of the blanket to reveal his right side. Her mouth puckered in concentration as she worked. Her eyes were grave.

"Is it bad?" he asked.

"It's getting a bit purulent. At least the arrow went all the way through and didn't break off inside."

"I pulled it through," he said.

"Oh my!" Lucie's eyes flickered to his face, then back to her work. "You have much courage, Micah. Not just because of the arrow, but in making that journey back to San Antonio."

"I didn't have much choice. It was either lie still and die or try to make it back," he answered matter-of-factly, but inside he was pleased she still thought highly of him. "Lucie . . . is it true about Tom? Is he dead?"

She nodded, keeping eyes intent on her work. "I'm afraid so."

"I'm beginning to think I'm just plain bad luck to anyone I get close to."

"Don't you even think such a thing!" she exclaimed, and in her emotion she pressed too hard on his wound.

"Ouch!"

"I'm sorry." She paused a moment, then added, "Micah, people die and that's that. I'm very sorry about Tom. He was a good man, but his death has nothing to do with you."

Micah shrugged, not convinced. Desiring to change the subject he asked, "Do you know what happened to Baker and Lowe?"

"Who?"

"The fellows that left me for dead."

"Oh, them!" her voice rose indignantly. "Captain Hays gave them a severe tongue-lashing. But if you ask me, it wasn't enough."

"I would have slowed them down, gotten them both killed. And me too."

"But you didn't die and neither did they."

"Well, I ain't gonna defend them. I thought about killing them both when I was crawling across the prairie." He sighed. It was very hard to be angry at anyone with Lucie's slim, soft hands caressing him. "Most anyone would have done the same."

"Not you."

He could not fathom how she could say such kind things about him. He just shook his head in disbelief. "Lucie, I don't know how you can say that when you know the kind of man I am. I am still completely befuddled that you took me in after what I did. Nothing I ever did was out of courage. You hinted at it the last time we saw each other. Anything I've done was from pure orneriness and hate, too. Honor, courage—they just have nothing to do with me."

"I'll agree you are ornery, and you have more than your share of hate in you, but it's only part of you. You have good in you, Micah. You'll never convince me otherwise." She finished her work and tugged the blanket back in place.

Micah smiled at her. He just didn't feel like doing any soul-searching at the moment. "You bring it out of me, if it's there."

"And don't you forget it!" she said with a tart smile, then gathered up her things and moved to the door. "I'll bring you some broth if you feel up to eating it."

"Yes, thank you." He didn't know if he could eat, but he'd take any excuse to have her return.

———

The fever hit hard in the night. Micah faded in and out of consciousness for two days. Nightmares assailed him. Goliad, San Jacinto, battle, slaughter, death. And, as nightmares will, his made no sense at all. The victims were not always soldiers, Mexican or Texan. Sometimes his father was one of the victims, sometimes even

Micah was cut down. But the worst nightmare was the one in which Lucie was hewn down on the battlefield.

Yet woven into and around the horror were moments that did not fit. He realized later that these were the moments when he came out of the nightmares into reality, a reality that seemed even less real than the nightmares. For they were moments of sweetness and peace. In them Lucie figured strongly, sitting at his bedside with her head bowed and her dear voice murmuring over him.

"Dear Lord, spare Micah that he might know you, that he might truly see you for the loving, merciful God that you are. . . ."

Micah never thought prayer could be so good. He never thought he might actually desire to reach out for it. It was like an island of calm in the midst of a hurricane. Was it just Lucie, or was it the words she was saying?

Finally the fever passed, and he woke again with a clear mind. Lucie was there at his bedside, and he wondered if she'd ever left. She wiped a cool damp cloth across his forehead.

"You were praying for me," he breathed.

"I have been praying for two days. I couldn't help it."

He smiled at the hint of apology in her tone. "Thank you."

"Really?"

"I just remembered something. . . ." He spoke dreamily, his eyes half-closed so as not to break the wonderful spell of the moment. "When I was a boy, before I came to Texas, I caught a bad fever. My mother sat by my bed as you are doing now, and she wiped me with a cool cloth and . . . and she prayed over me. I had forgotten how many times she . . ." He turned his head away as sudden tears sprang to his eyes. "I had forgotten. . ." he murmured, then he closed his eyes, his speech exhausting him. In a moment sleep engulfed him. A sleep without dreams, without nightmares.

He awoke a while later, and Lucie was still there. He gave her a weak smile but could not speak. He slept again, and when he awoke, she was still there. He continued thus for two more days, waking for a few moments, then sleeping. He had never slept so much in his life, nor had he ever lain still for so long, especially without a gun at his side, ever alert to danger. Yet he never grew restless, and he was never afraid. The sleep was delicious. And when he was awake he often did not talk, nor did Lucie talk much to him. They were simply quietly aware of each other. Sometimes she held his hand. But she required nothing more of him.

When he finally woke and felt truly rested, Lucie was gone. His disappointment went deep to his core, but he chided himself for his selfishness. It was probably the first time in days she'd left his side. He told himself this was for the best because he feared he was becoming far too dependent on her, on seeing her dear face each moment on waking. He could easily desire a lifetime of that.

She returned a few minutes later and seemed to immediately perceive that this waking was different from the others.

"So you have decided to join us for a while," she said.

"How long did I sleep?"

"Two days."

"And no nightmares," he said, amazed.

"Not after the fever passed."

"You knew—about the nightmares, I mean?"

"You talked a lot. They must have been terrible." She reached out and adjusted his pillow behind him. "Are you hungry?"

His stomach rumbled as if in response. Surprised, he said, "I am . . . mighty hungry."

"Juana has been dying to fatten you up. I'll tell her you are ready. Though we should start slowly. Some broth and a glass of milk, perhaps." She turned to go.

Micah laid a hand on her arm. "I wasn't dreaming, was I, about you praying for me?"

"No."

"I guess you have a captive audience now," he said.

"What do you mean by that, Micah?"

"Only that . . . well, I ain't going nowhere if you get the urge to talk religion to me, that's all." He smiled, abashed at his own words.

"I do declare, Micah! Maybe you are still delirious after all!"

Then she grinned, and he smiled, too, with abandon. And it felt good.

Thirty-Three

LUCIE DID NOT TAKE full advantage of Micah's offer. Oh, she had thought about doing just that at first. In fact, when he had first regained consciousness, she had even thought that now God had him where He could knock some sense into him—a captive audience, as Micah had put it. And then when he had actually given her leave to talk about God, well, she nearly attacked him with her zeal. But she remembered what he'd said once, that he knew a lot about religion. He had many Scriptures memorized and probably knew the Bible even better than he would admit to. She knew Micah did not need to be told anything about faith.

However, Lucie wasn't exactly sure what he did need or how to go about directing him. She prayed about it and realized that the best approach was to leave it in Micah's hands, let him do the reaching out.

And he did so, but slowly. A question here or there woven into a conversation. Often it was nothing deep or earth shattering. It seemed right now that Micah needed most of all to relax, to enjoy the moment, to rest from all intensity. God seemed to sense this as well. The talk was casual and even fun. They told each other stories of their adventures. Of course Micah had more exciting adventures. Lucie just had little tales of her growing up, but Micah listened as if hearing *The Arabian Nights*. They learned much about each other during this time, the kinds of things Lucie always wanted to know about Micah. And often matters of faith just flowed naturally from this.

Once Lucie brought Micah his supper and watched his eyes widen with wonder at the contents of the tray.

"Is that pecan pie?" he asked, indicating the dish next to his stew.

"Yes, and I made it myself."

"I thought Juana did all the cooking."

"Well, I confess I don't enjoy cooking." Lucie blushed at having to make such an admission to the man she loved, but she had to be truthful. "However, Juana has insisted I learn. Still, the men shouldn't be made to suffer more than once or twice a week."

"You can't be all that bad," he said.

"I'll cook for you tomorrow, and you can judge. But I do have one specialty—pecan pie. I love it and Juana hates it, so if I want it, I must make it, or so she says. Knowing Juana, she would make it if I pouted a bit."

Lifting his eyes from his tray, Micah gave her a sidelong perusal. "Somehow I just don't think you are the pouting type."

Blushing a bit, she shrugged. "I guess I've been known to use such methods to get my way. But in this case, I don't have to. I hate to cook, but I like to bake pies and cookies and pastries. I suppose it is my sweet tooth that drives me."

"Now, a sweet tooth, I can believe." He picked up his fork and impaled the pie, bringing a chunk to his mouth. He ate the pie with a look of deep scrutiny on his face.

She watched with breath more bated than she cared to admit.

Swallowing, he finally said, "I've had pecan pie only one other time in my life. My neighbor up in Cooksburg made it, and I fell in love with pecan pie. I asked my ma to make it, but she never got around to it. Those days she was feeling so poorly that we were lucky to have the basics to eat." He grew momentarily melancholy, then shaking it off, continued. "Well, I'm in love again! Lucie, this pie is even better than Mrs. Hunter's."

Lucie grinned. Micah liked pecan pie. He liked *her* pecan pie! There was something so wonderfully ordinary about it that it nearly made her weep.

Micah was attacking the rest of the pie.

"Micah," she scolded halfheartedly, "you need to eat your stew first."

"Who says?"

She screwed up her lips in thought about this. "It is just the right thing to do."

"It was only yesterday you were telling me that some things were just opposite of what we think they should be," he countered.

"We were talking about how the Bible says that with God our weaknesses can be our strengths, and how God's ways are often the exact opposite of the way people think things should be."

"Yes, and the order of my meal tonight is a perfect way to illustrate how I've learned that spiritual truth," he replied smugly.

Lucie picked up the napkin lying next to his plate and tossed it into his face. With incredibly quick reflexes for a man recuperating from near mortal injuries, Micah snatched the napkin and tossed it back at her.

Giggling, she said, "I think you are much too strong to fully grasp that notion."

"No," he said more solemnly, "I'm not." He lifted his gaze, smiling faintly. "When I was strong physically, I was very weak in my soul, my heart. Now I can't even walk. I guess I am not much stronger spiritually or emotionally, but I can see it now. My eyes are so much more open."

"That is a good place to be." Tenderly, she laid the napkin across his shirtfront.

"I don't know where I'm going," he confessed.

"It will come to you, Micah," she encouraged. "I'm sure it will."

Not long after that, Lucie began helping Micah get up. His wounds, the loss of blood, and the fever had taken a hard toll on him. He became exhausted walking just a few steps to the chair next to his bed. But within a week he was strong enough to venture outside. He asked Lucie to take him to the stable to see Stew.

"I just gotta make sure he's all right, with my own eyes, you know?" he said.

"I understand. But I have made sure that mule has been treated like a king. I personally give him a lump of sugar every day." She took Micah's arm as they walked outside. He probably did not need such assistance, but he didn't protest.

"How do you do it all, Lucie? You've been caring for me day and night, but I know your father needs help also. Then you have your chores. And still you take time for my old mule. You amaze me!"

"I don't consider a minute of it work," she explained simply. How could she tell him that every moment caring for him was sheer pleasure?

He was out of breath when they reached the stable, but he doggedly continued to the stall Lucie indicated was Stew's. He unlatched the door and went inside. Running a hand along the animal's flanks, he murmured affectionate words to the mule.

"You know," he said to Lucie, "I hate to admit it, but this ornery beast saved my life. It ain't nothing short of a miracle that he showed up when he did out there."

"I didn't know you believed in miracles," she said lightly.

"Don't think it doesn't make me angry that I just might have to change my perspective." He spoke with mock affront, then grinned. "A man can change, you know."

"I suppose anything is possible," she replied noncommittally.

———

Micah was sure he'd never been happier in his life. Sometimes he felt a little guilty about this, considering the loss of his two dearest friends. But he also thought that perhaps they, more than anyone, would understand. This was the first time in years that Micah was so completely removed from violence and strife. He didn't have to sleep lightly with a gun near at hand. He didn't have to move through the day in a constant vigil for danger. When he dressed for the first time—in some spares of the ranch hands because his own clothes had been tattered to shreds during his trek—he had momentarily felt naked without pistols tucked into his belt.

Yes, he had grieved the death of Tom, but it had simply not wrenched at the core of him as Jed's death had. Lucie said it was God's peace. Maybe so. Or maybe he just did not want to face the questions and deep down anger Tom's death would surely bring if he thought too intensely about it. Maybe it was hard to accept Tom being dead because he hadn't seen it for himself. That's what Reid Maccallum thought.

Micah smiled as he sat in the chair by the window in what had once been Juana's room. The housekeeper had vacated and was now sharing Lucie's room. Anyway, the thought of Reid was a pleasant one. The two men suddenly had much in common. Both were once strapping, strong men who were now invalids. Once Reid realized he was welcome, he often came and passed the time with Micah. And Micah enjoyed the visits almost as much as he enjoyed Lucie's visits.

Not a naturally verbose man, Reid could talk at great length if given encouragement. And he was knowledgeable about many varied subjects. Not a formally educated man, he still was well-read, interesting, and wise. It wasn't long before they became comfortable enough to talk about personal things. Reid talked about his son one day. This was another area Micah and Reid had in common, but from different perspectives.

"It wasn't easy for the boy," Reid said, "growing up as he did caught between two cultures. Unfortunately, I didn't see the depth of the problem until it was too late."

"Lucie doesn't seem to have problems in that area," Micah said.

"I can't exactly say why that is." Reid gazed a moment out the window. Lucie had moved another chair into Micah's room and placed it adjacent to Micah's. There was even a small table between the two chairs so the two convalescents could take refreshment together. "Maybe it was my doing. Fathers are different with sons than they are with daughters. I love them both to the depths of my soul, but I think a man expects more of a son. A son is an extension of a man far more than a daughter is. He has the potential to be everything the father could not be. It is a heavy burden to be laid on a boy. On the other hand, a son expects more from a father than a daughter does."

"A son wants to worship his father," interjected Micah. "I guess a daughter does, too, but only a son can hope to take that worship to the obvious conclusion of true imitation."

"Is that what you wanted to do? Imitate your father?"

Micah laughed dryly. "If I did, I failed miserably!"

"I guess that's really what I'm trying to say. All those high expectations fathers and sons have for one another—well, we are all doomed to fail. And it's probably just as well that we do!" He shook his head and, steepling his fingers, tapped them thoughtfully against his lips. "Joaquin did not feel he could ever be a respectable rancher, so he did just the opposite—became an out-law, and worse, a bandit politically opposed to all I and the other ranchers stood for. I know it isn't quite that simple, and there were other factors involved, but the end was the same. My son and I were driven further and further apart. We, who loved each other very deeply, became enemies of a sort. It tears me apart inside. I don't doubt it has been part of the cause of my heart going bad."

"Do you . . ." Micah paused, his eyes flickering to the window. Outside, the sky was a clean blue and the sun was glaring. The stableboy was chasing a couple of dogs around in the yard. Again, Micah felt life was too sweet now to sully with deep introspection, especially of painful topics. Yet he was curious about Reid and his son. Clearly there were many parallels between them and Micah and his father. Micah knew that sooner or later he must confront his own difficulties in this area or relinquish all the peace he was now experiencing.

He took a breath and went on. "Mr. Maccallum, do you still love Joaquin?"

"Of course!" the man said simply without hesitation.

"Why? He defied you during the war by fighting on the other side. He defies you every day by harassing the borders of your land. Surely his actions are a shame to both you and Lucie."

"I love him because he is part of me, Micah. Just as I am sure he loves me for the same reason. That kind of love does not die easily. It would be like hating yourself."

"Sometimes I do hate myself," Micah said flatly.

"And sometimes you love yourself. Life is not black and white."

"I've often wondered if my father loves me," Micah mused, only realizing he said the words out loud when they were spoken.

"I'm sure he loves you."

"How can you know that?"

"It was clear when I met him."

Micah blinked with surprise. "You met him?"

"He came last year after Lucie wrote to him about your being in prison in Mexico."

"Lucie wrote him?"

Reid smiled. "What do you and my daughter talk about all

those hours I've heard your voices from my room?"

"Everything and nothing," Micah answered. "But that never came up."

"I expect Lucie is reticent about broaching such a tender subject."

"Probably." Micah considered Reid's astounding words again. "He came here?"

"Yes, and he spent time with President Houston as well, no doubt badgering the man about your disposition."

"He did all that?"

"Sounds like a man who loves his son."

Micah rose from his chair and walked around it so he could stand facing the window. It was hard to let Reid see the sudden quandary of emotion his statement had stirred in Micah. Though part of him wanted to believe Reid's words, a part still sought to fight against them. Yet he knew that any peace he hoped to attain hinged on his coming to terms with both his father and his father's God. Having had a small taste of peace, he now knew he desperately wanted it. But could he sacrifice the hate that had sustained him for so many years? It seemed a twisted question. Who would choose hate? Micah didn't want it. But he feared the unknown more.

Thirty-Four

THREE WEEKS FROM the day Micah showed up half dead in San Antonio, Lucie deemed him fit enough to ride a bit. He still felt stiff and weak in the knees, but he was not going to argue. The restlessness that had been at bay during his recovery was beginning to creep up on him. This worried him a little, and he had confided it to Reid.

"I was beginning to think I was ready to settle down," he said. He didn't say that in his mind settling down almost certainly involved Lucie. Maybe Reid understood this, but nevertheless, Micah was not ready to approach the man about marrying his daughter no matter how congenial they had become. "I'm starting to feel itchy now—in my feet, you know."

"I sometimes get mighty restless myself," Reid said. "Might be you are just experiencing what is natural to most men. You've never had to lie on your back for long periods, have you?"

"In prison, but I guess that was different because I could still get around even if I was confined. But there were days when I wanted to scream from boredom."

"A man can only take so much," Reid agreed.

Micah hoped that was it. He hoped that the wild streak in him was finally getting tamed. He hoped so because Lucie Maccallum deserved a man at her side, not one roaming all over creation.

Regardless, he quickly dressed and met Lucie in the kitchen. She was placing some items in a basket. He peeked inside and found dishes of food—cold chicken left over from last night's supper, a loaf of bread, apples, and two slabs of spice cake, which was another of Lucie's specialties.

"What's all this?" he asked.

"A picnic."

"A real picnic?" He smiled. "I don't think I have ever been on a picnic. Not that I can remember. My stepmother took the young kids on a picnic once, but I wouldn't go. I was pretty ornery back then."

"Well, I am honored, then, to take you on your first *real* picnic." Lucie gave Micah a quick appraisal as she spoke. "But no guns on a picnic." She reached to remove the pistol he had in his belt.

Captain Hays had come to visit him a few days before and had brought him his weapons, which Baker and Lowe had brought from the battle site. Good weapons were hard to come by, and Micah was glad to have his back. He hadn't even thought about it when he had tucked the revolver into his belt upon dressing.

"But, Lucie, if we're riding any distance from the ranch, we gotta have some protection," he argued. "Against snakes or varmints, if nothing else."

"I decree there will be no varmints on this outing!"

He shook his head. "Ya just can't—"

"He's right," said Reid, who had just come into the kitchen. "That would be purely irresponsible, Lucie, and you well know it."

"But I don't want him troubled by such things today," she said.

"He'll be more troubled if you have no protection. As will I. One moment." Reid left the kitchen and returned with a rifle in hand. "Leave the pistol, but take this," he offered.

"That's fine by me," said Micah, looking to Lucie for final approval of the plan.

When she nodded reluctantly, Micah took the revolver from his belt and laid it on the table. It was with this very weapon that he had killed most of the Mexican bandits that awful day, the memory of which still burned painfully in his mind. He, more than anyone, wanted no reminders of that day just now. He was going on a picnic with Lucie. He wanted nothing to cloud the moment.

They rode about a mile from the house. The wind in Micah's face was as pleasant as the company he was with. He almost forgot the pain each jostle of the mule brought. The air of the early summer day grew warmer as the sun traveled high in the sky. And the wind was a dry Texas wind that bent the tops of the high grass and whistled through the cottonwoods on the edge of a little creek. Seldom did Micah take the opportunity to truly appreciate this country, but now as he did, he realized he loved it. His father had once told him, when he was pining for his Boston home, that Texas would eventually become home to him. Micah supposed it had, in spite of himself or his father.

He also thought of a conversation he'd had with Reid the other day, a rather cryptic conversation at that. They had been talking about the growth of Texas in general terms, about the appeal of wide open lands and such. Reid mentioned to Micah that there was some fine unclaimed land adjacent to the Maccallum ranch on the other side of Cutter Creek. He'd said no more, and Micah was afraid to make more of the words than their surface meaning.

He didn't know why he thought of that just now. They were far from the borders of Maccallum land. Yet Micah had been thinking more and more about his unclaimed land allotments. But it must be the height of arrogance—or at the very least, outlandish fantasy—to think that there might be more to claiming land on the borders of Maccallum land than simply being neighbors.

He glanced at Lucie, and an ache replaced the peaceful joy he had been feeling. He could never be fit for a woman such as she. There was simply too much blood on his hands.

They stopped on the shallow banks of the creek under the shade of a cottonwood. Micah secured Stew and Lucie's piebald in a place where there was good sweet grass, then he carried the basket to a place where Lucie had spread a quilt over the grass.

Micah eased down on the quilt. "I didn't think a man could get tired riding, especially after just an hour." He shook his head. "I wonder if I'll ever be good as new." He flexed his right arm. "There ain't much pain in my arm anymore. Guess that's something."

"You have come a long way, Micah, considering you nearly died." She visibly shuddered. "I can't imagine life without you around."

"Like I couldn't imagine life without Jed or Tom," Micah mused. "But life has a way of getting on one way or another."

"Yes, I know that. And God would have healed me. But I am glad I didn't have to find out." She opened the basket. "Come, let's eat."

Micah agreed heartily with that. He ate from hunger, for indeed his appetite was voracious these days, but he also ate by way of distraction. He'd tried to brush off Lucie's words about missing him, but they continued to echo in his mind, reminding him that once she had declared her love for him. Yet much had passed between them since then. Surely all she must feel now was friendship.

Micah ate more than his fair share of the food. When Lucie said she'd had her fill of chicken, Micah finished it off. Same with the bread. He ate two apples and one huge piece of the spice cake. He then eyed Lucie's half-eaten piece, which he thought had been sitting untended for long enough.

"If you ain't gonna finish that . . ." he asked subtly.

She laughed and pushed the cake toward him. "At this rate you will be fattened up far beyond even Juana's tastes!"

He ate the cake and, licking his fingers contentedly, lay back on the quilt. The sun burned down pleasantly upon him even as the wind wafted over him. This must indeed be the "good life" he'd heard others speak of.

Suddenly something snapped in the brush. Micah tensed and shot up, grabbing the rifle which he had laid next to the quilt. Cocking the weapon, he made ready to do battle. In a bush about ten feet away, two beady eyes peered from between the branches. Soon the head appeared. Masked like a raccoon, it had a long white muzzle.

"A raccoon?" Lucie breathed.

"No." He held his fingers to his lips and they both fell silent.

In another moment the critter scurried out from its cover.

"A coatimundi," Micah said when he saw the long, faintly ringed tail, which was easily half the size and weight of the animal.

"I've heard of them, but I have never seen one," Lucie said.

"Though they're not nocturnal like coons, they are shy enough."

The animal suddenly seemed to take note of its observers and, with incredible speed, retreated back to its hiding place in the brush.

"I'm glad you didn't shoot it," Lucie said.

"I wouldn't have. I usually look before I shoot." He gently released the cocking mechanism and laid aside the rifle. "But that could have been anything. I'm glad I had the rifle."

"Yet it wasn't."

"It isn't good to get too complacent in this land. It ain't tame."

Micah lay back again and tried to recapture the moment before the interruption. It was hard. His heart was still pounding, not from fear of danger, but rather because he might have been forced to kill again. In this wild country it was a delusion to think you would never have to kill to defend yourself, your land, or your loved ones. But Micah shuddered at the thought of having to do so in front of Lucie, of soiling her with violence.

"I haven't had any more nightmares," he said suddenly. "Not since the fever broke."

"That's good." She paused and looked down at him.

His heart clenched, for such was her expression that it almost gave him cause to hope.

"Would you like to talk about them?" she asked.

"Why wake sleeping dogs, as they say?"

"Because sleeping dogs do wake. I remember I used to have nightmares right after my mother died, and my father once told me that the best way to rid myself of such darkness was to shine light on it. Bring my fears into the light is what he meant. Talking about fearful things seems to have a way of shrinking them down to proper size."

"No doubt you and your father are right." He wondered how much to say to her. Then he decided he'd never had anyone he could say everything to, and because of that he'd squashed a lot down inside him. Maybe it would help to get it out. And maybe she could be that one person whom he could trust enough to tell.

He rolled over on his side and gazed at her. "I don't want to talk to you about it because the last thing I want is to drag you into the violence of my life."

"Micah, I washed the blood off your hands when you killed those bandits. I have just nursed you from wounds that nearly caused your death. I am part of your life—violence and all. You need not protect me. This is my choice. Besides, I am not as pure as you may think. I have seen violence and strife."

"Yet still you are pure. Somehow it has not touched you. Your mother's death, your father's illness, your brother's life, the rejection of the ranchers. Your purity and your faith have remained intact. How is that, Lucie?"

"I still think you have placed me on far too high a pedestal," she replied with a small tinge of pink on her cheeks. "But I will tell you this. My faith has not remained intact in spite of adversity. Instead it is the other way around. Adversity has strengthened my faith, and the reason, I believe, is because I don't call God into question for all the ill in my life."

"Why not? He is God, after all."

"I think you know the answer to that."

"Oh yes," Micah replied a bit too glibly. "Free will, as it is called in religious circles."

"Micah, I can't argue religious doctrine with you. You probably know much more than I, and I'll bet you are a far better debater than I. So rather than debate, I will tell you one thing from my heart. What sustains my faith is love, pure and simple. God's love for me. I feel it always, and it gives me assurance that He will always treat me well."

Micah closed his eyes. Yes, it would have been so much easier to bat around doctrines and such. But love? How does one argue with something that is not a concrete issue but fairly glows from Lucie's heart? He sensed that from the first moment he saw Lucie. It was that very love that had drawn him. Not specifically a love for him, but her simple capacity for love. And he could not now debate it. He didn't want to.

He kept his eyes closed, for it was hard to look at her and confess the deepest pain of his soul. "Lucie, I haven't known much love in my life, so . . . it's hard to see, really see, these things you say about God. You talk about a loving God. I know the Scriptures tell of these things, but to me . . . He is a stranger. I have feared God, but love? I just don't know."

"I won't say there is nothing to fearing God," she replied. "He is *God*, after all. But I believe it should be more of an awe-inspiring fear, not a shake-in-your-boots fear. The most awesome thing about God is His love."

"But how can I possibly understand that love?" Micah rolled onto his back and stared up into the sky, as if the very heavens might open up and answer him.

"I think I came to understand it because of my parents," Lucie said. "I always felt their love, even when I was naughty. And I came to see how God was like that. It was easy to understand what Christ did on the cross. There's a verse in the Bible that says that God showed His love toward us in that while we were still in sin, Christ died for us."

"I never had such examples," Micah said. "Maybe from my mother, but it is so dim in my memory now. I probably would have been better off if I had dwelt more on remembering the things my mother taught me than on hating my father."

"I wish you had."

He heard the sadness in her voice. He still did not have the courage to look at her.

"I wish you had some way to see love," she added softly.

He wanted so to open his eyes and look at her, but he was afraid to. He thought she spoke of more than God's love.

"If only I could," he breathed, barely above a whisper. "I think I'd know better how to give love as well."

They were silent awhile. A fly buzzed around Micah's face, and he brushed it away. It seemed to him there must be a way for even one such as he to solve the puzzle of God's love. He knew that all had access to that love, that a man wasn't left out of the club, as it were, just because his experience was so limited. The God that Lucie spoke of—the God Micah wanted so to believe in—would not hold out a gift that was limited to only a few lucky ones. There must be a way.

Now he did venture a glance toward Lucie. She had plucked a bluebell from the grass and was studying its pretty purple petals. Her face in profile was pensive, yet at peace as well. She did not have the look of one who feared her friend might be denied what she had found. She was so certain of God. Then he thought of a matter that had nagged at him since he realized Lucie had taken him in to nurse him.

"Lucie," he said, "I have been wondering and wondering why

you took me in after what I tried to do to you that night in the stable. And after all the other things I have said and done. I couldn't figure it out because I couldn't understand the reason for it. You did it out of love, didn't you? You couldn't turn me away because you love me. I wouldn't be so presumptuous as to say it was more than a Christian love, but that's what it was, wasn't it?"

"Yes . . ." she murmured, her eyes still focused on the bluebell.

"But it can't be so simple."

"Why not, Micah!" Her voice rose with intensity as her eyes lifted and met his. "Even Jesus said we must become as children to enter the kingdom of God."

Micah jumped up and paced to the edge of the clearing. He knew she'd tell him how simple it was, but it was too difficult to accept that. He turned.

"Lucie, I have never been a child," he said dismally. He came back to the quilt and dropped to his knees before her. "My father certainly never let me be a child. I was constantly made to be some kind of symbol of his religious perfection. I was full grown at thirteen when I watched my mother bleed to death on the trail after having run away from my father. I was an old man when less than a year later I stood at Goliad and watched my uncle and four hundred others massacred. Those nightmares, Lucie . . . they aren't just crazy visions of ghosts and goblins. They were the reality of my life haunting my dreams. Hardly a night went by that I did not relive horror after horror. Blood! It's all over me, not just on my hands. I am steeped in it. And it is not all innocent blood like at Goliad. I exacted much vengeance for that day. At San Jacinto I shot armed and unarmed men. That's what I dream about—a boy with hands raised, begging me with his eyes not to shoot. And feeling joy at pulling the trigger."

He stopped abruptly, shocked and dismayed at what he had revealed. But it was pity, not revulsion, he saw in Lucie's eyes.

"You were fourteen, Micah," she said. "Confused, hurt, and caught in the horror of war."

"Those banditos . . ." he began, and now he dared not stop. Let her know it all. "The last one . . . I . . . think there was a moment when, had I allowed myself, I could have let him live. But I didn't think. I acted on instinct—the instinct of a killer."

"You are not a killer!" she insisted passionately. "But even if you were, do you think you'd be beyond God's power to heal?"

"I don't know."

"He has healed your nightmares."

"For the time being."

"Oh, Micah!" she exclaimed in frustration, throwing down the flower in her hand. "You are as obstinate as that mule of yours!"

"I have always said we deserve each other—me and Stew, that is." He let a smile play upon the corners of his lips. This was supposed to be an enjoyable afternoon picnic. He was desperate to bring it back to that. Tenderly he picked up the bluebell. "I'll keep this, if you don't mind. A memento of my first picnic." His eyes searched hers, imploring that she accept a truce of sorts from the previous intensity.

A smile on her lips, slightly reluctant, but offered nonetheless, she said, "I'll pick you a bouquet, if you'd like."

"One is all I need." He looked at the flower, then back up at her. "Not that I'll soon forget this day."

Thirty-Five

IT WAS LATE AFTERNOON when they reached the house. A strange horse was tied at the post in front. And a rangy-looking animal it was. A charcoal with many flecks of white or gray, but most likely gray, because it appeared to be an ancient beast. The coat was matted and dull, either from ill care or simple age. Its head hung low and its body was bony.

"You know anyone with a mount like that?" Micah asked.

"I should hope not!" Lucie replied. "Why, he makes your Stew look like a stallion!"

They took their mounts to the stable, tending them quickly, then walked to the house. Micah hoped the visitor had nothing to do with him because he was exhausted and could only think of stretching out on his bed for a while before supper.

Lucie entered first. Micah heard her gasp just before he ran into her back as she stopped abruptly before the open parlor door. Micah was about to apologize when he glanced over her head into the parlor. Then he, too, gasped.

Unable to speak, he glanced at Lucie to ensure he was not imagining the sight that greeted him. Then he looked back at the guest in the parlor.

"Well, say something, boy, or I'm gonna think maybe I am a ghost!" Tom Fife stood, a grin plastered across his whiskered face.

"I—" Micah began, then shook his head. "You real, then, Tom?"

"Of course he is!" said Reid, also seated in the parlor. "Now come on in and give the man a proper greeting."

Lucie and Micah both came fully into the parlor, but Micah stopped just short of his friend, just short of throwing his arms around the man.

Lucie took Tom's hand and smiled. "This is so wonderful, Mr. Fife!" Tears welled in her eyes.

Tom graciously gave Lucie's hand a squeeze, then turned toward Micah. "Come here, ya ornery cuss!" He grabbed Micah and fairly crushed him in a mighty bear hug.

Micah just bit his lip. Shoot, if he wasn't gonna cry! But he blinked back the moisture as quickly as it rose. "Ya ain't dead" was all he could say.

Tom stepped back. "Not yet. And neither are you. Why, up until yesterday, I'd given you up for dead, too. Guess only the good die young."

"Like Jed," Micah murmured.

"Yeah," Tom said solemnly, then added more lightly, "You and I will probably live forever!"

"No doubt," said Micah. He grinned and gave Tom a more careful perusal. "You're scrawnier than a motherless polecat! Near as bad as that critter outside passing for a horse."

"I ain't had it near as good as you, all pampered and cozy in this fine house with the prettiest nurse in Texas."

"Micah didn't look quite so good when he first came," Lucie said.

"I know." Again Tom was serious. "I heard some in town about what happened to you. I still can't believe you walked near fifty miles. But even more amazing was what that mule of yours did. There's a story that will go down with the legends."

"What happened to you, Tom?" asked Micah.

Lucie interjected, "Why don't we all make ourselves comfortable, then Mr. Fife can tell us at his leisure."

"Yes," said Reid, "I want to hear as well. Tom's been here for an hour, but we put off his story so he wouldn't have to tell it twice. Would anyone like refreshment first?"

"No," said Micah. "I want to hear what happened to you, Tom—how you came back from the dead."

"It ain't much of a story," Tom said as he resumed his seat.

Micah noted that his friend was limping, but he said nothing and, after seeing Lucie to a chair, took a chair next to her and nodded for Tom to continue.

"I reckon those two varmints, Baker and Lowe, thought I was dead. I must've been out cold when they looked me over—anyway,

I'll give them that much. But what still sticks in my craw is that they left you knowing you was alive. They should've found a way. But what's done and all that."

He sighed, shaking his head, and Micah glimpsed some of what Tom must have suffered thinking Micah was dead. It fairly stunned him.

Tom went on, "So Baker and Lowe left me where I was behind a mesquite bush. I guess they took you across the river, so's you'd have more protection if the Comanches came back. Well, that's the irony of it, ain't it? We was that close, no more'n a stone's throw from each other, and we didn't even know it! I lay where I was all that day and most of the next, bleeding and dying of thirst. I couldn't move. My leg was shot up too bad. Finally I couldn't bear the thought of dying of thirst with a creek a few feet away. Maybe some of my strength had returned—I don't really know—but I crawled down to the bank. The water sustained me for two more days. I covered myself with some nearby branches and such, so when the Indians came back they didn't see me."

"I had already taken off by then," Micah said. "If I'd been in my right mind, I would have known better than to believe them varmints Baker and Lowe. But there was nary a sound or a movement from where you fell."

"Like I said, a real irony," Tom said. "I was unconscious most of the time, but when I came to, I didn't dare move too much, even if I could, for fear of the Comanches. But if you had seen me, I'll wager you'd have died for certain then because you would not have taken off without me, and I couldn't walk an inch. So it all worked out for the best."

"But if you couldn't walk, Mr. Fife," Lucie asked, "how did you finally get away?"

"Some traders happened by. They saw my body and was gonna bury me. Luckily, I had just enough life left in me to make 'em stop. Instead, they loaded me in their wagon and took me to Laredo. I tried to tell them to get me to San Antonio, but they were heading to Laredo, and it would have been out of their way. At any rate I wasn't in much of a position to be insistent. Leastways there was a doc in Laredo. But that varmint was gonna cut my leg off. I told him if he did that I'd come back and cut his heart out. I was half out of my head at the time and couldn't have been too awfully fearsome, but bless that doctor's heart, he saved my leg." Pausing, Tom stiffly moved his right leg. "For what it's worth. I reckon it'll never be the same, but at least it's still hooked on."

Micah stared at his friend in amazement.

Tom laughed. "It is a pure miracle, ain't it? I mean, you and me both coming back from the dead."

"You could call it that," Micah replied noncommittally.

"You mean to tell me, Micah, that you're still being ornery about God?" Tom turned to Lucie. "Ain't you talked no sense into him yet?"

Lucie smiled wanly. "He has a rather thick head."

"Yeah, I do remember seeing a Comanche arrow bounce off his head before I blacked out," Tom said.

Micah fingered the scar above his ear. It was still raw and tender. "It hardly bounced," he said with mock defensiveness. He looked around at the three people who had become, perhaps, the most important people in his life just then. They deserved more than a recalcitrant attitude. "I guess I've got to allow for the possibility of a miracle—well, more than a possibility!" But he couldn't say more than that, and he grew uncomfortable. "I'm sure parched, Lucie. If you'd like, I'll go ask Juana to get us some tea or something."

"I'll go," Lucie said, rising. "You and Tom can visit."

Tom stayed for supper and, in fact, was invited to stay the night in a spare bed in the bunkhouse. After the meal, Micah walked with Tom outside—or rather, Tom limped and Micah hobbled, for his wound in his side was giving him a painful stitch. Tom said he wanted to see the famous mule, Stew. Lucie gave them some sugar.

"That gal always spoiling your mule like that?" Tom asked as they came to Stew's stall.

"I guess so."

Tom reached in and rubbed the white patch on the mule's sandy face. "It's pretty clear she's mighty glad this beast saved your hide."

"Maybe . . ."

"You been here three weeks now recuperating. That all you got to say?"

"Tom, when did you get to be so talkative?" Micah asked, just a bit peeved.

"Near dying does that to a fellow. Makes you realize you better get your licks in while ya can." Tom held out his hand to Stew, a lump of sugar in his palm. The mule nearly nipped off his hand going for the treat. "Ouch!" Tom yanked back his empty hand. "And here I thought your heroic deeds might have made a decent creature of you!" He scolded the mule. Then he turned to Micah. "And same to you, boy! Didn't your experience teach you nothing?"

"Yeah. Never camp on a creek bank when there's high ground around!" Micah retorted, then his expression twisted in shame. "I'm sorry, Tom. I'm about going crazy with all the soul-searching I've been doing lately. And now to have you preaching at me—"

"The Maccallums been preaching at you a lot?"

"Nah, not really. Not even after I gave Lucie leave to preach all she wanted. It's not them. It's me. Wondering about it all, what it means." Micah went to a nearby stool and plopped down rather dejectedly. "I know something's gonna give soon, and I know it's gonna be me. And it scares me worse than dying did. Tom, what do you think about all this religion business?"

"You're asking a man who's just been hauled from the bowels of death. That ought to make a believer out of anyone." Tom turned and leaned against the wall, facing Micah. "But then again, you are also asking a man who never attended much church and such." He smiled suddenly. "Your pa once thought me a pure and simple heathen. Guess he wouldn't take too kindly to me giving you religious advice. I wish I would have gone to church more, and I just might do it now. But I always have had a mighty high opinion of God. I believe in Him, Micah, because living out in the wilds as I have, it's impossible not to. And I know it was His doing that you and I survived. Why us and not Jed? Can't say, except maybe Jed was more ready than us. And maybe God has something more He wants us for. That's a fearsome prospect."

Micah nodded. "It's all fearsome." He paused, hesitant. He picked up a bit of straw from the ground and rolled it thoughtfully between his fingers. Finally he looked up. "You ever worry, Tom, about what God thinks of all the killing we've done?"

"I ain't never shot at anything that wasn't shooting back," Tom answered.

"I have, Tom," Micah confessed. The admission did not get easier with repetition. "At San Jacinto."

Tom limped over to Micah and laid a hand on his shoulder. "That was a terrible, terrible time, boy. I should have kept you away from that slaughter, but I lost track of you. It was a confused time. Everyone's pain and anger ran so deep for what had been done in the past. I ain't excusing it, but ... somehow I think God would understand the heart of a fourteen-year-old boy caught in that horror."

"Lucie says God loves me in spite of what I've done," Micah said. "But I just don't think that's enough. I don't know how I can ever make up for what I've done, but there ought to be something to *do*."

"Seems like it, don't it?" Tom shifted uncomfortably.

Micah jumped up. "Sit here, Tom. You oughtn't to stand on that leg for so long."

"Thanks, Micah." Tom eased down on the stool. "I guess they'll be putting ol' Tom out to pasture now."

"Ya ever think about ranching?"

"I got my land allotments up near Austin. I always thought I'd retire there one day. Don't know a blessed thing about ranching, though. I wonder if it's true about old dogs and new tricks. And an old dog with a bum leg to boot!"

"I might give it a try. Reid Maccallum said he'd teach me what I need to know."

"You could do worse for a teacher—or for a father-in-law."

"We'll see about that. I'm a long way from being deserving of a gal like Lucie."

Silence fell between them as the evening shadows lengthened, and it grew dark in the stable.

With a groan, Tom lumbered to his feet. "Best get on before it's too dark to find my way to that bunkhouse." He started toward the door, then paused. "Micah, about that other matter, you know, about religion and all. I'm sorry I couldn't be more help to you."

Smiling, Micah strode up next to his friend. "Just seeing you today helped stir something like faith in me. I'm not ashamed to admit that when I saw you, Tom, I like to have cried."

"You don't say?" Tom was clearly astonished.

"Last time I cried was when my ma died, and I swore then I'd hate too much to ever cry again. Maybe . . ." he mused half to himself, "maybe something is changing in me. God must love me some to give me a gift like you coming back from the dead."

Side by side they hobbled from the stable, one leaning on the other. Micah was exhausted in his body, but there was indeed a stirring in him that seemed a lot like hope.

Thirty-Six

MICAH WATCHED JACK Hays ride away. They had just finished making a survey of a plot of land by Cutter Creek. Besides being a ranger, Hays was also a surveyor by trade. Micah was not making any commitments, but ... well, he was bored and needed something to do. It wouldn't come to anything, but thinking about it merely filled time. He certainly had made no mention of the outing to Lucie.

Micah remained in the area, taking another ride around the place. It was a good stretch of land, with abundant grass to graze a decent herd. True, cattle ranching was not going to make a man wealthy, but who could tell what the future might hold? Anyway, Micah was not looking for wealth. Just peace. Would that be found on a ranch? Or was rangering still what Micah wanted to do? Jack had spent most of their day together encouraging Micah to return to the unit now that he was pretty much recovered.

Micah simply did not know what he would do. One thing was certain, he had to move on from the Maccallum place. He no longer needed nursing, and he and Lucie were, well, just getting way too close. The last thing he wanted to do was hurt her. And right now he wasn't certain what would hurt her more, marrying her or leaving her. He knew what would hurt him. The thought of leaving her tore him up inside. Yet he could not think of himself and his own desires in this.

Though he'd had few nightmares in the last weeks, that gunfight with the banditos still haunted him. He still shuddered at the thought of how instinct and pure reflex had caused him to kill those men, especially that last man. He knew it wasn't exactly murder, because in such a position a man did not have the luxury to pause and debate his actions. Survival had propelled him, he hoped. Yet doubt nagged at him.

Regardless, if he was a man whose first instincts were kill or be killed, he was not the kind of man for a genteel woman like Lucie.

He thought of that day on the picnic when he had grabbed his rifle at a mere sound. He'd been ready to kill. There was such a fine line between simple survival and being a killer at heart. Especially in this untamed country where dangers were very real. On which side of the line did he stand? He did not know.

Micah rode up to an oak and reined his mount. He'd seen this tree from a distance while with Hays and wanted a better look. It was old and gnarled with twisted branches, and even with its summer foliage, its long sprawling limbs made it appear barren. It was standing in the middle of a grassy meadow, the only tree for quite a distance. He liked the look of it and was glad it was on his land. He felt akin to it in many ways. But this oak must have strength and deep roots for it to remain green and sturdy so far from water.

Suddenly Micah realized what he had just thought. *His land?* Could he make roots like the oak? Strong enough, deep enough to offer shade and shelter to the woman he knew he loved? Shelter and not strife. They had already had far too much strife.

Shots in the distance grabbed Micah's attention. Riders were galloping in his direction. He saw four Mexicans being chased by three gringos. Micah jumped off Stew and slapped the mule's rump, making him race off away from the chase. Then Micah took cover behind the oak. He could not outrun the Mexicans and he saw no reason to become embroiled in a situation until he knew more. The Mexicans were probably bandits, and the gringos might well be rangers. But the Mexicans *could* be locals, and the gringos could be mere troublemakers.

Not far from Micah, the Mexicans split up, two racing off south while the other two headed north toward Micah's position. The gringos were closer now, and Micah thought he recognized Big Foot Wallace's mule and Bert Long's chestnut. Wallace and one of the rangers took off after the bandits heading south. Bert Long raced north.

Long fired, striking one of the two bandits he was chasing. The Mexican hit the dirt. The remaining bandit took aim. He had a revolver, but Micah saw Long had only used his percussion cap pistol and was going for his second pistol. He could not possibly draw it before the Mexican fired. He'd be dead if Micah didn't do something.

Having no choice, Micah drew his revolver, but in the split second before he fired, he saw the bandit's face. He hesitated, and the bandit got off his shot anyway, and Long fell. Micah fired just as the bandit wheeled his mount around. His shot struck the bandit's horse and the animal reared, throwing his rider into the dirt. The bandit rolled once and, amazingly, as he gained a squatting position, still had his gun in hand and was aiming at Micah, who also hit the dirt. The bandit's shot went astray.

In the next instant both men poised to fire again and at the same moment saw they'd both end up dead if they followed through.

A grim smile twisted the bandit's face. "I think you gringos call this a Mexican standoff."

"It appears to be just that," Micah agreed.

Carefully, each eyeing the other, both men drew to their feet. The bandit cocked a brow, arrogance and disdain marking his features. "I recognize you. Sinclair, isn't it? The man who killed six of my best men in one bloody battle."

"And you are Joaquin Viegas," Micah said coolly. "You've killed a few of my friends as well."

"So now what?"

Suddenly Micah threw his gun into the grass. Viegas could have killed him instantly then but was obviously too stunned to react to the unexpected gesture.

"I ain't gonna kill you, Viegas, so no sense drawing this out any longer." Micah hadn't realized until the instant he tossed down his gun that he was going to do it, but now he realized it was all he could do. All he would do.

"¿Qué es?" mumbled Viegas. "Why?"

"I'm plain tired of killing. Besides, killing you would hurt too many folks I care about."

"What do you mean by this? Speak clearly or I will shoot. I have every reason to kill you for what you did to my men."

Viegas's eyes were hard and steely, but Micah saw something

else in them. More than a hint of Lucie's eyes were there. And around Viegas's nose and chin there was Reid Maccallum. But how could Micah explain all he was feeling to his adversary when he didn't understand half of it himself? He could have killed Viegas five minutes ago while he was mounted and aiming at Bert. But he hadn't, and he knew his skill well enough to know when he had fired, he'd missed on purpose, even if at the time he had not pointedly told himself to miss. Had it been instinct? To miss? To spare a life instead of take it?

"Speak, gringo!" hissed Viegas. "My patience wanes."

"I'm acquainted with your family."

"A mere acquaintance would not cause a man to do what you have done, risked what you have risked. Perhaps I have been lured into some trap."

Micah shook his head. Why would this man, this enemy, believe him? Yet if Micah didn't become more convincing, he was going to die. "I happen to be in love with your sister," he admitted. It was the first time he'd ever ventured such words of love, but Micah knew they were true. He wished it could be Lucie hearing this remarkable confession and not a bandit poised to kill him. "I'd marry her if I thought I was good enough for her," he added, feeling suddenly rather cocky.

"You?" exclaimed the bandit.

Micah could not tell if it was shock or fury in the man's tone. Micah snorted dryly. "Guess you'll kill me for sure now. But if it's gotta be that way, then so be it. I'd rather that than risk hurting her."

"And does my sister feel the same toward you?"

"Maybe, but I wouldn't want to speak for her."

"But if she does, would not your death hurt her as well?"

Micah hadn't thought of that. "I only know if you die, especially by my hand, it could destroy her."

Viegas eyed Micah somewhat dubiously but also with a perplexed crease in his brow. His gun hand, however, was still taut and ready.

"I think you speak truly, gringo," Viegas said slowly and thoughtfully. "But I have never known a ranger to be squeamish about killing an enemy—for any reason. And knowing who you are, I realize you could have killed me before. Stories of your abilities have spread, and I doubt you would have shot my horse if you hadn't been aiming at him."

"Well," Micah said, "it's true I wasn't aiming at you, but neither was I aiming at your horse. He turned and got the round that was supposed to go over his head."

"Still, you did not aim at me."

"You and I, Viegas . . . maybe neither of us are killers deep down. Lucie believes in us, anyway. I don't know about you, but I realize there ain't nothing I want more than to live up to her faith in me."

For the first time, Viegas's expression softened. He lowered his gun. "Find your mount and be on your way, Sinclair, before I decide I prefer a different future brother-in-law."

"Gladly, Viegas." Micah whistled, and Stew, who had not wandered far, trotted up to him. Micah mounted.

"Before you leave, Sinclair, I have one piece of advice for you," Viegas said somewhat wryly but also with a note of earnestness. "Get out of the rangering business. I do not want to see my sister made a widow."

"I'll give it serious consideration, amigo." Then Micah added, "And here's some advice for you. Go see your father. He ain't gonna live forever, and it breaks his heart more every day thinking he might never see you again. He loves you, and he don't deserve the pain you've been giving him."

"I, too, will consider—" Viegas stopped suddenly and smiled. "No, I will do it. Very soon."

Micah rode up to where Bert Long lay. He was still alive. Micah hauled him up with him on the mule. Glancing back before he rode away, Micah saw that Viegas had mounted his dead comrade's horse with the man's body secured behind. Viegas then rode away toward the south. Would he go to the Maccallum ranch? Perhaps he was just going south to take care of his fallen comrade's body and then to tie up loose ends, get his affairs in order. It would be a risky prospect for the bandit to go to the Maccallum ranch. It might be his death warrant. Yet Micah felt certain Viegas would go. Viegas did not hate his father.

Micah took Bert to the Maccallum ranch to get patched up. It was the closest destination, and besides, Micah wanted to see Lucie.

"You two gals ought to hang out a shingle," he said to Lucie and Juana as they followed him to his old room. He had Bert Long slung over his shoulder.

"Imagine that!" Juana laughed. "Dr. Juana Herrera ... hmm, I like the sound of it."

Micah deposited Bert on the bed. The ranger groaned. "Hey, Micah! I ain't no sack of potatoes. Watch it!"

"I don't reckon he's hurt too bad if he can complain like that," Micah said with a chuckle.

Bert had taken a shot in his calf, but the lead had gone cleanly through. There was little bleeding. His worst wound was a nasty gash on his head, which had struck a rock when he fell from his horse. Assured that his friend indeed was not too badly off, Micah beckoned Lucie out into the hall.

"Lucie, I saw your brother today," he said.

"Joaquin!" Fear and excitement collided in her face.

Micah told her about their meeting. "Ain't that the most amazing thing you ever heard?"

"I . . . I simply don't know what to say!" Then, seeming to come to herself, she threw her arms around Micah. "Thank you, Micah!"

"It felt good, Lucie. I know sparing one man don't make up for all the others, but then again, in a funny way that I can't explain, it does. Inside me, it does. But I don't want to analyze it. It was a good thing. That's all that matters."

She lightly kissed his cheek before dropping her embrace and stepping away. "Yes, Micah." She was fairly beaming. "I am so proud of you!"

"I just wanted to let you know I'll be going away for a while," he said. And when the light dramatically faded from her eyes, he quickly added, "Just a few days is all! I'm heading north. I figure its time I took the same advice I gave your brother."

Thirty-Seven

IN NINE YEARS the place had not changed much. Well, that wasn't exactly true. There were some bright flowers blooming in a small garden by the front steps. And cheery curtains in the windows. There was an altogether inviting look to the place. But still Micah feared that invitation might not be extended to him.

At the edge of the yard he dismounted and walked the mule the rest of the way. He'd barely gotten to the middle of the yard when a squealing little girl came racing toward him from the woods by the house. She fairly screeched to a halt upon seeing him, and all her merry squealing ceased. She appeared to be about ten years old, chubby and rosy cheeked with a mop of golden curls on her head.

Before Micah could address her, another girl jogged into the yard.

"Leah, you give that back to me! I found it—"

Then this girl stopped abruptly as well. Slender and pale with hair the color of strawberries streaked with sunshine, Micah knew her immediately. And she, incredibly, recognized him.

"Micah!" Isabel cried, racing past her sister and throwing her arms around him.

"Yeah, it's me, but I can't believe you recognized me," he said. He felt he surely must have aged a hundred years in nine.

"Of course I do!" She stepped back and smiled up at him. Micah's heart clenched. She looked so much like their mother. Then she held a hand out to her sister. "Leah, this is our brother Micah. You were too little to remember him."

Leah bent her head back to get a good look but still said nothing.

"I have never seen her so quiet," Isabel said.

307

As if to defy that remark, Leah finally said, "You can't be our brother. You're taller than Papa."

Micah shrugged, not quite knowing how to answer that. "Well, I am your brother, and I am glad to meet you, Leah. You were nothing but a slip of a thing when I last saw you. And you, Issy!" He gave her an astonished look. "You're nearly a full-grown woman. How old are you?"

"Sixteen."

"Well, you've grown into a beautiful young lady, that's for sure." It warmed him that she blushed with pleasure at his compliment. He remembered when she used to look up to him as a big brother. It appeared as if she still might, though he knew he didn't deserve it.

Isabel took his hand. "Come on into the cabin and see everyone else."

"Everyone. . . ?" His throat turned dry as the real reason for his visit suddenly reared before him.

"Except Papa," piped up Leah, appearing to warm to the stranger who was her brother. "He's down to the Hunter place, but he'll be back by supper."

Relief washed over Micah. He knew he was going to have to face the man eventually, but he just couldn't feel disappointed about a delay.

"Lead the way," he said, tying Stew to a post before following the girls up the cabin step.

Inside he was greeted with a buzz of activity, though not chaotic as he remembered when his father had been caring for household matters. Rather, it was a pleasant sound of children's voices, the sizzling of some good-smelling thing on the stove, and the gentle purr of a woman's voice.

"It's all right, Oliver, don't worry, there's more milk." Elise, Micah's stepmother, was bent over the table, her back to the door, a cloth in her hand mopping up obviously spilt milk.

"Mama," Isabel said, "we have a visitor."

Micah was both touched and inexplicably disturbed by his sister's casual reference to Elise as "Mama."

Elise turned, and a look of surprise was immediately replaced by a warm, welcoming grin.

"Micah! Oh, my goodness ... Micah!" Sudden tears welled in her dark eyes.

" 'Pears I haven't changed much at all in nine years," Micah said dryly.

Elise came up to him, took his hands in hers, and gave him a close appraisal. "Well, you've grown a foot at least. And my"—she let go of one of his hands and fingered the fringe on his buckskin coat—"you certainly have filled out the coat, haven't you?" Her eyes briefly rested on the place on his shoulder where one of the bandito's shots had penetrated and which he had clumsily patched.

"It's served me well," he said, suddenly wanting to turn away so she would not question the damage. But he forced himself to keep on facing her.

"I remember how you had to hitch a belt around you so it wouldn't billow out like a tent," she remarked.

"Yeah." He tried to smile and not remember the life of violence his coat had seen since then.

"Well, you've met Isabel and Leah, now let me introduce you to the rest of the family." She turned to the boy at the table. "This is your baby brother, Oliver."

"Mama, I ain't no baby!" Oliver said.

He was, by Micah's reckoning, nine years old. His hair was light brown and straight except where it curled around his ears and collar. His eyes were blue-green and remarkably like their father's. He now looked up at Micah with what might well be awe in those eyes.

"Papa says you are a ranger, that you've fought in wars with Mexico and against Comanches."

"I've done some fighting," Micah said uncomfortably.

"That a revolver?" Oliver's eyes focused on the Colt tucked in Micah's belt.

Micah now realized his oversight in not leaving the gun in his saddlebag. It had been wrong to come into this cabin armed. "Yes, it is," Micah said.

"Can I hold it?"

"Not now ... maybe later." The boy's eagerness disturbed

Micah. Did the child with the name that meant peace take more after his brother than his father?

By now three other children had come into the circle, and though they were staring with unabashed curiosity at Micah, they were clinging to Elise.

Elise placed an arm around the oldest of the three. "This is Hannah."

Hannah smiled, gave a little curtsey, but said nothing. She would be ten now, and she was even more pale and frail-appearing than Isabel. Micah returned the smile, and because the girl suddenly began to blush, he thought better of saying anything.

"And these two little darlings are your half brother and half sister," Elise said. "Joseph is four, and Beth is two."

They also smiled shyly but said nothing.

"I'm pleased to meet all of you." Micah looked around the room. "You got any more hiding in the corners?" he asked lightly.

Elise laughed. "Well . . . one where you can't see it yet."

Then Micah noted that Elise was in the family way. Her apron camouflaged it pretty well, but it was plain there was a slight bulge in her midriff. He quickly shifted his eyes away, cursing the heat he felt rising about his ears. He hadn't been so young when his mother had gotten into such a condition not to notice how miserable she had been, especially with Leah and Oliver. But Elise was glowing. The new baby would make seven children for her to care for, even if they weren't all hers. Yet she was still young-looking, even beautiful. It actually seemed as if she was thriving on her circumstance. Part of Micah resented this, yet another part for the first time in his life wondered if his mother had not somehow brought some of her misery upon herself.

No, it couldn't be! His father had been a monster. He had heaped burdens and expectations upon his family that none could bear. Yet why did he sense none of that oppression now in this family?

"Micah," Elise was saying, "we'll be having supper in a couple hours, but would you like something to tide you over? I'm sure you've had a bit of a journey today."

"I did skip lunch," he replied.

Elise had him sit at the table, then she set a plate of cookies and a glass of cool milk before him. As he ate every cookie on the plate and had another glass of milk besides, they visited. Isabel joined them, but the younger children, except Oliver, who remained at the table as well, grew restless and were distracted by other activities.

In less than an hour Micah had heard all the news of neighbors he had known. He shared what little political information and news he'd heard. But the conversation waned, mostly, he realized, because he kept avoiding anything to do with his personal life. Finally he could bear it no longer and lurched to his feet.

"I better see to my mount," he said. "He's been on a long road today, too."

"Oliver can take care of that," Elise offered.

"No," Micah answered quickly. "I mean, my mule is kind of temperamental, so I better do it myself." He headed for the door. Whether Elise, who he recalled as being rather intuitive, understood his need to get away or not, she made no further protest.

She did ask as he reached the door, "You will be staying on for a few days, won't you?"

"If . . . I'd be welcome."

One did not require any special mental abilities to know exactly what he meant.

"I know you will be, Micah."

He knew what she meant, and he hoped it was true.

Thirty-Eight

MORE MEMORIES FLOODED over Micah as he walked Stew to the little stable. He remembered when he and his father and Uncle Haden had built it. He remembered the huge fight that the two men had over him. Haden had left that very day, not to return until the day he took Micah, his mother, and sisters away—away from Benjamin Sinclair.

Now that Micah thought of it, Uncle Haden had never said why he had returned. Benjamin had told him never to come back. But Haden had. And during all the time Haden and Micah had spent together afterward during the war, the subject had never come up. Now Micah wondered. Had Haden come to reconcile with his brother? Had he had a change of heart? One thing Micah did recall of the time spent with his uncle was that he had not once bad-mouthed Benjamin. He had even gently rebuked Micah when he would denigrate the man.

At the time Micah was far too filled with hatred for his father to hear any defense of the man. But now Micah didn't know. He'd come home because he felt he had to, yet he had not consciously decided to forgive his father. He wasn't certain he would, though he had no idea what he would do. Perhaps that was the place Haden had been in when he had returned. He didn't know exactly why he was doing so, only that he had to do it.

Micah took his time with Stew. He removed his saddle and set it on a rack, then he found a brush and meticulously brushed the animal's coat. When he finished, he tied Stew to a post. There was a horse, a different one from any Micah remembered, in one of the two stalls, and Micah figured the other stall would be for Benjamin's mount. He was filling a bucket with some oats when he heard a sharp creak. His hand shot to the pistol still in his belt.

Then he remembered there were no dangers in this place, none at least that need be faced with a gun.

"Micah" came Benjamin's resonate voice.

Slowly Micah turned. "Pa."

The two men eyed each other, both wearing impenetrable masks that were hauntingly similar. Micah had thought of a lot of things to say to his father on the journey up from San Antonio, but speech fled him now. Accusations, apologies, venom, sorrow, regret. It all seemed so empty and futile in the face of the man who must surely be Micah's greatest enemy—and his greatest salvation.

It felt as if the silence would crack right down the middle. Then Benjamin spoke.

"I'm glad to see you, son."

"Guess it's time I came back." Micah was yanking words, it seemed, from his very guts, past a lump in his throat as large as a boulder. "I'm glad I'm welcome."

"You were always welcome. No one made you leave."

"Didn't you, Pa?"

Sudden tension sparked like flint striking rock. Then Benjamin smiled, a gesture both ironic and sad but devoid of ire.

"I guess there are ways of pushing a person away without actually doing so. I did make you leave, and I have never stopped being sorry for it."

Micah did not know how to respond to that. He wanted to reach inside himself and find that anger and hatred that had sustained him for so long. But now he knew, if he hadn't before, that he had not come home to stir old flames. God only knew, he could. He wouldn't have to reach down too far to find them and fan them into a mighty conflagration. This man had hurt him—even Benjamin himself did not deny it. The wounds were deep and some even as tender as the arrow wound in his side. The past could not disappear in a word or a gesture. Yet if Micah had learned nothing else from Lucie and from the painful realities of life, he knew it did no good to cling to the destructive forces of hate. He'd come home to make a start at least of quenching flames, not fanning them.

"We've both made mistakes, I reckon," Micah said.

"You were but a child, and I made you learn to hate—" Benjamin's voice broke with emotion. His eyes glistened.

"Don't, Pa!" Micah softly entreated. "We don't need to dwell on the past. Why don't we just start over?"

"The past will always be between us, son. We can't hide from it. Perhaps we don't have to talk about it right now, but we will need to sooner or later. Nevertheless, Micah, I want you to know I love you. Did I ever tell you that ... except when I was beating you into submission? May God forgive me for that! I love you and always have."

Sudden moisture rose in Micah's eyes. He blinked hard to push it away. Was this new path of his going to turn him into a blubbering idiot? He turned his attention to the bucket of oats, placing it where Stew could easily get to it. He rubbed the mule's face.

In another moment, confident of his control, he said, "I guess we're part of each other, Pa. We can't change that or what it means, for good or ill. I'm sorry I refused to see the love that was always there. I'm sorry I never told you the same." He looked at his father. Still, the words "I love you" were difficult to speak.

Benjamin seemed to understand that. He approached the mule and laid a hand on its flank. "So is this the famous mule that saved your life?"

"You heard about that?"

"Quite a bit after the fact, or I might have come to see you while you were ill. But by the time I heard about the exploit, you were on your feet, and I didn't want to upset you by showing up." He looked over the animal's neck at his son. "You've become fodder for legends, Micah."

"How much have you heard?"

"Enough."

"I ain't proud of any of it."

"I don't judge you, son. Honestly, I don't." They were silent for a few moments, then Benjamin added, "I think supper is nearly ready. Why don't we get back to the cabin?"

––––––

In the next three days it was fairly easy for Micah to keep interactions with his father on a safe, light level. Six children offered ample distractions, and all wanted a piece of Micah's time. And he was quite willing to give it. He wanted to get to know his brothers and sisters. He went on walks with them, swam in the creek, and joined them in their daily chores. Oliver, especially, wanted to dog Micah's every move. He nagged Micah about his guns until Micah finally relented and let the boy handle them. That wasn't quite enough, and he got Micah to take him hunting.

The boy's fascination about these things disturbed Micah. Finally one evening after all the children had gone to sleep and he was sharing a quiet cup of coffee with his father and Elise, Micah broached the topic.

He tried to speak casually and lightly. "That Oliver sure has a powerful attachment to my revolver. I found him playing with it the other day, so I hid it up on a high rafter in the barn. It wasn't loaded, but still . . ." His voice trailed away, for he didn't quite know how to verbalize his disquiet.

"Thank you, Micah," Elise said. "He is a bit young for such things."

"I've tried to teach him a bit about guns," Benjamin added. "But, if you remember, I am practically hopeless at shooting, or at least hitting a target. I manage to keep us in meat, but it isn't easy."

"You are better off that way," Micah said grimly. "Sometimes I wish—" He stopped and shook his head. "It ain't no use wishing for what'll never be. I just wouldn't want Oliver to follow in my footsteps."

"I think it might only be that he is enamored with you," Elise said. "He's never had a big brother. And well, with three older sisters, I am sure he is simply in heaven to be around you. He's heard about you. You are kind of a hero to him."

Micah gaped at her with incredulity. "That's terrible!" He jerked his gaze around to meet his father's. His eyes were filled with sudden fire. "You can't have told him about the things I've done! And I can't believe you would have held them up as heroic! I've lost count of the people I've killed, and I certainly can't say now if them or me was on the right side. And even if I thought I was right, no one—no one!—should be as proficient as I am at killing. I'm not a hero! Please tell him I am not a hero!"

"No matter what we tell him, he hears things," Benjamin said. "I've tried to impart to him a sense of right and wrong. But, Micah, I am proud of you, of what you have become in the last few years, especially. It is good to hear that you don't enjoy the taking of life, but you have been a protector of this republic. You have sacrificed greatly to keep this land safe for folks like me and my family here. Perhaps you have crossed some lines and had to deal with matters that were not always black or white, and I see clearly the toll it has taken on you. But because men like you faced these demons, men like me can live in peace. I thank you for that, and that is why you are a hero."

"You don't know everything about me, Pa," Micah murmured, shame still nagging at him.

"I don't need to know," Benjamin replied with intense confidence.

Micah was silent for several minutes as these profound words sunk into his head and his heart. He thought about the things Lucie had told him about God's mercy. He'd been wrestling so with wondering if he could really be accepted by God, if he could ever deserve peace and the genteel life Lucie offered. Then it suddenly occurred to him that his father, if anyone, would know. Micah understood now a little more about how Benjamin had suffered when Rebekah had died and how he'd finally been humbled and changed. If Micah could accept the change in his father, then perhaps it was indeed possible for him to change as well.

"Pa," he said, knowing that the time had finally come to impart to this man what lay on his heart, "Lucie told me that God loves me no matter what I've done. I know she doesn't lie and that she truly believes what she says. But . . . I've done some bad things. It just can't be that easy."

"We punish ourselves far more than God would ever think of doing," Benjamin answered. "And the worst way we punish ourselves is by our inability to accept the simplicity of faith. There is only one requirement to embrace God's love, and that is to believe in it."

"But ain't there some things that are even too much for God?" Benjamin and Elise exchanged an odd expression, then Elise reached out and laid her hand on Micah's.

"I know for a fact there isn't," she said.

He shook his head, his skepticism obvious that this near saintly woman could not possibly have even a hint of what he meant.

She went on. "Micah, I don't think you know anything of my life before I came to this house."

All he knew, he admitted to himself, was that she showed up one rainy day with a half-dead child in her arms. He knew there were some unsavory men after her at one point, and they had kidnapped her. He'd heard the word "slave" mentioned in undertones, and at fourteen he had come to the conclusion it had something to do with that. But he'd been far too wrapped up in his own misery at the time to take much interest in anyone else's.

He continued to eye her skeptically, almost daring her to shock him. She did.

"I was a prostitute before I came to your home," she said quietly, with a hint of shame in her tone.

Micah's mouth fell open, and he quickly snapped it shut. Then he said, "I thought I'd seen and done it all, that there was nothing out there that could discombobulate me." And he didn't know what stunned him more, the fact that God had accepted Elise or that his father had.

Amusement twitched at her lips, but her eyes remained solemn. "I did not think even God could wipe clean the filth of my life, my very body. But look at me now, Micah. I am clean! Not perfect by any means, but clean. And if that wasn't enough, God also gave me happiness. Have you heard that God's love covers a multitude of sins? Well, I am proof those are more than mere words."

Micah glanced back and forth between his father and Elise. He did not doubt that what she said was true. But for him? Lucie had said so, too. It must be so.

He focused on his father. "Pa, you are sure, then? All I got to do is want that love, that peace, and believe?"

"I am positive, son."

"Then I want it."

Micah stayed on at his father's house for two more days, then felt he was ready to go back south. He saddled Stew and led him out into the yard where the family was gathered to see him off. He hugged his brothers and sisters and promised he'd come back to visit more often. Elise gave him a packet of food, then encircled him with a fond embrace. He put the food in his saddlebag and turned toward his father. There was still a reticence between them. It could hardly be helped after so many years, but Micah was certain he'd be back often now and the healing between them would continue.

He held out his hand, and Benjamin shook it stoically.

"I'll be back," Micah said. He paused, then added, "And you can come south anytime to visit me. In fact, it might be in a few months"—heat began to rise in his neck, but he went on—"well, I might be getting married, and I'd like it if you came. Maybe even . . . you could perform the ceremony."

By the look of joy on Benjamin's face, Micah's halting, awkward words might have been a boon from a king.

"I'd be proud and honored to do so, Micah!"

"I guess I'll be going, then." Micah started to mount the mule, then stopped. He jerked around to face his father once again. "Pa! I do love you!"

Now Benjamin's jaw went slack, but he recovered quickly. "Forgive me, but I've got to hug you, son!" And he did so.

Micah had never felt such a thing in his life. There was power and fierceness in that embrace, but a tenderness, too, as can rarely be found except between two men who are part of one another, bone, blood, heart, and soul.

Thirty-Nine

MICAH WATCHED LUCIE ride ahead. She had challenged him to a race, but he had slowed so he could take a moment to observe her gallop across the grass. He remembered the time he had first seen her riding with the herd of horses he had been intent on stealing. So much had passed between them since then, but Lucie had not changed. She had been the gentle constant over the years, the light beckoning him through the abyss.

She slowed to a trot and, turning in her saddle, called to him, "What are you doing, slow coach! Don't you dare try to humor me! I can win you in a fair race."

He smiled and spurred his mule up alongside her. "You have won, Lucie! You've won my heart, fair and square."

"Have I? Well, it is the first time you have admitted to it." Her eyes held an impish glint.

"I thought you knew."

"You have been acting mighty peculiar since you came back from your folks' house. But you know me. I never want to be pushy."

He laughed outright, unable to contain his mirth.

She stared at him, a look of utter astonishment on her face. "Micah, I have never seen you laugh before, not like this."

He tried to control himself. When he spoke, just a few bubbles of amusement escaped. "And at your expense, no less. I am sorry."

"Don't be sorry. You must know I love it." Her eyes swept over his features, seeming to see him for the first time. "For a minute there you looked like a boy."

"Maybe I ain't a twenty-three-year-old wizened old man after all. Leastways, I don't feel like it anymore." He stretched his arms out wide and gave a whoop. Stew, misinterpreting the sound, reared, then lurched off at a run. Micah had to fight the reins to get him under control. "Why, you addlebrained, no-account, poor excuse—"

"Micah!" Lucie interrupted in a scolding tone as she rode up next to him. "Don't you say another unkind thing to this dear mule! I won't hear of it!"

"Harrumph!" Micah snorted. "And she says she ain't pushy!" Then he grinned, and his eyes filled with the overwhelming love that was filling his heart. "Lucie, let's ride over to those trees and get off for a spell. I want to talk to you."

They dismounted, tied their mounts, and found a level place in the grass to sit. Lucie brought her saddlebag. Micah brought nothing—no gun in his belt, no rifle in his hand.

The afternoon was warm with a light breeze carrying a fragrance of prairie grass. A flock of white-winged doves flew overhead.

"A feeding flight," Micah said. "We used to hunt them by firing into the swarm. They make good eating if you are hungry enough."

"I like better 'La Paloma,'" Lucie said. "The old Mexican ballad about the doves." She hummed a tune, then in Spanish softly sang a verse.

Micah gazed at her and was reminded of her other heritage. How naturally the Spanish language flowed from her tongue. He had come to have a fair understanding of the language of his old enemies as well. But he felt no enmity for them now. That had all seemed to die with his other old hatreds. He felt no hesitation at all in reaching out to this woman. She represented only love and life and peace to him.

"Micah," she said softly as he continued to stare after she had finished the song, "you look like you have swallowed one of those birds whole."

"I feel a bit like I have, too. Not since I told my father I loved him has there been such a lump in my throat."

"Why is that?"

Her impish grin indicated she must already know the answer to her question. But she had a right to hear it with her own ears, just as his father had.

"Words like that don't come easy to me, Lucie."

"I well know!"

"Anyway, I been wanting to tell you since I came back yesterday. But there was so much else to talk about regarding those amazing days I spent with my family. I still can't believe it went so well." He caught a new glint in her eyes. "You needn't look so smug, even if you knew all the while it would be so. Though I do think you are the wisest, smartest woman—no, person!—I know. I probably won't always listen to you even when I should."

"You probably won't."

"It's already been established how thick-skulled I am."

"Yes . . ."

"You don't have to agree so quickly!" He shook his head and laughed. "All right. See if you agree with this. I love you, Lucinda Maria Bonny Maccallum! Ya hear?" He paused long enough to gasp in a breath as the full import of his own words struck him. "I do love you!"

"And I love you, Micah!"

"But you always have, haven't you?"

"When I wasn't angry at you or confused about you."

"Same here. I've loved you from that instant you fainted in my arms."

"I didn't faint!"

"Oh, maybe you was just faking so I'd hold you." He reached toward her, gathering her into his arms. "Like this . . ."

"Very likely!"

She melted into his embrace, and he marveled at how well they seemed to fit together.

"Only now there is no confusion," she added.

He nodded his agreement.

"Do you want to hear when I first knew I loved you, though I was afraid to admit it?"

Micah nodded his head, his cheek still pressed against her soft hair.

"It was when you gave that little Hornsby baby to Mrs. Wendell. She thought you ran out because you were so glad to get rid of a little nuisance. But I knew better. When you rescued me, I thought there was more to you than a rough horse thief. But in that moment with the child, I was certain. It's funny, but in spite of all the confusion you have caused me in the last couple of years, I was always certain of your tender heart, Micah. You tried so hard to hide it, but you were never very successful."

"That's one thing I'm glad I failed at, then." Reluctantly, he let his arms drop and moved a safe distance from her. "I wish I was better—" Stopping suddenly, he shook his head. "No, I won't go down that road again. I know now I'll never ever be deserving of what God gives me. I'm just gonna accept it."

"That's good to hear."

"Lucie, I want to marry you. You know that?"

"That's also good to hear," she replied just a bit dryly. "Especially since I want to marry you as well."

"I would have been back sooner from Cooksburg, but I made a little side trip. I went by the capital to file some papers. I made claim to a parcel of land."

"You did!" She beamed, then tried to temper it as she added, "I wouldn't have required it of you. I mean, if you felt as if you should continue to be a ranger—"

"What! And be off roaming all over the republic when I got the prettiest, sweetest woman in the world sitting at home? Never!" His expression saddened briefly. "I know it wasn't the whole problem with my parents, but I do know my father's circuit riding took an awful toll on their marriage. I won't make that mistake. But there is more to it. You see, Lucie, I *want* to settle down. I want to be with you and with the family we'll someday have. I'm so tired of roaming. I look back at the long road I've been on, and it no longer has any draw for me, not when looking ahead I can see the light of your smile at the end."

"My goodness! And I thought you were a man of few words!"

"There's one thing, though. . . ." He hesitated over his next words. They were difficult but had to be spoken. He jumped up and paced a bit, wondering if he could find a way to avoid what he meant to say. But he loved her too much to avoid something so important. He turned and faced her with resolve. "Well, I think we should wait a bit before we get married. For your sake, Lucie, because so much has happened to me that I just want to be sure it's all gonna take. Do you understand?"

"Yes, I do, and I love you all the more for saying it. But let's not wait too long. I want my father to walk me down the aisle." She rose, walked to him, and took his hands into hers. "But to be honest, Papa has been so greatly restored since his reunion with my brother, I think he may live forever!"

"Well, don't you worry, Lucie, I don't intend on waiting that long!" He brought her hands to his lips and gently kissed them. "I just don't know how I'm gonna be able to handle all these good things, Lucie!"

"We'll find a way, as we always have."

Forty

MICAH WAS NERVOUS, scared, and exhilarated—all at the same nerve-wracking time. He tried to sit on the couch in the Maccallum parlor, then nearly jumped out of his skin at the sound of a sharp knock at the front door.

Both Micah's father and Reid Maccallum were with Micah. Benjamin volunteered to get the door, telling Reid to rest easy. Benjamin rose, strode to the door, and answered it. Micah heard the voices in the entry.

"Why, hello, Tom," Benjamin said.

"Afternoon, Reverend Sinclair. I heard you was visiting for the Christmas holidays, and I hoped I'd get back from patrol in time to see you."

"So you are still a ranger?"

"Captain Hays talked me into it. How could I refuse when he said he'd rather have me with a bum leg than some green new recruit? But I'm only signed on till the end of the year, then I'm gonna try my hand at ranching."

"Well, come on in. I'm not the host, but I am sure you are welcome."

"How is Mr. Maccallum?"

"Come see for yourself."

In another moment Benjamin and Tom Fife came into the parlor.

"Looks like everyone's here—the menfolk, at least," Tom said. When Reid Maccallum rose and extended a hand, Tom shook it heartily. "You're looking fine, sir."

"I should be. Everyone is waiting on me as if I were a king," Reid replied.

Tom turned to Micah. "But you look awful, boy—like maybe you swallowed a cactus whole."

"Well, how do you expect a fellow to feel who's about to become a father?" Micah snapped.

"Well, sure, I expect—" Tom stopped suddenly and gasped. "Ya mean now? It's happening right now?"

Micah jerked his head toward the back of the house. "Back there."

Now Tom turned pale. "Sakes alive! I didn't mean to intrude—"

But a cry from the back cut him off. Micah jumped up and, pushing past his companions, headed toward the sound. Benjamin caught him.

"Micah, now you can't go rushing in every time there's a sound. You've got to give your wife time to do what she has to do. Elise and Juana are with her and will let you know when to come."

"But she's in pain!" Micah said miserably. "I can't just sit here and listen to her cries." He turned desperate eyes toward Tom. "Tom, she's been at it all night. How much longer can a man stand such a thing?"

Benjamin chuckled. "It's a bit hard on her as well."

"You can do it, boy," Tom said. "Why, I've seen you survive a lot worse."

"Nothing like this. Every time she cries out, I like to die inside." Micah started pacing.

"Let's have some coffee," Reid said helplessly.

But Micah had already consumed several pots of coffee. If he had more, he'd jump down someone's throat, maybe his own. A year ago on Christmas Eve when he and Lucie had married, it had been so wonderful, and each day since had been more wonderful than the last. They'd built a little cabin on their land, an hour's ride from the Maccallum place. They'd even planned on the arrival of their first child. Micah had been lulled into believing life would just be a peaceful Sunday afternoon ride. He'd never imagined that now that he and Lucie were together, he'd ever feel so torn up inside.

"We ain't having no more after this," Micah declared suddenly.

Benjamin and Reid laughed.

"You'll change your mind once it's over," Reid said. "I'll wager Lucie will want more, and she's the one doing the real suffering."

"So, Tom, what brings you out today?" Benjamin asked.

Micah knew it was an attempt to distract him, and he was glad for it.

"I got news, that's what. Texas has been voted in as a state in the Union!"

"That is wonderful!" Benjamin said.

"I was never in favor of statehood," Reid said, "but even I can see that economically we could not have made it alone. And to show my support, I offer a toast." He poured coffee for everyone, and they lifted their cups. "To the twenty-eighth state in the Union. The biggest state and always the best!"

"Here, here!" They all chimed in, even Micah.

"Ya know, Pa," Micah said, "I ain't never told you this, but I'm glad you dragged me here. I love this place, and I am truly glad that my child's gonna be born on this auspicious day." Another cry from the bedroom turned his smile into a grimace. "It will be today, won't it?" he asked shakily.

Suddenly they heard a very different cry. No one stopped Micah now when he nearly dropped his cup and raced toward the room. They all followed instead.

The door opened, and Elise poked her head out. "There you are, Micah—oh goodness, and everyone else, too!"

"Lucie!" Micah said anxiously. "Is she all right?"

"Yes, she is, and she has brought a wonderful, healthy child into the world." She held up the bundle in her arms for all to see.

All the blood in Micah's body rushed right to his head, and suddenly Elise, the door, and everything began to spin. He swayed back. Luckily, the wall of his three friends behind him kept him from falling.

"Are you all right, Micah?" Elise said.

"I think he was about to faint," Tom said, alarm and amusement vying in his voice.

"I-I'm fine. Just fine...." Micah stammered. He made himself stand firm, like a man. Like a ... father. The thought made his head light again, but he remained stable on his feet.

"Micah, you can come in now," Elise said. "I hope the rest of you gentlemen don't mind waiting a bit so the new family can have some time alone."

Micah did not need another invitation. Brushing past Elise with hardly a glance at the bundle, he strode quickly to Lucie's bedside. She was pale and obviously worn. Her dark eyes seemed larger than usual and were ringed with circles. Her hair lay in damp strands about her face. Yet for all her fatigue, she seemed to glow. Her smile, as always, was like cool, fresh water on a hot summer day. Micah drank it in, reveling in her beauty and in the deeper beauty of the love on the wings of that smile. The love for him! That would never cease to amaze him.

Taking her hand, he sat in the chair by the bed. "You are truly all right, Lucie?"

"Oh yes! Micah, we have a son! I didn't think I could be happier than I was on the day we married, but I am."

"Same here," he said, then her words sank in. "A son?"

"And our Lucie was very brave," Juana said, wiping a cloth across Lucie's forehead. "Now we will leave you two—I mean you three—alone."

Elise brought the baby to the couple. "Would you like to hold him, Micah?"

"Me?" he squeaked, all his fears flooding over him again.

"I happen to know you are quite proficient with babies."

"But this one's different. . . ." His eyes skittered to Lucie. "This one is mine . . . ours. I'm . . . a father."

"Come on, then," Elise prompted. And before Micah could say another word, the bundle was tucked in the crook of his arm.

The two older women then left, and Micah gazed at the child. Impulsively he lifted the blanket wrapped snugly around the infant. A tiny hand popped out. Micah touched the fingers, then looked at the other hand. Then he loosed the feet and counted ten toes.

"He's perfect, isn't he?" Lucie said.

Micah nodded. "It doesn't surprise me at all that anything that is part of you would be perfect. But, Lucie, I can hardly believe I am part of this as well. Something so perfect has come from me! It is far too amazing to even ponder."

"It doesn't surprise me at all, Micah, my love. I always knew there was more to you than met the eye. And in addition to that, our God is the giver of perfect gifts."

"Yes. I among all men should know that!"

"We will name him Jed, like we agreed."

Micah nodded again. And for the first time since that terrible time in Mexico, he was able to smile when he thought about his friend. "I'll bet he is grinning ear to ear over this. Thank you for letting me have this way, this joyous way, to remember my friend." He paused, then added, "But if you recall, what we really agreed on was Jed Joaquin Sinclair. A child of two proud cultures. Oh, and Lucie, there is more yet. Tom just came to celebrate the fact that today Texas has officially joined the Union."

"How wonderful!" said Lucie. "I love the symbolism it all represents. Our little Jed will be a special child, Micah. I know it."

"He *is* a special child!" Micah tucked the blanket securely back around the baby. Out of the corner of his eye he saw Lucie gazing at them. "What is it, Lucie?"

"Oh, I was just wondering what we will name our next special child."

"Next child! Then it's true what everyone said, that you quickly forget all the pain?"

"I forgot the moment I laid eyes on him."

"I kind of did, too." Micah bent down and kissed the babe's forehead. And he meant it in the broadest sense. The past could never be changed, yet God had found a way to heal many of the wounds.

"Well, if you can handle so much happiness, so can I!" Micah said, brushing her smiling lips with his.

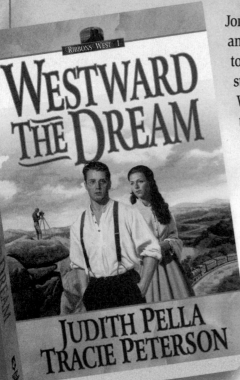